DANGERS, TOILS AND SNARES

Julia Courtney

Quotation from The Collected Works of C.G. Jung, Volume 9 (Part1) : Archetypes and the
Collective Unconscious, by kind permission of Princeton University Press.

'Girls were made to love and kiss' by kind permission of United Agents LLP on behalf of the
Executors of the Estate of Jocelyn Herbert, MY Perkins and Polly MVR Perkins.

Matador
Unit E2 Airfield Business Park,
Harrison Road, Market Harborough,
Leicestershire. LE16 7UL
Tel: 0116 2792299
Email: books@troubador.co.uk
Web: www.troubador.co.uk/matador
Twitter: @matadorbooks

ISBN 978 1805140 801

British Library Cataloguing in Publication Data.
A catalogue record for this book is available from the British Library.

Printed and bound in Great Britain by 4edge Limited
Typeset in 11pt Minion Pro by Troubador Publishing Ltd, Leicester, UK

Matador is an imprint of Troubador Publishing Ltd

For my grandfather, Hans Hirter

Through many dangers, toils and snares
I have already come.
'Tis grace has brought me safe thus far
And grace shall lead me home.
(John Newton)

A curious combination of typical trickster motifs can be
found in the alchemical figure of Mercurius; for instance,
his fondness for sly jokes and malicious pranks, his powers
as a shape-shifter, his dual nature, half animal, half divine,
his exposure to all kinds of tortures, and—last but not
least—his approximation to the figure of a saviour. These
qualities make Mercurius seem like a daemonic being
resurrected from primitive times, older even than the Greek
Hermes.
(Carl Gustav Jung)

PART ONE

From 'Im Frühling', Ernst Schulze

O wär ich doch ein Vöglein nur
Dort an dem Wiesenhang!
Dann blieb' ich auf den Zweigen hier,
Und säng ein süsses Lied von ihr,
Den ganzen Sommer lang.

Oh, if only I were a bird,
there on the sloping meadow!
Then I would stay on these branches here,
and sing a sweet song about her
all summer long.

Very few people come to Tarnheim now. Although Eastern and Central Europe is once more open to tourism, it is too far off the beaten track, and too unremarkable, to attract visitors. The castle itself is in ruins, having been mistakenly bombarded by the Russians as a guerrilla stronghold. As before, farmers, craftsmen and shopkeepers live in the village; increasingly, the younger generations opt for life on the land. It is not a bad place to be.

Everyone knows that, if you follow the mountain path, checking on the cattle, doing a bit of hunting or climbing, picking berries and herbs, well, then you will encounter the children. It's said that they have always been there, although opinions on that vary. Usually they are hiding in the bushes or in the undergrowth near the pool. You hear them laughing and they may peep out at you. Sometimes, though, their pale bodies flash behind the waterfall and disappear. More rarely, you actually see them in the open, although they are always at a distance.

The girl, who is the taller, is wearing a dirndl, the boy an open-necked shirt and lederhosen with faded embroidered braces. He scrambles along the steep path, trying to catch up with her. Sometimes, though, they are holding hands. People say, too, that you can hear him singing, but perhaps that is only birdsong after all.

A SUMMER AT TARNHEIM, 1902

Karel von Tarnheim asked to see Miss Flora Drake in her sitting room.

He began by asking the governess about his daughter Christa's progress.

This, she said, was quite satisfactory. Christa really preferred to be outdoors, but she did her lessons conscientiously and showed a real aptitude for drawing; had the Graf considered extra lessons for her? It was a pity, Miss Drake added, that Christa had so few friends or companions of her own age. She was of course to go away to the convent school when she was thirteen, but that was still four years off.

--Ah, yes.

Karel eagerly seized on her point.

--This summer, Miss Drake, she is to have a companion, and I am afraid that your responsibilities will be increased. You know that I have a nephew?

--Yes; Christa has spoken of her cousin Jiri.

--That is his name in the family. His full name is Jaroslav Felix von Tarnheim Zellek; he is the son of my late sister Gisela, and is thus the last male von Tarnheim. He is being brought up in Pallin by his father and stepmother. But, as he is now seven years old, I am anxious for him to spend time here at Tarnheim; it is agreed that the mountains are better for his health, and so we are to have him for this summer, while Herr and Frau Zellek are at Marienbad.

--A boy of seven! Two years younger than Christa.

--Yes, Miss Drake. Do you think you can undertake the charge? He will of course be looked after by the old nurse Grushenka and I will also find him a body servant as he is becoming too old for a nanny. You would be responsible for his lessons and daily activities, as you are for Christa. I should add that as yet he knows no English, so to begin with you will need to explain things to him in German. But he will soon learn, and English will be of benefit to him.

At exactly eight o'clock, there was an imperious knock at the schoolroom door.

--Come in! called Miss Drake.

The door opened to reveal a very small boy with a thin, heart-shaped face topped by thick, curly dark hair.

--How Do You Do, Miss Drake, he pronounced slowly and clearly. I Am Very Pleased to Meet You.

He then looked at Christa, who gave him a nod of approval. She has taught him that, thought Flora Drake.

--I am pleased to meet you too, Jiri.

The child then turned to Gustl, a strong lad of about fourteen, whom Karel had decided should become his nephew's body servant. He stood hovering in the doorway, holding a rather battered toy bear and a folder of music. Jiri took these from him, and addressed Miss Drake; his German had a cultured accent with a noticeable lilt of the

4

Principality in which they lived, a tiny state long since absorbed into the Austrian Empire: it came very far down in the Emperor's list of titles and possessions. Indicating the bear, the boy announced, This is Wolfi. And these are the pieces I have been practising. Would you like to hear them now?

--Thank you, Gustl. You may go, he added in lordly tones.

Flora soon found that dealing with two children was far more complicated than she had imagined. To begin with, there was the language situation. Although both children spoke German, it was not in fact their only, or indeed their first, language. This was the tongue spoken in the Principality, a separate language rather than a dialect, and they spoke it with the servants, with peasants and villagers, and with each other. Flora could not follow it, and ruled that in the schoolroom only German or English was to be spoken. She had begun teaching Christa French, which would be needed at the convent, but that was still four years away, and Jiri would have enough to do learning English.

Jiri was in fact managing to pick up this new language quite readily, but there was constant private whispering and consultation that excluded Miss Drake, so that often she did not know what the two of them were plotting. For so small a person, Jiri was an extremely disruptive element. He was rarely silent; if not chattering he was singing, and wanted to interfere in all Christa's doings. He could be obedient, but only if it accorded with his wishes, and needed to be constantly occupied, as when bored he always found some mischief to do.

Flora Drake was tidying the schoolroom when the children returned from riding. She could hear angry voices before they entered, and as they did so she saw Christa raise her riding crop and give Jiri a smart whack on the arm. He let out a howl, flung himself at Miss Drake and clung around her waist.

While trying to quiet him, Miss Drake turned to Christa, with whom she rather sympathised.

--Christa, she began, I know Jiri can be a naughty, annoying little boy...

She was about to continue along the lines of, But as the elder you should show him a good example and allow me to correct him if necessary. Of course, Jiri had heard her words, and flung away from her, shouting and stamping.

--I'm not, I'm not. I hate you I hate you both.

This quickly became a screaming, kicking tantrum, reaching cries of, I want Mutti, I want my papa, and passionate weeping.

At this point Karel entered.

--Jaroslav! Stop this noise at once. At once, I say! Is this any way to behave before ladies?

Jiri was by this time beginning to wind down anyway, but he clearly made an effort, although his whole body was shaken by sobs and hiccups.

--Good. Wipe your face and blow your nose.

Karel handed him his own large, clean handkerchief.

--Now, apologise to Miss Drake.

Jiri bowed and clicked his heels.

--Dear Miss Drake, I humbly apologise.

--And now to Christa.

--Christa, I humbly apologise.

6

Karel retrieved his snot-soaked handkerchief and threw it with force and accuracy into the waste basket.

--Now, we will go outside for a while. Perhaps we might go as far as the lake and look at the fish. Miss Drake, where is the boy's hat?

Taking Jiri by the hand he led him from the room.

Again, Karel sought Miss Drake's sitting room.

--I must apologise for my nephew's appalling behaviour. I must also ask you whether he is often like that.

Miss Drake was glad to be able to answer honestly that it had never happened before. --He is certainly naughty, sometimes very naughty, but he has been taught good manners, and he is an affectionate and spirited child. You must know, too, sir, that he is remarkably talented. He obviously has an excellent piano teacher in Pallin, and he never has to be reminded to practise, which is most unusual in a child of that age, and especially one like Jiri... I mean, he is very active and easily bored.

--Yes, at least I am aware that his father encourages what is, I accept, a precocious aptitude. I suppose it keeps him out of mischief, at least to some extent. I admit, Miss Drake, that sometimes that child is more trouble than a regiment of Ulans.

Karel's grim smile accompanied this admission.

--If I had my way, he would be off to a military academy as soon as he is old enough, but as it is... he is my nephew, not my son, and his father must have the final say as to his future.

--Forgive me, Herr Graf, but he is only seven, and in some ways a very little boy...

Miss Drake was pleased to see that Karel von Tarnheim seemed to take notice of her suggestion of drawing lessons for Christa. One morning as they were on the terrace, Miss Drake reading and Christa engaged in sketching the view, he joined them and talked to his daughter about her work.

--Where is Jiri? he asked finally.

--He is playing somewhere... Miss Drake looked around and was horrified to see Jiri running along the terrace wall, on one side of which was a drop of about eight feet to the courtyard, and on the other a sheer fall down the mountainside. Karel signed for silence; he knew better than to startle the boy, but he moved quietly towards him in time to catch him as he made the leap from the wall into the courtyard.

--Thank you, Uncle. If you lift me back onto the wall, we can do that again.

--No, Jaroslav, we cannot. I am ordering you not to climb on that wall ever again. Do you understand me?

--It's nice up there.

--That is not the point. Tell me, what is a junior officer's duty?

--To obey his commanding officer.

--Well then.

--But what if he doesn't like his commanding officer's order?

--Be quiet, Jiri. Here are Miss Drake and Christa. You have given Miss Drake a fright. Now say you are sorry and promise never to do it again.

Jiri did so.

--Where is that oaf Gustl! bawled Karel. He is supposed never to let the boy out of his sight.

Gustl must have received a severe warning, as after this he was constantly in evidence. Having a body servant was not entirely good for Jiri, Miss Drake thought. He added Gustl to his list of minions, and the words 'I want' or 'I don't want' were even more frequently heard. On the other hand, she was less anxious about his physical safety, although...

One afternoon she came upon Gustl, Jiri and Wolfi sloshing towards the kitchen entrance, all three of them soaking wet.

--What?

--He was too quick for me, Fräulein.

--Tell me as we go along, Gustl. We need to get Master Jiri inside; he is shivering.

The story was that they had been fishing from the bridge over the lake, an activity suggested by Gustl as likely to keep Jiri happily occupied. Wolfi had been placed on the bridge to watch; a gust of wind had blown him into the lake, and Jiri had instantly scrambled up and jumped in to rescue him. With some presence of mind, Gustl ran down, waded in and, swimming to the middle of the lake, was able to haul Jiri, now clutching Wolfi, to the side, where he vomited up the water he had swallowed.

Flora Drake took charge.

--Grushenka, please give Master Jiri a bath, get the mud out of his hair, give him a hot drink and put him to bed. You, Gustl, had better go and get dry, she added to the disconsolately dripping lad. You have probably saved Master Jiri's life, although of course you should not have let him fall in the first place.

--I didn't fall. I jumped in to save Wolfi.

Gustl squelched off. Meanwhile, Jiri was protesting that

Grushenka would not let him take the sodden Wolfi into bed with him.

Clearly, trouble was brewing, until Christa, who had come to see what the fuss was about, told him not to be such a baby, which had immediate effect, and promised, less wisely, that Wolfi would be dry in time for proper bedtime.

Miss Drake handed Wolfi to the nurserymaid. Please make sure that he is dry, by whatever means necessary, she ordered.

Fortunately, he was, although the bear was never quite the same again, having paid for his exploits by spending time in the bread oven.

--I think we need to teach Jiri how to swim, was Christa's final comment on the episode.

Another problem was food. As the children did not come down for dinner, Karel had decreed that they should have luncheon with him. Jiri was perched on a pile of cushions, with Gustl standing behind him.

--Come now, Jaroslav. You want to grow, don't you? urged Miss Drake.

--Yes.

--Good. Then eat what is on your plate.

--Must I, Uncle?

--Yes. You must do what Miss Drake tells you.

--I think I shall be sick if I eat that.

--I have told you, Jaroslav, obey Miss Drake.

Jiri shrugged, a piece of rudeness that went unrebuked. Picking up his fork, he thrust a piece of meat into his mouth, and immediately began to heave.

--Quick, Gustl! called Christa. Put him outside.

Gustl picked him up bodily and made for the French windows opening onto the terrace. Unmistakeable sounds of vomiting reached the dining table.

--He did warn you, commented Christa.

The equally difficult question of bedtime was eventually solved by Miss Drake.

Christa had explained that, Jiri is very naughty at bedtime, Miss Drake. He won't go to bed, says he does not like going to sleep, and even when Grusenka has put him to bed, he gets up and runs around.

--Does he say why he doesn't like it?

--All he says is that it is a waste of time. You know, he only goes to sleep when he absolutely has to. That's why he has a rest after lunch. He usually goes to sleep then because he is so tired.

--I wonder, Christa, whether he would like to come to my room with you when I read to you in the evening.

--We could try. He might not understand all the story, though.

--So much the better.

So that evening Jiri, in his sleepsuit and dressing gown, accompanied by Wolfi, sat on the floor at Miss Drake's feet while she read *The Little Duke*. He had been running around all the afternoon, he had been for a long ride with Christa and the groom, and he did not, indeed, understand all of the English words in the story. Gradually his eyes began to close and Miss Drake felt his head weighing heavier on her lap.

Gustl appeared at the door.

--Madam, it is Master Jiri's bedtime.

Both Miss Drake and Christa signed for silence. Gently Gustl picked him up and tiptoed away, Jiri's curly head resting on his shoulder. By some dexterity, the boy was rolled into bed without waking… and so it set the pattern of almost every evening.

There was much discussion of whether they should accept an invitation to a children's party in the valley. It was to be held in the park of the largest local town, which would be closed to the public for the day; there would be games, luncheon and a chance to play in the gardens, ending with tea. Given the Tarnheims' (tenuous) connection to the imperial family, and their reputation for exclusivity, securing the presence of the two children was important for their hostess, and, in a sense of noblesse oblige, reluctance to appear discourteous, and perhaps thinking it might be good for Christa and Jiri, Karel gave his permission.

The unknown quantity, of course, was Jiri, and it was impressed upon him that the slightest misdemeanour would bring such disgrace on the House of Tarnheim as had not been seen since the Middle Ages, and that he himself would be a marked individual for life. It says a lot for his buoyancy of spirit that his enthusiasm seemed undiminished. As he would be missing his after-lunch rest, he was put to bed early on the night before the party, with warning that any protests would mean that he would be left at home. Christa forbade him to take Wolfi to the party, saying that this would make them appear babyish, but added with one of her flashes of insight that he would have fun telling the bear all about it when they got home.

That morning Tarnheim was at its most beautiful. As

they got into the pony trap, Flora Drake and her charges were a sight to be proud of. She wore a simple summer costume with a large, flowery hat, all purchased in Paris thanks to the generosity of a previous employer: suitable, subdued, but unmistakeably elegant. Christa had a white lace dress with a blue sash, with matching blue ribbons and flowers in her hat. Jiri's outfit was also white, a sailor suit with a broad-brimmed hat.

It was a sparkling drive, down the hillside, through several villages, where the balconies of the houses were bright with geraniums, and past the prosperous suburbs of the town, with attractive villas set in colourful gardens.

Because of this rather long distance, most of the other guests had arrived by the time they appeared.

Lorgnettes were raised and heads turned discreetly towards them. Flora had begun to sense that, in this corner of the empire, the von Tarnheims were the nearest thing to royalty, and would be under constant observation.

Both children greeted their hostess in their customary polished manner.

Miss Drake was introduced to a formidable row of mothers, grandmothers, and other governesses. Most of them wished to practise their English, usually learned from English governesses like herself, although one or two had visited England or Scotland (for the shooting). Had she visited Sandringham? And was King Edward quite recovered from the illness that had postponed his coronation?

While answering such queries, Flora Drake tried to keep an eye on the children. She soon realised, to her surprise and relief, that Jiri was evidently much more used to playing with other children than was Christa. Although used to getting his own way at home, here he was willing to wait his turn, to give way to others, to share toys and to help those even smaller than himself. She guessed that in Pallin the Zelleks had a wide circle of friends and neighbours, and that Jiri, sociable by nature, had learned early how to enjoy the company of children his own age. Christa in fact, was finding it more difficult to fit in, but soon she had joined a group of girls, some of them a little older than herself.

--You are Miss Drake, are you not? The governess of Gräfin Christa? And is that...?

--Yes, Frau Essen. He is her cousin; he is staying with us for the summer.

--Ah. How old is he... about six years?

--Actually he is seven; we are hoping that he will grow somewhat in the mountain air.

--Ah. Yes, of course, his poor mother... he is certainly small for his age, but he looks healthy enough.

--Oh yes, thank you...

--That's good. They are after all, the last of the von Tarnheims. Tell me, Miss Drake, does the little Gräfin ever speak of her mother?

What the garrulous Frau Essen went on to say threw light on some unspoken questions in Flora's mind... she had assumed that Christa's mother, like Jiri's, was dead, and she had sometimes wondered why Karel von Tarnheim had not married again, providing a stepmother for Christa, besides some half-siblings for her, and relieving little Jiri of the burden of being the sole Tarnheim heir. Now she knew why.

Before luncheon, the children were taken by some of the attendant nursemaids to a pavilion to wash their hands and tidy up.

Christa ate with her usual hearty appetite, and Jiri did better than at home, perhaps because others were eating and perhaps because the food, attractively served in small portions on delightful plates and dishes, appealed to him.

The afternoon appeared to be going equally well, when Flora became aware of Jiri's hand tugging hers.

--Miss Drake, Miss Drake... please... Jiri pulled her face down towards his. I need...

--Now, Jiri?

--Yes, Miss Drake. Jiri was hopping from one foot to the other. Now.

--Very well.

There was no time to seek out the appropriate buildings, and Flora looked around.

--You will have to go in the garden. Here.

She hurried him down a secluded path.

--Did you not go before luncheon?

--No. I didn't need to then. But I do now.

--Those bushes.

Jiri headed off, and the sounds that followed proved that matters were indeed urgent, and that he had done well to hold on this long.

Flora looked up and saw... John!

--Miss Drake! Flora! What...

Before she had a chance to reply, Jiri emerged from the bushes, pulling up his drawers with a look of relief, and took his usual proprietorial grasp of her hand.

--Who?

Having adjusted his clothing, Jiri bowed and clicked his heels.

--Jaroslav Felix von Tarnheim Zellek.

--John Loudon. They shook hands.

--Come, Jiri, said Flora, we should find your cousin.

As they marched off Jiri put his other hand into John Loudon's.

The two adults were thus able to converse above his wide-brimmed white hat.

--He's Christa's cousin, explained Flora. We have him for the summer.

--I hope they're paying you extra.

--Shh! What are you doing here?

--Climbing holiday with some old friends from medical school…

The rest of the afternoon was delightful; the children had more games with small prizes, and Flora could not believe her eyes when Jiri, who adored sweets and was rarely allowed them on the grounds that they would spoil his appetite or make him sick, gave his box of bonbons to a child who was crying because his had been spilled on the ground.

Tea, coffee and cakes, amazing patisserie, were served at tables spread with dazzlingly white cloths, on delicate Austrian china.

Several gentlemen had now joined the party, including John, introduced by the friend whose young sister was one of the guests.

--Like old times, Flora? Afternoon tea in your parents' garden?

--Yes, although I don't think we were serving Linzertorte!

As the servants cleared away, Flora thought of the drive

ahead. She beckoned to Christa, and extricated Jiri from a group chasing each other around a fountain. Apart from a few grass stains he seemed none the worse for the day, and did not argue when Miss Drake told him it was time to leave. He was, she suspected, getting tired.

Both children thanked their hostess most correctly, with Christa's slight air of condescension offset by Jiri's heartfelt, Thank you. I have had a lovely day.

So have I thought Flora.

In the pony trap, Jiri discarded his hat, and leaned against Miss Drake.

--What have you in your pockets, Jiri?

--Some chocolates. *Auf der rechten*, one for Uncle Karel and, *auf der linken*, some for Gustl. He will have missed me.

With this he put his arm around her and went to sleep.

Christa chatted on. Some of those girls were very nice. Elsa and Alys von Stroen are so funny! They both have ponies, Miss Drake, and they have three dogs… Do you think Papa would let me invite them for a day, Miss Drake? And didn't Jiri behave well today?

--Yes, he has, agreed Flora, suddenly aware that a whole day had passed in which Jiri had not fallen off, into or out of anything, had not hit anyone, thrown any missile, screamed, stamped or vomited…

The next day, as they took their usual mid-morning break from lessons, Flora looked towards the terrace and saw Karel walking with Jiri, who was holding his uncle's hand in his customary way; presumably he did this to stop his hearers from escaping. Karel looked at the tower clock, and evidently sent Jiri off to return to the schoolroom.

As Flora too turned to go, Karel called her.

--A moment, Miss Drake! I wish to congratulate you on the success of yesterday's outing. I gather that the children both enjoyed themselves and behaved most creditably. Jiri has even brought me a souvenir! He held up a rather squashed chocolate in a shiny wrapping. I particularly thank you for your care of Jiri, which must have averted an... unfortunate accident.

--Oh, you mean when—

--Yes. He has told me about that. Incidentally, perhaps I should explain, just in case he starts talking to you about the Emperor.

Miss Drake looked bemused.

Karel smiled. Well. Of course Jiri should have used the lavatory before the luncheon. I have told him that he should always make sure to... even if he thinks... At all events, I told him that when they are on public visits members of the imperial family lose no opportunity to pass water if the facilities are available. Whether they need to or not. Of course, Jiri asked whether that applied to the Emperor himself. I told him that it does... and that if in doubt he should Remember the Emperor.

It was another brilliantly sunny morning. The two children, dressed in clean summer clothing, greeted Miss Drake politely and sat down at their desks. Christa was set a translation exercise, Jiri a page of arithmetic.

--Christa, the sooner you begin, the sooner it will be completed. Jiri, sit up properly and stop tapping your feet.

Silence. With some deep breathing which Flora hoped signified concentration.

She too sat at her desk, and was enjoying an interlude of peace. Someone knocked on the door, provoking loud barking from the two dogs, Christa's borzoi and a small hairy terrier that had attached itself to Jiri; these sat mournfully outside the schoolroom during lessons.

--Come in!

It was John.

--Children, this is Dr John Loudon. You may remember him from the garden party.

They stood up and, in careful English, wished him good morning.

--Good. You may get on with your tasks.

Flora felt justly proud of her charges, neat, polite little aristocrats...

John drew her over to the window.

--What are you doing here? I thought you were mountain climbing.

--Flora, I had to see you... look... I know we agreed...

--Miss Drake, I have finished my sums.

--Already? Wait a moment, Jiri, and I will come and look at them.

--Flora, you know how I feel. I want you to think carefully. CRASH!

Jiri was standing on a chair, a ruler in his hand and around him on the floor an array of heavy books that he had levered from the shelves above. One of them had dislodged a pot of ink, which was slowly spreading across Christa's desk and onto the floor.

--My translation! shrieked Christa. You naughty boy, I shall have to do it all again.

--You'd only just started it.

--I hadn't; I'd done masses!

--No you hadn't.

--Jiri, said Miss Drake in amazingly calm tones. Get off the chair and sit down at your desk.

He did so, treading in the pool of ink and thus leaving a trail of footprints across the floor.

Take off your shoes. Be careful not to get ink on your socks and Do Not Move until I give you permission.

--Miss Drake, shall I ring for Tasha to come and clean up the ink?

--Yes, Christa. That would be a good idea. Meanwhile perhaps you could pick up some of these books, if you can do so without getting ink on yourself. Jiri, what were you trying to do? Those books are very heavy and could have fallen on your head, you know.

--I thought I would get them down and use them to build a house for Wolfi.

Miss Drake sighed. How had a scene of peace and contentment degenerate into a chaos of spilled ink, scattered books and quarrelling children?

--John, this is all your fault. You had better go.

--MY fault? These children are insufferable. Christa is not as innocent as she looks, and as for Master Jiri, if I had my way he would feel that ruler across his backside. But all right, I'm going...

After this, things got worse. Christa became adept at provoking Jiri into a screaming tantrum, during which he would hurl missiles at her. She purposely urged him to run, jump, climb and ride further than his strength allowed, and he became fractious and uncooperative, even when she was not present. On a more positive note, John and Flora had made friends again after an interval of some days and one afternoon Christa had gone, rather against her will, to try on a dress which was being made for her, and Jiri was playing under the trees while John and Flora shared coffee and cakes on the lawn. Several times Flora told Jiri to stop climbing on the edge of the fountain, to stop throwing stones into the water, to stop swinging on, and thus damaging, the lower branches of a tree, not to climb any higher.

--I can climb that high! I know I can! You can't stop me! You can't... you want to stop me having fun and you can't... you can't even say German properly!

--Enough, Jiri! You have been intolerably rude, and grossly disobedient to Miss Drake. John Loudon seized Jiri by the collar, threw him across his knee and smacked him very hard several times.

When he thought the child had had enough, he set him on his legs. Jiri's expression of total amazement and outrage was so funny that both John and Flora had to restrain smiles.

--There, said John. I hope I shall not have to do that again, if only because it has hurt my hand almost as much as your bottom. But remember...

Jiri's lip began to tremble.

John ruffled his hair. It's over, Jiri. Off you go.

Miss Drake led him away; with one hand Jiri clasped her hand and with the other he cautiously rubbed his backside.

I'll have to tell von Tarnheim, thought John. But when he did, Karel smiled. So, Master Jiri has met his match! I am sure it will teach him a valuable lesson. You have my full permission to chastise him again, although I hope you will not need to do so. For myself, while I often reprimand the boy, I cannot bring myself to do more; it would be like striking my sister, he so resembles her. But, now we are conversing, Dr Loudon... I gather that you are a childhood friend of our esteemed Miss Drake. I would be most happy if you would remain here at Tarnheim as my guest for the rest of your stay in our Principality. It will be excellent for the children to hear more English spoken, and Jaroslav may benefit from having more superintendence.

As for Jiri, for a few days he was wary of John. But he evidently bore him no ill will, and before long he was seeking out his company, and asking his opinions, almost in preference to Miss Drake's; the words Herr Doktor Jonni told me, or Herr Doktor Jonni said, were heard with annoying frequency.

Now that he was a guest at Tarnheim, John Loudon set himself to help Flora with the children, if only because it meant that he could spend more time with her.

--As usual, he commented one afternoon, Madam Christa is correct. We should teach Jiri to swim; can Christa herself swim, Flora?

--I think she can; one of the maids taught her a while ago, although, after the girl left, there has been no one to take her.

--Where can they swim? That lake is not at all suitable; I don't at all like the look of the water.

--A little way up the hillside. There's a waterfall, not a very high one, and a pool beneath it, which then flows into a stream. I have been there with Christa. It is a lovely spot, and the water is absolutely clear, although I think it may be cold.

--By afternoon, when the sun has been on it, it may not

be too chilly. I think I'll take them and see how we get on; but first I will look at the pool.

--Flora, you are right, it is a lovely spot. And quite an interesting one... I see local people have been there, and left flowers, herbs... and at one time it must have been a bathing place for the von Tarnheim family... there are some sculptures perhaps brought back from Italy... and an antique tombstone, *Vocatus atque non vocatus, deus aderit.*

The party was made up of John, the two children, and a maid carrying their towels. Gustl was given a break, as John felt confident of taking charge of Jiri, and the maid would help Christa. Flora too remained at home, enjoying an hour or so of peace.

When they returned, she noticed that John was carrying Jiri on his shoulders, although as they neared the gate he put down the boy, who ran off with Christa. However, Flora could tell from their faces that it had been an entirely successful activity. While the maid took their things to dry, and the children went off, Jiri to do piano practice and Christa to her sketching, Flora looked questioningly at John.

--Christa is a natural athlete! If she can climb, ride and skate as well as she can swim, well, few girls – or boys either – can match her!

--And Jiri?

--Absolutely fearless, and determined to keep up with Christa. But, Flora, I tell you as a medical man, that child is much too thin. I'd known he was a lightweight, but when I saw him undressed, well, if he was in my care, I would be

23

concerned. And the walk there and back, together with the swimming, was too much to ask of him...

--He has grown a little since he arrived. I measured them both at the beginning of the summer, and I have promised to do so again before he leaves. But I am sure he has grown, and of course that makes him look even more skinny.

--Grown or not, Master Jiri will never be a big strapping fellow. But he could certainly develop into one of those wiry, active chaps who can outstay the heavies. It's just that we need to fatten him up a bit before he faces a winter of coughs, colds and Lord knows what... Of course the trouble with both those children is that they are the products of centuries of inbreeding; at least Jiri's mother had the sense to marry outside the clan, although when I look at him I wonder...

--No, John, you are imagining things. That musical talent must come from Herr Zellek, there is none in the Tarnheims, I assure you! She paused. Jiri and Christa are first cousins...

--What does that comment imply? Flora, you don't mean that von Tarnheim has any ideas of securing the family line in that way? It would be eugenic disaster! My dearest, if you have any influence at all with any of them, do all you can to prevent such a marriage, however far in the future it may be! I wonder, though, that von Tarnheim himself does not marry again; I know that like the wretched imperial family he would not look at anyone further removed than a second cousin, but even so there must be someone.

Then Flora told him, in strict confidence, what she had learned at the garden party.

--Well, Flora, just make sure he doesn't expect you do a Jane Eyre! Although leaving Karel von Tarnheim for a life of

24

sexual licence on the French Riviera is not, now I come to think of it, any indication of insanity.

At intervals during the summer, Jiri had heard from his parents via postcards of bandstands, mountains, parks and the like, with brief clearly written messages on the back. He made up his mind to write a letter, and this was a joint exercise for them all, with Christa ruling lines on a sheet of paper, and Miss Drake helping with spelling and orthography. This in turn produced a letter to Jiri from his father, which of course pleased the boy greatly.

From things he had said, and from conversations with the housekeeper, Frau Trinkel, Flora had the impression of the Zelleks as cultured, sociable people, well-off and musical. Anton Zellek's grandfather had founded the glassware factory that had laid the basis for a business empire; his father had built the comfortable villa on the outskirts of Pallin, which he furnished in Biedermeier style. Under Anton himself, the factory had specialised in the newest artistic style of glasswork, the villa had acquired decorations in aesthetic taste, and Gisela von Tarnheim had married into the family. Anton had two sisters: one was a nun, the other married to a merchant in Bremen. Gisela and Karel von Tarnheim had been very close and the von Tarnheims disapproved greatly of Gisela's marriage into the bourgeoisie; in fact, had Karel not been away serving with the Ulans at the time, he might have managed to prevent it.

Grethe had been imported as Gisela's companion and later, nurse… and, after Gisela's death in Switzerland, where she had gone for medical treatment, she had become Anton's second wife, and thus Jiri's stepmother. Both Anton and

25

Grethe evidently cherished Jiri and worried, perhaps with cause, about his health; this, together with Karel's insistence on seeing more of his nephew, had persuaded them to part with him for the summer. Jiri had told Flora proudly that in the autumn he was to go to the parish school; Karel had mentioned this with distaste, saying that the boy should have his own tutor rather than mix with the bourgeois children of Pallin. Flora carefully avoided debate, although she thought the Zelleks' decision a wise one, especially given the boy's sociable nature and quick intelligence.

Jiri sought Miss Drake's help in reading the handwriting of his father's letter... he says that there are some big toy shops in Marienbad, and if I have been good, he will choose something for me... Only, Miss Drake, I haven't always been good, have I?

Honesty compelled Flora to admit that, no, he had quite often been naughty, although (sounding more positive) his behaviour had improved lately. (She did not say, since John had taken Jiri in hand.) His parents would, she was sure, be pleased to hear this.

--I have tried hard, Miss Drake. Truly.

--I know you have, darling. She drew him towards her and kissed his forehead. As she did so, she recalled John's comment about Jiri's fragility.

--I think, too, Jiri, that they would be pleased if you could be a little bit more... sensible... about mealtimes.

Later she thought hard about this. Remembering the garden party, she decided to try small portions, cut into bite-sized pieces, arranged on attractive plates. There were some, she thought, with soldiers on them... Unfortunately Christa would be likely to complain that this was babyish, and giving in to Jiri's silly ways... one would have to speak separately to Christa...

As so often happened with Christa and Jiri, while apparently simple requests provoked uproar and drama, more potentially tricky moments passed off effortlessly. At the garden party Christa had noticed that Jiri was smaller and thinner than other children of his age; he would be even more fun to play with if he could grow a bit taller and stronger and, she added wisely, perhaps he would behave better if he was less tired and finicky. She stopped teasing and distracting him at mealtimes; she praised him if he cleared his plate and even, although Miss Drake rather disapproved, sometimes helped him to do so by feeding him the last few mouthfuls.

It was this that led to the children's private game, completely secret and conducted only in their own language. Nothing was ever to be committed to writing, all traces of their activities had to be obliterated and no one else, however nice, was allowed to play. Big Bird and Little Bird was entirely, and exclusively, their own.

Even so, their relationship remained complex and volatile. As part of the plan to strengthen Jiri, during the morning break from lessons, simple refreshments were given to the children, usually outside on the terrace. Often Karel joined them, and his presence did not always prevent unpleasantness.

As Gustl put down the tray, Jiri's eyes widened in horror.

--*Where is my special mug?*

--Never mind that now, Jiri, said Miss Drake. You promised Doktor Jonni that you would drink your milk every morning.

--I promised him that I would drink it every morning from the special mug he gave me. I didn't promise to drink horrible milk from any old mug. I want my mug with the dogs on it, they are called Fritzi, Mitzi and Hansi.

His voice began to rise in pitch and volume.

--Shut up, Jiri, shouted Christa, reinforcing her words with a vigorous kick.

Jiri then solved the milk problem by throwing it over her.

--STOP! Karel seized a child in each hand, holding them apart at arm's length.

Miss Drake, please take Christa to change her clothes. I will take Jiri for a walk and speak to him about his behaviour. I wish to see everyone in my study before luncheon.

Later:

--Now, Jaroslav, I want you go away and think about what I have said. Then I want to see you in my study with Miss Drake and Christa.

As he walked slowly towards the deserted schoolroom, Jiri's world darkened around him. His uncle was most displeased. He had said that Jiri was not fit to associate with civilised people, and that any invitations to treats or parties would certainly be refused. If he was so very bad, thought Jiri, Miss Drake would not love him, Christa would push him away, Doktor Jonni would be cold and stern and maybe Mutti and Papa would get to hear of it and refuse to have him back... He stumbled to the piano and pounded on the keys with his fists. Tears fell on the keyboard. Almost without thinking, he began to pick out the notes of a tune he had heard one of the gardeners singing... he tried to remember the words, there was a proud rider, a dear horseman... and a nice chorus that cheered you up...

By lunchtime things had calmed down.

--Now, Jiri and Christa, I want you to apologise to each other and to Miss Drake.

--Miss Drake, we humbly apologise.

--Jiri, I'm sorry I kicked you so hard.

--Christa, I'm sorry I threw the milk over you. I hope it hasn't made your hair stink.

--No; Miss Drake and Grushenka washed it for me.

Christa's hair, which was thick, wavy and a few shades lighter than Jiri's, was shining, tied back with a ribbon rather than in its usual plaits.

--It's very pretty. He put out his hand to touch it.

To everyone's surprise, Christa gave him a hug; over his shoulder she looked straight at her father.

--Papa, he really has been very good about the milk. He does hate it, and he can only manage to drink it when he thinks about Fritzi, Mitzi and Hansi.

--This is all that oaf Gustl's doing, fumed Karel. He will be made to understand that Master Jiri's milk must always be served in the correct mug.

At the next swimming lesson, John Loudon asked how Jiri had come by the bruise on his leg.

--I kicked him, Christa admitted cheerfully.

--I got my own back. I threw milk over her, added Jiri with equal insouciance. John decided to pursue the topic no further.

Now that the school room party numbered four, it was easier to play card and board games. Rather to John's surprise, Jiri proved more amenable than Christa, who hated losing and would often slam down her cards in disgust. If Jiri lost at a game of chance, he would shrug in his characteristically Viennese manner, saying, Oh, that was bad luck! With games of skill, he would become thoughtful, before pronouncing, That was silly, wasn't it! Of course, what I should have done…

--I wonder whether you might teach him chess, suggested Flora.

--Well, on condition that at the first sign of bad temper or inattention the board goes away, and I will never, ever let the boy win.

Nor did he, but Jiri never seemed to mind, and learned fast.

I suspect that the little rascal is beginning to work out how I think and what are my favourite moves… I'm going to ask Karel to play with him sometimes, if only to prove that Jiri is capable of sitting quietly for more than five minutes at a time!

After this, Karel seemed to spend more time with his nephew, although things did not always go smoothly.

One morning as Karel entered the hall after his morning ride, his nephew, half dressed and followed by Christa, Gustl and Grushenka, cannoned into him.

--What is this? He held Jiri at arm's length.

--It's his hair, Papa, explained Christa. He won't have it combed.

--She pulls it, said Jiri, indicating Grushenka.

--It's so thick, master, and curly, it gets all in a tangle, added the nurse.

--It should not take three people to make one small boy presentable…

--I'm not a sm—

--Be quiet! Karel's glare made Jiri feel that actually he was very small indeed.

The boy's hair is far too long. It is like mine, and should be kept short. The barber in Strelitz who cuts the servants' hair will do at short notice. I do not wish to interrupt Miss Drake's duties, and I suppose there is no one else I can trust him with. Hans and I will take him. Gustl, have him ready at nine o'clock. With his hair combed. And, Jiri, the ride on Nero I promised you if you are well-behaved? From what I have seen of you this week, there is no prospect of it. Christa, I will not have you running after your cousin with the servants. You may come and have breakfast with me.

Taking her hand, he led his daughter away.

Promptly at nine, the pony trap set off for Strelitz. Jiri was wedged between Karel and his uncle's valet Hans, but he was in high spirits, if rather over awed by the company. No lessons, a sunny morning, a ride to Strelitz, a look at the town.

Hans took Jiri into the barber's shop. Jiri had never been in one before, as at home his hair was usually cut by his father's valet. Hans was evidently above such tasks.

--The Honourable Graf wants Master Jaroslav's hair cut.

The barber cranked his chair up as high as it would go, placed a cushion on it, and lifted Jiri up. He tied a towel around him.

--Now, sir, how would you like it cut?

--I would like it exactly as my uncle has it, please.

Jiri was looking around at the mirrors, the other customers, the rows of oils and colognes.

--Keep still, young sir, or I'll cut your ears off.

Jiri looked at the scissors. He sat rigidly still.

Dark curls fell rapidly to the floor.

--How's that?

--I think the master will approve, noted Hans, who had re-entered the shop after having a smoke outside.

--Macassar oil, sir?

--Let me smell it. No; it is nice but Christi will say it makes me stink.

Jiri became aware that he was the only person in the shop who did not have a moustache. He knew that men, or at least most of them, had moustaches, and boys did not; at what point did the transition occur?

--Excuse me, he said, how long do you think it will take me to grow a moustache... like... like... that gentleman's? He indicated a stout customer with an impressively waxed moustache.

--I'd say it would be some time, sir, replied the barber; seeing Jiri's look of disappointment, he added, But for dark-haired gentlemen like you and your honoured uncle, it is easier than for those with blond hair.

The barber untied the towel and lifted him down. Master Jiri, said Hans, before we meet your honoured uncle, do you need to go pipi?

--Yes Hans, that is a good idea. Jiri had been too excited to remember to go before leaving home, and time was getting on. The barber indicated the door and Jiri trotted off.

--You were lucky, said Hans. That one can be a little devil when he chooses.

--I can see that! But the bit about cutting off their ears always works. Like his uncle, isn't he? And I expect he's company for the young lady.

--Yes; those two fight like cat and dog, but they soon make it up, and then they get up to all sorts...

Jiri reappeared.

--Come along, Master Jiri. Your uncle will be waiting for you in the café.

Hans put Jiri's hat on the boy's head.

--My hat feels loose now I've had a haircut!

--Be careful that you don't lose it... here...

--NO, I'm not having the strap under my chin. It looks babyish and it makes me feel sick.

Christa would have told him sharply that the Ulans secured their czapkas with a chin strap; it did not make them look babyish, and if they felt sick, they put up with it in soldierly fashion. But Hans was less quick, and wished to avoid trouble.

He gave in and, taking Jiri's hand, marched him off. There were a couple of toyshops in Strelitz, but Hans allowed no distractions, ignoring the constant stream of Oh Hans, did you see that, Oh Hans, look at those dogs, Oh Hans, listen to that...

In the café, Karel had drawn out his watch several times.

--Ah. At last. Take off your hat, Jiri. Much better. I hope you have behaved yourself.

--Yes, sir. Master Jiri has been a perfect gentleman.

--I am glad to hear that, Hans. You may go and have some refreshment. Now, Jiri, you may choose a cake. I have waited for you, and I am having Linzertorte.

The cropped hair revealed Jiri's small, well-shaped head, and accentuated his delicate, animated features. Really, thought Karel, he is not a bad-looking boy; if only he were a little more robust and less wilful... Meanwhile, Jiri was tucking into a cream cake, which Flora would never have allowed him to have in case it made him sick on the way home, something that occurred to neither Jiri nor Karel.

--Good. Now stop staring around – that is not the way a gentleman behaves – and finish that last piece.

As they got into the pony trap, Hans took care to jam Jiri's hat down over his ears. Even so, before they reached Tarnheim it blew off and was last seen rolling down the mountainside.

--Why was the boy's hat not secured, Hans?

--I'm sorry, sir. It was overlooked.

Jiri did not hear this piece of kindness. He was too much interested in the progress of his hat, and wondering whether a goat would eat it, or an eagle use it for a nest, or perhaps it might float down the river until it joined the Danube, and then it would go all the way to Vienna, and the Emperor might see it and wonder who it belonged to...

--Well, when we reach home you must find him something to wear. The boy cannot run about bareheaded.

--Very good, sir.

Nothing much was thrown away at Tarnheim, so that over the next few years Jiri often wore garments made for Karel in the 1870s; many of these could be described as *Tracht*, and in fact suited him very well. Hans would find him some headgear that would do until Flora could replace his white sunhat. It was not too disastrous. And overall, it had been a most successful morning.

Summer began to end. The quality of the sunlight became golden. The sunsets over the mountains were magnificent displays of red, purple and gold; autumn flowers bloomed in the Alpine meadows, and the children picked berries for Grushenka to make into jam. Soon the cattle would come down from the Alpine pastures, their horns garlanded with flowers, to a welcome from the village band.

Flora and John sat together at the schoolroom window, which was open. On the terrace below, the children were occupied. Christa had her paintbox and was filling in the countries in a map of Europe, which Flora hoped would serve some educational purpose. Jiri had been given a box of Christa's outgrown toys; these included a number of coloured bricks, which he was using not to build with but laid out to form a complicated design that evidently meant something to him, as all patterns did. The floors in Tarnheim were mostly made of parquet wood, tiles or paving stones; this meant that Jiri could rarely simply walk or run from one place to another, but had to execute a series of steps, hops or jumps demanded by the patterns. Flora had come to realise that Jiri's mind did not work quite like other people's. When he had spoken of the days climbing to Friday, the year going level in August, or a piece of music tasting strawberry, she had at first corrected his apparently bizarre English. But he used the same mode of expression in German and this was clearly how he experienced and visualised the world.

Flora knew that the peaceful atmosphere was fragile. At any moment Jiri could upset Christa's water pot, she could kick over his design, they might get bored and run off to some piece of mischief, or they might protest noisily at being called inside.

The moment was fleeting; John looked up.

--What's that he's singing, Flora?

Jiri's clear, high voice could be heard as he arranged his bricks.

--OH! It's a folk song… he has only to hear something once and he can sing it perfectly… I expect he likes this one as it has a horseman in it and that little nonsense verse beginning Juvi, which sounds a bit like Jiri, I suppose!

It was 'Drei Lilien'.

Drei Lilien, drei Lilien,
Die pflanzt ich auf mein Grab.
Da kam ein stotzer Reiter und brach sie ab…
Juvi, Juvi vallerah…
Ach Reiter, lieber Reitersmann…

At the end of the summer, John left for England, and Jiri went back to Pallin. A nursemaid arrived to collect him: a rather grim-faced person who Miss Drake hoped would stand no nonsense, although she did not envy her the three-hour journey ahead. Jiri greeted her with evident delight, and said goodbye to everyone in a gratifyingly courteous and grown-up manner. He was lifted into the pony trap and waved his (new) hat until they disappeared down the drive.

--It will be quiet without him, commented Christa.

JIRI IN LONDON, 1904

In autumn 1902 Jiri entered the parish school. Several of his contemporaries were there already; children could be admitted shortly before they were seven, but as his birthday was in June, just before his summer visit to Tarnheim, his parents had decided to wait until the beginning of the new term. They took the decision to educate Jiri in this way only after considerable thought, and in the face of Karel von Tarnheim's disapproval. Experience had shown that Jiri got on well with other children, and in a group he was often more amenable, less demanding and even likely to eat better. In addition, the district was a prosperous, respectable and cultured one; the children were uniformly clean, well-dressed and good-mannered. The sisters did not look for great educational achievements; the school was airy and bright, filled with flowers, plants, pictures and music.

Jiri loved it. He was delighted with his tasselled cap, short jacket with red facings and gold buttons, and his little knapsack. Even so, the first few months were not plain sailing. Jiri was convinced that he was Exercising Self-Control when he threw things (inkpots were especially satisfying) at the walls or through the window rather than at the teachers or the other children, and felt that he should be commended for this restraint. Unfortunately the opposite seemed to happen. If sent to fetch a cloth or mop to clear up, he would disappear until the end of the lesson; usually he would just sigh and trot meekly to the little stool in the punishment corner. The sisters prided themselves on never having failed with a child; Jiri Zellek was beginning to test this, when the headmistress, noticing that he would always comfort or stand up for anyone in trouble or distress, told him that she counted on him, as a member of an honourable family, to set a good example to those less fortunate. While this did nothing to mitigate his tendency to arrogance and bossiness, it did work in regulating his outbursts.

In some ways the family had a relaxed attitude to Jiri's education. Given his mother's ill health and early death, all Anton and Grethe wanted was that he should be healthy, happy and reasonably well-behaved. In addition, Anton, who was an accomplished pianist and had a beautiful baritone voice, wished his son to develop his musical talents; as for Grethe, she and Miss Drake had both given Jiri simple lessons, and she felt that anyone who could read and write basic German, do quite well in English, speak a few words of French and tackle lengthy problems in arithmetic, all at the age of seven, might have a successful career in business. Karel von Tarnheim, of course, had him destined for the Ulans; a soldier was more likely to kill foreigners than to converse with them, but the officer caste was totally anglophile, and any gentleman should be able to bandy a few Gallic phrases.

So, Anton and Grethe had no hesitation in taking Jiri out of school each summer for his months at Tarnheim, and in spring 1904 they also proposed to take him with them on a visit to London. This was their second trip to the English capital. The first had been most promising. Anton had heard of the Fabergé branch in Bond Street, and felt inclined to follow the Russian goldsmith's lead; he got on well with Henry Bainbridge, manager of the showroom, and had asked his advice about the English market for luxury items. Mr Bainbridge had presented Grethe with two of the firm's gemstone animals, a British bulldog and a carthorse, which Jiri longed to get his hands on, but which were firmly locked in a vitrine in the Pallin villa. Anton also purchased an enamel cigarette case, at reduced price because of a barely perceptible flaw, which he intended to present to Karel.

They had also opened negotiations with Liberty and Co. Here the merchandise would be rather different; affordable glass tableware together with more expensive items like vases, lampshades, dishes and ornaments in *Jugendstil* shapes and colours. A first shipment should have reached the Regent Street store by now, and Anton was keen to see how it was selling; should they concentrate on supplying Liberty, or set up their own showroom? In any case, the progress of the Liberty sales would give an indication of what best suited English tastes.

So late spring saw them in a London hotel, having survived the train journey across Europe, a sea crossing, and another train from Dover to Victoria Station. They had brought Anton's valet and one maid with them, and this bodyguard of four adults had kept Jiri from falling under various trains or overboard in mid-Channel. Although he seemed as active and cheerful as ever, both parents felt that he was still too thin and tired easily, so very soon after their arrival they asked John Loudon to examine him.

Jiri was delighted to see Doktor Jonni, who was able to reassure the Zelleks that the child's chest was absolutely clear, and that care, rest and encouragement to eat was all that could be done; they all knew that any attempt to make Jiri take any form of tonic was not even worth trying.

John also realised that the Zelleks had a full business agenda, so that they could not actually have Jiri with them all the time. As he was free the next day, he offered to take Jiri to see something of London, asking the boy what he would like to do.

He was rather disconcerted to find that at the top of Jiri's list was a visit to Buckingham Palace to see dear Queen Alexandra, whose picture he had seen and whom he was convinced must be a relative of the von Tarnheims. After John explained that she was currently at Sandringham, and would be unlikely to be able to return to London even to meet Jaroslav Felix von Tarnheim Zellek, the Palace slid down the list, although Papa had promised to take him to see the Changing of the Guard. What else was there? The Zoological Gardens, or perhaps the Tower of London?

A tower? Could one see the mountains from there? Well, no… but the Bloody Tower had a gruesome history (which John summarised in two sentences), beefeaters, ravens, the crown jewels… Jiri could not wait.

The visit to the Tower was a huge success. It did not, perhaps, add much to Jiri's understanding of English history, but they both had a wonderful time, and as Jiri had made up his mind to speak only English (as far as possible) while in London, his incessant chatter certainly added to his language skills.

At the same time, John felt that there was a limit to the amount of time he could allot to the visitors. Slightly against his better judgement, and perhaps to add to the interest of his letters to Flora (which tended to consist of comments on his patients and colleagues), he paid a visit to his mother and sister in Bayswater. Would they, he asked, be willing to host Jiri for a day? Anne spoke a little German; Jiri could cope with a certain amount of English conversation and his behaviour at the Tower had been good, if rather exhausting.

So, a taxicab containing Jiri and the Zelleks' maid dropped the boy at their door. As the cab and the maid drove off, Jiri and the Loudons surveyed each other. Anne Loudon was tall and athletic, like her brother; she had a similarly mobile, intelligent face; her mother was shorter, plumper, grey-haired but active and lively.

Jiri bowed and clicked his heels.

--Good morning, Frau... Mrs... Loudon and Miss Loudon. Thank you for your invitation.

He looked around their drawing room.

--Please, I may play your piano? I have not done any practice today.

This got though about forty minutes very successfully, and the ladies were impressed by Jiri's ability.

They then offered him refreshments, biscuits and would he prefer milk or lemonade?

--Lemonade please, was the decided reply.

Jiri was by now quite at his ease, and told them about his friends, his cousin, his uncle, dear Miss Drake... he had been given some pocket money, which, he added, was supposed to last the week (his parents were determined that he should learn the value of money; so far he viewed running out of cash as a life hazard to be accepted along with grazed knees and the occasional smack); he had seen some interesting-looking shops in London, and it would be nice to buy presents for everyone, did they not think?

Yes, they did, and Anne suggested that she would take him to the Bayswater store Whiteleys until lunchtime.

Again total success; Jiri was thrilled with his purchases, which he insisted on showing to Mrs Loudon while Anne and their only maid, Beatrice, prepared luncheon; after that, Mrs Loudon read aloud to Jiri from one of John and Anne's childhood books, as she was convinced that children should not run about immediately after eating. He listened intently; Mrs Loudon became aware of his dark curly head resting against her knee, and thought that maybe one day Anne or John might make her a granny...

--Perhaps we might go to the park; would you like that, Jiri?

--Yes please, Miss Loudon.

--I think I will come too, said Mrs Loudon; it's a fine day, and I would like a walk and some fresh air.

Anne settled her mother on a park bench and sat beside her. Jiri ran off; he had seen some children playing by the pond with boats and, although he hadn't got one himself, he wanted to see what was going on and as far as possible to offer comments and advice. Language appeared to be no barrier, and soon he was part of the group... mothers and nursemaids relaxed in the sunshine...

Suddenly Anne heard raised voices... as if in the slow movements of a dream, she saw Jiri push a far bigger boy into the pond... before the splash had ceased, another boy shoved Jiri and he too fell into the water... he emerged clutching a handful of mud and stones, which he flung at the boy who had pushed him, achieving considerable damage to the lad's white sailor suit.

The uproar around the pond was stilled by a stocky young man in a dark suit, who ran forward, hauled Jiri out, said something to the boy who Jiri had pushed (it sounded like, That served you right, now be off) and made a comment to the nursemaid who was in charge of both lads, one of whom was sopping wet and the other covered with mud and slime...

--I saw that, he said to Jiri. If you want to pick a fight, especially with someone bigger than you, watch your back. You were so pleased with yourself that you didn't see his brother coming. Nice job with the mud, though; not bad aim. Looks like you belong to these two ladies...

--Is this yours? he asked Anne and her mother, holding Jiri by the collar.

--Oh Jiri, cried Anne.

--You'll need to get him home. Far to go?

--No, no, not at all... he doesn't actually live with us...we have him for the day...

--Well, I'd rather have him for a day than a year! I'd better carry him.

He could not help looking down at his suit... Anne understood...

--Oh, your suit... She took off her knitted jacket and wrapped it around Jiri, who was now beginning to shiver... and I'll take his boots, so that will keep the worst off.

--Thanks. It's my best suit. But anyway the interview was this morning, so it doesn't matter so much.

Anne now poured the water out of Jiri's boots, causing a

43

cry of, Oh, if there are *kleine fische*, they must go back, *arme Kleiningkeiten*…

--No, no, it's all right.

--Come on, then… Jerry, is it? Let's get you back to where you belong.

--Jiri, we must take you upstairs and get your wet things off.

--Only Granny Loudon and Beatrice… not Miss Anne… I don't want…

--All right, my dear. That is very gentlemanly of you, and Beatrice and I can manage quite well. Anne, why don't you make some tea and thank this gentleman for his help?

--Do you mind coming into the kitchen? We have only Beatrice and a daily girl…

--Kitchen? That's where I like to be!

They looked at each other.

--We haven't been introduced.

--Well then. You go first.

--Anne Loudon.

--Ralph Battrill.

--Where are you from, Mr Battrill?

--People here keep asking me that. I'm from the Island… the Isle of Wight.

--Oh! Forgive me… it was just that I didn't recognise the accent.

--I'm not the only one with an accent, though, am I? Where is young Jerry from?

Anne told him the name of the Principality, adding,

--No, I'd never heard of it either! It's somewhere in Austria–Hungary. My brother's… friend… is a governess there. Her pupil is Jiri's cousin.

44

--Little toff, then?

--Well, yes, perhaps. But it doesn't stop him getting into trouble.

--How old is he? About seven?

--Actually he is eight and will be nine in June. I know he is small for his age, but he is very bright.

--Hmm. More pluck than sense, I'd say. Stuck up for that little lad whose boat got smashed and got himself shoved in the pond.

--So that's what—

--Yes. Kettle's boiling.

They took their tea into the drawing room.

--What are you doing in London, Mr Battrill?

--I'm here for a job interview... that's why the suit! I'm an engineer, been working across in Southampton; going for a job, marine engineer, prospects in Canada.

--Oh.

--And you, Miss Loudon? You live with Mrs Loudon?

--Yes. My brother John is a doctor, at the Royal Midchester Hospital; he has his own rooms near there. I'm attending extension lectures, and I do some research in the Reading Room... at the British Museum... she explained... for some people who write for magazines and so on. I'm a suffragist, she added rather defiantly.

He nodded; if there were any suffragists on the Isle of Wight, they kept a low profile.

And, she continued, there is quite a lot to do here, helping Mother and Beatrice...

Beatrice appeared.

--Please, miss, can the gentleman come and help with Master Jiri?

The help required was to carry Jiri downstairs. He was wrapped mummy-fashion in a blanket; Ralph dumped him on the sofa.

--There, nipper. You look like a gurt mallyshag.

--A what? asked Anne.

--A mallyshag; that's what we call a caterpillar.

Everyone laughed, including Jiri.

--I'd better be going, Miss Loudon, Mrs Loudon... I'm staying with family in Croydon, and they'll be wondering how my interview went.

--We can't thank you enough.

--I might just look in tomorrow, just to see how...

--Yes... yes... please do...

--What a nice young man. Not quite a gentleman, perhaps, but most helpful.

--Yes, mother.

John arrived later to find Jiri still immobilised, being read to by Anne.

--What?

--Doktor Jonni, don't worry, I am quite *in Ordnung*. Mr Ralph says I am a mallyshag. Mr Ralph was right; I was most foolish, I should have seen that other boy... It was so cold, but the fishes are *perfekt*ly well.

--Jiri, that's enough. Be quiet. Miss Anne will tell me what has happened. And we must get you back to your parents.

--Doktor Jonni! hissed Jiri. I cannot move. There are

46

ladies and I HAVE NO CLOTHES ON just this blanket. *Es juckt ziemlich…*

One of Jiri's foibles was that he would not bear anything itchy or scratchy next to his skin, but John was merciless.

--If it is itchy, Jiri, it is your own fault and you will have to put up with it.

--The thing is, John, his clothes are still wet, and I really don't want him to have damp things on, especially after he was shivering so much. My dear, Beatrice and I had to undress him, he wouldn't let Anne be there, and the child is really very thin, poor little fellow…

--Poor little fellow my foot! Mother, this is too much for you…

--No, John, it has been quite pleasant to be a grandmother for one day, even if he is a little… active…

Anne and John considered sending to the hotel for some dry clothes for Jiri, but in the end John lost patience; it had been a long shift on the wards, and he said that he would just take Jiri as he was, with his belongings bundled up, take a cab and get him into the hotel by the back entrance.

--What's this? he asked as a brown paper parcel was added to the bundle of damp clothes.

--His shopping. We went to Whiteleys, and he bought presents for everyone at home. In fact, John, he didn't buy anything for himself; he spent the last of his money on a really pretty pencil case for Flora.

The next day Anne said that she was worried about her mother being overtired, and that she would stay with her instead of going to her extension lecture. So, she was at home when

Ralph Battrill dropped in, on the way to or from Croydon, apparently, to check that all was well. As Anne showed him the sights of Bayswater, he mentioned that he was thinking of spending an extra day or two in London. He'd heard that the Crystal Palace at Sydenham was worth seeing; perhaps, if they took Jerry as a chaperone, it would be all right with Anne's mother?

Later, the Zelleks received a note asking whether they would allow Jiri to visit the Crystal Palace with Anne Loudon and a friend. Gladly, and Anton provided a generous donation to cover the entry and refreshments for all of them.

Once more, Jiri was deposited at the Loudons'. His stepmother had bought him some new clothes; the others, Jiri explained, were good enough to play in, but would never be quite the same after the pond. Now, he said proudly showing off his new Norfolk jacket and knickers, I am a real English Boy, which was a most unlikely statement.

--Would you like to be one? asked Mrs Loudon rather unwisely. Even Jiri realised that this required some diplomacy.

After thought, he responded, Of course, I am a subject of the Emperor. But if I was not, I would choose to be a subject of King Edward and dear Queen Alexandra. I like London very much. And English people are mostly very nice. Except when they push you into the pond.

It was arranged that Ralph would travel separately from Croydon and meet Anne and Jiri at Sydenham Station. Anne explained to Jiri, who was almost (but not quite) speechless with excitement, that they would need to take a short train journey to a place called Sydenham.

--Is that where the peasants live? he asked. I mean, it is not in the city?

Thankful that Ralph Battrill could not hear this exchange, Anne explained that in England there were no peasants.

He looked incredulous. Then, who works on the farms? And who milks the cows? And who chops the wood?

--Well, of course, people in England do those things. But we do not call them peasants.

--But, Papa has a big dictionary, and *Bauern* are peasants.

--It is a matter of... usage... do you know what that means?

--No.

--It means what is said and what is not said.

--Ah. That is understood. What is correct; what is polite. I see. But, then what does one call people who do such work?

--We call them the working classes.

--Thank you. *Ich verstehe*. When in England you say the working classes you mean the peasants.

Anne felt that this conversation had little future, and was glad to see that they were nearing Sydenham, which certainly did not appear to be inhabited by peasants.

Having met Ralph and obtained a map, they looked at the grounds, the fountain (where both Ralph and Anne kept fast hold of Jiri) and the Egyptian Hall. Rather guiltily, Anne had wondered whether the cultural gap between her and Ralph would cause awkwardness; she was determined not to seem superior, or a know-all, but... in fact, Ralph was able to explain things which she could not, while appearing intelligently interested in anything she had to say.

Knowing that they had a long day before them, Anne thought of refreshments.

--Jiri, would you like a bun?

--I certainly would, said Ralph.

49

--Can I try that? asked Jiri, looking at the cups of tea that the adults were enjoying.

--All right. You can have a sip of mine, when it's a bit cooler, offered Ralph. Meanwhile, eat up your bun.

Jiri began it with enthusiasm, but left half of it, distracted by the antics of two nearby children.

--No. It's all crumbs.

--Jerry, said Ralph, there are lots of children who are hungry, and would be glad to have that.

This statement had as much impact as it ever does, that is, none.

--Perhaps I might wrap it up for them. But it will get even more crumby.

--All right. I will eat it. But you are having none of my tea.

Jiri shrugged. He would try tea some other time. This was far too lovely a day to spoil by insisting, and besides, he had the measure of Ralph as someone who would not be trifled with, any more than Doktor Jonni or Uncle Karel.

Shortly afterwards, Anne visited the ladies' cloakroom. As she came out, she could not immediately see Ralph and Jiri amongst the crowd.

An attendant touched her arm,

--Excuse me, madam, your husband and little boy are over there.

Of course, it was the colouring. Both Ralph and Jiri were exceptionally dark. She turned towards them: Ralph had his hand on Jiri's shoulder and was pointing something out to him; the boy was looking up, his face alight with interest.

Suddenly Anne knew that Ralph would be an extremely good father. Just then, he saw her coming towards him and his expression revealed that, as far as he was concerned, at that moment only one person in the vast building meant anything to him. Anne felt herself smile as she ran to them.

It was a lovely day.

It was long remembered by all three of them.

By the time they set off for Sydenham Station on the return trip, Jiri could hardly keep going. He held hands between them and fell silent.

--Scramble up, nipper, said Ralph, crouching down. I'll give you a ride for the rest of the way. Mind you keep still and behave yourself.

--Yes, Mr Ralph. Thank you.

--You know, Anne, said Ralph, glancing at an advertisement showing a group of impossibly red-cheeked children playing leapfrog, you could try Virol for that nipper... build him up a bit?

Jiri fell asleep in the train.

--I'll need to go back to the Island tomorrow or the next day. They'll be sending the letter there, to say whether I've got the job.

--Why don't you go into the shipping office tomorrow, Ralph? Then you can find out whether they have sent the letter, and what's in it.

He took her hand.

--I'll do that. Then we can talk.

When the train stopped, Anne's head was on Ralph's shoulder and Jiri's head was in Anne's lap. None of them wanted to get out.

Anne consulted her brother about the Virol.

--Could do worse; we use it on the children's ward. I don't think we have a hope of getting him to take a proper spoonful, but maybe a teaspoon every day if you want to try.

Jiri paid several more visits to the Loudons', where he asked eagerly about Mr Ralph, to be told that he had gone back to see his family on the Isle of Wight before preparing to leave for Canada. Anne was most willing to talk about him; she found Jiri an old jigsaw puzzle of the British Isles showing the different counties, and patiently pointed out the difference between the Isle of Man and the Isle of Wight, a vital piece of information probably unknown to most Austrian eight-year-olds. She also came back from the chemist's with a jar of Virol.

Jiri viewed this with great mistrust. It was Mrs Loudon who produced a very special silver teaspoon with the end shaped like a little figure, supposedly Saint Peter. This, she said, could be used only for Virol, and only if Jiri would take a tiny dose of the brown, sticky substance, which, he discovered, did not actually taste too bad.

She was even willing for Jiri to take this spoon back to Pallin with him, on condition that its specialist use continued.

--I don't suppose they have Virol in Austria, Mother.

--In that case, Anne, his parents must be told to take a supply back with them.

The Zelleks had found it very convenient to be able to leave Jiri with the Loudons; it was impossible to have him with them during their busy schedule, although Anton fulfilled his promise of the Changing of the Guard, which enchanted

Jiri even though the King and Queen did not conduct it in person, and Grethe took him on some of the few social visits she undertook; Jiri behaved well and played happily with any children they met. But the Loudons' Bayswater house became his second home, with a supply of clean play clothes readily available and a financial arrangement made with Anne Loudon for the boy's supervision and a few English lessons. John realised that despite his fears that Jiri would be too much for his mother, in fact, the lad brought a new interest to both Mrs Loudon and Beatrice; the older lady pronounced him a delicate child requiring careful management, while Beatrice declared that he needed a firm hand, preferably across his backside. Between them they kept him happy and generally well-behaved. Mrs Loudon also attempted Jiri's moral education.

--Jiri, dear, we can't always have what we want.

--Why not?

--Because it's not good for us.

--But people are usually nicer when they get what they want. I know I am.

Jiri knew that it was babyish and ungentlemanly to scream, kick and throw things when thwarted. But it was a quite effective method of getting one's own way, and things were so much pleasanter when life went according to one's desires.

Mrs Loudon continued.

--You are a little boy and still learning how to behave properly. Grown-up people know better than you what is good for you.

This reminded Jiri of an equally unsatisfactory conversation with one of the sisters at school; he asked her why his prayers so often went unanswered. The gist of her reply was that he was praying for the wrong things.

--Oh. So how do I know whether I am praying for the right things or the wrong things?

--If they are right, then your prayers will be answered. If not, then you will know that you are praying for the wrong things.

Jiri opened his mouth to point out the flaws in this argument, *ABER*...

Sister glared sternly at him.

--The Prayers of Good Children Are Always Answered, she pronounced, putting Jiri in his place and providing an instant answer to his question.

Still, Granny Loudon had offered a distant hope.

--You mean, that when I am grown-up I can have what I want and tell other people what is good for them? Like the Emperor, or King Edward, or Uncle Karel?

--Well... not exactly, dear... would you like to have your elevenses now?

Mrs Loudon had been brought up as a member of the Church of England, and made sure that Jiri learned an English version of the grace, which she made him say before luncheon; she even tried introducing him to the vicar.

--Come in, Jiri dear, said Mrs Loudon. This is our clergyman, Mr Russell.

Jiri stood to attention.

--Good afternoon, Father.

(It's Mr Russell, dear, corrected Mrs Loudon).

--Good afternoon, Mr Russell. May I have some of that cake?

--No, Jiri, not now; it will spoil your supper.

--Very well. I will ask Beatrice later, replied Jiri good-naturedly.

Mr Russell surveyed the boy. Well, Gerald...

--My name is Jaroslav Felix von Tarnheim Zellek.

--Well... er... my boy, are you a good child?

This question was always posed by representatives of religion. It was a sin to lie to the clergy, but the truth usually resulted in much unwelcome information about eternal punishment.

Jiri drew a deep breath.

--No. Not always.

--We are all sinners, more or less, responded the vicar, his tone leaving Jiri in no doubt about their relative positions.

--Do you say your prayers, and go to church?

This was safer ground.

--Yes, I say my prayers every night, except sometimes when I fall asleep without meaning to.

(Well, that could happen to anyone.)

And Papa has found a proper church near the South Kensington Museum.

--What does he mean by a proper church? Mr Russell asked his hostess.

--I'm afraid he means a Roman church, whispered Mrs Loudon, but Jiri had caught the question, and explained.

--Where you can light candles, and there are statues. Our Lady, she is always *sehr hübsch*, and St Laurence with his... his... (what might be the English word for gridiron?) frying pan... and St Peter with the big keys.

--Ah. Perhaps he knows the Scriptures. What can you tell me about the Apostle Peter, my boy?

55

--He is the first Pope. That is why he has the keys. He can unlock the gates of Heaven and let the good people in. Then he locks them again, to keep out Freemasons, and Protestants and people like that. The other one is for Hell. He puts the bad people in there and locks them in for ever and ever, in burning fires, said Jiri with relish, thinking of one or two on whom he would personally like to turn the key.

Mr Russell seized the moment to ask,

--And what about you? Where will you go when you die, my child?

--I shall go to Purgatory for years and years. Although I think there are ways of getting a few thousand years off, but I can't remember them now. Perhaps you know all about that? he asked hopefully.

Suddenly the Roman concept of Purgatory made sense to Mr Russell. It was listening to Jiri Zellek for several thousand years. Rather ostentatiously, he pulled out his watch.

--How time has flown, dear Mrs Loudon! I must be going. I will come back soon… perhaps when you are alone… I will pray for you, my boy, he added.

--Oh, thank you! cried Jiri, Please could you ask for…

But the clergyman was gone.

--Are you sure I can't have just a very little piece of cake, dear Granny Loudon? asked Jiri.

Anne was at a lecture; Mrs Loudon needed peace and quiet to go through the household accounts.

--I'll take him into the kitchen with me, m'um. He can help shell the peas.

This was a new experience for Jiri, and at first he was delighted with the task. He compared the number and size of the peas as they nestled in their pods; he liked the colour, and he tried the taste. It was satisfying to see the pile of empty shucks on the table, and the pile of peas in the bowl, growing. Then he began to wonder how far one could flick the peas across the kitchen. Doktor Jonni said that scientists learned by doing experiments. He could be a scientist with the peas. Or he could be an artillery officer, shooting the enemy.

--Whatever are you doing, Master Jerry?

--I am making... *so*... with the peas to see how far they will go.

--Wasting good food and making a mess, that's what you're doing. Now get down and clear it up.

Beatrice handed him a dustpan and brush, both handy items, he thought. Busily he began sweeping the floor.

--Beatrice, here is a big... *Spinne*... I don't know in English... they have some legs and eat flies.

--URRGHH! It's a spider, that's what it is!

--If you are frightened, Beatrice, I will squash it. But that would be a pity and make mess.

--No, we don't kill them. If you wish to live and thrive/ Let a spider run alive.

--Oh, that is nice! Please say it again so I can learn it.

Beatrice repeated the rhyme and he said it after her.

She looked at the kitchen clock.

--Look at the time! Why does everything take twice as long when this child is about? Master Jerry, leave the peas, go and wash your hands and then you can help lay the table.

--Jiri, where are you?

--I am in the bathroom, Miss Anne. I have been washing my hands and now I am blowing bubbles.

--Who said you might do that?

--No one. I thought of it for myself.

--It is a waste of soap. Dry your hands and come down.

--*Jawohl*, Miss Anne.

--Beatrice, there do not seem to be many peas in this dish.

--No, m'um.

--Jiri, have you been a good helpful boy?

--Not really. But I have had a nice morning.

Ralph Battrill returned to Croydon for a few days; apparently he needed to make some further arrangements, and buy some equipment, for his move to Canada. Calling in at the Loudons', he suggested that he and Anne might take Jiri to the park.

Immediately Jiri wandered a few steps away.

--Want to play?

--Yes, yes!

--Come on then.

Jiri looked at Anne and Ralph, who were having one of their important conversations. They would not miss him.

He ran over to the group of boys, mostly rather bigger than himself, with one or two younger lads.

--Can you bowl?

Jiri looked confused; he saw no such receptacles.

The tall, fair boy tossed a ball up and down.

--Ah. Throwing.

--No, that's for girls and little kids. Like this.

He demonstrated. Jiri took the ball.

--Aim at the stumps.

Again, Jiri was puzzled. All the trees looked quite intact.

--Over there.

Jiri copied the boy's action and managed to hit the row of sticks indicated.

--Not bad. Can you hold a bat?

--Bet he can't. He's a foreigner. They can't play cricket.

--I can! Jiri seized the bat and twirled it around his head.

--No, no! You'll brain somebody like that!

Jiri had rather thought this was the point of a cricket bat. He was thinking that it was quite a handy weapon.

--I know you! It was you who pushed that cad Ted Browning into the pond. Then his brother shoved you in and you threw mud at him.

--Yes. I did not like him. Or his brother.

--Nobody does. But you were the first person to push him into the pond.

--Did you get a hiding?

--No. But next time… Jiri recalled the lecture he'd had from John Loudon.

--Well, I reckon if you can do that, you can learn to play cricket, said the tall lad.

You see Ginger there? You just do what he tells you, and if you don't make too much of a mess of it, we'll let you join the team.

Time passed quickly. Apart from a tendency to dispute the umpire's decisions, Jiri got on well, although he could not be said to understand all that went on.

Anne and Ralph eventually woke up to the fact that he

was no longer with them; fortunately he was not far away, and clearly quite happy with his new companions.

--Jiri, come along, we must go, called Anne.

He ignored her.

--Jiri, I said it's time to leave.

No sign of recognition.

Ralph stepped forward.

--Jerry! Now! Look sharp or it's a clip on the ear.

Jiri did not know what this was, but judging from Ralph's tone and expression, it was nothing good.

Reluctantly he waved goodbye to the cricketers.

--Now. Say sorry to Anne.

--I am sorry, Miss Anne.

--Apology accepted, Jiri. Try to be more obedient in future.

--Yes. I will try. Mr Ralph, how much does a cricket bat cost?

--One your size, and just for playing about with? He named a figure.

--Thank you. I shall save up. But it will take a long time.

--Perhaps your father will help you. But I don't suppose many people in Austria play cricket.

--I can teach Christa and Gustl, and you can use a bat for other things.

At about this time, the three of them became enthusiastic cinema, or rather *kinema*, goers. Anne and Ralph would put Jiri between them, and their hands would meet across the back of his seat. He was absolutely enthralled by the screen. Daredevil escapes, dramatic encounters, dastardly doings, cowboys, swordfights, high-speed train journeys and news footage of royalty all appealed to him greatly. He also escaped and scrambled into the orchestra pit, where he introduced himself to the pianist.

--I could do that, he told Anne and Ralph, if I grow a bit taller.

--Do what?

--Play the music for the pictures. I need to be tall enough to be able to see across to the screen, so I'd know what was happening. Then I would choose what to play. If I played 'God Save the King', for King Edward, would everybody have to stand up? So would 'Rule Britannia' be better? Or 'He's a Jolly Good Fellow'? And something very, very beautiful for dear Queen Alexandra. We are related to her, you know. It would be nice if she was *eine Tante*, but I think she is a faraway cousin.

--You mean a distant cousin, Jiri, corrected Anne.

--Oh yes, and my uncle's the King of Siam! laughed Ralph.

--Oh! cried Jiri, I thought...

--Stop it, Ralph, you know he believes everything you say.

--More fool him, but he shouldn't tell such whoppers.

--Actually it's probably true. The von Tarnheims, the four of them, are somehow related to lots of people like that; John was telling me.

--Four?

--Yes: Jiri's uncle, his cousin Christa, Jiri himself and Christa's mother, but no one talks about her. Anyway, they are in the Almanach de Gotha.

--The what?

Anne grinned wickedly.

--It's a sort of stud book of European families with titles.

Ralph and Anne had, after much discussion, come to a series of decisions, which still needed to be shared with her mother and brother. This would not be easy, but it was made more urgent, and even more difficult, one day about two weeks before the Zelleks were due to leave.

It began, as such things often do, with coincidences and honest mistakes.

Anne was at the British Museum; Mrs Loudon was called to a friend whose husband had fallen suddenly ill. Beatrice had charge of Jiri when Ralph Battrill arrived unexpectedly; he hoped Anne would be at home, but if she was not, it might be a good opportunity for the talk he needed to have with her mother. He found Beatrice rather flustered, and Jiri eyeing up the apple tree, which he had been forbidden to climb, but now that everyone's back was turned... A letter had arrived for John Loudon; it was marked Urgent, Please redirect, and Beatrice was at a loss as to what to do.

--Don't worry. I'll see to it, offered Ralph. And I'll take the nipper along with me, keep him out of your way.

Jiri put on his cap and jacket, and they left, Beatrice presumed for the post office.

But, when both ladies returned, there was no sign of them.

A thought struck Anne. You don't think, she said, that they might have gone to find John at the hospital?

--What? You mean he has taken that child to the East End? To that den of infection? He would not be so irresponsible, even if he is—

Anne broke in.

--Ralph... Mr Battrill... knows nothing of London; he is as ignorant of the city as Jiri! Why, that first time when we

62

met in the park, he was only there because he had taken the wrong train.

Meanwhile, Ralph and Jiri had got out of the omnibus at a stop which Ralph hoped was close to the hospital where John worked. He was used to the dockside areas of Portsmouth and Southampton, but he had never been anywhere like this. How could people live like that? The smell… the filth…

--Hold my hand, nipper. Keep walking.

People were following them. A woman's voice called out, I'll look after the kid if you want a good time.

Reaching the hospital was a relief. Ralph handed in the letter, took Jiri back outside, and was preparing to rethink their route home, when John himself appeared, letter in hand. (It concerned a sudden problem with John's intended purchase of a medical practice.)

He was clearly furious.

--Battrill! What are you about?

The two men faced each other. This was when a gang of street urchins started shouting abuse at Jiri; one knocked off his cap and, when he bent to retrieve it, sent him sprawling on the pavement.

Jiri could swear fluently in his native language and in German and did so now, adding a few terms he had picked up in the hotel stables. While most of this could not be understood, the general drift was clear. He was looking around for something to throw, when John seized him by the collar, and with a few kicks and well-chosen words sent the other lads on their way.

--How could you, man! If this boy has picked up infection or disease, it is your doing! Don't you see, you dolt, what a serious illness could do to him? When you get him home, make sure Anne gives him a bath with carbolic soap and changes his clothes, if you've got the sense to remember that.

--Hold on. I know he's a bit undersized, but what's so wrong with him that he needs wrapping in cotton wool?

--In a word, inbreeding. That's something you ought to know all about, coming from where you do.

Ralph was used to more or less good-natured jokes about the Island, and the interconnected nature of its inhabitants, but these came from workmates, sailors and the like, not from some superior middle-class bastard who thought himself mighty because he had a medical degree.

--That does it, Loudon. I'll marry your sister and I'll take her to Canada, and when I do I'll never set eyes on your smug face again; and if I do, I'll sock it. Come on, nipper, we're going. I don't like the company here.

Fortunately for Ralph's dignity, a cab had just deposited one of the surgeons and was looking for a return fare. He shoved Jiri inside, slammed the door and gave the Loudons' Bayswater address. After a while, he realised that it was quite a considerable journey, and he hoped he had sufficient money.

--Jerry?

--Yes, Mr Ralph?

--Have you got any money?

--No. It is Thursday.

Ralph did not immediately see the relevance of this, but realised that Jiri had his pocket money every Saturday. There was little hope of it lasting beyond Wednesday.

--Are you all right, nipper?

--Yes, Mr Ralph, but not my knee.

It had been grazed, and blood dripped down onto his sock. They both looked at it with interest.

--Here. Ralph tied his handkerchief around it.

--Thank you. And thank you for saving me.

Ralph knew that at least he was a hero in someone's eyes.

--Mr Ralph, what's a friggin' eyetie? And am I one?

--What?

--That's what that boy was calling me.

--Well, Jerry, it means an Italian. And you aren't. But don't say that in front of the ladies, will you?

--No. I expect it is Strong Language.

When they arrived in Bayswater, Ralph had to leave Jiri in the cab while he went inside to ask for the price of the fare. Finally he lifted him out, and with a set expression, repeated John's instructions…

--Beatrice, said Anne, take Master Jiri upstairs, give him a good scrub with carbolic soap, including his hair, and change all his clothes. And do something about his knee.

--I don't want iodine, noted Jiri firmly.

--You'll have what's good for you, snapped Beatrice. You don't want it to fester, do you?

--What's fester?

--Going bad and having to be chopped off.

Jiri thought of those whose limbs he hoped might fester, and the sooner the better, but Beatrice was hauling him away.

--I will take his jacket and knickers into the garden and give them a thorough brush in the fresh air, said Mrs Loudon; it was as well she did, as a couple of fleas hopped out in search of the cat.

--I'll get us all some luncheon. Anne turned towards the kitchen.

--Never mind the nammet, Anne. I've had words with your brother. We're changing our plans.

--Ralph, we have thought and thought. We have agreed; you are going to Canada, and you will look for suitable employment for me. Meanwhile I will make sure mother and John are used to the idea. Very soon, Flora and John will be married, he is buying a practice, and they will have mother to live with them. Then, when the passage is available, I will join you.

--No. You are going to marry me now and come as my wife, for better or worse. If you stay here, they will persuade you that I'm not good enough for you, that we wouldn't be happy, and you'll be better off without me. I know how it will be. It's now or never, Nance.

There was silence. In the garden, Mrs Loudon could be heard brushing Jiri's clothes.

Upstairs, the boy's voice was raised in protest, answered by Beatrice,

--No more of that, Master Jerry, or you'll have soap in your mouth. Now stand still while I dry your hair.

--I'm not having iodine.

--Yes you are. Sit still and be a brave boy.

--I don't want to. I'm not brave. It hurts.

A burst of sobbing followed. Anne felt like joining in.

--Ralph, you're not being fair. I need time, time to make arrangements here, to see mother settled.

--My dearest, I know you are a good daughter... but you are like me, not the only child in the family. Dad was a seaman and understands that I can't stay on the Island all my life; Mum will miss me, but she's got Stan round the corner and his missus, and Elsie will be going into service at one of the big hotels, she wouldn't move away... Your mother has John, soon she'll have Flora, and they'll start a family. If we go, we go together, away from all of that... that...

A new life, thought Anne. It was true; her mother liked Ralph, but thought him below her. John actively disliked him. She was two years older than Ralph; she would never meet anyone she could love so much, and she did love Ralph. His dark hair, his strong, stocky body, his direct ways and dry, country humour, the way he took her for herself, Anne Loudon, not as a young (or now, not so very young) lady, not as a bit of a blue stocking, not as a would-be New Woman, not as someone keeping up appearances with one maid and a daily girl, accepting money from the Zelleks for looking after their son... but herself... or, at least, herself as he saw her, and that was something she would need to live up to.

It had gone quiet upstairs. Beatrice drew Anne aside.

--Miss Anne, the boy is asleep on your bed. He has a nasty graze on his knee, and that Mr Battrill got him overtired. And he was upset, miss. He said the two gentlemen were angry and shouting; he couldn't understand it all, and he thought it must be all his fault, although he hadn't meant to be naughty.

--Oh dear. What did you say, Beatrice?

--I told him not to believe that the world revolves around a silly little boy like him, and it was likely nothing to do with him. I didn't want the mistress worried by his crying, so I kept him on my lap for a bit and he nodded off. I put him on your bed with the eiderdown. You can all have your luncheon in peace, and I'll give him something afterwards.

Anne was surprised, considering that Beatrice generally described Jiri as a spoiled child whose whims should not be given in to.

Still, it was good to have time to talk things over with her mother, although no one ate much luncheon.

Beatrice reappeared.

--I'll go and rouse the boy, now, m'um. He's had a good hour, and if he goes longer he won't sleep tonight, I'll be bound.

--Wake up, Master Jerry.

--Oh! Beatrice! Have I missed lunch? I'm so hungry!

--Well, get up then, and wash your hands. I've saved some for you.

Jiri got up, looking longingly at the floppy rabbit from Anne's old toybox, which Beatrice had let him hold while he had iodine on his knee.

He knew that it would be babyish to take this downstairs; he would not do it.

--Beatrice, do I have to wash my hands? I've had a bath.

--Yes, you must. You know that you must wash your hands before every meal.

Jiri obediently followed her to the basin.

--Good. Now you can have your luncheon.

--May I have it on *mein Lieblingsteller*? The one with... the... tall... high... cows... with hair...

--You mean the plate with the highland cattle?

--Yes, that's it! The highland cattle! Please.

--We'll see. I'm not promising. And you must behave yourself for the rest of the day, although that will be a miracle, as we all know.

68

Afterwards, Mrs Loudon read aloud to Jiri, who still smelled faintly of carbolic.

--Beatrice is going to do some shopping, and you may go with her, said Anne.

--Oh! But am I correct? He looked down at the play clothes he was wearing.

--Yes Jiri. You are clean and neat. You have your woollen jersey and the tam mother knitted for you. You are perfectly dressed for the butchers and the greengrocers. And here is sixpence. Beatrice, he may spend it as he likes, although perhaps not all on sweets.

Jiri looked longingly at the money. Finally, 'I have had my pocket money this week' was wrung from him.

--That is all right, Jiri. I am sure your father will be quite in agreement. You have been a very good boy.

Jiri was faintly surprised by this, but pocketed the money before anyone could change their mind. He and Beatrice left.

When they returned, both of them had distended cheeks and smelled of peppermint. Jiri offered a paper bag of bullseyes around. Mrs Loudon refused on account of her teeth; Ralph said, Yes, bullseyes were his favourite, and Anne asked to have hers later, if any were left.

Jiri had also bought some soldiers. He was delighted with these, saying that they were just like the ones at the Changing of the Guard. Tea was a much more lively meal. Afterwards Mrs Loudon got on with her knitting as she hoped to finish a striped stocking cap for Jiri before he went back to Austria. Anne and Ralph sat holding hands on the sofa and Jiri played relatively quietly with his new soldiers. It was a contented scene until John Loudon appeared, still with a face like thunder. He refused a bullseye.

--You still here, Battrill? I don't know what I am going to tell his parents. I am going to watch him carefully for the next forty-eight hours. If he shows no signs of infection by then, we may be clear, although I shall not feel secure until a fortnight has gone by.

--Anne, said Ralph, we have spoken to your mother. Now, are you prepared for me to tell your brother here what is to happen?

Eventually, the Zelleks prepared to return home. Although they had managed to have Jiri with them for some of the time, it had been more difficult than they had expected. Anton decided that his next two trips, which were shorter ones to Munich and Berlin, should be undertaken alone, leaving Jiri and Grethe at home; besides, he wanted to find a singing teacher for Jiri, and to prepare the boy for a couple of piano competitions; it would be good to get him used to playing in public.

--I want to say goodbye to Granny Loudon and Miss Anne, Papa.

--He is right, Toni; they have been so good to him, and we ought to thank them.

So the two large, blond Zelleks appeared in Mrs Loudon's drawing room; really, Jiri is a changeling, thought Anne, but of course everybody says he takes after his late mother. They had brought a beautiful vase (one of their samples) as a parting gift; Jiri said a courteous goodbye and thank-you, and at the last moment threw his arms around Mrs Loudon.

She felt his skinny, fragile little body; so far the Virol had not made him any fatter, but it was early days, and perhaps he did have rather more stamina.

The white cliffs of Dover grew distant as the cross-Channel steamer headed for Boulogne. Before long, the sea grew choppy, then rough; most of the passengers, including the four adults in the Zellek party, were soon prostrate. Jiri, who on land seemed able to throw up at will, was unaffected. He was handed to the care of the overworked steward.

--Here, Fenton! he called to one of the sailors, look after this lad for a minute. I've got the whole of first class calling for basins.

The sailor told Jiri that he must behave himself or he would be thrown overboard to the sharks who infested that section of the English Channel.

--Sharks! How big are they? Where are they? Can I see them?

Jiri raced to the ship's rails. Fenton caught him in time, uttering some interesting new English words, which Jiri resolved to remember.

--Come here! Do you want me to tie you to the funnel?

At the *kinema* Jiri had seen the story of a noble cabin boy who had been lashed to the mast of a storm-tossed ship. When they arrived in port everyone else had been swept overboard and drowned, and... with difficulty he wrenched his mind back to the present.

--It's very cold here, he complained.

--All right. Fenton surveyed the shivering child, a small figure in a little reefer jacket, with a hand-knitted stocking cap pulled own over his ears. Let's go to the galley. I bet no one's eating much, so Cookie might find you some cocoa.

The ship's cook wedged Jiri into a corner, and, realising that the combination of a lurching ship, a full mug of cocoa and a small boy could be disastrous, he tied a tea towel around the child before giving him the hot drink.

Jiri fell silent, sipping the hot, sweet liquid. He thought about his stay in London. It seemed to him that he had been there for ages, and that English was almost his native language.

It would have been nice to have met dear Queen Alexandra, and to have got his own back on those boys outside the hospital. He must remember their technique, though: first knock the cap off and then... and it would have been nice to have a cricket bat, which his father had refused him on the inaccurate grounds that he would have little use for it in Austria. But he was realising as he grew older that one could not have everything, and as consolation he had been given a wonderful wooden castle, with a little cannon that really fired. It was now packed away in the trunk, but he would make sure that it was The Very First Thing Anyone Unpacked. And he had seen the Tower of London, and the Changing of the Guard, and the Crystal Palace, and the *kinema*; he now had a career planned as a *kinema* pianist, and somehow he would teach Christa and Gustl cricket.

FRIENDS AND FOES, 1905

John Loudon continued to visit Tarnheim each summer; his understanding with Flora Drake was that they would marry when Christa left for the convent. Meanwhile, John was working in one of the big London Hospitals; this meant that he could arrange to spend the summer months on the Continent, visiting clinics and laboratories, using Tarnheim as a base. Karel was happy to welcome him on this footing.

The summer when Jiri was ten and Christa twelve was his penultimate stay. John continued to enjoy climbing expeditions with various English and German friends, and Jiri listened eagerly to his tales of these outings. Eventually John began to teach Jiri to climb; he stressed that a climber must concentrate on what he is doing, and obey the orders of the leader implicitly, neither of which came easily to Jiri, but the boy was fearless, agile and keen to learn, so that John was pleased with his progress and decided that he was ready for his first proper climb. This was to be undertaken with two other boys, a guide, Gustl and John himself. It was, John reassured Flora, not at all a difficult route; Jiri would be challenged, but not beyond his abilities, and if he became overtired John would bring him down immediately. The idea was to introduce Jiri to climbing as part of a team, with ropes and a guide, rather than to scale any peaks. He will be roped to me and to Gustl the whole time, declared John. Nothing can happen to him.

The other lads were Theo, a twelve-year-old from Strelitz already at the Oberschule, and Ferencz, whose family was holidaying in the mountains. Jiri remarked that he had already met Theo, that he was not a very nice boy, but perhaps he would be better on the day. It was not until later that they learned that Ferencz, aged eleven, had a fear of heights that this relatively easy climb was supposed to cure.

John, Gustl and Jiri set off early in the morning, complete with climbing gear, a map of the route and adequate refreshments.

Towards the end of the day Flora was in her sitting room, when John knocked at the door and entered. He looked exhausted. She did not need to ask how things had gone.

--Jiri? she asked anxiously.

--He is in bed. I have given him a mild sedative, and told Grushenka to keep him there in the morning, at least until I have seen him. No, Flora, it is better that you don't go to him; in any case, I am sure he is asleep now.

Apparently all had gone well at first, at least as far as Jiri was concerned.

--I was quite proud of him, Flora. Not a word of complaint, tackled anything he was asked to do, got on neatly and carefully and was really enjoying it, too, unlike the other two lads, I'm afraid.

Theo is, as Jiri told me, not a very nice fellow. He is one of those big, clumsy lads, maybe not very sure of himself, but given to bossing, bullying and grumbling, although quite an adequate climber, really too good for the others and disgruntled at being sent on an easy climb. They have met at a couple of parties in Strelitz, although so far Jiri has been below his notice as young, small and rather babyish, although he has never tried to bully him.

--I'd like to see anyone try to bully Jiri! exclaimed Flora.

--Well, yes, that's the trouble. Flora, Jiri is in danger of... anyway, it turns out poor Ferencz is scared to death of heights. What his parents were thinking of sending him on this climb I can't think. Well, again I have to say I was proud of Jiri. Patient, encouraging, praising Ferencz for every step he took, although Theo started to take it out of the poor lad, calling him a coward, to which Jiri, who is afraid of little or nothing, ups and says he isn't, in fact he is very brave as a real officer does things even if he is scared, and it's not brave to do things you're not scared of, only if you are really frightened, which piece of philosophy, delivered in Master Jiri's inimitable manner, with which we are only too familiar, doesn't go down well with Theo.

We keep going till lunchtime. Poor Ferencz can't eat much, Theo stuffs himself, Jiri really tucks in, and I'm thinking fresh air and exercise is all that the child needs.

Then I suggest we set off back, as going down is always more difficult and I know Jiri will be tired by the time we reach the only tricky bit. When we get there, the guide goes down with Ferencz, leaving the rest of us at the top. Jiri was roped to me and Gustl, but Theo wasn't; he's been told not to move until the guide comes back for him. Stupid idiot stands at the top, taunting poor Ferencz, who has frozen about halfway down. Well, you can imagine. Jiri tells him to stop;

Theo starts calling Jiri names, and he gives more than he gets. I couldn't understand all of it but well, Flora, I suppose he must have picked up that language at the stables; you will have to talk to him about it. John passed his hand wearily across his brow. Then Theo says something pretty vile about Christa's mother and the von Tarnheims in general.

I should have stopped it before then, but Jiri loses his temper...

--Oh no!

--Yes. Picks up a rock, in both hands, it was that big, and runs at Theo ready to brain him, and Theo's at the edge, not roped.

--Oh, John.

--Thank God, I was roped to Jiri and able to grab him while Gustl, bless him, got the rock out of his hands. By now he's kicking me. Goodness knows what my legs will look like tomorrow. I spoke to him pretty sharply, told him he was endangering all our lives (which was a bit of an exaggeration) and that I would never take him climbing again. That worked. But you can imagine the state he was in by that time. Gustl and I got him down, leaving the guide with the other two. I did go back later to make sure they were all right.

--Oh, John, no wonder you are worn out!

--I had a word with the guide; of course, he'd seen and heard it all; I gave him a tip and asked him to be discreet. I think he will, said Jiri was a plucky little fellow, all the von Tarnheims had a temper on them, he was a real von Tarnheim, etc. By the time we got near home, Gustl and I had to take turns to carry Jiri; it was emotional as well as physical exhaustion and perhaps I had asked too much of the boy. But, Flora, he could have killed that lad Theo, he wanted to, and I keep asking myself whether he'd noticed the fellow wasn't roped...

--John, he's only ten! And very small for ten.

--Yes, yes, I know and that's part of the problem; you know how small chaps can be very aggressive, and poor Jiri hasn't got much self-control. Anyway, Flora, I'll talk to him in the morning. I've had enough for one day; I'm going to bed.

And, rising rather stiffly, John left the room.

Next morning he found Jiri sitting up in bed, finishing his breakfast and swallowing the herbal concoction flavoured with honey that Grushenka had convinced him would make him grow as tall as his uncle. It was several years before Jiri realised that it didn't work.

--Good morning, Jiri. How are you?

--Good morning, Herr Doktor Jonni. My legs are tired and my arms hurt.

--Let me see them.

They were covered with bruises from John and Gustl's restraining hands.

--I will ask Grushenka to put some arnica on them. Perhaps she will spare some for me. John grinned and showed Jiri his legs, which bore the marks of Jiri's climbing boots.

--Did I do that? I'm so sorry... Jiri seemed on the point of tears and clutched the bear Wolfi, who was in bed beside him. Quickly John interposed,

--In England we call it a fair fight and shake hands.

--A fair fight, said Jiri holding out his hand, and they shook.

--Jiri, I need to talk to you about yesterday. Before he could start crying, John hurried on.

77

I was very pleased with you for most of the time.

Jiri was evidently astonished.

Yes. You climbed well, you obeyed my instructions perfectly, you did not complain when you were tired, and you were extremely nice to Ferencz.

--It was all Theo's fault, muttered Jiri.

--No, it was not. You forgot that, when one is climbing as a team, personal differences must be overlooked for the sake of all. And, Jiri, you lost your temper.

--He made me. He was horrible.

--He may well have been horrible, but he did not MAKE you threaten him with a rock. It was your own bad temper and lack of control that made you do that, Jiri. And, I have to ask you, did you realise at the time that Theo wasn't roped?

There was a brief silence.

--Yes, Doktor Jonni. I did see, and I didn't care, I just wanted to hit him. I hated him. And I still do, although I wish I hadn't behaved like that.

--You do understand, my boy, that you could have killed him?

--I do now, and I suppose I'm glad I didn't. You would all be sorry if I was executed as a murderer. And perhaps he will be nicer now. But I don't want to see him again.

--I don't suppose he wants to see you ever again, Jiri.

--Will Uncle Karel be very angry?

--Ah. I will speak to your uncle. I shall have to tell him that you lost your temper on a climb, and that is very serious. I shall also tell him about the better aspects of your behaviour.

--He'll say that I need to go to cadet school as soon as I am old enough.

John did not reply to this; for the first time he began to

78

wonder whether army training might after all be the best way of channelling Jiri's anger and aggression.

--Now, as your doctor, I'm going to examine you. I think I shall ask you to be a good boy and stay in bed this morning. Perhaps Miss Drake and Christa would be kind enough to come and read to you. Gustl can bring you your luncheon here, and then you may get up in the afternoon. By the way, you might think about apologising to Gustl for spoiling his day.

One reason why John had prevented Jiri from joining the usual luncheon group was that he did not think him in a fit state to face interrogation from his uncle. As he had predicted, Karel took a very dim view of Jiri's loss of control, but, in view of his age, and his otherwise exemplary behaviour, he was willing to give him another chance if John could see his way to taking just Jiri and Gustl on an easy climb. The exact content of Theo's comments on the von Tarnheims was not disclosed. Christa was told only that Jiri was very tired after the climb, at which she said scornfully that she would certainly never have needed a day in bed after such an easy one. What passed between the two of them remained private. There were no repercussions from Theo's parents. The guide kept his mouth shut and Theo himself perhaps felt that he had emerged with little credit.

Unexpected support came from Ferencz. He was an intelligent, imaginative boy, although not physically brave. He had taken a liking to Jiri and for the remainder of their stay his family encouraged the two boys to play together. His father visited Karel, praised Jiri's courage and spirit, and obtained permission to take him on trips and outings as company for

Ferencz and his little brother Mikki. It suited Jiri not to be the youngest, smallest member of a group; he did not need to prove himself, or push himself beyond his strength and, perhaps backed by dire warnings that any bad behaviour would instantly put a stop to the visits, he showed that he could be really good, even for days at a time. In addition, Ferencz's family was musical; Madame Balinkay played the piano and Ferencz himself was learning the violin, so Jiri's talents were appreciated. He began to pick up a few words in Hungarian, and took teasing about his accent in good part. The father, who appeared only at weekends and who had suggested the unfortunate climb, was a Hungarian government official whose huge black moustache fascinated Jiri, although he knew it was rude to stare and tried very hard not to. Ferencz, with the graceful courtesy he possessed even at the age of eleven, said that, horrible as the climbing experience had been, it was almost worth it to have met Jiri, and they all said how much they would miss him when they returned to Budapest. He is a very suitable friend for the boys, remarked Madame, although all those von Tarnheims are rather arrogant, even little Jiri at times; they think themselves a cut above other people.

--Jiri doesn't think himself a cut above other people because he's a von Tarnheim, corrected Ferencz. He thinks he is because he's Jiri.

At about this time, Jiri received an invitation to an afternoon party given by Theo's parents.

--I'm not going.

He was rather deflated by Miss Drake's response.

--No, Jiri, it is better that you do not go. I'm afraid I cannot quite trust you.

--Oh, Miss Drake, you can trust me; if he insults Ferzi Balinkay or our family, you can trust me to kill him.

--That, Jiri, was my point.

--Miss Drake, that is not logical.

--Shut up, Jiri. Christa aimed a kick at him, which he dodged.

--Now, Jiri, you will write a note declining the invitation. You can write a draft, I will correct it, and you can write it out properly.

He did not argue, but muttered something Miss Drake could not understand.

--Jiri, you know that I will have only English or German spoken in the schoolroom.

--*Jawohl*, Miss Drake. Christa what is the German word for ****?

--Jiri…

--Miss Drake, how can I write it in German unless I know what the word is?

--Be quiet, Jiri, and do your best.

Silence followed, broken only by the scratching of Jiri's pencil.

--What are you writing, Jiri?

--I am writing that I would rather put my head in a bucket of shit than spend an afternoon with Theo Holtzner.

--Me too.

--Silence, Christa. You have not been invited.

--Thank goodness.

--Jiri, that will not do.

Miss Drake tore his draft in two and threw it into the waste basket.

--Here is a clean sheet of paper. With lines ruled on it.

You will write down what I will dictate.

A look of glowering rebellion threatened trouble, until Christa interposed.

--Jiri, I bet your handwriting is already better than that lout Theo's. You write what Miss Drake tells you, then we'll ask Papa for some headed paper and one of the special envelopes, you write the letter out as nicely as you can, and That Will Show Them!

Seeing this as a practical, if not particularly ethical solution, Flora Drake backed her up.

--That is a good idea. We will keep it short, she added.

Rather annoyingly, Jiri could usually do anything he set his mind to, and, although it took some time, a suitably impressive note, signed with his full name, was sent off to the Holtzners'.

Flora recalled that she really needed to take Jiri to task for his colourful vocabulary, but after the narrowly bought success of the note-writing she quailed at the thought of the semantic and moral discussion that would ensue.

Meanwhile Jiri's visits to the Balinkays continued. While he played chess and shared music practice with Ferencz, he also enjoyed the company of six-year-old Mikki, who adored him. Mikki was not unlike Jiri, in that he was a mischievous, daring child who was often in trouble. Madame Balinkay shook her head over him; he was so unlike Ferencz.

--Don't worry, Madame Mama, said Jiri, He will soon be more sensible. I was very naughty when I was his age.

--Not as naughty as Mikki, surely?

--Oh I was MUCH, MUCH worse.

--Why, Jiri, what did you do? asked Mikki with interest.

--I shall not tell you, as it might give you ideas, and I would not like to be a Bad Influence.

This was said with such an air of conscious virtue that Ferencz and his mother exchanged smiles.

--Actually, Jiri, whispered Ferencz, it's too late. You are one already.

Ferencz revealed that he had also been invited to the Holtzners' party; under duress he had gone, and had not enjoyed it. The really unfortunate aspect of this was that Madame Balinkay felt obliged to host Theo for an afternoon, and, unaware of Jiri's feelings towards the older boy, she invited him also. Ferencz had not told his parents of Jiri's murderous attack on Theo, if indeed he had fully taken it in at the time; they knew only that Jiri had been kind, considerate and helpful to their son.

This time there was really no escape. Both John and Flora had been extremely disturbed by Jiri's rage on the climbing expedition. The temper tantrums, which were perhaps understandable in a rather spoiled, overactive child who was physically frail and often overtired, seemed to have mutated into an episode of uncontrollable violence. He was still only ten; what would he be like when adolescence rocked his personality? Especially if the longed-for growth spurt was slow in coming, and John was adamant that Jiri would always be short and slight, with the vein of aggression often seen in men of that build. They had agreed not to discuss the matter with Karel von Tarnheim; Flora now recalled the various tales she had heard, and dismissed as idle legend, of von Tarnheims who had killed animals, servants and even kinsfolk in maddened rages. They both took any opportunity to talk to Jiri about the need for self-control; he would otherwise be a danger to himself and others, and they used every possible argument to convince him to try to act responsibly. Perhaps as a result, Jiri had been exceptionally good recently; Miss Drake and John Loudon were also to be of the party at the Balinkays, since Christa was at the von Stroens for the day, and surely Jiri could be kept under control.

For most of the afternoon, things were, if not exactly pleasant, at least reasonably civilised. John undertook to supervise the three boys plus little Mikki, on a walk, engaging them in conversation and avoiding any direct confrontation. Jiri was clearly making a huge effort, the only question being how long he could keep it up.

At last came the time for Theo's departure. The whole party gathered to say goodbye to him in the hall. As he prepared to leave, he hissed something at Ferencz, referring to him as a girlish coward, and to Jiri as a runt from a crazy family; his aunt was a whore and everyone knew that the von Tarnheims were homicidal maniacs who fucked their sisters. Ferencz held Jiri back, but, looking out from the smart pony trap sent to fetch him, Theo made a rude gesture.

It was too much. Jiri snatched up a stone, which he flung, scraping paint off the vehicle.

--Good riddance! Bugger off, you fat-arsed motherfucking wanker, he bawled.

A horrified silence fell.

John Loudon grabbed Jiri and took him into the corridor. Resounding slaps were heard, causing Ferencz and his mother to flinch, Miss Drake to suffer acute embarrassment, and Mikki to open his eyes in horror. Suppose something like that should happen to him? He would be a good boy from this day forward.

Shortly John appeared, holding Jiri, who was fighting back tears, by the shoulder.

--Now apologise for using such language before ladies and an innocent child, he ordered.

Jiri did so, although even in his shattered state he did not think Mikki so very innocent.

John released him and he ran to Miss Drake, who, rightly or wrongly, took him in her arms.

She and John exchanged glances. We shall take Jiri home, she announced.

At this Jiri broke loose and rushed to Madame Balinkay.

--I am truly sorry. Please say that I may come again, Madame Mama—

Madame Balinkay earned a reward in Heaven.

--In Hungary, she said, a gentleman's apology is always accepted. If you can behave yourself properly, you are welcome here, and she drew him towards her and kissed his forehead.

Jiri was allowed to visit the Balinkays again. With exquisite tact, neither Ferencz nor his mother mentioned the unfortunate incident.

Mikki asked Jiri whether it had hurt, to which he replied that it had, very much, but that was what happened if one was naughty, so Mikki had better be careful.

Mr Balinkay looked down at Jiri.

--I hear you stepped out of line last week, Master Jiri.

Jiri was NOT frightened, but Mr Balinkay was very large, and that moustache... And that English doctor gave you a damn good hiding, which you took like a man… that should teach you… but no more strong language in front of the ladies, understand?

--Yes, sir, I understand, replied Jiri in Hungarian.

Mr Balinkay was delighted; swinging Jiri into the air, he roared, Well said! We'll have you in Budapest to liven up Ferzi and keep Mikki under control!

Setting Jiri down, he ruffled his hair and strode off, leaving Jiri somehow reminded of his own papa, and how good it would be to see him at the end of the summer.

At Tarnheim, John had to explain things to Karel, who was of course shocked by his nephew's unmannerly behaviour, and quite agreed that instant punishment had been the right thing to do.

Rather to John's surprise, and perhaps relief, he went on to say that as neither John nor Flora were native German speakers, and that English society, although most admirable, was rather different from that of the empire, he would speak to Jiri about correct forms of language and address.

Both John and Flora thought that, especially when they were away from home, Christa and Jiri had much more formal, polished manners than most English children. However, Karel embarked on a programme of social etiquette that involved sessions with the major-domo and the housekeeper on titles, precedence, seating arrangements and so on. The children pored over an Almanach de Gotha, thrilled at finding themselves listed and determined to establish links, however tenuous, between the von Tarnheims and various European royal houses. They collected pictures of royal personages, cut from illustrated papers, or bought as *cartes de visite* in the village, and discussed endlessly which of the Russian Grand Duchesses was the prettiest, and what a nice little boy the Tzarevich looked, although not so much fun as Mikki Balinkay. Flora encouraged this enthusiasm as a means of teaching history and geography; compared with some of the children's activities it seemed relatively harmless.

At luncheon, Karel would spring questions along the lines of,

--Christa, you have to invite the cardinal archbishop for light refreshments: how would your letter commence? Good. Now, how would that differ for an archbishop who is not a cardinal?

Jiri, if the Archduke Franz Ferdinand were to come in now, how would you address him?

One day the discussion turned to how the children would establish precedence amongst the royal houses of Europe if they were hosting a dinner party. Jiri, who had a decided *schwarmerei* for Queen Alexandra, maintained loudly that she would rather sit next to him than to Kaiser Wilhelm; from what we know of Edward VII's consort, he was probably right.

Meanwhile his luncheon lay neglected on his plate.

--Come, Jiri, said Flora, finish your food.

--It's cold and greasy; not even Lord George would eat this.

--You mean Mr Lloyd George, Jiri, corrected Flora.

--Like I said, Mr Lord George.

--Doktor Jonni, I didn't think you could be a mister AND a lord, asked Christa.

John began, patiently, to untangle the misunderstandings.

--Jaroslav, barked Karel, eat your luncheon or leave the table now. Understand that if you do so, you will have no dessert.

--I don't WANT... began Jiri.

--GO!

With what dignity he could muster, Jiri got down, clicked his heels, bowed and made for the door, which Gustl opened for him.

Flora wondered whether he ate anything at the Balinkays; she had explained rather shamefacedly to Madame that Jiri's capricious appetite ranged from non-existent to ravenous, and that he was easily distracted at mealtimes. She also impressed on the boy that he must behave well when being a guest. You may be sure, she said, drawing on the current enthusiasm for the British royals, that when King Edward is invited out to luncheon with his friends he does not poke his food with a fork, say it is disgusting, and leave it on his plate. Thinking of His Majesty's impressive girth, she felt quite safe in this assertion.

--May we ask Mikki Balinkay to come with Ferencz on Tuesday, Miss Drake? I think he is missing his little friends in Budapest, and he feels left out when Ferzi comes to see me.

--That is a kind thought, Jiri. But how will we amuse him?

--There is a box of toys upstairs. I am too old for them now, of course, but Mikki could play with them.

Jiri thought of the contents of the box. He thought particularly of the wooden St Bernard. It had a little cart in which milk churns, only one of which was missing, tiny chickens, ducks and vegetables, could be carried. You could also fit in some little soldiers if they were tired or wounded. And, if you took off the cart, the St Bernard could have a barrel of brandy for lost travellers fixed to his collar. Jiri had made some very successful mountains out of furniture, books, bricks and some rocks smuggled in from the garden. The intrepid dog had frequently scaled these and…

Miss Drake was saying:

--And of course there is a children's hospital in Strelitz. When Mikki has finished with them, we might take the toys there.

--NO!

--Jiri, cried Christa, I know what this is! You want to play with those baby toys yourself! The Balinkays will think you are so babyish, and sometimes YOU ARE.

Jiri turned scarlet, took a deep breath and looked around for something to throw.

Miss Drake put her hand firmly on his shoulder.

--That is enough. No more from either of you; another word and I will tell Madame Balinkay that you are both too naughty to have visitors. How shaming would that be?

In the end both Balinkays came for the day. Christa quite liked Ferencz, and in the morning the whole party walked around the gardens, fed the ducks, had refreshments on the terrace and listened to Ferencz and Jiri playing the violin and piano. Luncheon passed off quite well; a few days before, Jiri had stated firmly that It Would Be Better Not to Have Soup; when asked to explain, he uttered the single word 'Mikki'. Soup was not on the menu, and Gustl was instructed to look after Master Mikki Balinkay; his adroitness, honed by long attendance on Jiri, prevented any disaster. There were none of the altercations, digressions or threats common at luncheon in the von Tarnheim household; Christa and Jiri behaved as if they were entertaining royalty, as they had often done in imagination. Afterwards the elder boys played chess while Miss Drake supervised Mikki with the toys. Eventually Jiri could not resist joining him, and kept the child very happily occupied while Miss Drake read aloud to them all.

Sensing that Mikki was at last getting bored, Jiri said he would take him to the stables while the others finished the story. He knew the ending anyway.

Christa went to fetch her sketch pad, leaving Miss Drake alone with Ferencz. The boy looked thoughtful and rather sad.

--Things are most unfair, you know, Miss Drake.

--I am sorry that Jiri has left you alone, Ferencz. It is rather impolite of him.

--Oh, I didn't mean that, Miss Drake! Jiri is so kind to Mikki, just like he was to me on that climb. And generally (he did not say *always*) Mikki is very good when he is with him. No, I meant that it is so unfair that Theo Holtzner gets away with everything and poor Jiri is punished and blamed.

--As for that, I am sure Jiri has forgotten all about it; at least I hope he has not forgotten that he must not swear or damage property, and I am sure he remembers that Doctor John would discipline him again if necessary, but I don't think he worries or thinks much about it.

Miss Drake could not know that Jiri prayed nightly that something horrible would happen to Theo Holtzner. He reasoned that if God dropped Theo off a mountain or down a deep hole, the deed could not be pinned on Jiri Zellek.

Ferencz shook his head. He had never been tempted

to swear or to damage property, and the memory of what Doctor John had done to Jiri made him shudder. Existential awareness of the injustice of life clouded his soul.

--Ah, here come those two!

Mikki and Jiri could be heard approaching, hand in hand, swinging their arms and singing a regimental song in German, *Wir sind die k und k uhlanen...* and then switching to the Hungarian version...

--Oh, that's Papa's old regiment! Christa had reappeared.

--What is *k und k*? asked Miss Drake?

--Oh of course, you are English!

--Yes, Ferzi, Miss Drake is a subject of King Edward and Queen Alexandra! Miss Drake, k is *kaiserlich*, that is me, because I am a subject of the Emperor. Mikki is königlich; for him it's *császári és királyi* because he is a subject of the Emperor too, but the Emperor is also the king of Hungary, he has a special crown with a wonky cross like someone has dropped it, and bits hanging off it.

Ferencz leaped to the defence of St Stephen's crown.

--No, Jiri, you must not say that. It is a really special symbol of the Hungarian nation. The Emperor cannot be king of Hungary unless he has been crowned with it, in Budapest. The cross is not symmetrical because the crown is so old and it has been changed many times.

--I humbly apologise, Ferzi, although I don't see why someone couldn't have mended it. Jiri was glad that he had not added that anyone, even the Emperor, would look an idiot wearing that crown. Seeing that he was on dangerous ground, he changed the subject slightly. And, Miss Drake, you could be *k und k* too.

--How?

--Well, actually King Edward is the emperor of India AND the king of England. So your army is *k und k*. Although India is quite far away.

Mikki had been quiet for long enough.

--Ferzi, Ferzi, Uncle Graf Karel was at the stables and he gave me a ride on Nero!

--Did you have a ride too, Jiri? asked Christa, knowing that a ride on Nero was a great honour.

--No; Uncle had only time for one, and Mikki is a guest.

The Balinkays went to prepare for their return home.

Jiri looked as he did when about to make a huge effort.

--Miss Drake, Christa, may I give the St Bernard to Mikki? He really likes him, and I too old for him now, and at least I can play with him at Mikki's sometimes; that's better than him getting blood and sick all over him at the hospital, AND I don't need to play mountains anymore. When we were at the stables, Doktor Jonni told Uncle Karel that before he goes back to England next month he will take me on a short climb, just him and me and Gustl, but with ropes and a map and everything, because I really have been less naughty.

--Well done, Jiri! Why didn't you tell us at once?

--Didn't want to mention climbing when Ferzi was listening.

The Balinkays' pony trap disappeared down the path. Jiri leaned against Miss Drake, who put her arm round him.

--You really have been a good boy today, Jiri.

--Yes, I know. It has been very tiring.

Once again, summer drew to its spectacular alpine close. The Balinkays returned to Budapest; at some level, Ferencz was not sorry to be going back to a life of normality, as it had been before the arrival of Jiri von Tarnheim Zellek. For Mikki, Jiri's doings assumed legendary status, and Madame Balinkay thought often of the little boy who had called her Madame Mama and played the piano for her.

Jiri, very little taller, but slightly sturdier and certainly browner, prepared to rejoin his father and stepmother; a new school term would begin, he had been promised a pony of his own, and he looked forward to learning some new piano pieces.

He shook hands with his uncle, and with John; he kissed Miss Drake affectionately and said his goodbyes to Christa in private. In public the children scarcely looked at each other as his luggage was loaded into the pony trap.

Christa never cried. Or hardly ever.

--Well, Flora? One more year? They sat on the terrace watching the sunset on the mountains. Are you sure you want to stay on?

--Yes, John; I have agreed; but, you know, perhaps it is time for you to start looking again for a practice to buy, as that first one fell through; it will take some time to find exactly the right one, at the right price, and this time next year I shall have another year's salary in hand. There is not much to spend one's money on, up here!

--Those children. What's going to become of them, Flora? You've given them more of your love and attention than they deserve.

--Well, I have had almost sole charge of Christa since she was eight. And in some ways I feel I know her very little better than I did then. Perhaps I've failed her, John.

--Nonsense, Flora! She is certainly self-contained, but there is little harm in that.

--Perhaps you are right. And Christa will be very different after five years at the convent; she will be there from next year until she is eighteen. It will do her good to be with other girls, of her own age and class; really here the von Stroens are the only family she is allowed to visit. At least Jiri goes to school in Pallin, and is used to mixing. Look how good he was with little Mikki Balinkay, and with Ferencz, although those two brothers are so different from each other. In fact he has always been able to get on with other children.

--Apart from Theo Holtzner.

--Well, yes. I don't like to think about that.

--I was talking with von Tarnheim after dinner the other night. He is determined that Jiri should go to military academy, or at very least into officer training at some point; the more I think about it, military training would probably develop him physically, and military discipline, though it would come very hard, would be good for him. And if he has to kill someone, it's better one of whoever the empire is fighting at the time!

--What a waste, though, John. I'd hate to see him one of those mindless young officers one sees in Vienna.

--It also seems that, on the other hand, Herr Zellek is keen to develop Jiri's musical talent. He sees his son as a professional pianist or singer and, von Tarnheim tells me in disgust, Frau Zellek in her turn would like her stepson to take over management of the family glass factory and business interests.

--I've sometimes thought, John, what if we could, somehow, take him with us…

--What? Flora, these children are not yours; in time we shall have some of our own. And Master Jiri would not last a month in an English public school. And even if his parents agreed, von Tarnheim would never let him out of his sight. He is remarkably attached to the boy. No, Flora; I know you are fond of him, but his life is here, like Christa's. In years to come, she will marry some princeling in Austria or perhaps Germany, she will hunt and fish, and you will get pictures of her children. When Jiri is Karel's age, he'll be a sharp-tongued little martinet commanding a cavalry regiment: we can put a picture of him in uniform in pride of place.

AT THE BALINKAYS', 1906

Flora was not the only graduate of her year at training college to choose the option of teaching abroad. One of her friends now contacted her to say that she was currently a governess in the family of a wealthy Hungarian family; they were holidaying on one of their estates, and Flora would be most welcome to join them; the extra participant in English conversation would be ample recompense for her keep. Meanwhile, after much deliberation, Karel had allowed Christa to go on a walking and skiing holiday with the von Stroens. This all coincided with another of the Zelleks' business trips; Jiri had a standing invitation to spend time with the Balinkays; could Flora take him to their home in Budapest on her way?

So, amid general enthusiasm, Jiri was delivered to the Balinkays. He felt extremely grown-up, had decided to leave Wolfi at home, and was determined to behave at all times as befitted a von Tarnheim.

When he arrived in Budapest it was still winter and much colder than at Pallin. Jiri wore a little fur coat and hat that Ferzi had outgrown; it was being kept for Mikki, although the brothers were of quite different builds. He adored this outfit, in which he looked so like a small furry animal that passers-by gave him smiles of amusement that he interpreted as admiration.

Ferencz was being educated by a private tutor, and Mikki by a nursery governess, both of whom visited daily. The problem of where to place Jiri was solved by asking the governess to teach him Hungarian, using the simple stories and writing exercises she set for the younger boy. Meanwhile spring came to the beautiful city. Jiri thought Budapest superior to London, and, perhaps for patriotic reasons, preferred the Danube to the Thames, although the Tower of London and the Crystal Palace took some beating. There was a great deal to do there; they went shopping, skating, and swimming in the famous thermal baths. Mr Balinkay could not help contrasting Jiri with his own two sons; the boy was such a poor little shrimp compared with Ferzi, who was well made, although tall and slim, and stocky, sturdy young Mikki. They would soon build the boy up, he thought. They also went riding, which was a great success. Jiri knew of course that Hungarian horses and Hungarian riders were the best in the empire and so in the entire world. Although English racehorses were, he gathered, worth watching. Mr Balinkay gave him a pair of wonderful Hungarian boots, counting them as a very early birthday present. When he collected the boys from the stables Mr Balinkay asked the groom how they were shaping up.

--That little Austrian is a plucky lad; I could make a rider of him in time! Does what he's told, will try anything; took a tumble and got straight back on with no fuss. Master Mikki, he's a strong one for his age, I must say! And, like his friend, not scared of much!

--What about Ferencz?

--Beautiful seat and hands, sir, just needs a bit more confidence over the jumps.

Meanwhile Mikki and Jiri were saying goodbye to the ponies; they were both in high spirits, although Ferzi looked less cheerful. He really did not like jumping, and seeing the two younger boys taking to it so readily made him feel depressed.

--That is a wonderful pony, Jiri was saying. Much faster than dear old Tonie at home, and he can jump! The groom's name is Arpad and he's helping me improve my jumping position. I only fell off once and I didn't hurt myself, not really, only my elbow a little bit, and Mikki and Ferzi are such good riders, Mikki is much better than I was at his age, and please sir when can we go again, because Arpad says I need to practise quite a lot, and I don't suppose anyone has got a biscuit or some sweets in their pocket, as it has all made me very hungry...

Perhaps realising that Jiri was too well brought up to talk with his mouth full, Mr Balinkay took the hint and purchased silence at the nearest sweet shop.

Jiri enjoyed his lessons with Mikki. If they had not behaved too badly, the governess ended the morning session by reading them a story. Jiri's standards of literary appreciation were not high, and he was, after all, operating in a fourth language, so both boys were entranced by an endless series of tales about a family of dogs: papa, mama and five puppies. Mikki and Jiri acted these out, with exciting additions and a lot of barking, howling, yelping and snarling; returning rather earlier than usual, Mr Balinkay heard the racket.

--That's enough! You are right under the drawing room window; you will give Mama a headache! Silence! Now! Understood?

--Yes, Papa. Yes, sir. And he strode off.

The boys looked at one another.

--I know, said Jiri. We can go hunting. We have to creep up to our prey in Absolute Silence. He spoke in German but Mikki got the drift. Dropping to all fours, they padded into the bushes. They were still there, crouched and ready to pounce, when Mikki's nanny hauled them off to get ready for luncheon. By now Jiri's hair had attracted many twigs, leaves and insects. His protests as these were combed out were heard throughout the house.

Eventually, clean and neat, the boys appeared in the dining room.

Jiri marched Mikki up to Madame Balinkay.

--Madame Mama, we were too noisy. We are sorry; aren't we, Mikki?

--Oh... yes, Mama. Only, we were being dogs, and...

--Well, well, boys. I am glad you were having a nice game. But try to be a little quieter in future.

--You weren't exactly quiet when you were having your hair combed, Jiri, noted Ferzi.

Mikki spoke up.

--I bet you would have yelled if nanny had pulled your hair like that! And there was a big beetle in it, wasn't there, Jiri?

--Yes. But please do not worry, Madame Mama, we put it outside, and it ran away quite safe.

Mr Balinkay indicated their chairs and they sat down. Mikki began to protest when a napkin was tied around his neck.

--Actually, Mikki, it is quite a good idea, said Jiri. Otherwise you might have to change your blouse again, and you know what a bore that is.

Luncheon at the Balinkays was both less formal and more civilised than at Tarnheim.

The Balinkays' tableware was daintier than the weighty antique von Tarnheim cutlery, which Jiri still found unwieldy at times. Compared with Mikki's, his table manners were a model of refinement. The conversation, between the Balinkay parents, Ferzi and his tutor (a thin, serious man with drooping sandy whiskers) was conducted in Hungarian or French, presenting a slight language barrier that prevented Jiri from offering his opinions quite as vociferously as usual. Everyone was listened to, everyone took their turn in conversation, and the topics generally concerned matters of culture or daily interest; altogether a contrast to the protests, threats, altercations, insults and reprimands that characterised the von Tarnheims en famille.

Flora's holiday ended. On her return to the Balinkays', she was shown into the salon. There was, she thought, a slight air of awkwardness; Ferzi was with his tutor, she was told, and Mikki was in the park with his nanny. And Jiri?

--He is in bed, Miss Drake. Really, he is much better now, although...

Flora learned that all three boys had caught some seasonal illness, perhaps influenza. Ferzi, who was always his mother's chief concern, had been most unwell and required careful nursing. The other two had it more lightly, and seemed to be over it when Jiri suddenly developed a cough and a very high fever; for some nights, Madame Balinkay and the nanny had sat up with him, and they had considered contacting his parents, but just as the doctor had warned that Jiri's body could not take much more, his cough abated, his pulse was stronger and his temperature went down, at least in daytime. Miss Drake must be their guest until the boy was well enough to leave.

Flora found Jiri sitting up in a bed which had been moved into the nursery from the room that he had been sharing with Mikki. He was looking through some illustrated boys' papers; when he saw Flora his face was radiant.

--Oh, Miss Drake! He scrambled to his knees and held out his arms; she held him and he began to cry.

--I'm sorry to be so babyish… but I haven't been very well. Everyone has been so kind to me… Doctor Dukay, he isn't like Doktor Jonni, but he is a nice old gentleman, but oh, Miss Drake, I am so glad you are here!

He rested his head on her shoulder in complete contentment.

Jiri! My own boy.

Flora felt an overwhelming sense of fiercely protective, unconditional love. It was unlike any previous emotion, more powerful than the love she bore for her parents, for John Loudon, or the affection, pride and yes, pity, that she held for Christa. It would be years before she recognised it again. His stepmother, she thought, cannot love him like this. He has no one else.

They stayed like that for some time, until she realised that Jiri was falling asleep. She kissed him on the forehead and gently laid him down.

The door opened quietly; Mikki stood there, holding Puppi, his toy dog, a battered creature whose ears needed frequent replacement.

--It's Jiri's turn to have Puppi, he explained. He hasn't got Wolfi with him, and we've been sharing Puppi while Jiri is ill. I'll need him back at bedtime.

--Yes, of course, Mikki. I'll make sure he is returned safely.

Mikki carefully tucked the dog in beside the sleeping boy.

--And thank you, Mikki. Jiri always says you are a good comrade.

Flora felt somehow resentful towards the Balinkays, although reason told her that they had actually given Jiri all possible care and attention. She was now able to observe the workings of the household, and to talk with Madame Balinkay, who told her that apart from a few boisterous episodes with Mikki, Jiri's behaviour had been excellent (better than at Tarnheim, thought Flora with a pang); they had been to solemn High Mass in St Stephens Cathedral, and Jiri, whom they had feared would be bored and fidgety, was rapt. When this came up later in conversation, he said only that it was *wunderschön* and that he thought about it often. He is like Ferencz, he has music in his soul, concluded Madame.

Comparing the two boys, Flora thought this was both correct and incorrect. Jiri was not really like Ferencz, who had a developing aesthetic appreciation of the arts: music, painting and especially literature. He already wrote poems, which he and Jiri attempted, not always successfully, to set to music for Jiri to sing. As for Jiri, although he could read fluently in German, he preferred to be read to; he was drawn to beautiful things, which he categorised simply as *hübsch* or *sehr hübsch* but music was an integral part of his being, rather than an enjoyable pastime or accomplishment among other interests.

Despite the four-year gap in their ages, Jiri and Mikki were closer than ever, their joint propensity for trouble and mischief-making tempered by mutually protective instincts. Flora perceived that Jiri was in some ways for Mikki a more congenial older brother than Ferencz, while having to look after Mikki, and live up to an element of hero-worship, was very good for the irresponsible Jiri. Ferencz was a more complex character than either of the younger boys, although, as Flora knew, Jiri required a great deal of management and understanding. Ferzi, in his turn, spent time with Jiri during his convalescence, showing much tact in distracting him, sensing when he was flagging or irritable, coaxing him to eat and relieving his mother and Miss Drake from sitting with the boy. Jiri was certainly recovering. Mr Balinkay came to see him.

--Better today, Master Jiri, hey?

--Yes, sir, thank you.

--I'll bet you are bored with staying in bed. Lili, find something to wrap him in. Good; now hold on to me…

Jiri was always a lightweight, and he had now become alarmingly thin. Mr Balinkay scooped him up and carried him downstairs; the man smelled of cologne and cigars. It was nice to be back in the salon.

--See who I have here! Mama, Miss Drake, make him comfortable on the couch. There! Master Jiri fancied a change of scene; I'm off to the bureau now, but I'll run back to take him upstairs when you're tired of his company!

The boy had, in John Loudon's words, lost a great deal of ground. Flora had never known him quite so thin and easily tired to the point of listlessness. She consulted the Balinkays' doctor, who said that he had been seriously worried about the boy and was still concerned, especially by his tendency to run a temperature in the evening. He prescribed a febrifuge and a tonic, while urging the greatest possible care of the child's health. By the time Jiri was pronounced able to travel, his parents had returned from their business trip; the month or so of his planned visit had long expired, and Flora undertook to take him to Pallin before she returned to Tarnheim. Despite the anxiety of the past few weeks, the Balinkays were sorry to part with him; a summer on Lake Balaton, said Mr Balinkay, would be just what the boy needed, and they would be happy to take him there, as Madame had recently inherited a villa at the lakeside resort. He gave Jiri a book of boys' adventure stories to read on the journey, and entrusted Miss Drake with a carton of sweets: he knew that the boy was not really allowed them, but surely there was no harm in one now and again.

Flora thought that Jiri was in some way altered, although perhaps it was her feeling for him that had changed. During his illness he had actually grown a little, and in some ways he seemed more mature. He had been profoundly affected by the sung Mass in St Stephen's; he had never heard anything like it, and remembered it all his life as his first transcendent musical experience. He had also developed in another way. Flora had huge admiration for anyone able to cope with the combination of Jiri and Mikki, but apparently the governess had done so, backed only by a couple of warnings from Mr Balinkay, with the result that Jiri was now quite fluent in Hungarian. This meant that he had another language to add to his native tongue, to German and to the reasonable command of English and smattering of French that he had acquired from Miss Drake.

He was not, though, completely transformed. On the homeward journey the bottle of tonic prescribed by Doctor Dukay fell out of the train window somewhere between Budapest and Vienna; Jiri said that this did not matter, as he was NOT going to take any more of it; he had only done so to set a good example to Mikki, and now that Mikki was out of sight, the tonic could go.

SUMMER, 1906

Flora Drake was climbing the path to the children's special bathing pool. As she approached, Jiri's high, clear voice could be heard protesting,

--Christi, can't I put my drawers on? This rock is hurting my bottom.

--No. The ancient Greeks didn't wear drawers. But you can get your towel and sit on that.

--Thank you. So the ancient Greeks had towels?

--Shut up, Jiri.

--Of course they must have, or they would have dripped everywhere.

--Shut up, Jiri. Hold the stick out, like I told you.

Beside the pool below the waterfall, the naked boy was sitting on his towel, holding a stick at arm's length. Christa was sketching him hurriedly, aware that it would be only a few minutes before he began to complain that his arm was tired, and why couldn't he have a proper spear?

This summer, the children were obsessed with the classical world; Flora felt that the crowned heads of Europe had been preferable, as, judging from the children's interpretation, the ancient Greeks shed their clothing at every opportunity and the Romans threw missiles and stabbed enemies whenever possible.

Christa was attending art classes in Strelitz; the teaching was decidedly old-fashioned and consisted mainly of copying photographs of Greek statues. But she was determined to study art, either in Vienna or preferably Paris, a plan of which her father would have disapproved, and therefore knew nothing about. She also read everything she could find about entry to art schools; it annoyed her to find that while men could draw unclothed models, women were not allowed to do so. Determined to get around this stupid regulation, she turned to the only model available, and he was very far from ideal. He fidgeted, complained, chatted incessantly and also had nothing like the god-like male body of the ancient Greeks. He would have to do, and as the only time he sat still was when he was playing the piano, she did numerous clothed sketches of him there, which she planned to work up to a painting titled *At the Piano*, which would rival Renoir, Manet, Morisot and in fact every known artist.

Jiri was more interested in the Romans. Ferzi Balinkay, from whom he heard quite frequently, had been learning Latin for some time and Jiri was delighted when his own father suggested that he might begin, so that he would be well ahead at Oberschule. With his natural facility for languages, he loved the way in which Latin connected with other tongues, and he was intrigued by the more bloodthirsty aspects of Roman history.

--Jiri, called Flora, Get dressed. You will catch cold.

With evident relief, Jiri scrambled off his rock and began to put on his clothes, calling to Gustl to help him with the buttons. Christa looked very annoyed.

--Miss Drake, I had not finished sketching him. He was being a Spartan warrior.

Flora thought that anyone less like a Spartan warrior than poor Jiri could scarcely be imagined, but said nothing. She looked at Christa's drawing. For a girl of her age, who had very little guidance, it was rather remarkable. She had captured Jiri's birdlike fragility, so that he appeared to have perched briefly on the rock before taking flight, and with the branch he held, and the lightly indicated waterfall, he seemed part of his surroundings, far more like a Slavonic nature spirit than a classical figure.

Meanwhile Christa stood up and put away her sketching materials. She stretched, took off her light summer dress, stepped out of her chemise and drawers, and dived gracefully into the pool.

Flora felt disquiet. Noticeably, Christa's body was beginning to change; she was tall for her years, not small and skinny like her cousin, and her breasts were already developing. Jiri, of course, was used to seeing her naked and would take no notice, but Gustl was a young man of eighteen.

--Are you not rather a big girl, Christa, to be swimming without a bathing dress?

--Oh, Miss Drake, of course I would wear one if anyone was here. But there is no one, only Jiri and Gustl.

--Jiri is still quite little I suppose, but Gustl?

--Oh, Miss Drake, of course Gustl is only a servant.

--Miss Drake, Miss Drake, is there anything left in our

basket? All this swimming and being a Spartan warrior makes me very hungry, and my feet are cold now.

--I will see, Jiri. Meanwhile stamp your feet to warm them up.

--Oh, Jiri, said Christa, you have such big feet for such a little boy and they are always cold. You are such a nuisance.

--I'm not. If it wasn't for me, you would have no one to be your model.

--You're no use anyway. You fidget too much.

--No, I don't.

--Yes, you do. She splashed him with water and climbed out of the pool. Flora quickly wrapped her in a towel.

She then dried Jiri off as far as possible and consoled him with the remains of the picnic.

Gustl began to gather up their belongings, shrewdly finding Jiri's bathing costume stuffed into the bushes: the boy had hoped that it would be forgotten. In fact, Jiri had originally wanted a bathing costume. He suffered a dread, which he would confess to no one, of what a predatory fish might do to his manhood, and felt that a swimsuit might offer protection. But now he hated the one-piece woollen garment, complaining that it was scratchy and itchy, especially around his... he used local words, but the wriggling and tugging left one in no doubt. They trailed off down the track. Christa and Jiri ran ahead, chattering in a mix of German and their own language. Both had rather high, clear voices; Jiri's showed no signs of breaking, and from time to time he sang, his surprisingly strong notes echoing around the mountain landscape.

This was the last summer that Flora Drake would spend at Tarnheim, as in the autumn Christa was to enter the convent school where all the von Tarnheim Mädchen had gone for centuries. Flora would return to England; John Loudon had at last purchased a medical practice in Shropshire. His mother and her maid, Beatrice, were preparing to leave Bayswater and get the house ready for them; John's sister Anne was in Canada with her husband Ralph Battrill. To Flora's dismay, John had refused to attend their wedding, which had been a very quiet affair, although Mrs Loudon seemed to have come to terms with the situation, and was clearly enjoying the move to the country. Flora wished the Battrills well; she foresaw that their marriage would not be without problems, but in Canada the difference in their social origins would be less significant. Sometimes she contrasted their bold, swift decision with her own protracted courtship.

Christa was now thirteen and Jiri just eleven. Both of them seemed younger than their years, Christa because of the exclusivity of her upbringing and Jiri partly because he was still small, and worryingly thin, so that people tended to treat him as a younger child. In some ways he was much the same as always: his appetite was capricious, he was reluctant to sleep, and kept going on nervous energy, which would suddenly fail, leaving him ravenous or exhausted. He had perhaps more self-control, in that his wilfulness was less evident and his rages fewer. Flora had been greatly impressed by the improvement in his spoken and written English since his stay in London as well as by his command of Hungarian, acquired at the Balinkays'.

On his arrival at Tarnheim he and Christa had at once settled into their close but turbulent collaboration, persisting in speaking their native language and sharing complicated and mysterious games. Flora felt that this must end after

Christa went to school (and Jiri had only a year or so to go before entering Oberschule) and perhaps it was no bad thing. She had at the back of her mind John's warning about Karel von Tarnheim's possible plans for them, and as they entered puberty their strangely intimate relationship might have its dangers; she had only recently become aware, through something Grushenka had said, that they were sometimes to be found in the same bed, with Christa explaining that Jiri had woken from a bad dream, or that he was cold or upset, and needed her. *Two little birds in the same nest*, murmured the old nanny.

Meanwhile it was probably Flora's imagination that made this summer seem particularly poignant, with every action and event meaningful and unlikely to be the same ever again. She resolutely pushed away thoughts of parting from Jiri; she had to accept John's verdict; her fantasies of taking the boy to England with her were just that: fantasies; his life was here, and although perhaps no one loved him in her deeply maternal way, he was, after all, surrounded by people anxious for his welfare. And he would soon cease to be the little boy who nestled against her shoulder, held up his face for a goodnight kiss, looked into her face with that mischievous, enquiring glance, took her hand as they ran along a mountain path...

At this time, she was in sole charge of the children. Karel von Tarnheim was on one of his trips to Prague; John was in Vienna, where there were some fascinating medical discoveries.

Jiri rather took advantage of their absence. One morning, provoked by Christa, he flew into one of his rages and hurled a heavy glass paperweight at her head. She dodged, and the missile shattered the window, landing on the terrace some feet below.

Flora took Jiri by the shoulders and made him face her.

--Jiri, you know what Doktor Jonni would do to you if he were here.

--Yes. But he is in Vienna.

--Your uncle will be most displeased when he hears of this.

--Yes. But the window will be mended by the time he comes back.

--So, Jiri, I shall have to punish you. I shall not allow you to go to Elsa von Stroen's birthday party, and I shall write to her mother explaining that you are being punished for an act of gross naughtiness, and that until you have learned to behave properly, you will not be permitted any treats or visits.

Both children began to protest.

--But Miss Drake, cried Jiri.

--Really, Miss Drake, I ducked in time, it was only the window. May we go down and see what has happened to the paperweight?

--No. You will both go and get ready for luncheon.

--Come on, Jiri, said Christa, putting her arm around his shoulders. Honestly, your aim is really improving.

Until almost the last moment, Jiri had hoped that the governess might relent. But when Christa appeared wearing her Sunday dress, he knew it was useless, and burst into tears. Christa embraced him and declared she would not go without him. By some huge effort of will, he told her that she must go; Flora unwound him from his cousin, and Christa drove off in the pony trap, looking both glum and relieved.

Jiri followed Flora into the schoolroom. He sat at his desk and tears dropped onto his French exercise book. He was really being very volatile and babyish again these days; Flora thought this might be a mix of the deep humiliation he felt at having his behaviour known to the von Stroens, his distress at her displeasure, and the underlying anxiety of Christa's departure. She fought against the desire to put her arm around him and read him a story; having come thus far, she must carry the punishment through to the end.

The best she could do for him was to ignore him, before saying,

--Jiri, we have done very little work this morning. It is almost breaktime. Can I trust you to run outside and gain control of yourself? I will send Gustl for you in time for the next lessons.

--Yes, Miss Drake. I will be good.

Jiri was rather listlessly rearranging the pattern of pebbles, sticks and snail shells that he and Christa had been working on in one of their secret corners of the garden. Hearing a rustle behind him, he turned around, jumping to his feet and taking off his hat.

The visitor could not help feeling pleased by the rapt expression of wonder and delight on the child's face; apart from that, he was in no way impressive.

--Who are you? she asked… clearly the vision spoke German.

--Jaroslav Felix von Tarnheim Zellek. He bowed and clicked his heels.

--Ah, Jiri! And who do you think I am, Jiri?

--Well, at first I thought you must be Our Lady, but she only appears to good people. Then I thought you might come from Mount Olympus, but you are wearing clothes. Then maybe you are a (he gave the native word for a garden spirit)…

--Enough! I can see that you have some ideas in your head. I am your cousin Valerie.

--My cousin? Can I kiss you, then?

--What a little flirt! You are sharper than you look!

--But may I?

Mindful of the damage this could cause, she replied,

--I think you might kiss my hand.

With huge reverence, he bent over her ungloved hand. It was beautiful, and he caught a faint scent; later he realised it was of heliotrope.

--You've been crying, she observed.

--Yes. I have been crying all the morning. It is hard to stop, when one has started, although I know it is babyish.

--What's the trouble?

--I have been naughty. So Miss Drake said I could not go to the von Stroens' with Christa. And she has told them why.

--I shouldn't worry about that. Those von Stroens were always a boring lot, and not up to our standards. But does that mean that Christa is not here?

At once Jiri perceived that it was Christa who the visitor wished to see, rather than himself. This was rather a blow, but at least he was here with her now. To his shame, he found that tears were gathering once more.

--Haven't you got a handkerchief?

--Yes. But it is wet already.

--Here.

Her handkerchief was, of course, tiny, lace-trimmed, embroidered and fragrant. It was far too good to blow his nose on, so he used his sleeve. She looked away.

--Yes, Cousin Valerie. Christa is at the von Stroens'. Can you wait until she gets back?

--No, I cannot do that. Do you tell her everything?

--Mostly.

This was not quite true; in fact, Christa was the only person from whom Jiri had no secrets; there were one or two things he was ashamed to tell her, but she always found them out.

--Well then. Let's see what she makes of it. There is no point in my staying any longer.

--Will you kiss me goodbye? And will you come back?

--No, and possibly. Well… I will kiss the top of your head. That looks fairly clean. Come here. Close your eyes.

For one enchanted moment, she was very close to him; he caught the scent of heliotrope once more, and was enveloped by the shadow of her beautiful hat. The light kiss on his dark, curly hair was all too brief, and she was gone when he opened his eyes. If it had not been for the handkerchief, which he was still clutching, he might not have totally believed in her; at times his grasp on what was generally called reality could be idiosyncratic, but this was proof.

When Gustl escorted him back to the schoolroom, Jiri looked far less woebegone. Although she was not in favour of eating in lesson time, Flora knew that Jiri had refused breakfast, and had provided a few small pieces of buttered bread with his favourite raspberry jam, which he ate with some appetite.

She told herself that this was not spoiling, merely concern for his health, and much-needed encouragement to eat.

--Now, Jiri. I see that you are calmer and more sensible. Shall we try some French and arithmetic before luncheon?

--Yes, Miss Drake. Anyway, those von Stroens are a boring lot and not up to our standards.

This might, she thought, be an example of sour grapes, but at least Jiri seemed to have come to terms with things. His concentration was not, perhaps, at its best, but he was probably worn out by hours of emotional turmoil; at least he was polite, willing and even, as the morning wore on, cheerful.

Later that day, Flora was pleased with both of the children.

As soon as the pony trap could be heard, Jiri ran out to greet Christa.

--Oh, I have missed you! Did you have a lovely time?

--It was quite amusing. Frau von Stroen (who mistakenly believed Jiri to be A Dear Little Boy) sent her love and this box of bonbons.

--OH! It is *sehr hübsch*! The little dogs. Oh!

--I will take care of it for you, Jiri, said Flora, but you may have one now.

--And Christi, and you, Miss Drake!

--And, said Christa, LOOK!

She had been invited to choose a small gift. Miraculously, the selection had included some Roman soldiers. Saying that these were for her cousin, Christa had secured them. The children rushed off to play with them in the short time that remained before Jiri's bedtime.

It was not until the next day that he could tell Christa about the visitor. By now even Queen Alexandra had taken second place in his imagination and his description of the visitor was ecstatic. After a while, Christa told him to Wait There. I am going to get something from my box.

This box was kept in Christa's room and Jiri was forbidden by her to touch it. She would know if he had, and she would then cut Wolfi into small pieces and burn the fragments before flushing the ashes down the water closet. He made sure to stay several paces away from it.

When she returned, she was holding a small photograph with torn edges.

--Did she look like this?

--Yes; she did, only much more beautiful.

--Well then. That's not your cousin. It's my mother. So I suppose she must be your aunt. Not that you are good enough.

--I want her to come back.

--So what are you going to do about it?

--What the ancient Greeks and Romans did. Build a shrine and offer burned offerings. And chant. Like this.

--Shut up, Jiri. But I suppose we could do that. I had to copy a picture of a Roman altar.

--We could try praying in the chapel as well.

--No. I've done that and it doesn't work.

Jiri was not surprised. He did not like the chapel, which was one of the oldest parts of Tarnheim castle, being built into the rock of the mountainside; it was very plain, and used only on Sundays, when a very old retired priest came from a neighbouring hamlet to say Mass for the household; gone were the days when the von Tarnheims had their own

117

personal chaplain. Jiri often fidgeted and was told off by his uncle. It was quite different in the church in Tarnheim village. This was like the one in Pallin with plenty of colour, ritual and, best of all, music. Jiri attended to every moment, which was just as well. The von Tarnheims had their designated area, near the ranked memorials to departed members of their family, and when they attended on special feast days the entire village watched their every move, later discussing their clothing, appearance and deportment. In Pallin Jiri had made his first communion, and for a while aspired to be an altar boy, until a series of incidents involving candles, incense and holy water caused him to be banned. He was in fact far more useful in the choir, where his behaviour was impeccable except perhaps during the sermon.

He continued,

--Christi… she left her handkerchief behind… as she is your mother, do you want it for your box?

They both looked at it.

--Thank you, Birdie. I should like that. But you may keep it for the moment. I will tell you when to give it to me, and you will have to do so At Once.

--Yes, Christi. Where shall we build the altar?

Christa waylaid the housekeeper.

--Frau Trinkel, I wish to speak with you.

--Certainly, Madam Christa. What can I do for you?

--You know that Master Jiri sometimes gets ideas into his head?

--Well, yes, madam! We never know what the boy will come up with next!

--He thinks... perhaps he has heard that... my mother is somehow his cousin...

Frau Trinkel had been told not to discuss Christa's mother with the girl. But she would keep this brief and matter of fact.

--In a way, he is right, madam. You see, your mother and your honoured father were... are... cousins. You mother's late father was the old Graf Johann's brother, thus uncle of your honoured father. Of course, Master Jiri's mother, Gräfin Gisela, was your honoured father's sister. If you look at the family tree in the library, madam, you will see that many years ago Graf Felix and Gräfin Adelheid had two sons – two that lived, that is: Johann, father of your honoured father, and Ulrich, your mother's father.

Christa nodded.

--So, your mother is... was... cousin to the late Gräfin Gisela. Strictly speaking, then, she is not just Master Jiri's aunt by marriage; she is a sort of cousin to him, although whether it is a second cousin, or a cousin once removed, I'm sure I can't say! It is all in the family, though, madam.

--Well, Flora, your management has been most effective! As you thought, I would have given Jiri what Mr Balinkay describes as a good hiding, and I'm sure he would have taken the point, but your punishment seems to have made him reflect on his behaviour and its consequences. He and Christa seem rather calmer with each other.

--Yes. He is ready to be guided by her, although perhaps that is not always a good thing. And perhaps he is a little more grown-up. At least, so he seemed when he left the Balinkays'.

--In general, yes. But I am not sure that a boy of eleven should be quite so... well, I mean Wolfi.

--John, he has tried valiantly to break himself of the habit. When he went to the Balinkays, he left Wolfi behind.

--Ah yes, the Balinkays! We both know, Flora, that if it had not been for that Hungarian doctor, little Mikki Balinkay, and your timely arrival... we are lucky to have that boy still with us, Flora, however much of a nuisance the little chap may be!

--Yes, and of course in his mind it just reinforced how much he needed Wolfi. At least it is only at bedtimes now, and actually, John, I am sure it will pass in good time. After all, I don't suppose many officers in the Austro-Hungarian Ulans take their bears to bed with them!

--True. And is Jiri prepared, do you think, for his uncle's plan?

--At present, he has confided to me that his ambition is to become a *kinema* pianist. But somehow I do not think that either Karel von Tarnheim or the Zelleks will let that happen.

Karel had decreed that on mornings when he was at home, Jiri must do half an hour of physical exercise with him before breakfast; this would, he said, strengthen the boy, give him an appetite for *frühstück* and not interfere with his morning lessons. Generally these exercises took the form of the callisthenics popular at the time, but after a while Flora noticed that they had changed.

Karel positioned the boy with his skinny legs in a wide squat, and took him through a series of movements.

--That's cavalry sword drill, explained Christa. In the Ulans, you have a lance. When that gets stuck in someone, you leave it and you draw your sword. There are four basic moves; watch. Upper right, for a mounted opponent on your right; lower right, for an infantry opponent on your right;

then the same on the left, but that is more tricky. You have to do it mounted, holding the reins in your left hand; that's why they are squatting. Jiri will have to do it on his pony; he's sure to fall off.

Karel had now given Jiri a stick to simulate a sword, making him go through the moves again. Flora noticed the look of set concentration on Jiri's face. He will do this till he drops, she thought.

Eventually,

--Sheath sword! Attention! At ease! bawled Karel. Very well, Jiri; now go and have your breakfast.

--Yes, sir. Jiri went. His legs were shaking and his arms felt about to drop off.

It may be easier tomorrow, he told himself.

Both children were also being taught how to shoot. They had Austrian hats, each with a tiny *gamsbart* and little jackets with lots of pockets. Christa wore a loden skirt, and Jiri had shorts and long stockings just like the Emperor. Karel declared that an ability to shoot would be required when they were invited on hunting parties later in life; it was a necessary aspect of civilised education. Meanwhile the children daily expected an invitation to Sandringham and Flora, realising that it was the same for children of their class in England, made no comment. She wondered, though, how Jiri, who could not bear to listen to a story in which animals were unhappy or suffering, (*No, no, Miss Drake! Not that one. I don't like it. It is too sad*) would react when expected to kill birds or beasts; so far they were aiming only at targets, and with any luck she would have left Tarnheim before actual blood was shed.

Although Flora was entitled to use the library at Tarnheim, she rarely did so. The children hardly ever entered it; Karel was no bibliophile, in fact, he read only newspapers, periodicals and popular novels, but even he could see the dangers of a combination of Christa, Jiri, ladders, dust, spiders and heavy volumes. The children were forbidden to enter unescorted.

But one afternoon, the steady downpour of rain meant that no one could go out, and rather at her wits' end, Flora suggested that they might go to the library and select some books about the Greeks and Romans. Christa was encouraged to wear her painting smock; Jiri would just have to be found a clean blouse later.

As Flora and Christa were looking through some likely volumes, Jiri moved away; Flora turned to see him kneeling in front of one of the largest books she had ever seen, gazing intently at a picture.

It was evidently the size of the book that had attracted him, and it must have been on one of the lower shelves, otherwise he would not have been able to pull it out without attracting notice.

--Miss Drake, Miss Drake, he called in his clear imperious tones, please come and explain this picture to me!

It was a full-page woodcut, perhaps three or four centuries old. A craggy landscape, possibly modelled on that around Tarnheim, filled the background. Crowded into the foreground, a ram with huge curved horns peered from a fantastically grotesque thorn bush. On a rudely constructed altar lay a boy in a tunic, bound down by cords; over him stood an old man in long robes, with flowing hair and beard. He brandished a huge knife. Bundles of sticks were propped against the altar, and a lamp with a burning flame stood nearby.

--That is a Holy Bible, Jiri, and the picture is of Abraham and Isaac.

Both children looked completely blank. Flora realised that while they could have answered questions about the saints, angels, and the rosary, Bible stories were largely unknown to them. Although she, John and, she suspected, Anne Loudon prided themselves on having moved beyond the teachings of their Anglican childhoods, they were familiar with every aspect of Scripture.

She made the children sit down, drew up a chair, and told them the story. Silence followed.

--Well, Christa, what do you think we can learn from this?

--He didn't know much about perspective.

--Who didn't? asked Jiri.

--Him. Christa pointed to the monogram in the corner of the picture. But, she added, it's not bad. Miss Drake, how was this picture made?

--It is a woodcut. We can find out more about the process if you wish. Now, Jiri?

--My Papa wouldn't do that to me, he said confidently, and I don't think Uncle Karel would.

--But if God told them to? insisted Christa.

--Papa wouldn't. He wouldn't want anyone to stick a knife in me and set me on fire.

Jiri's lip trembled.

--It's all right, Jiri. No one is going to do that to you. And, remember, God told Abraham to untie Isaac, and they went home and lived for a long time after that.

Jiri relaxed. So the story had a happy ending. Except for the sheep.

Flora took out her watch, and was relieved to see that time had moved on.

--Christa, gather up those books we have chosen. Jiri, I will help you to put this one back.

She felt that perhaps it was good that he had not selected any even more disturbing illustrations, Adam and Eve for example, or the burning fiery furnace. Even so, both children were unusually quiet as they returned to the school room.

Despite Miss Drake's reassurance, Jiri was shaken by the experience. Isaac was evidently a good boy, at least he had carried those sticks all the way up a mountain, and yet even he had had a narrow escape. Jiri began to have nightmares, in which a malevolent old man, an amalgam of Abraham in the picture and God the Father in the painted glass window in Tarnheim Church, was chasing him across a rocky landscape, threatening him with a sharp knife and a box of Lucifer matches. Every time he seemed to be escaping, a huge thorn bush appeared in his way, and he felt compelled to stop and try to free the struggling ram. There were variations: at times the avenger wielded a blazing cricket bat, and once, hideously, the sheep bore the leering face of Theo Holtzner.

Jiri lost ground, as John Loudon put it, and took to falling asleep during the day.

John was horrified: in these enlightened days, no child should be exposed to the terrors of religion, he pronounced, especially not to the horrors of the Old Testament; even fantasies about angels and saints were preferable to that!

This led Flora to a course of action of which she was greatly ashamed. She went into the village and obtained a brightly coloured picture of a guardian angel, with a German prayer for protection on the back. Jiri, whose aesthetic sense for any art except music, was rather undeveloped, was delighted: it was *wunderschön*! He believed of course that he had a guardian angel, but the picture gave this concept shape and reality.

He also knew what the angel's name was, although he would tell no one, not even Christi... in fact, especially not Christi.

Each night, he would say the prayer and sleep with the picture under his pillow. That way, the angel would protect him during the night and drive away any bad dreams. Abraham would not stand a chance.

As might be expected, Christa was scornful of the artwork, but as often happened when there was any real cause for concern over Jiri, she proved helpful, sitting with him while he said the prayer, and even staying with him until he fell asleep.

Jiri now slept all night, ate what was for him a hearty breakfast, and seemed to be his usual self.

Flora felt that yet another unexpected obstacle had been surmounted.

It took the children a long time to build a satisfactory Roman altar. They searched the gardens for fragments of statuary and flat stones; a major find was a figure of Mercurius, probably brought back from the Grand Tour by some eighteenth-century von Tarnheim. More of a statuette than a full-scale piece, it bore a slight resemblance to Jiri; at least, it was more like him than the heftier deities. This was balanced by a grotesque carving of some kind of Wolpertinger (a Wolpertinger is a fantastic creature made up of disparate animal parts).

Suddenly Jiri was reminded of the woodcut that had frightened him so much. But it was now too late to protest, and anyway, it was not him who was to be sacrificed. He had some idea that perhaps the handkerchief left by Valerie should be offered as a means of magicking her reappearance, but he was reluctant to part with it at least until he had to surrender it to Christa, so he said nothing.

--It's not working. I think we need to sacrifice something alive. That rat, and the crow, were both dead when we found them, complained Christa.

--They had maggots, and they were alive.

--Shut up Jiri. Maggots don't count.

He wondered why not, but accepted that discussion was probably useless.

--Well, anyway, they stank.

--Shut up, Jiri.

Much as he had enjoyed building the altar, it really did remind Jiri a little too much of the woodcut. So he was not sorry when Christa seemed to lose interest in the game.

There was now a period of glorious alpine summer. Flora encouraged the children to be out of doors as much as possible, riding, walking and climbing as well as swimming under her supervision. Flora thought she would always remember them like this, Christa in a dirndl and Jiri in an open-neck shirt, his shorts suspended by a faded pair of embroidered braces that had belonged to Karel as a boy.

Under this regime, quarrels grew fewer, Jiri seemed sturdier and had more appetite, Christa was more cheerful and forthcoming than she often appeared, and the classical obsession faded somewhat.

Flora's memories of those days also included the sound

of Jiri playing the piano; back in Pallin he had won a local competition and had acquired a taste for public performance. If he still saw himself as a *kinema* pianist, he kept quiet about it. Karel had been horrified by the suggestion that the children should go to the *kinema* in Strelitz, his experience of the moving pictures being limited to things that were definitely for men only. In fact, Jiri was beginning to aim higher, seeing himself as a six-foot-tall virtuoso in immaculate evening dress playing before dear Queen Alexandra, and of course Valerie.

John and Flora often accompanied the children, and during the long afternoons they planned their future life in Shropshire. In retrospect, these weeks were among the happiest any of them had spent.

Inevitably, the days passed. Flora was amazed that no one had thought of taking Christa to see the convent school for which she was destined, to meet the Mother Superior and the teachers and get to know the buildings and grounds. Karel was quite taken aback by the suggestion; the nuns had sent a list of things that Christa would need; surely Miss Drake had enough to do finding so many pairs of stockings, dresses for a range of occasions, a suitable trunk, not to mention scores of handkerchiefs, and every item embroidered with Christa's initials and the family crest. There was absolutely no call for the girl to travel all the way to Vienna, when she would be going there permanently before long.

Flora found out as much information as she could about the convent; she showed the children pictures, and explained to Christa what sort of lessons there would be, and how many other girls she would be living with. They both met this information with silence. Jiri once exclaimed at the picture of the chapel organ; he would dearly love to be able to make the all-encompassing sounds one would produce, but so far no one had let him anywhere near a church organ, probably with good reason.

Christa told him sharply to Shut Up, and he did.

Abruptly the mood of the household changed. Christa was decidedly morose. Jiri looked dejected and played dismal music in minor keys, finally confiding to Flora that he was afraid that once Christa had gone to school, she would not want him anymore.

Flora decided that she needed to speak to Christa on her own.

--We shall all keep in touch, my dear, and we can visit you, and there will be holidays, and you will have so many new friends; in fact, poor Jiri is quite unhappy; he thinks that you will not want him anymore.

--That just shows what a stupid little idiot he is. Whether I want him or not, I've got him, haven't I?

Before Karel left for Prague, Flora had obtained his permission for the children to be photographed. John had a Kodak, and took various snaps of them all on the terrace, the children with their ponies and dogs, informal and wearing *Tracht*, but Flora wanted something more permanent and professional to take with her when she left the Principality.

So they drove into Strelitz, Christa wearing a simple, expensive and rather old-fashioned white dress, with lace inserts around the square neck; she had white stockings, and bar shoes instead of her usual light boots. Her abundant hair was caught up in a wide ribbon. Jiri was in knickerbockers and a short jacket, with a floppy bow under the broad collar of his white shirt. Had Karel been at home, he would have insisted that the boy had a haircut before being photographed, but Flora had rather a fondness for Jiri's curls, and left them uncut.

The result was fairly satisfactory. The children stood to attention before the studio's painted backdrop of mountain scenery. Two pairs of dark eyes stared out from two solemn von Tarnheim faces. Relatively expressionless, they looked more alike than usual without Christa's purposeful, and Jiri's mobile, glances.

Jiri had been enchanted by the whole process, and asked Flora if he could send a copy to Mrs Loudon, *So that she can see how very much I have grown.* He kept up quite a regular correspondence with Mrs Loudon, encouraged by Flora: the skill of writing a letter in English was a useful one, and Jiri always worked better at a self-chosen rather than an imposed task.

So an envelope arrived at the Shropshire home that Mrs Loudon and Beatrice were preparing for John and Flora. It contained a letter from Flora, a letter from Jiri, and the photograph.

--Where are my spectacles, Beatrice? asked Mrs Loudon, and, when they were found, she unfolded Jiri's letter, which was short but very painstakingly written.

--See, Beatrice! How very neatly Jiri has written this!

--Well, yes, m'um... I don't see any blots or crossings out... to think that scamp could sit still long enough!

Mrs Loudon now read aloud:

Dear Granny Loudon!

Hearty greetings! I hope you are well and that your new home is nice. Miss Drake says Shropshire is very pretty and you can see the mountains. (He must mean the Welsh Hills, Beatrice.) I send a photograph. I am with my cousin Christa. You will see that I have grown very much. I hope my English writing is correct. I have written this letter by myself. I send kind respects to Beatrice. Goodbye now honoured lady,

> *Yours faithfully with a kiss,*
> *Jaroslav Felix von Tarnheim Zellek.*

--Well! That is quite as good as many English boys could have written. He is really a credit to Flora's teaching. Now, let us look at the photograph.

She adjusted her spectacles. We must find a frame for it, then it can go in the drawing room. I do so miss being able to run into Whiteleys for things like that! For now it can be on my table... Well! How well they hold themselves! You can see that they come from a good family. And how nicely Flora has dressed them.

--Is that Master Jerry's cousin, did you say, m'um?

--Yes, Beatrice. She is a good-looking girl, and what lovely wavy hair!

--I see Master Jerry still has his curls. I wonder if he still makes a fuss about having it combed.

--Oh, I expect now that he is such a big boy...

They both looked at the photograph. Jiri was not really such a very big boy.

--He has filled out a bit, don't you think, m'um?

--Yes, I am sure he has, and he says he has grown.

--It's nice they are company for each other. Both being onlies, I mean, m'um. And they are alike, aren't they?

--Well, of course, Beatrice, they are cousins. And I think

they are fond of each other; see… I have only just noticed…
They are holding hands.

--We've got to do something. I've only got another two
weeks before I have to go there. I wrote to my mother. But the
letter came back; it was a wrong address.

--You didn't tell me.

--I don't tell you everything, Birdie. I'm not supposed to
write to her. But I got Gustl to smuggle it out.

--He didn't tell me.

--He doesn't tell you everything, either. Anyway it came
back. No one saw it. But if she knew, I know she would come
and take me away with her.

--What about me?

--I haven't decided. I don't suppose she would want you,
as you are such a little nuisance. And you do have your Papa
and Step-mutti.

--Yes. They would miss me.

--Well. When she takes me to Paris, and I am studying
art, I will have my own studio. And you can come and live
with me, if you promise to behave yourself, and you can have
a singing teacher from the Paris Opera, and a piano. We shall
need quite a big studio.

--Oh yes! And Papa and Mutti, and Miss Drake and
Doktor Jonni can come and stay as long as they like.

--I didn't say the studio would be THAT big. But we'll
see.

Jiri was silent, contemplating this wonderful future. Then
he added,

--But we have to get her back here first.

Flora heard an extraordinary sound. She was used to hearing Jiri singing, which he did at all times, and at this point his voice was quite remarkable. It had taken Flora a while to realise that his treble had nothing of the ethereal quality of an English choirboy; the tradition in which he was being trained to sing was quite different, a good deal more robust and powerful with some force behind the high notes. But what was he singing?

It was one of the Great O Antiphons that the Catholic Church uses in Advent. He must of course have learned it while in the Pallin church choir, but it was not Advent now.

It was the first O: 'O Come, O Come Emmanuel'... but after O Come, or as he sang it, *Ach Komm*, the words were unfamiliar... they were surely in his native language?

Singing, Jiri walked around the Roman altar. He repeated the words again and again... O Come, O Come.

On the altar, a battered toy bear lay wrapped in a dainty lace-trimmed handkerchief. A hunting knife protruded from its chest.

Soon an acrid odour filled that corner of the garden.

Ten days later, Christa left for Vienna.

1906–12

Note: Prince Felix Felixovich Yusupov 1887–1967, assassin of Rasputin.

After Christa left for the convent, Jiri returned to Pallin for his last year at the parish school. He was now in the top boys' class; after the age of ten, the boys and girls were in separate groups. He was apprehensive about the harder lessons he would face at the Oberschule, but Mother Jerome assured him that if he concentrated and applied himself, he would manage very well. His father told him that as long as he did his best, no one could require more.

That Christmas, he and Christa were reunited at Tarnheim while the Zelleks visited their relatives in Bremen; they hesitated to subject him to an arduous journey to north Germany in the depths of winter, and as Karel had particularly wanted the boy, they allowed him a mountain Christmas. He had been promoted to a big bedroom at Tarnheim, in fact that traditionally allotted to the male heir; it had a carved walnut bedstead, and long windows opening onto a mountain view. He and Christa stood watching the snowflakes and listening for the singers from the village.

His twelfth birthday came in June 1907. Christa had made some friends at the convent, and had been invited to spend the holidays travelling in Italy, a chance that could not be missed. Meanwhile, the Balinkays reiterated that a summer on Lake Balaton was just what a growing boy like Jiri needed. They were right. With Ferzi, who was nearly fourteen, and eight-year-old Mikki, Jiri had a wonderful time swimming, sailing, sunbathing and playing on the sandy shores of the beautiful lake. He made firm friends with the Takacz family after rescuing their Bichon, Za Za, from the lake, almost drowning himself and Mikki in the process. Peter Takacz was seventeen and took Jiri under his wing; he had three younger sisters, all of whom got on well with the little Austrian and the Balinkay brothers.

Jiri began his new school in excellent health and spirits, and at first things were not too bad. There was a great deal of military-style drill as all the boys would be called for army service at some point, but, schooled by his uncle, Jiri did not object to this. The lessons were challenging enough to be interesting but not impossibly difficult. The music master made full use of his talents, and taught him a great deal. He was generally popular with his classmates, and although often in trouble, had fewer disciplinary problems than might have been feared. In fact, overall the Zelleks were confident that they had made the right decisions about his schooling. Christmas 1907 passed happily in Pallin; Jiri was thirteen in June 1908; he had spent Easter at Tarnheim and as Christa was in Paris perfecting her French at the mother house of her school's order, Jiri again passed the summer in Hungary. As before, it greatly benefited his health, and by the autumn he had clearly begun to mature physically.

His voice showed signs of breaking, which seriously disoriented him; at school there was a new set of masters, and lessons began to seem boring; Jiri formed part of a disreputable group of boys and was increasingly insolent and disobedient.

Finally, in the spring of 1909, the headmaster made an example of him by thrashing him in front of the whole school. It was the worst thing that Jiri had ever experienced. The pain and humiliation were beyond imagining. It must never ever happen again. He would jump out of the window, he would run away to Tarnheim, he would stab the headmaster with the hunting knife that he now took to carrying with him at all times. As his fourteenth birthday approached, Jiri, still small and skinny after a rather modest growth spurt, became the target of bullying by a group of older boys, all much larger and stronger than himself.

This was when he used the knife. The ringleader received a serious cut on the cheek; in later life Jiri admitted freely that he had actually aimed for the boy's throat, but had missed because he was so shaken and manhandled. At all events, this led to Jiri's expulsion or removal from Oberschule, aged just fourteen. At this point his formal education ended.

Anton dealt with the situation by reminding the 'victim's' family that their son had nothing to be proud of in attacking a younger, smaller boy. He claimed that Jiri had been systematically bullied, his body covered with cuts and bruises, although he had never complained. Too honourable to tell tales, he had taken the matter into his own hands and tried merely to protect himself. Put like this, Jiri appeared as a frightened child (he was barely fourteen) rather than as a deranged lunatic fit only to be locked away for life, as his assailant maintained. Anton also confiscated the hunting knife, which caused one of Jiri's rare outbursts against his father.

He had no right. The knife was a von Tarnheim one, given to him by his uncle. It was to be carried only by a von Tarnheim. His father was not a member of his real family. Uncle Karel should hear of this. He would never have allowed all this to happen.

Anton rode the storm. He was in no hurry for Karel to know about these events. He would inevitably use them as evidence that Jiri should be enrolled in a military academy without delay. When Jiri had calmed down, Anton assured him that the knife would be returned to him once he had proved that he could act responsibly. Meanwhile, as the boy would not be attending school (*No. Never. I am never going back there*), it was time to concentrate on his music. Until his voice had settled down, he must work on his piano technique, strengthening his fingers, and acquiring a better knowledge of harmony, music theory and the classical repertoire. He must hear more instrumental music and perhaps join a chamber group. He must practise diligently for the next few weeks. Then Anton would take him to the Pallin Conservatoire for an entrance audition and, despite his youth, he might be allowed to enrol in a few classes and study with an advanced teacher.

Music was Jiri's salvation. He was soon attending the conservatoire daily. Later that summer, Anton, Grethe and Jiri travelled to Italy, where the elder Zelleks wanted to see the famous glassworks on the island of Murano. For the boy it was a formative experience. He heard opera sung in native Italian for the first time, and with his facility for languages was soon able to make himself understood, especially with the girls.

This was the last summer of Anton Zellek's life. He died suddenly just before Jiri was fifteen. For the next few months, Grethe struggled to maintain control of the firm, and Jiri was at first completely prostrated by his father's death and then acted wildly, roaming the town with the worst elements of his age group, smoking, drinking, who knew what else?

Then suddenly, perhaps at a word from his piano teacher, he applied himself to his studies as never before. It was clear that, following Anton's wishes, and using the substantial sum of money that he had left in his will for the purpose, he would be able to progress further. After one more summer with the Balinkays, Jiri left for lodgings in Vienna.

When Grethe visited him towards the end of spring 1912, she was seriously concerned about him; he was absorbed in his studies to the point of overwork, and she did not take to his two particular friends, Heinrich and Max. Both were Jews, a couple of years older than Jiri. Max she suspected of leading her stepson into licentious ways and dubious political opinions. She could not quite define her antipathy to the elder, Heinrich, who was devastatingly handsome, appeared protective, even proprietorial towards Jiri, and evidently drove him hard in his studies. The boy seemed to be running a temperature every night, and admitted to feeling faint and dizzy from time to time. Christa, she knew, was at Tarnheim having now left the convent; she contacted Karel and arranged for Jiri to travel there at once. Rather to her surprise, he did not argue, and two days after reaching Tarnheim he collapsed while on a walk with his cousin, who came into his room the next morning.

--Christi, I'm so glad to see you!

--You must be bored, then!

--Yes, I am. Terribly.

--Have you been sick again?

He nodded.

--My uncle wanted me to try that horrible tonic again. I told him I'd much rather not, and he said he was sorry, but it was an order, so I did try. And the thing is, now I keep tasting and smelling it all the time.

--Would you like to look out of the window and get some air?

--Yes! Jiri swung his feet out of bed and holding onto the chevalet, stood up shakily.

Christa helped him to the window and they stood there together.

--Oh that's much better.

--They are so silly giving you that medicine. You are supposed to have it after eating and that only means that you've got more to spew up.

He shuddered.

--Come back to bed. I'll read to you.

--Thank you. Wouldn't you rather be outside, though?

--Yes, but if I read to you, you'll go to sleep and then I can go out.

--Papa, does the doctor know what is making Jiri ill?

--I don't think he does. Gives me some nonsense about outgrowing his strength.

Father and daughter looked at each other and laughed.

--Well, Papa, he told me he had grown half an inch. We measured, and he is only two inches shorter than me now, so I suppose he has grown. Does he really have to take that medicine? I think it's making him worse and he's so skinny now... please, Papa, could I go and fetch Grushenka?

--For goodness' sake, the boy's far too old for a nanny, and she'd probably try to poison him with some peasant herbal muck.

--I'd make sure she wouldn't. And you know she is good at looking after sick people, and you will want to take Hans with you when you go away next week... or perhaps we had better send for Grethe?

--No. You may fetch Grushenka.

Christa drove the dog cart into the village, where her old nurse now lived with a granddaughter.

As Christa and Grushenka approached Jiri's room, Hans was coming out holding a covered bowl. A smell of vomit hung in the air and Jiri lay curled up, his arms over his stomach muscles which were strained with retching.

Grushenka shooed Christa out.

--Well, said Hans two days later, I know she stayed up with him all night, and who knows what she dosed him with, but this morning he asked Gustl to give him a bath and a clean shirt. The poor kid's skin and bone, but he never was much else anyway, and once he can eat a square meal and keep it down, I think the master can go away with an easy mind. Madam Christa is as pleased as punch: getting the old girl was all her doing, and she's up there reading to him and keeping him amused like a real little nurse, which ain't like her at all!

The doctor, unaware that the rest of his tonic had been flushed down the water closet, took credit, and a fee, for Jiri's recovery. The boy should not get overtired and should be encouraged to eat, he added.

Given Jiri's capricious appetite the servants took to leaving small amounts of delicious and easily-eaten food in his way: his favourite Linzertorte, some peeled and sliced fruit, small slices of bread with morsels of ham and cheese… under this regime, he gained strength; his uncle wrote to Grethe that her stepson had indeed been unwell but was now much better, and Jiri wrote along the same lines.

Karel von Tarnheim left, confident that his nephew was almost recovered, and that another three or four weeks, by which time he would be back in Tarnheim, would see Jiri as well as ever.

So Jiri and Christa were left alone. After a couple of days, they resumed their usual activities, walking, riding, fishing, reading together. Jiri practised the piano and Christa sketched. One afternoon they went into the library, where the day's post was regularly displayed; perhaps there would be a letter from Grethe or Heinrich for Jiri, for Christa from one of her old school friends, or one for them both from Karel von Tarnheim.

Jiri picked up a large, ornately decorated envelope.

--What's this?

--Oh! We must have forgotten it while you were ill. It's an invitation to a dinner and fancy-dress ball. It's impolite to leave it unanswered; I had better attend to it. With a businesslike air, Christa seated herself at the desk.

--Who's it from?

It came from the family of a rich businessman who had bought a house and estate in the valley. Karel had considered that they were not the sort he wished to mingle with, but they clearly continued to try to lure the von Tarnheims into their social circle.

The Zelleks, of course, would have had no such scruples, and Jiri looked with interest at the card.

--Did Uncle Karel say we couldn't go?

--Surely you don't want to. People like that? But no, he didn't say anything about it; I think he was too worried about you, though he tried not to show it. Jiri, don't you ever dare get ill like that again, especially as we are the last two von Tarnheims.

--I suppose we are. But, if we didn't go to the dinner, I don't think I could manage that, it would be such a bore, couldn't we go to the dance? It might be fun, and if Uncle Karel didn't say we mustn't...

--You really want to?

--Yes, Christi, I think I do.

So Christa wrote a gracious little note, saying that as her cousin had been ill recently, it would be sadly impossible for them to attend the dinner, but that they would appear at the ball afterwards.

The response was enthusiastic. Gräfin von Tarnheim and Herr von Tarnheim Zellek would be heartily welcome for whatever part of the evening they were able to attend.

--We need fancy dress.

This was a problem. Time was short, and anyway they had no money to order costumes from Vienna or anywhere else.

--We've got *Tracht*.

--Oh, Jiri, that's so boring.

--Well, yes and no. Jiri looked at her pensively. We are almost the same height now that I've grown, he announced proudly. We'll go as each other. I'll be you and you be me.

Christa took this in.

--Oh… but… anyway our *Tracht* isn't really for evenings. Although…there might be some old pieces, with the silver and gold lace, in the *Kofferzimmer*.

Up in the *Kofferzimmer*, they opened a few trunks without finding more than the accumulated clothing of several generations of Tarnheims. Finally, layered with rosemary and lavender… AHA!

Jiri took an old curtain and threw it on the floor.

Let's lay them out on this, he suggested, pulling out elaborate items of national costume, evidently designed for evening wear, festival processions and the like. It might even be that some eighteenth-century Tarnheims had worn these at the imperial court, participating in some fantastical masque or entertainment.

Jiri held a beautifully embroidered bodice against himself… how's this?

--It's pretty… but Jiri, I think you will need to be shaved! She reached out her hand and touched his face, where, given his dark colouring, it was not surprising that he had the early beginnings of a moustache. Jiri caught her hand and kissed it.

There was a moment's silence.

--Let's try some of this stuff on.

Both took off their outer clothing; as children they had been naked together, and even now they were used to seeing each other in underwear; during Jiri's illness he had worn only a shirt. Now he was in his drawers and undershirt and Christa was in her chemise.

--Ugh, Jiri, I'd forgotten what big ugly feet you have.

Given his dapper physique, Jiri had quite large capable hands, and relatively long, bony feet.

Suddenly he sniggered rather unpleasantly.

--You know what they say, Christi, about men's feet? If you've got big feet you've got a big (they were speaking their first language). When I was at the Oberschule...some fellows... they said a little rat like me couldn't have... and they tried to tear off my drawers...

--Oh, Birdie. Christa pulled him towards her.

--I kneed two of them in the balls, and brained the other one with my history textbook. A couple of other fellows heard the racket and joined in. I was angry... you know... and it was quite a fight and I had my hunting knife, the one Uncle Karel gave me. Papa took me away from the Schule after that and I don't think they wanted me back anyway.

By now he was pressed against her.

--Birdie, is that...?

--Yes.

Then things happened very quickly. Christa could hardly believe that it was Jiri making those sounds, and that it was Jiri who was on top of her, it was Jiri who was inside her... Jiri who lay there half on her and half off.

--Have you done this before?

--Yes. A few times. With a woman, I mean.

--Is it always this messy? And I thought it would have lasted longer.

--It's meant to. But...

Jiri's experiences in a Viennese brothel had not got as far as that.

Reaching for his everyday hose he pulled out a handkerchief and handed it to her, horrified when he saw it stained with blood.

--Christi! I'm sorry! I've hurt you!

Suddenly he remembered that it had hurt him the first time, with Heinrich.

--A bit late for that. But I think it's only because this was the first time. Jiri, I don't want to see you again today. I'm going. You can sort out these things yourself.

That year Karel had purchased an Austro Daimler, but decided not to take it to Prague. It caused quite a sensation when it arrived at the colonnaded mansion where the fancy-dress ball was in progress. The lights festooning the trees and entrance were glowing in varied colours; the scent of flowers, both from the garden and the huge floral displays in the hallway, perfumed the midsummer dusk. The von Tarnheims' cloaks were whisked away.

The hostess had arranged that guests should enter the ballroom down a staircase so that their costumes could be admired. There was a pause in the dancing, which had already commenced.

--Herr von Tarnheim Zellek and Gräfin von Tarnheim! announced the footman.

The two figures who now descended the staircase hand in hand were of equal height since one of them was wearing high-heeled buckled shoes. Both were masked. They formed a strange contrast to the crowd of Pierrots, Chinamen, shepherdesses and Spanish gypsies clustered below. They appeared as fantastical, archaic figures from an eighteenth-century French fairy tale, or as two of the magical host who, in local folklore, emerged from caverns in the mountain to bewitch mortals with their dancing at just this time of year.

They were alone on the dance floor. They had practised; because of her height, Christa was used to leading during dancing classes at the convent. Jiri, as he said, had to learn how to do it backwards and in high heels, but thanks to his neatness and economy in physical movement he soon mastered a skill that was to prove useful over the years. As the night went on, their identities became more evident, but many of the guests played along with the game so that according to the choice of their partners, they danced in both roles.

--Jiri, whispered Christa as they passed each other, we are not the most important people here after all. I hear that there is a Russian prince, visiting incognito, who has been lured in!

Finding that his shoes were not as comfortable as they had been at the beginning of the evening, Jiri took a glass of champagne, which he loved, and stepped into an alcove shaded by potted ferns. Someone came up behind him and put a hand on each side of his waist.

--Now, turn round so that I can see who and what you are, little elf!

Jiri turned. He saw a slim man of medium height in his early twenties, as dark as he was himself, clean-shaven and wearing evening dress so impeccable that Jiri's breath was taken away. It was just how he would like to be seen. He was being offered a cigarette, a Russian cigarette, from a case that he recognised as Fabergé. The man took it from him, placed it between his own lips, lit it and placed it between Jiri's lips in turn.

--Your Royal Highness. Jiri knew no Russian but instantly resolved to learn. By some instinct, he spoke in English.

--Ah. How did you guess that I am studying in Oxford this year? But those English fellows can be somewhat boring so I have escaped for few days. Although, as I have no fancy dress, and I have always loved dressing up... my Mama used to get so cross when I borrowed her jewels... I have been finding this evening less than exciting. Perhaps you might change that for me, whoever you are.

--Jaroslav Felix von Tarnheim Zellek. The bow and clicked heels were an odd conjunction with the skirt and floral headdress.

--Felix! Then we have something in common besides an inclination to female dress. My name is Felix also. As was my father's. We must celebrate that. More champagne.

It appeared as if by magic. Being a prince seemed to have many advantages.

--My mother is from an old Tatar family, he continued. Let me see you without your mask. Though, with it on, you are like a creature imagined by Aubrey Beardsley.

He took it off and threw it into a corner.

-Ah. Not a typical Austrian. A fellow Slav.

He drew Jiri towards him, tilted his face and gave him a long, lingering kiss, laughing at the boy's instinctive response.

--You, Felix the Less, are evidently gifted with the ability to gain enjoyment wherever you wish; I guess you have already tried what we in Russia call gentlemen's mischief. You are here with your... sister, is she? Surely not, although...

--Christa von Tarnheim is my cousin, Your Highness.

--Ah yes. Cousin marriages can be very convenient, and I assume that yours is an old family, as is mine; how nice to know that one is actually of better lineage than the ruling house! You and I can cock a snook, as the English say, at the Habsburgs and the Romanovs!

At this moment the clock struck two.

--I am like Cinderella! Although a couple of hours late! My chauffeur is ordered for two o'clock. I must make my farewells. But, dear little Jaroslav Felix, I think I shall give you one more kiss to remember me by.

An advantage of wearing a skirt, Jiri realised, was that no one could see you having an erection.

--Jiri, Jiri, I suppose you have not eaten anything. There are some delicious refreshments downstairs, do come! Christa too had discarded her mask, or had it taken from her. She seized his hand and led him to a salon, where every type of cold delicacy was arranged in dazzling colours on shining dishes between pyramids of ice carved into wonderful shapes.

--Ice cream! And some more champagne.

He surveyed the ices, which were in silver scallop shells, each with its own little spoon.

--Which flavour? Oh they all look so pretty! What is this one, Christi? I haven't had a pale green one like that before.

--It's pistachio. I had it in Paris.

Jiri took one. And then another. He closed his eyes as he sipped from the silver spoon. The music seemed at once far off and near; the blend of colours and sensations overwhelmed him; he might float away.

--Jiri! I think you have had too much to drink. How much champagne have you had? And two ices...or maybe three? Let's go; we must say thank you to our hostess. She is very pleased with us; apparently as he was leaving Prince Yusupov told her how enchanted he'd been to make acquaintance with the von Tarnheim family!

She got him into the motor.

--Christi, he said as they approached Tarnheim, I think I'm going to throw up.

--No! Not in the motor! They will never get the smell off the upholstery! Papa will never forgive us. Stop, stop!

He tumbled out by the roadside and was violently, horribly sick. But by the time they had reached home he had largely recovered, little the worse save for a lifetime's aversion to pistachio ice cream.

They stood in the early summer dawn. Already the sun was beginning to shed pink, silver and blue light on the mountains.

--I don't want to go to bed, Christi. Why don't we have a swim in the bathing pool?

--What about all these things?

--We can wrap them in one of the cloaks and pick them up later.

They took off their finery and, huddled together under the remaining cloak, they set out. Both knew the way so well that they did not stumble; Jiri had kicked off his shoes, and Christa had her arm around him.

Naked, they plunged in. Oh! It's so cold! They dived beneath the water and swam to the area where the waterfall splashed into the pool; they surfaced, clasped hands and jumped up and down in the foam, their white bodies rising out of the dark water. They clasped each other and separated, then clasped again.

The sun rose. They lay together by the side of the pool, covered by the cloak.

In the early morning, Gustl looked towards the mountain path and saw two figures running hand in hand towards the castle.

--Gustl, Gustl! called Jiri as soon as they were in earshot. We must have breakfast immediately; bring it to my bedroom at once.

Snuggled up in Jiri's bed, they shared hot chocolate, rolls with fresh butter and Grushenka's berry jam, and honey cakes. They played the old, secret game of Big Bird and Little Bird, then, folded in each other's wings, they slept into the afternoon.

Karel van Tarnheim returned at the end of the summer. He arrived home quite late, when both Christa and Jiri were asleep. He had breakfast in his room, so neither of them had yet seen him when the major-domo announced that the master would like to see Herr von Tarnheim Zellek in his study.

Normally this summons would have made Jiri's heart sink. While his uncle had never physically punished him, he had given him numerous unpleasant tellings-off. But he was not usually addressed in the household as Herr Zellek, even less by his fuller name.

--Jiri... Jaroslav...I am pleased to see you looking so much stronger.

Jiri was still skinny, but he was sunburned, lively and active.

--Sit down. I wish to speak to you.

Jiri said nothing.

--Jiri... you are now seventeen years old. We need to speak of your future. You must be aware that if I had my choice you would have been at cadet school for the past two years at least. But your late father was adamant that you should pursue musical studies, first in Pallin and lately in Vienna. And there is no doubt that you are talented, Jiri. But

I must ask you to remember that you and Christa are the last two von Tarnheims. You, in fact are the last male Tarnheim, and at some point, perhaps, we may arrange for you to drop the Zellek from your name, and eventually to assume the title.

--But, interrupted Jiri. That single *aber* was the only word he was allowed to contribute. His uncle signed for silence, and continued.

--I must ask you, do you really contemplate a life as a performer, in public, even on the operatic stage?

This was a question to which he clearly did not anticipate an answer.

--While I have been away, I visited your stepmother.

--Mutti? How is she? asked Jiri eagerly.

--She is very well, and I must say, she is making an excellent job of managing the glass business. That is exactly the kind of thing she is eminently fitted for. We agreed, of course, that much as she may wish it, the life of a factory manager is not fit for a von Tarnheim.

Jiri remained silent. Much as he loved the processes and products of the glass factory, the idea of going there every day, overseeing it all, sitting in an office… this did not appeal to him. He was also aware that his time in Vienna had made him look afresh at his own musical capabilities. Perhaps knowing that he had no financial need to make music his profession, his professors had made it clear that as a pianist, he was indeed rather precociously talented, and with study and practice he could give great pleasure to his hearers; if he had needed to, he might well eventually earn a living as an accompanist, a repetiteur, a teacher, but the concert platform was already crowded. His voice was only just settling down but promised to be bewitching in its way given his tone, range and musicianship. But he would never be a *heldentenor*; he would never have the physique or force for opera roles; one cannot earn a living from lieder and folk songs, and the little count, as he was nicknamed, could hardly become a cabaret singer or join the opera chorus.

The extent to which this had worried Jiri, even shattered his dreams, is not known, even to himself...

His uncle was continuing.

--Your stepmother fully agrees with me, Jaroslav. The von Tarnheims have always been officers in the Kaiserlich und Königliche Armee. You will be returning to Vienna shortly, for a few weeks before joining an officer training course. When that is completed I shall secure you a commission in my own old regiment, the XXth Ulans, in which von Tarnheims have served the Emperor for three centuries. I will also provide you with a suitable mount. I do not need to make you an allowance, as you will have sufficient from your late father's estate. Is that understood?

--Yes, sir. There was really little else that Jiri could say. And it is just possible that the thought of being one of the smart young Ulans seen flirting with the ladies in the Ring, or riding a top-grade horse, or parading before the Emperor was not unattractive.

--One more thing. His uncle looked, for once slightly ill at ease. Women. You are growing up. A young man must gain some... experience.

--Uncle, I have.

--Good. Karel was evidently relieved. Given Jiri's habit of causing chaos, he was glad that the task of taking the boy to a brothel did not fall to him. Just be careful, my boy. Those

151

places can harbour disease, and young women of the lower classes can cause embarrassment and entanglement.

--Yes, sir.

Gustl discussed events with his fellow servants.

--So little Master Jiri is off to be trained for the Ulans.

--I don't think he's got much choice!

--He'll be all right. At least he's got plenty of guts. And the army will make a man of him.

--It's a bit late for that! Ask Madam Christa.

--You don't mean to say that those two innocents—

--Innocent my foot. While the master's been away those two have been at it every chance they get.

--Let's just hope there aren't consequences.

--That maid Odile has been keeping an eye on madam. But the sooner our little stallion is packed off, the better!

The groom spoke for the first time.

--I'll tell you one thing. That boy thinks he can ride, but a proper cavalry instructor will make mincemeat of his arse.

1913-14

Bold, outspoken, optimistic, physically robust and intelligent rather than scholarly, Mihaly Balinkay had always liked the idea of joining the Hussars. So, at about the time his elder brother began his university studies, Mikki was entered in a military academy. Here he was popular and successful; in the early autumn of 1913, he was one of a group of cadets selected to take part in a parade in Vienna. In between rehearsals and lectures, the cadets were allowed some free time to visit the sights; Mikki and his friend Lajos decided that the place to go was the Prater; here, surrounded by a crowd of fashionable, elegant and sophisticated Viennese strolling in the sunshine, warm at last after a disappointing summer, they felt rather young, insignificant and out of place, although they tried to convince themselves that they were enjoying it.

Suddenly a clear, resonant voice called.

--Mikki! Mikki Balinkay!

And, looking round, they saw a group of Austrian Ulan officers, in their blue and red uniforms. One was hurrying, almost running towards them.

--Jiri! I hardly recognised you, you look so much taller!

Coming from the guileless Mikki, this delighted Jiri, and he replied graciously,

--It's the czapka! Christa says that is the only reason I joined the Ulans!

--And… the moustache.

--It is easy if one is dark. When you are my age, Mikki… but I shall never rival your father! He is well? But, Mikki, we are impolite. Please present your friend to me.

--Hortai Lajos. They were speaking Hungarian, and Mikki used the inversion of given and family names.

Jiri drew off his glove and English fashion offered his hand, which was brown, capable and unexpectedly large. On his little finger, he wore a simple gold band with a tiny lapis seal.

--Jiri von Tarnheim Zellek.

They shook hands.

--Cadet Hortai, you are fortunate. Mikki Balinkay is the finest comrade a man could have. Now, would it bore you to join me for coffee and cakes? If you have no other engagements, of course. I know a café near here, where the pastries are excellent and where we can sit and watch the world go by.

He was careful not to say the girls, although of course that was what had been on the boys' minds.

Wonderful! Jiri stepped between them, linked arms, and off they went. It was now clear that even with the czapka, Jiri was not tall. By now even he had reluctantly admitted that he had reached his full height of just under five foot five. He always gave his height as five foot six. He could not really be said to have filled out, but he had lost his air of boyish fragility, for army life had made him upright and extremely well-muscled. Dr John Loudon had been right: wiry, active and surprisingly strong, he could hold his own on the parade ground and on manoeuvres.

Mikki and Lajos felt that they were much more visible in the company of a dapper young officer, who was being saluted by a couple of Ulan troopers.

--Now... Mikki, do you still like chocolate? Dobostorte? And... may I call you Lajos? For you? I shall have Linzertorte. I used to have it when I was studying here.

Lajos had noticed Jiri's fluent, correct but not unaccented Hungarian, and asked him where he had learned it.

--In Mikki's family! His governess taught me, but we were sometimes very cheeky, weren't we, Mikki!

Lajos could believe that.

--Yes; we have been friends since we were children, explained Mikki. Although Jiri is a few years older than we are, of course. He was commissioned this year, on the Emperor's birthday.

--That's right! I was glad to get out of officer training, I can tell you! I have never been to military academy, like you cadets; I did just over a year of officer training.

It was hard. I was a spoiled brat, wasn't I, Mikki? And being told what to do, and how to do it, every minute of the day and much of the night, was most irksome and boring. I'm afraid I got rather a reputation as a nuisance. Finally the Commandant handed me over to the riding master, on the grounds that I'd missed training by not being in cadet school. He was Hungarian, like you: of course, you are the best riders in the world. The man was terrifying! He worked my arse so hard that at the end of the day I had no energy left to make mischief, or not much, anyway. But at last I now have some idea of military discipline, and am a tolerable rider, and we have been on manoeuvres, which was great fun. But tell me, Mikki, how is Ferzi? I have not heard from him lately.

Jiri's entry into the *k und k* had been rather variously received by the Balinkay family. Mikki was simply proud. Mr Balinkay was one of those like John Loudon, who thought that army discipline might be a good solution to the problem of Jiri Zellek. Madame Balinkay and Ferencz, in contrast, felt it to be an appalling waste of Jiri's musical talents and wondered how far it had been his free choice.

--I saw Ferzi when I was on leave. He's studying philosophy now, and keeps talking about the meaning of life and the nature of reality. Is that something that always happens when you get older, Jiri?

Jiri paused before replying,

--I don't think so. Anyway, we are Catholics so we do not need to ponder the meaning and purpose of life. That saves a great deal of time and breath. And, Mikki, we are soldiers with a duty to the Emperor, to our fellow officers, and to our men.

--And you are a von Tarnheim, added Mikki.

Jiri shrugged as he agreed, That also.

Suddenly they noticed a commotion: people were stopping and looking upwards; a strange whirring, chugging sound came from the sky.

It's a flying machine!

The pilot was showing off, swooping, circling, dipping, rising... Men waved their hats, women waved their handkerchiefs, a ripple of excitement and national pride, a murmur of voices some cheering, and then the machine was gone, up, up into the clouds.

--It's a Lohner Traube! cried Mikki.

--Here we go, sighed Lajos. Really, Mikki, you talk about nothing else.

--Well, it's better than debating the meaning of life, isn't it, Jiri? Anyway, they make them here in Vienna, and in Hungary too, and there's a fellow, Major Emil Uzelac, he came to talk to us about aviation; it's the future for the *k und k*.

Lajos interrupted.

--That's not what our Commandant thinks! He says it's all new-fangled nonsense, useful for reconnaissance maybe but nothing else.

--Our Colonel says the same, added Jiri. But, it must be wonderful to go up in one of those, mustn't it... it is so wonderful to be up high, anyway, in the mountains, and, well, if one can have a motor, I don't see why one cannot have a flying machine also!

Here the patron appeared in the doorway, greeting Jiri, whom he evidently knew well.

--Herr Leutnant! Pavel is not back from his pause; would you care to have the piano?

Taking off his czapka to reveal close-cropped, dark curly hair, Jiri went to the piano and began to play popular songs, dance music and the tango, which was the newest craze.

--The Kaiser has forbidden any German army officers to dance the tango in uniform! he announced – but we are all right, the Emperor has not said anything! So let's see what you lot can do.

Two girls who had been sitting by the window smiled at the cadets. They were kids, but they looked cute in their uniforms; they must have some pocket money, and might be up for some fun before the evening's serious work began.

Tables were cleared away. Those who knew how to tango offered to teach those who didn't. Jiri pounded cheerfully at the piano.

Eventually three of his fellow Ulan officers burst in.

--There he is! Jiri, you are on duty in ten minutes. Let's hope Steffi can cover for you, or the Colonel will have your guts for garters, again.

Two of them lifted him almost bodily from the piano stool, while the third rammed his czapka onto his head and retrieved his sword from under the piano.

--Servus! Got to go! An honour to meet you Lajos! Mikki, I'll write and tell you where we are posted.

And he was gone.

The two senior officers stood looking down at the sunlit parade ground.

--It takes me back, said the General. A smart young officer inspecting his troop of lads before morning exercise.

The Colonel was slightly concerned to notice that the smart young officer referred to was Zellek. But, when he concentrated, Zellek was actually very prompt and neat, and he was mounted on his unsensational but reliable horse Bruno, prudently selected by Karel von Tarnheim.

Jiri's was one of those voices that carries clearly across distances without giving the effect of shouting or bawling.

Evidently he was not satisfied with the troop's appearance and turnout. They gave the effect, he told them, of a complete *Gurkentruppe*, an insult that had some slight results. Not enough; Jiri now addressed them again, this time with success; the troopers straightened up in their saddles, squared their shoulders, quietened their mounts.

--That's more like it! Now I'm not ashamed to be seen with you! Trot!

And they clattered out of the enclosure.

--What on earth was that language? demanded the General.

--I think it was Ruthenian, sir. Many of our lads are Ruthenian peasants: not a bad lot.

--That officer; surely he is not Ruthenian. We both know the regulations forbidding officers to command troops of their own nationality if it is other than pure Austrian.

--No fear of that, sir. Von Tarnheim Zellek is from the Principality.

--Then how comes he to know Ruthenian?

The Colonel was at a loss, which he would later take out on young Zellek.

--I respectfully suggest, sir, he perhaps just happens to know some of the language.

--No one just happens to know Ruthenian. This could be a case of fraternisation. He must be reprimanded. This sort of thing undermines the discipline of the army.

--So, Zellek, said the Colonel next morning. You are aware that, although the giving of basic commands may be in one of a variety of languages, the provision of instructions must be in German, and German only.

--Yes, sir. Respectfully observe, sir, that this was not an instruction. It was a description.

--Zellek, this insolence will find you in the punishment cells. You spoke to the men in Ruthenian, did you or did you not?

--Yes, sir. I told them that their uniforms looked like a line of washing in a farmyard, and that they were wearing their caps like birds' nests on a row of turnips. They smartened up at once, sir.

--Enough! He glanced at Jiri's record sheet, which lay before him on the table.

Zellek, you are guilty of using a language other than the permitted amount of German on the parade ground. You are guilty of gross insolence in your answers to me. It is only the fact that you have not yet worked through your latest set of extra duties that prevents me from punishing you severely. You must realise that this sort of thing looks like fraternisation and can undermine the discipline of the whole army.

This seemed a rather tall order for the slight figure standing before him.

--May I ask, he continued, How is it that you can speak Ruthenian?

--Oh, I do not speak it fluently, sir. But, if one hears a language spoken all around one, it is difficult not to pick up a few words, don't you find, sir? Anyone must do that, and then, I do have an interest in languages. Ruthenian is really not so very difficult if one knows Hungarian, Croatian and some Russian; of course, I know the men laugh at my accent behind my back! But then they do laugh at us all, sir! And actually, I have thought that sometimes it is quite useful to know what the lads are talking about among themselves; without breaking any confidences, of course.

Suddenly the Colonel thought of a way the affair might be represented to the General.

--Zellek, he announced, I am overlooking this incident to some extent. I am issuing you with a serous reprimand, which will be entered on your records; it will be noted should you ever seek promotion. And you will not speak Ruthenian on the parade ground or in my hearing other than, as I have said, to utter the basic words of command.

(He didn't say anything about singing, thought Jiri. Or when he isn't listening.)

Meanwhile, dismissed!

--Well, Jiri?

--He told me that I am undermining the discipline of the entire *k und k*.

--What, you? By yourself? Or have you got help?

--No. Just me.

--Really Jiri? I would have thought that required someone a little taller.

--Don't be cruel, Toni!

--But how, my boy, are you accomplishing this?

--It's because I know some Ruthenian.

--Right. Shall we go back to the beginning?

--I was telling the lads off. They were really a disgrace, Steffi: sloppy, slouching, nothing polished, collars undone. I'm not having it. I hate it when the Germans accuse us of Austrian sloppiness.

--I would have thought that was promoting discipline, not undermining it.

--Thing is, I find they take more notice if I throw in a few Ruthenian insults; actually they are nothing to what one could do in Hungarian, but…

--Yes, yes, let's stop you there; so, you're using Ruthenian on the parade ground? You know that all instructions must be given in German.

--Of course, but as I told the Colonel, this was not an instruction. It was a description.

--You told the Colonel that?

--Yes, of course.

--I'll bet he loved that.

--It did seem to upset him rather.

By now they had a larger audience.

--I'm amazed you're not in the punishment cells right now, Jiri!

--He did mention that. But he thought better of it. After all, as I explained, it's almost impossible not to pick up a few words of a language when one hears it all day. And I did remind him that it can be quite handy to know what the lads are gossiping about… you know, I'd never have heard about Binstein and that landlady if his orderly hadn't mentioned it to one of the grooms while I was checking Bruno… it can be so interesting… I'll bet none of you knows the latest about how Rudi raised the money for his tarock debts.

--Jiri, you little horror.

--No, tell us…

In the summer of 1914 Jiri's regiment went on annual manoeuvres. Most of the young officers thoroughly enjoyed the change from the usual routine; they rode, marched, bivouacked, swam naked in lakes and rivers, enjoyed the hospitality of local landowners, and flirted with hordes of admiring young women. The enjoyment was slightly marred when, in the final days, Captain von Klinsturm broke his leg badly in a fall from his horse: most unexpected and regrettable since he was one of the best riders in the regiment and an admired and popular officer.

When they were back in quarters, once again the Colonel sent for Leutnant von Tarnheim Zellek.

--What's this, Zellek, that I hear about the steeplechase?

The regimental race event, featuring the famous annual steeplechase, followed by a grand dinner and ball, was in preparation.

--Sir?

--You and Von Klinsturm's horse.

--Yes, sir. Captain von Klinsturm has been kindly letting me exercise Grazia for some time. She's wonderful, sir! Such a mover, such heart, so full of…

--Yes, yes. And?

--Well, sir you know about poor Klinsturm's accident. He has told me that he would like me to ride Grazia for him.

--Well, Zellek, if he has settled that, he must have some confidence in your riding ability.

Zellek seemed to grow an inch taller. Sometimes, the Colonel thought, especially with renegades like von Tarnheim Zellek, a word of encouragement works wonders. So he continued,

--I have just been reviewing the reports of the manoeuvres. You have been commended, in fact highly commended, for your initiative, leadership and efficiency. Especially in that matter of the unexploded grenade. Your fitness reports are all good or satisfactory, and you performed creditably in the shooting and fencing competitions. Well done, Zellek. Dismissed!

This was the first time that Jiri had left the Colonel's office other than in dire disgrace. With a clear conscience he applied himself to preparations for the steeplechase. In fact he was distinctly nervous, if only because von Klinsturm, at a testy stage of convalescence, had told him that if Grazia was harmed in any way, any way at all, not only would Jiri's army career be over for good but he would be facing civilian life minus two important organs. But exercising Grazia was a delight. She was the best horse he had ever ridden: a grey mare, light, spirited and very responsive; fast, brave, a talented jumper. She had also been very expensive, and the steeplechase was notoriously perilous for a relatively inexperienced jockey to negotiate. Bruno was not built for speed, and Jiri had never raced him; informal contests trying out remounts and playing around on manoeuvres were his only previous practice. While he ardently longed for a chance to show off Grazia's paces, he knew that von Klinsturm had the right to change his mind at any time; for this reason he did not mention the steeplechase to his uncle or Christa, who would be attending the celebrations.

They arrived in Karel's motor with a valet and a maid, plus a huge amount of luggage following with a footman by train and trap. Numerous changes of clothes would be required for the two days of their stay.

When they arrived at their hotel, it was discovered that the majority of the luggage had failed to appear; the train had been delayed, so they lunched at the hotel, waiting impatiently for Karel's reserve officer's uniform and Christa's race-going outfit; by the time they were changed and ready, the races had already begun. Christa looked around for Jiri. As she did so, a young officer approached them and respectfully introduced himself; Jiri, he said, had asked him to look out for them. It was excellent that they had managed to get here in time to support Leutnant von Tarnheim Zellek in the steeplechase.

--But there must be some mistake. Jiri would never enter Bruno in such an event.

--Ah. Well, sir, he is not riding Bruno.

--Good heavens, Christa, the boy will break his neck.

--His riding has improved, Papa.

--It will need to!

--Let's go to the stand; can you escort us, Leutnant?

As they took their seats, the runners were approaching the start. Raising her opera glasses, Christa made out Jiri; she gathered that he was riding the restive, evidently nervous grey. They got off to rather a bad start but cleared the first fence in excellent style, while two of the less skilful riders were already unseated. It was evident that Jiri was attempting a safe, rather than a fast, race. Von Klinsturm had spoken very kindly to him, stressing that this was a first for both horse and rider; it should be seen as experience, and all he required of Jiri was, as he had previously said, that Grazia should get round unharmed. Jiri too, preferably.

Staying with the main group rather than with the leaders, Grazia jumped faultlessly; by a process of attrition, the field both narrowed and became more strung out so that eventually Christa could see four leaders quite closely followed by a tight group with the stragglers falling behind, one or two of them being pulled up. Jiri and Grazia were well up in the mid-group.

Then they made what seemed a disastrous mistake; it was Jiri's fault; Grazia wanted to go and he tried to hold her, meaning that they approached the water jump awkwardly, stumbled and had to scramble out, with Jiri only just still on board. They had lost ground as they headed for a really fearsome fence, the penultimate obstacle. Gathering pace, they approached it, only to see absolute carnage. A tangle of fallers on the other side meant that landing was hazardous… Given the gap that had opened between Grazia and the group ahead, Jiri was able to move to the extreme outside; they jumped the fence clear, landing to the left of the pile of horses and riders in the centre. This meant that they had open ground to the final fence and Grazia, no longer held back, gave her all. They went over the last one looking as fresh as when they had started and now only three horses competed on the straight to the finish. They overtook two of them while the crowd cheered at one of the most exciting finishes for years. With a couple of lengths to go, Grazia gained on the leader, but this horse, a powerful bay gelding, found a final ounce of strength to hold her off, winning by half a length. Grazia and Jiri were a close, creditable and plucky second. Those who had backed them each way as an outsider were jubilant. Christa and Karel felt as exhausted as if they had ridden the race themselves. Jiri was overjoyed by Grazia's performance. He also knew that he had been extremely lucky. His mistake at the water jump, which he'd thought must lose them the race, had actually both saved them from serious injury at the hedge and enabled their clear gallop to the finish. Von Klinsturm muttered something about the Devil looking after his own, but he was actually delighted, and was able to do Jiri a few good turns in the future.

At the ball that evening, the winner of the steeplechase and his partner had the honour of leading off the dancing; after they had done a circuit of the floor, the riders who had come second and third followed in turn before the rest of the company joined in. So it was that Jiri and Christa stepped out, watched by the entire regiment. Although he knew Christa so intimately, he had never seen her like this. Short-sleeved and low-necked, ending just above her ankles, Christa's dress had been made by one of Vienna's foremost couturieres. It was of shimmering gold net embroidered thickly with gold beads in a pattern of stylised foliage and roses, their petals very lightly touched with pink silk thread. She was not a beauty like her mother, but she was handsome by any standards and remarkably so for a von Tarnheim; etiquette decreed that as an unmarried woman she could not wear the main family tiara, but the lighter one, with its droplets of yellow diamonds, nestled and scintillated in her wavy hair. Jiri, with his cropped dark hair and neat moustache, suited the Ulan dress uniform in his neatness and perfect proportions. Years ago Karel had thought him not a bad-looking boy, and now he was certainly quite a good-looking man.

As they danced, their absolute physical accord and intimacy was palpable. They did not need to speak, and in fact did not do so until later.

--Darling, you deserve champagne and I know you want ice cream. But I shall not let you have both together.

--You are right, as you always are! Let's go outside.

Coloured lights were strung beside the pathways and throughout the bushes. They stood close together.

--Birdie, it's been such a long time.

--I don't want to crush your dress. It's the most beautiful thing I have ever seen.

--It was terribly expensive! And the fittings… I was never so bored in my life! It's just as well that you were one of the first three; at least everyone got to see it. I told Odile not to wait up for me.

When they entered the hotel lobby, Jiri ordered champagne to be sent to Christa's room. They embraced in the elevator, among the veneered and gilded mirrors. Inside, he helped her out of the golden dress, which he spread reverently over a chair before wrestling with the complications of his dress uniform; at last he reached his underwear and socks, which he removed, singing and casting the garments about the room. He was naked by the time the second bottle of champagne arrived.

--Jiri... what are you doing? I mean, what are you doing now? I know what you've just done.

--I'm getting my ring off. I'm having to spit on it. Where's your finger?

--Urgh, it's wet, that's your spit! It won't go on that finger, it's too small. Try my little finger, then.

--It must fit that. It goes on mine all right, though it was tight. Anyway, it's just for now. I'll get you a big diamond or whatever we fancy, or you can choose one from the family stuff.

--No. I like this. It's Aunt Gisela's ring, isn't it, that your father left you. And you've worn it since then, since you were fifteen.

--Yes. She's wearing it in both the portraits. I think Uncle Karel gave it to her. All her other jewels went back to Tarnheim but Papa must have kept this; perhaps it is not worth much.

--It's very old, though, at least the little seal is; I think it's Mercurius.

--Do you remember who he was? I'm not sure I do.

--I think so. There's that statue of him near where we built the altar that time; we thought he looked a bit like you; skinnier than most of those Greeks! So I'll have you on my ring, won't I? It's nice to get this settled, isn't it?

--Oh yes! And we should celebrate… if you can let me get out of bed, I'll see if we have any champagne left… and if not, I'll ring the bell.

--Excuse me, sir. Your servant is outside with your regular uniform. He says you are on duty.

The hotel valet shook Jiri awake.

--Oh God! What time is it?

Jiri rolled out of bed; he was rather stiff, slightly hungover and very thirsty. Taking a gulp of water from the carafe, he gathered up as much of his dress uniform as he could carry, opened the door and thrust it into the corridor, where his batman stood holding a bag. Stumbling back into the bedroom, Jiri seized his sword and czapka, dropped those outside also, and closed the door behind him. Christa had not stirred. Her golden dress was still draped carefully over the back of a chair. The only article of Jiri's clothing that remained was one black silk sock which hung rakishly over the mirror, where he had flung it in the early hours of the morning.

Outside, he tried to locate his vest and drawers in the pile of clothing.

--Best hurry, sir, said the batman as Jiri struggled into his underwear. There are people coming up and down here.

By the time they reached the post, Rudi was waiting for them.

--Toni is taking your duty; he's out with the troop. The Colonel wants to see you *now*.

During the next fifteen minutes, Jiri's only positive thought was that at least the Colonel was not giving him a dressing down in public, as had happened before.

In fact, the interview was not entirely private, as to those gathered outside the door the Colonel's voice could be clearly heard.

--So, on the strength of riding a superior officer's horse in a steeplechase, Leutnant Zellek saw fit to absent himself without leave; it was an offence punishable by court martial and dismissal from the *k und k*, in which case the Leutnant could sink to his proper level, that of a jockey in a third-rate racetrack, a life for which his appearance, language and breeding fitted him.

This last was a particularly hard blow, as in the regiment it was not the done thing to remind Zellek that he was in fact only half a von Tarnheim.

There was much more of the same.

Eventually:

Dismissed. Out of my sight.

--Yes, sir. Thank you, sir.

Jiri, looking green, came out and leaned against the door.

--Well?

--Two weeks' extra duties and confined to post.

--Phew... what you need is a strong coffee and a cognac.

--I'll have to write notes to my uncle and cousin to say that I can't say goodbye to them at the hotel.

--Just tell them that you've got unexpected duty. Rudi signed to his servant for writing materials. Say, Jiri, where's your ring?

--Oh…

--Don't tell me… you and cousin Christa?

--Yes. We're getting married.

--I knew it!

--This calls for champagne… lads, the boy's got himself engaged!

Captain Count von Kalm sauntered over.

--Your cousin? Well, one has to do these things for the sake of the family, but from what I have seen of you two, I think duty and inclination are combined!

--Yes; she is lovely, Jiri. That was some dress!

--Don't mind me asking, but is she a kid like you, Jiri?

--Christa is two years older than I am.

--When did you decide?

--Oh. We didn't. We have always been together.

--I know he's a kid, but it's about time he got married! You know what they call him at the Pear Tree? No? Leutnant Two for the Price of One. It seems Toni called in there one night and asked for Katze.

--Sorry, Herr Oberst. She's with the little Leutnant.

--Oh well, I'll have Suzi then. They're always giggling together, and one's as good as the other.

--A thousand apologies, Herr Oberst, but she is with him too.

It seems the girls got scrapping about who was going upstairs with Jiri; he says (passable imitation of Jiri's high-pitched, cultured Principality accent): 'Oh, ladies, I hate unpleasantness! Madame, I'll take the two of them.'

Very well, she says, but you'll have to pay for them both. 'As you wish,' says Jiri, 'but I *do* think you might make a reduction for quantity.'

When they had recovered a little, the first speaker continued, You haven't heard the best bit. Toni rises to the occasion and asks her if there's room in the bed for another one!

--At least, gasped his friend, Gräfin Christa won't be disappointed!

--Indeed; in fact I'm sure she knows what to expect: what do you think they were doing last night?

Jiri wrote to his uncle, formally asking permission to marry Christa. He knew she was willing, and he gathered that his uncle would approve. He thought he would ask Toni to be his best man, in memory of that night at the Pear Tree.

Karel spoke to his daughter: she displayed Gisela's ring, which she suggested might be enlarged to fit her third finger, and said she was happy for Jiri to remain in the Ulans; they could make a home in Tarnheim for the time being.

Karel felt that the future of his house was assured for the next fifty years. The Colonel had told him over dinner that, rather surprisingly, Jiri had the makings of a good officer; early marriage and perhaps fatherhood would settle the boy down and time would bring promotion. Karel prepared to announce the engagement. But before he could do so, war was declared, Austrian forces were mobilised, and Jiri's regiment was deployed to Serbia, with the possibility of seeing further action on the Galician Front.

PART TWO

1919

A wounded bird cannot sing
(Jerry Hadley)

Flora Loudon slowly mounted the steps of the Mühlethurnen Institute. Her suitcase was heavy, and she was relieved when a smartly uniformed porter ran down and took it from her.

--Frau Doktor Loudon? Please come inside.

The entry hall resembled a clean, spacious hotel; at the reception desk she was asked to sign a guest book, and was given a key.

--I will take you to your room, Frau Loudon. The Herr Direktor will see you in half an hour; I will send someone to accompany you.

The view from Flora's room reminded her of Tarnheim, but, this being Switzerland, everything was somehow neater, cleaner and more organised than that remote corner of an empire that was now in the process of being dismantled.

Flora looked in the mirror and was dismayed. She took off her jacket and removed the blouse she had been wearing for the past forty-eight hours; there must be some arrangements for laundry, she thought. After using the washbasin, she took a clean blouse from her suitcase, transferring the brooch she always wore, brushed her jacket, dusted her shoes and tidied her hair. She was having a swift drink of water when a knock at the door announced her escort to the office of the Herr Direktor.

--Please sit down, Frau Loudon. May I offer you coffee?

Flora accepted.

--You are happy to speak German, Frau Loudon? She nodded.

His accent was pure north German, in contrast to the Schweizerdeutsch spoken by the porter, receptionist and maid she had met so far.

Despite her half-hour of tidying, Flora looked, and felt, very tired.

--You have had a long journey; it is surprising that you have got here so quickly.

--Yes. I left as soon as I received Gräfin von Tarnheim's letter.

--You were not in England?

--No. I have been in Belgium. I am looking for my late husband's grave.

--Ah.

--It was fortunate that Christa von Tarnheim had the address of the pension where I was staying, otherwise...

--Indeed. I have some good news; Leutnant – or as we should call him now that he has been discharged from the army, Mr – Zellek was operated on three days ago, at the time when Gräfin von Tarnheim left; it was entirely satisfactory. As yet he does not know that his cousin is no longer here; we have a letter from her to give him when he is ready for it. It is here.

176

He handed her the letter, which she put into her handbag, next to her own letter from Christa.

--Meanwhile it will be excellent for him to have you with him.

--How is he?

--The Herr Leutnant has been lucky.

--Oh?

--Yes. Firstly he is still alive. Next, he has all his limbs, and we hope that by the time he leaves us they will all be in reasonable, even good, working order. Unlike many of our patients, he is not disfigured, nor is he suffering from shell shock, which is perhaps remarkable considering what happened when he was wounded.

Flora's mouth went dry; she took a sip of coffee.

--What happened to him?

--He is able to give quite a clear account, which is another good sign. His unit was attacking the Russian forces; he received a shot to his leg, so that when his horse was hit by shrapnel he was unable to fully dismount; the horse fell onto him, which is how he sustained his back injury. At that point, he was trapped beneath the horse, and in fact it is well that he was. He remained there for some hours, during which the Russians covered the field of battle, shooting any wounded who showed signs of life. He was then still conscious, but unable to move and of course was shielded by the remains of the horse, and after the Russians had left he was eventually found by an ambulance unit.

There was a brief silence.

--He was also fortunate in being well looked after, both then and subsequently; when he came here, he had both his cousin and Augustus Kreutzer with him.

--Aug… ah, Gustl?

--Yes. Kreutzer has also been lucky; he has quite a tale to tell. At the beginning of the war he was conscripted into the infantry, and served on the same Galician Front as Leutnant Zellek. Kreutzer was captured by the Russians, but managed to escape and make his way back to Tarnheim. Of course, he could have been shot as a deserter, but by the time he came to official notice the war was over. I gather that his sweetheart had given up hope and sought consolation elsewhere, but it seems that he has found someone here. He has been invaluable in lifting and moving Mr Zellek, and also some of our other patients.

--And Jiri's treatment?

--Has generally gone well. We have given prior attention to his back; to speak frankly, there was some risk in the procedure my surgeons undertook, and if it had been unsuccessful, there would have been little point in working on his leg. However, the long period of immobility he underwent in hospital and at Tarnheim allowed some natural healing to take place and although the operation was, shall I say… tricky… it was entirely successful. We allowed a period of recovery, and have now worked on his leg. Again, he was extremely lucky; the bullet did not penetrate the knee joint but passed below with little damage to the joint itself; he should be able to flex his leg to a useful extent; I gather much of the stiffness was caused by lack of movement while his back was healing, and the recent operation, if followed by a course of massage and exercise, should help considerably.

There is one thing, however, where we shall need your help.

Over the past two years, Mr Zellek has had a great deal of morphine. This has had two consequences. Firstly, it is now ceasing to have much effect. Secondly, his system is quite dependent on it. Our answer is to withdraw the drug gradually, and this we are now doing; with good management, all should go well, but there may well be moments... hours perhaps... of difficulty... you understand?

--Yes. Thank you, Herr Direktor.

--We have taken X-ray photographs of his back and leg, of course, and if you wish to see those at any point they can be made available, but perhaps you would like to see Mr Zellek himself first?

Flora had mentally rehearsed the moment when she saw Jiri again, but the one thing she had not been prepared for was that he had grown a beard. It was of course to be expected; it was quite neatly trimmed and he did not look neglected or unkempt, only quite ageless. In fact, she realised later, he greatly resembled a sixteenth-century von Tarnheim from the gallery of family portraits.

He was partially propped up with a backrest and pillows; a cage supported the bedclothes over his left leg.

His eyes were closed but she could not tell whether he was asleep.

--Jiri... she took his hand, and he opened his eyes.

--Dear Miss Drake! You have come to look after me.

--Yes, Jiri. I am here.

Then, as if the thought came from very far away:

--Herr Doktor Jonni... have you found him?

--No. Not yet.

--Where's Christi?

179

Flora assumed the firm tones of the schoolroom.

--Christa cannot be here just at present. But I am here, and I will stay with you.

That seemed to content him. Flora sat beside him; the chair was comfortable, the room was sunny, and the fatigue of the interminable train journey began to catch up with her; she nodded, and was soon asleep.

She woke to feel a hand on her shoulder.

--Fräulein Drake! I beg pardon, Frau Doktor Loudon!

--Gustl?

--Yes, Gnädige Frau, it's me!

Whatever Gustl had been through, and, as Flora came to realise, that was a great deal, it had changed him from a large, shambling young servant to a strong, capable man of about thirty. He wore the white jacket of the institute's nursing staff, with his name, Augustus Kreutzer, embroidered on the pocket.

--I am afraid you have had a long journey, Frau Loudon. But it is most good that you are here. Since Herr Jiri had his operation, and Madam Christa left, we have managed quite well, as he has been sleeping most of the time. But that will change.

--Gustl, do you know where Madam Christa has gone to?

--No, ma'am... perhaps you do?

--No. Her letter to me said only that she had gone with Captain Westenberger, that they were to be married, and that she was to accompany him to America. She asked me to come here to be with her cousin. That is really all I know.

They looked at each other.

--Gustl, the Herr Direktor has given me another letter, one which she left for Mr Jiri; I am to give it to him when we judge that he is ready. That may have more details. I wonder, too, whether she has written to her father?

They were interrupted.

--Frau Loudon, there is a lady at the reception desk, who says she is the Countess von Tarnheim. She asked for Gräfin Christa, and when she heard that the young lady had left, she called for the Herr Direktor. He is on his way to her, but if you could get to her first...

--It might be better, said Flora, and she succeeded in doing so.

Valerie von Tarnheim was not at all as Flora had pictured her. She must have been in her early fifties; quite tall and slender, dressed perfectly for a morning visit to a Swiss sanatorium in a light jacket and skirt with an elegant yet not over-elaborate hat. Her face was made up, but with such subtle artistry. In all she presented that correct, understated, effortless 'rightness' to which Jiri had always aspired. She turned towards Flora, seeing a middle-aged Englishwoman in a good, but well worn, summer costume.

--Good morning, said Flora. I am Mrs Loudon. Countess von Tarnheim, I presume?

--Mrs Loudon... ah, yes, the former Miss Drake! Valerie's voice was high, clear and cultured. Would you prefer if we speak English?

--Thank you, but I am quite comfortable with German, unless you wish for French?

--German, or at least a version of it, seems to be the language here...so...let us proceed with that. I am told that my daughter is no longer here. I assume that Jiri Zellek knows where she is?

Flora had to play for time.

--I'm afraid Jiri is still unable to see anyone; it is only days since his latest surgery. I'm sure the Herr Direktor will confirm that.

--Surgery? He is not... disfigured... like some of those... people... I saw outside?

Flora realised that, like Jiri, Valerie could not bear anything damaged, ugly or distressing.

--No. No he is not disfigured.

--Good, although he was never anything to look at. He was the ugliest baby I ever saw, a scrawny little thing that never stopped screaming. At least Christa was a pretty child. But surely an exception can be made? I am after all, a relative.

--I understand that you are his aunt by marriage.

--Yes, but he is also my first cousin once removed. His mother Gisela was my cousin, and she was my husband Karel's sister. My father was the brother of Graf Johann, Karel and Gisela's papa. We three are all first cousins; is that plain enough?

Suddenly Flora realised what had been troubling her. She had expected Valerie to resemble Christa, as indeed she did; what had surprised her was a marked likeness to Karel von Tarnheim, and to Jiri himself. Karel and Valerie were, then, first cousins as well as husband and wife. Had John known that, or only suspected it? And was that partially why he had been so horrified by the prospect of marriage between Jiri and Christa?

The Herr Direktor now joined them and confirmed that Jiri was unable to have visitors as yet, suggesting that Valerie return the following day. Both he and Flora knew that, for good or ill, Jiri must now read the letter left him by Christa.

Flora and Gustl waited outside Jiri's room. She had tried to explain to him that Christa had left at the time of his latest operation, but had asked that her letter be given him when he was well enough. He seemed to take this in, presumably assuming that Christa's absence was temporary.

There was a long silence. Then a cry: an anguished howl, shriek, groan such as Flora hoped never to hear again, followed by a crash.

They went in. Jiri had knocked over the bedside table in an attempt to get out of bed; Gustl took hold of him, while Jiri continued to shout, sob and scream in his native language, which Gustl could understand, and which Flora could not.

--What was he saying, Gustl? she asked later, after Jiri had been held down and given an injection that eventually quietened him.

--He was saying that he would track down Captain Westenberger and kill him. That he would do many... things... to him first... there was much that you do not need to hear, Frau Loudon.

--I did not realise that he would be quite so distressed. Of course, he and Christa have always been close.

--Yes, Frau Loudon. They were. And of course after you left Tarnheim, as they grew up, they were, I mean they did...

--Gustl. Flora spoke slowly and clearly. I think I know what you are trying to tell me.

--And of course, he added quickly, the master always planned for them to marry. They are the last of the von Tarnheims, and if they were... already... well, it wouldn't really have made much difference, would it?

--But Gustl, did Graf von Tarnheim not think that they were, well, too closely related?

--Beg pardon, ma'am, I don't know how it is in England, but all the old families with us, they always marry relations.

They wouldn't want to marry just anyone, would they? That was the trouble with Herr Anton Zellek, at least I always thought so.

By now they were sitting on the terrace.

--Gustl, I am not asking you to be disloyal to the family. But, if we are to help Jiri through this, it is best that I know as much as you feel able to tell me.

--*Jawohl*, Frau Loudon, but please excuse me if I do not always use the polite words.

She nodded.

--It was the summer before Mr Jiri went into officer training, for the Ulans, you understand. He had been studying in Vienna; when he came to Tarnheim, he was not well. Madam Christa had left the convent the summer before. She had been travelling, staying with one of her school friends, I think. But she came back just before he arrived. As I said, he was not well. Hans said that the master dealt wrongly with his illness; I know he was very worried, and he tried to make Master Jiri take some sort of medicine the doctor ordered, but he was being sick all the time and got worse. It was Madam Christa who took matters into her own hands and brought back old Grushenka, you remember her, Frau Loudon?

She dosed him, and we poured the tonic down the water closet and he perked up; I remember one morning he asked me to give him a bath and bring him a clean shirt, and I knew he was better, although I'd never seen him so thin, not till now. Well, the master was keen to go on one of his visits to Prague, and he'd delayed because of Mr Jiri being so ill. Once he was getting better, the master was off. That left the two of them on their own.

As I said, Mr Jiri had been living in Vienna. I don't know what those students get up to but... well, ma'am, as his body servant I could see that he was, as they say, a proper man, well hung; he was seventeen by then and from some of the questions he asked Hans, I'd say he'd discovered what it was all about, if you see what I mean.

I'm not sure when it happened, or how willing she was; maybe not at first, and he may have been sudden, rough; he's always been stronger than he looks when he's roused. Look at how hard it was to hold him down just now, and he's been nearly bedridden for months... But after that, they'd be off all day, riding, swimming, walking, climbing... and forgive me, ma'am, fucking.

They'd get me to put the phonograph in the big hall and they'd dance, and then there was that party down in Strelitz... something happened there. And the two of them were in Mr Jiri's bed all the next day. So it went on until the master came home. That gave them a scare, I can tell you! But while he'd been away he'd made arrangements for Mr Jiri's training; apparently Frau Zellek, his stepmother, had finally agreed to it.

So off he went back to Vienna, and then to the training camp.

Madam Christa... I only know what the others gossiped about... but at that time she had a French maid, Odile, that she'd brought back from her travels. And about six weeks after Mr Jiri left, Madam Christa was... ill... for a couple of weeks... she'd not been looking right... and then she seemed back to herself, got on with her painting, all that.

Next thing, Mr Jiri's in the Ulans, and the master and Madam Christa went to the regimental races and ball. I went with them to help Hans, and you never saw anything like it. It was like fairyland. She had this golden dress, and the diamonds in her hair. You never saw Mr Jiri at that time, did you, ma'am? I wouldn't say he'd filled out exactly, but the army must have suited him. In his uniform... and a good rider... anyone would have been proud to own him. A real officer, a real von Tarnheim. After that, the master seemed set on them marrying.

That was in 1914.

I got drafted. But I heard Madam Christa was nursing in the mountains, in Italy... she's a wonderful climber, you know, even better than Mr Jiri, though he is never scared, just doesn't have a very long reach.

--That must be where she met Captain Westenberger, said Flora. I believe he was in the American Medical Corps on the Italian Front.

What had Christa's letter said? *Bruce has made me realise that it would be wrong to marry Jiri even when he is well again. He will take me to America with him. Dear Mrs Loudon, I am asking you to look after my Jiri until he is better.*

Gustl continued.

--Mr Jiri was in the military hospital for a long time, and then the master wanted him moved to Tarnheim. I'd got home by then and lucky we were there, as that flu, the sickness they said came from Spain, started killing people off. It would have done for Mr Jiri, I can tell you. But none of us got it at Tarnheim; it was poor Frau Zellek who caught it, down in Pallin, and it polished her off. I can't say the master was too upset, but of course Mr Jiri was. She'd been a good mother to him all his life; I dare say he wouldn't remember his real mother, the master's sister. (And Valerie's cousin, thought

186

Flora.) I suppose Madam Christa heard from the master; she left the hospital in Italy and came home. I never thought she had the makings of a nurse, but she was wonderful with Mr Jiri. He couldn't do without her, that's why she came here with him.

--And Captain Westenberger?

--Well, really we didn't know anything about him; I didn't until he turned up here.

It was a couple of days before Mr Jiri's second operation, the one on his leg. It wasn't nearly as serious as the one they'd done on his back; that was a real masterwork, I'll tell you, no one could believe how successful it's been, so if this next one went as good, he'd be able to start exercise, and massage, and be able to... well, to get back to what happened, this American army doctor turns up. Not, as it looked, in the line of business, but searching out Madam Christa. Been trying to find her ever since she left the Italian Front. Of course who knows what went on there, but in a war...We'd been told to keep Mr Jiri quiet, calm, not taking quite so much morphine so it might work better after his operation, so I suppose she made the decision not to tell him anything. Packed her kit and off they went.

--What's he like?

--Typical Yank. Big, full of himself, speaks English that you can't understand a word of. Only person he talked to here was Dr Alte.

--Dr Alte?

--Yes. He's what we used to call a mad doctor.

--A psychiatrist?

--That's it. He works here with the poor fellows who have Kriegshysterie and the rest of the time he's got a big sanatorium near Lausanne, for people with mental trouble. He's a nice enough gentleman; took an interest in Mr Jiri from the first, although don't ask me why, anyone can see it's his back and leg that need fixing. I don't know how the master will take this, he added. Mr Jiri getting wounded hit him hard.

Valerie had of course charmed the Herr Direktor. He told her that after some weeks of correspondence, Jiri, Christa and Gustl had arrived at the institute, Gustl carrying Jiri and several porters following with their luggage. Jiri it seemed, had progressed well after discharge from the military hospital but recently this had slowed. Almost any exertion caused extreme back pain, and he was not able to walk far because his leg had little flexibility. They had become desperate, and the Direktor had received the impression that they would take any level of risk, having decided that Jiri would leave the institute with the chance of leading a relatively normal life, or not at all. Should his medical team fail, he would watch closely for the suicide of at least one of them.

But, fortunately, up until this point, all had gone unexpectedly well. The Countess, he felt sure, would not wish to jeopardise the recovery of her relative, and now that Frau Loudon was here, it was hoped that Herr Zellek would come to accept the departure of his cousin and concentrate on rehabilitation.

Of course, yes, what really interested her was the whereabouts of her daughter, quite understandable, but he had no information to give her. And he could assure her that Frau Loudon was also in ignorance. If they could give Mr Zellek one more day of recovery, he might well be able to help.

Flora could not help liking Valerie, just as she had not been able to resist loving Jiri, and for some of the same reasons. All the von Tarnheims were arrogant, but with Jiri and Valerie this was tempered by a rather charming, slightly childish naughtiness. Valerie was by far the best-looking of them but even with her, the appeal lay less in the actual cast of features than in the animated expression that was so like Jiri before the war.

She had asked Flora to have coffee with her while Jiri was being got ready for the day.

Flora sensed that she was anxious about seeing him.

--He has a beard, she explained, thinking of her own initial reaction. Of course, it's been too difficult to shave him. And… he is having injections.

--Oh yes. From what I gather, the poor kid's a morphine addict by now.

--He's had constant pain ever since he was wounded. Once he's better…

--Good luck with that. I've seen it and it's not attractive. But really that's not my problem. Mine is… Christa. Look, Mrs Loudon, I'm sure you do not think well of me… in fact, you have probably been told that I am insane at best, and wicked at worst… if not both. As for insanity, I ask you to consider whether anyone of sound mind would agree to spend the rest of her life halfway up a mountain with Karel von Tarnheim. I'm not the mad one in this; if anyone is insane, it is Karel; and Gisela. Especially Gisela. As for wickedness… this escape of Christa's, I'm beginning to think, is something that runs in the family… as does so much else. I made a sudden decision, and I think that is what she has done. But I need to find out more about it, and if possible, where she is now.

--Forgive me, Countess, said Flora, but, as you have been

189

so frank with me, may I ask why it is now that you wish to be with Christa? You have surely had little contact with her.

--Actually, over the past few years, I have seen her a couple of times, and have corresponded with her. There is no reason, of course, that you should know this; Karel, I am sure, does not, and as for little Jiri, well, he was either racing around Galicia on horseback taking pot shots at the Russians, or lying at death's door in some military hospital. Christa may have told him later, or she may not. Frau Loudon, it would have been a very bad idea for those two to have married, as Karel, the stupid idiot, wanted. It is almost a good thing that Christa has followed her heart (if that girl has one) and decamped to America. I had made up my mind, as these things often happen, to accept that my daughter would not be part of my life; then, we met by chance. She was staying with a friend from the convent, and that family took her on a trip to Paris... she's obsessed with art, you know. Well, once I saw her, I thought, Why not? She was quite presentable, especially considering the upbringing she'd had. I assume Karel wanted to protect her; he'd put it about that I was crazy and of course that was the gossip in the Principality; he wouldn't want her to hear that. Then, too, he thought she might follow in my footsteps as a loose woman; plus, of course, his conviction that no one lower than the imperial family is good enough to mingle with the von Tarnheims. So Christa saw almost no one except her governess and Jiri until she went to school. But actually we got on well. I suspect she saw me as a means of escape and, even more importantly, a way to study painting, which of course I would not permit any more than would Karel. Then, I gradually realised over time that there was something going on between her and Jiri. The old, old von Tarnheim story.

We lost touch towards the end of the war. On opposite sides, really; I have French citizenship now, of course. Then, I heard from a friend who was holidaying in the Oberland; hotel gossip about who comes and goes... someone von Tarnheim, and von Tarnheim Zellek, at the Mühlethurnen Institute. So here I am, just in time to find my daughter's eloped with a Yank. Do you think Jiri's in a fit state yet?

It could not be put off indefinitely. Valerie leaned over the bed and touched his hand.

--Valerie! You have come after all! It's been a long time. But I knew you would.

She was taken aback, but spoke calmly.

--Yes, Jiri. Can you tell me, where is Christa?

--Oh yes, it was Christi you wanted before. I thought you'd come for her. I expect she's getting the studio ready.

--Studio? What studio?

--In Paris. We knew you'd come back, and take her to Paris. Then I could come, she told me I could; there would be room for a piano. Have you seen it yet?

--Jiri, dear boy, I don't know what you are talking about. Perhaps you don't either.

--Valerie, you are so beautiful. You know, that's what the angel was called, wasn't it, the one Miss Drake gave me? And then I wasn't frightened anymore and I could go to sleep. I'm so tired now, Valerie darling; please stay with me.

It was useless.

AT PALLIN, 1920

Come back, even as a shadow, even as a dream.
(Euripides, Herakles)

When the Austro Daimler 14/32 was returned after war service, it was not the immaculately impressive motor that Karel had purchased in 1912. Years of delivering supplies, ferrying the wounded and homeless, damage from strikers, weather and neglect, as well as the obsolescence of eight years of engineering development, had all made it difficult for Karel's chauffeur to get it into working order, and even so the journey from Tarnheim to Pallin had been interrupted by breakdowns and emergencies.

It was late afternoon when they reached their destination. Karel was amazed to see his nephew running down the steps of the villa, hands outstretched in greeting.

--Jiri!

He could hardly believe that this young man, in neat civilian dress, sunburnt and clean-shaven, moving swiftly towards him, was the same as the frail figure that Gustl Kreutzer had lifted into the train for the journey to Switzerland eighteen months before.

--Uncle; wonderful to see you, sir! And Hans... he greeted Karel's familiar valet.

--It is good to see you so much better, sir, said Hans quietly.

--Thank you! It is good to be able to move about! And, Uncle, you have a new chauffeur? You are?

--Gregor, sir.

--Welcome, Gregor! You have driven all the way from Tarnheim? That is heroic! Come in, come in...

Karel, Hans and the luggage mounted the steps, while Gregor saw about the disposition of the motor. Meanwhile a small shaggy white dog of the useless, yappy kind that Karel particularly disliked, was barking frantically.

--Quiet, Otto! I am afraid he hates motors. Down, down! I hope you will be comfortable, Uncle. I think you have never actually stayed here before.

Karel was now able to observe a slight irregularity in Jiri's gait, but really, compared with what he was before...

In fact, the older man had stayed in the villa; but that was many years ago, and since then, although he had visited the place, he had avoided spending a night beneath its roof, until now, when his nephew had professed himself unable to come to Tarnheim. The boy's letter had not actually made his health an excuse; he had mentioned business affairs that must keep him in Pallin, but Karel could not imagine what these might be, and he had assumed that Jiri was not well enough to travel. But looking at him now, he began to wonder; Jiri had always been wilful and capricious, at least before he joined the Ulans, which had been the making of him. Unfortunate that his medical discharge had been inevitable.

Later, coffee and cakes were served in the salon. Karel tried to dismiss memories of the awkward, upsetting, even tragic conversations he had experienced in this room, which was in fact airy, sunlit, and comfortably furnished in now outmoded Biedermeier style. Karel tried not to gaze at the portrait of his sister that had been painted just before her marriage; she was wearing a blue dress and the gold ring with the antique lapis cameo seal.

--With your permission, sir, Jiri was saying, we shall dine informally tonight. I have no other guests, and you must be tired after your journey.

--Yes; Very well. Jiri, I have come all this way... to... but first, my boy, I must say that I am delighted to see how improved you are; is all well with you?

--Thank you, Uncle. I do not wish to go into accounts which must be boring, even to myself, but as you see, I am doing well. I am told that all I need to do is to build up the muscles supporting my back, also my leg muscles, and exercise enough to maintain the flexibility. It is taking time, but I see progress, and on the good days, indeed I have nothing to complain of.

--Good days?

--Yes, and they are becoming the majority! I am even beginning to ride again; in fact it is good exercise; as yet I cannot do very much, but should you wish for a mount, sir, I know where we can obtain one. Perhaps, though, it is well to say that sometimes I am tired, and then there is nothing for it but to rest, annoying though that is, of course! So, in that case, you must excuse me. But that is quite sufficient on this boring topic.

Jiri thought that his uncle was looking much older. It was eighteen months since they had last seen each other, and perhaps at that time he, Jiri, had not been sharply observant, but, if he'd been badly affected by what had happened, his uncle might have been even harder hit.

And Karel seemed to be thinking along similar lines.

--Jaroslav, he asked, you have had nothing from Christa?

--No. The letter she left for me at the institute was the last I had from her. He glanced at his left hand.

--Ah, said Karel, you still wear your mother's ring?

--Yes. Christa enclosed it in her letter.

In fact, Flora Loudon had retrieved it from the floor of his room at the institute. He continued,

--And Flora, Mrs Loudon, had heard nothing when I last saw her; you know she came here with me after I left Mühlethurnen; she has now gone back to Belgium.

--Ah yes. I believe she is still seeking her husband's grave…?

--Yes, although she hasn't been successful yet. I think she will go back to England for a while soon. Have you had any news, Uncle?

--No. Nothing.

Jiri felt almost guilty. Although the loss of Christa had been so terrible that he could not bear to think about it… well, that was what he did, not think about it; and meanwhile, to be alive, to be without constant pain, to be able to walk, ride a little, play the piano and attend to the affairs of the factory, which were surprisingly interesting: all this made him actually happy. He had, too, a sense of independence such as he had never before experienced; for the first time in his life, there was no one who could tell him what to do, not even Uncle Karel as the head of the family. Meanwhile, Karel was alone and could see his known world disintegrating about him.

--I suppose, sir, that you are following developments in Vienna.

--Yes. The Emperor has gone, although one hears that he may try to regain at least the Hungarian throne. And as for us, it seems that we are still Austrians.

--Yes; I was not really able to concentrate on our situation at the time of the peace settlements, but it seems that Austria won us from the Poles and the Czechs. I wondered whether one might perhaps have managed a Czech passport but, well, the moment has passed, and here I am.

--Jaroslav, I must speak seriously with you.

--Yes, sir. But may I suggest that we wait until you are thoroughly rested; perhaps tomorrow?

Karel was taken aback. Jiri was very much the master in his own home; it would have been better to have waited until the boy could, or would, come to Tarnheim. In fact, by the time they had dined, Karel was really feeling tired, and was not sorry to part with Jiri after sampling some very fine old Tokay laid down by Jiri's late father.

Early the next morning, he woke to hear Jiri practising scales, then playing with what to the unmusical Karel seemed to be much of his former skill.

At breakfast, Jiri ate well and then apologised to his uncle, saying that he expected a designer from the factory to call on him that morning; his uncle must excuse him; the matter could not wait but would be quickly despatched. The housekeeper would be on hand should he want anything. Meanwhile, Karel would find newspapers in the study, or he might like to stroll around the gardens? He was doing this when Jiri called to him through the French windows:

--Sir! May we have the benefit of your opinion?

Karel entered to find Jiri and the designer looking at an array of small glass figures.

Made in opaque golden brown glass, they were bears, in differing attitudes and with slight differences of expression and feature.

--I know they are kitsch, but they are rather delightful, really, exclaimed Jiri. Suddenly he thrust away the memory of Christa, teasing him about his lack of refined aesthetic taste: *Birdie, you are the Prince of Kitsch, you are like a provincial hausfrau, you shall choose nothing for our studio when we live in Paris!*

Karel regarded them in horror. Surely Jaroslav, a former Ulan officer, the last male von Tarnheim, was not taking this sort of thing seriously?

--You see, sir, he was saying, we need some new lines. During the war, we switched to utensils and so on for the military; when Mutti died in 1918, she was just getting ready to return to more normal production, and of course tastes have changed, and most of what Papa and Mutti commissioned looks old-fashioned now, although I still like the colours, and people want cheap, pretty things and, although we lost our foreign customers, well, Zellek is not a recognisably Teutonic name, is it... we could indeed be from Poland, or Bohemia, and we still have our London and Paris contacts... But, Uncle, what I want to ask you is, which of these fellows reminds you of Wolfi? I mean, really captures his spirit?

Wolfi? Of course: the wretched toy bear that Jiri had clutched throughout his childhood, and which had disappeared during the last summer before Christa went away to school. Karel remembered that the adults at Tarnheim had been rather pleased when Jiri had at last broken the habit of dependency at the age of eleven.

--Of course, poor Wolfi is long gone; if I were a Wagnerian, which I am not, I would say that he is riding with the Valkyries, but I was able to find this photograph to show Gestner here!

Jiri reached for a photograph album, which his stepmother had kept throughout his, and her, life. It fell open at a page showing himself, aged about three, with Wolfi. Suddenly Karel realised which photograph must be on the preceding page. Gisela.

But Jiri chatted on:

--Ah, he was in his prime then, it was before he fell into the lake at Tarnheim and had to be dried out in the bread oven. Let's see… which one is going to make our fortunes, Gestner?

Karel could stand no more. These were the affairs which Jiri had said were keeping him in Pallin. The thing that he had most dreaded, that his nephew would sink to his father's bourgeois status, seemed to be happening…

For the next two days, Jiri flitted cheerfully about the place; he took a short ride with his uncle, he borrowed the motor to go to the factory, where he remained for almost a whole day, he played the piano and was even heard singing. Karel could not pin him down for the discussion for which he had come to Pallin.

Then, Jiri did not appear at breakfast; he sent his apologies, saying that he had not had a good night, he hoped his uncle would not be bored, he would be down as soon as he could.

Karel went out and spent the morning at a coffee house in the town. He returned before luncheon, and entered the salon to find Jiri on the couch. His nephew's cane, which he generally used only for long distances or uneven ground and seemed more of a fashion accessory than a walking aid, was propped against the arm. Jiri was asleep; his rosary was in his hand and he had evidently been saying it when his eyes had closed. The effect was rather horrifyingly like a body laid out for burial. Karel noticed again that he was wearing Gisela's ring; he had always had it on his little finger, but now that his hands were thinner, it was on his third finger. Karel looked at him. In boyhood, Jiri had always been worryingly thin, but in the army he had become well-muscled and strong, though slightly built. Now, though much better than before his stay in Switzerland, he was clearly still fragile; Karel had been so pleased with the general improvement, and so distracted by Jiri's constant activity, that he had not really noticed this until now.

Jiri must have heard Karel come in; he was awake at once, and made as if to rise.

--No, no, my boy; don't get up. I am sorry you are not well.

--Oh, I am better now that I have had a nap. But last night seemed rather long; and sir, if you permit, perhaps I will stay here a little while and rest my back.

Perhaps it was unworthy, but Karel saw that Jiri was a captive. He sat down, facing the couch.

--Jaroslav, he began.

Jiri knew that tone of voice. His heart sank. He wanted to heave himself up and escape, however much it hurt. Last night had not been good; these days, or rather nights, the pain was no longer so all-consuming that all one could do was to endure moment by moment; but sometimes it kept him awake and miserable... it was hard not to think of Christi, especially at about two o'clock, when he was at his lowest, and tears were not far away. Especially at such times, he missed Gustl dreadfully. He had encouraged Gustl to stay behind at the institute; the man had found his vocation as a valued and well-paid member of staff, and would marry Nurse Vrenni in a few months. Jiri no longer needed to be lifted and carried, and his new valet Ernst was a good boy, but Gustl had seemed to know by instinct when Jiri needed him, to change his position, massage his shoulders or even read to him. They shared a weakness for trashy romance novels; while they both knew that real life was not like that, at three in the morning, when one's back hurt, a happy ending with no deep thoughts or long words could be quite comforting. That one *Love in Springtime* had been nice; he would not mind hearing it again, but the books had all been left in Switzerland.

Now his uncle was looking at him seriously.

I'm in for it, thought Jiri.

--My boy. We have to accept that Christa has left us. I am trusting that what you have told me of her letter to you is the whole truth.

--Yes, sir. She left with Captain Westenberger at the time I had my second operation, the one on my leg. I was not well enough to be told of this; that is why Christi sent for Mrs Loudon, and left me a letter with our ring. Some of what she said was between ourselves. I have destroyed the letter. *(This was not true.)* But the main thrust was that she had decided to marry Westenberger, that they had little time before he sailed for America, and because of Christa's nationality it was imperative that she went as his wife. They would be married at an American embassy. She did not say which one.

As he explained this, Jiri felt that someone else was saying these things, that they were not true, that they were part of a story someone else had invented.

--This was a blow, an unexpected one, to your plans.

--Yes. You had given your consent before the war, and as soon as I was better we would have been married *(And, Uncle, we would have been far away.)*

--Is it your understanding that she met this Westenberger when she was nursing in Italy?

--Yes; he was, as you must know, serving with the American Medical Corps. When I was discharged from the military hospital and came to Tarnheim, of course she left Italy to be with me.

--Did she mention Westenberger?

--Yes... not much... you know that I really can't recall then...

--Yes, yes, my boy. Do not distress yourself. I still do not fully understand her decision.

--No. *(But she's mine, and I will kill him.)*

--Jaroslav, we must accept that she is married. And, though you may not wish it, you are free. To marry.

Jiri looked amazed.

Suddenly Karel was embarrassed.

--I suppose, Jiri, that there is no reason why you could not...

Jiri grinned.

--Sir, I can reassure you that I am in full working order, at least when I have had a night's rest! I have had a couple of trial runs, as one might say.

--Well then. You are the last of our family. It is your duty. I know it is difficult to find... Karel was seized by the awful thought that Jiri might be entangled with some bourgeois provincial Fräulein, and he added,

I hope there is no one...

--No, no, Uncle. Purely professional.

--Well then. There are one or two young ladies distantly but distinctly associated with us by birth, who might...

It had not been easy. One in particular had looked perfect on paper, but when Karel met her and realised that she was a strapping six-footer he had faced the fact that Jiri's dapper size narrowed the choice of possible brides.

--Uncle, no.

Karel looked at him. What was this?

--Jaroslav, I am still the head of our family.

--Yes, sir. But I am twenty-five years of age. *(Christi is now twenty-seven...)* I have been through the war and I am still alive. I have inherited a business, which I must at least stabilise for the sake of my finances and the livelihoods of my employees. I may still have, foolishly perhaps, some musical ambitions, at least for further studies. I do not think that I shall stay here, in this house, for ever *(we were going to live in Paris... she would paint, I would make music and sing...)* but at least until I am rather stronger, I shall do so. Then I shall decide for myself what to do and where to go. But, sir, it will not be to live at Tarnheim *(as if I could do that without her)* and it will not be to marry to order. Things are changing; we are no longer part of an empire. I shall always be a von Tarnheim, but that may no longer mean so very much, since the new government abolished the titles of nobility in 1919. And now, sir, I think it is time for luncheon. Thank you; I can get up by myself.

Karel was disposed to leave the morning after his conversation with Jiri, but his nephew begged him to stay on for a few days, pleading rather touchingly that he would enjoy company while getting over his recent bout of back pain. So he remained at the villa for a further week, playing games of chess and discussing developments in Vienna and Tarnheim. By the time he left, Jiri was fully recovered. On Karel's last Sunday, they went to Mass. Afterwards the prosperous and respectable sections of Pallin society strolled in the park, meeting and conversing. Karel was introduced to honest bourgeois citizens whom he had avoided meeting for the past twenty years, and hoped never to meet again; they then went to the Daisy Café, where Jiri ate half a piece of *gugelhupf* and flirted with everyone in sight. Karel felt sure that the boy would get hooked by some ambitious parent for a pretty and socially ambitious daughter. What was as bad, he had not stopped receiving messages and messengers from the factory, and borrowed the motor and the chauffeur for a final trip there the day before Karel left. The extent to which the affairs of Zellek and Co occupied his nephew displeased Karel; either the boy should appoint a manager at once or sell the business and have done with it. But he seemed as wilful as ever, as well as unusually stubborn. However, they parted on good terms with Jiri promising to come to Tarnheim as soon as he felt able.

The evening after he left, Jiri had dinner, spent some time at the piano, and walked in the garden with Otto. It was a lovely night. There was a moon, and roses and honeysuckle scented the trees. All day Jiri had been trying not to think about her. But perhaps tonight he would allow himself; he must not do it too often. He had a bath, told Ernst to find his new silk pyjamas, said his night prayers and got into bed. Which one should he choose? The regimental ball was the best one, with her golden dress with the bead embroidery, and afterwards in the hotel bedroom, but sometimes if he just let things come, he remembered new ones so that he had more to choose from later.

--*Birdie, I think you like being in the Ulans.*

--*I suppose I do. I didn't like the officer training, but I like the regiment.*

--*I know why. You vain little thing, you know how adorable you look in your uniform. And you have all those wonderful friends, you all stick up for each other and call each other* du. *And you ride those expensive horses... and all the girls and some of the boys swoon over you... and you are so proud of being a real von Tarnheim, although you are only half a one...*

--*Birdie, did you understand what the Herr Direktor was saying, before you had your injection?*

--*He thinks they can make me better.*

--*Yes. He does. They can. It may take a long time. But after that... what are we going to do, Birdie?*

--*We are going to Paris.*

--*Birdie, Birdie, hurry up! Miss Drake will be waiting.*

--*I have to find Wolfi a storybook to read while I'm at lessons.*

--*Oh, all right! Here. Now come on, do...*

--*Can't you run faster? Gustl will catch up with us and I want us to be at the pool by ourselves... that's right! Oh what do we have for our picnic? Mahlzeit! Open your little beak...*

--*Never mind, Birdie dear. I know you have been naughty but it's not your fault. You can't help it sometimes. Don't cry. Here. I'll come into bed and hold you.*

He had fallen asleep; now he was awake and felt very lonely. He had felt like this when he first went to Vienna. His hands moved to his cock. Suddenly he thought not of Christa but Heinrich, Heini who had come to his bed that September night when he was sixteen, and had just returned from a summer by Lake Balaton with the Balinkays. *Jiri, you're brown all over... Yes, we all sunbathe and swim there, we don't bother with bathing suits...*

A few days later Jiri was sitting in the garden drinking coffee and reading. The pageboy Fritz appeared with a letter which had just been delivered; it was from Ferzi Balinkay. There was a page about the events of the new Horthy regime, followed by the news that Ferzi's first novel had found a publisher and should appear shortly: Jiri would be sent a signed copy. Finally Ferzi asked what his friend thought of recent developments in German literature, and asked what he was currently reading.

Jiri thought rather guiltily that the last book he had read was *Stenographer Hanna*, from the Edelweiss series of romantic novels. The stationer in Pallin had just begun to stock these, and Jiri had bought several on the pretext of getting them for the housemaids. Actually *Stenographer Hanna* was quite a good story, as one did not know until the last page whether the heroine would run away with the handsome, dashing and rather caddish commercial traveller or accept the proposal of her tall, dark, stern and inwardly vulnerable boss. Fortunately she made the right decision.

Jiri had just begun *The Garden of Kisses*, in which young, fair-haired Lisa leaves the city to care for her ailing grandfather, gardener on a remote estate. Frequently among the roses she glimpses the moody, reclusive landowner, whose heart has been broken by some past tragedy. As an experienced reader in the genre, Jiri had a fair idea of where this one was going, but he liked the cover design and was willing give it a go. He would just tell Ferzi that he was still convalescent and up only to light reading, leaving Ferzi to interpret that as he might.

Hearing footsteps, Jiri hastily thrust the novel under the cushions of his chair. It was Gestner, the designer from the factory, reminding Jiri that he had business to attend to, and a mound of correspondence.

Next morning:

--We are running out of headed writing paper; I must have been sending a great many letters.

Wearing a light summer suit with a rosebud in his buttonhole, Jiri took his hat and stick, called Otto, and set out to walk into town. It was a beautiful early summer morning; the air was clear, the gardens of the villas lining the road were in full flower, and Jiri felt that he could walk for miles. Ernst had been taking his boots and shoes in relays to the shoemaker, who was adapting the left shoe of each pair to Jiri's slightly irregular gait; when it was time for him to make a completely new pair, the fit would be even better.

As he entered the town, Jiri began to see people he knew, exchanging greetings, raising his hat to the ladies and making sure that Otto was still with him. At the stationers, he ordered his paper to be sent as soon as possible, and wandered around the shop to see what else he might fancy. Now that they stocked the Edelweiss series, the shelves displaying these popular romantic *Taschenbucher* were an attraction; Jiri looked around to make sure that he was unobserved before locating some new titles. He had picked up *Lakeside Lovers* and was scanning the description on the back (*Fisherman's daughter Etta, wild and wilful, is tamed by a mysterious yachtsman*) when he realised that he was being watched by a young lady in a simple flowered dress and matching cloche.

--Good morning. I suppose that you are selecting something for your sister... or perhaps your housemaids? She was looking at him with a very knowing expression, and Jiri decided that concealment was useless.

--Actually, I quite enjoy these. They are rather delightful when one wishes to relax.

--Have you read many?

--Er, well, several...

--And which ones did you like?

--*Love in Springtime* is nice, and *Stenographer Hanna* is a really good story. One does not know until the very end which proposal she will accept, and at one point I really thought...

--Oh I see that you do like them! Who is the author of *Stenographer Hanna*?

--I see it's Irma Fendl. She wrote *A Restaurant Romance*, too, didn't she?

--And did you enjoy that?

--Oh yes! I loved the bit when the young waitress poured soup over that customer who threatened her honour, and then the patron wanted to sack her, which would have been terrible as she had her little brother to support, but the kitchen porter that she loved secretly turned out to be a baron in disguise, I don't know how I missed that right up to the moment when...

By now the young lady was laughing quietly.

--Well now! I think I have just met one of my fans!

--You don't mean that you are Irma Fendl?

--Not quite; that is my pen name, among others. My real name is Ilse Treichler.

She held out her hand.

Jiri took it, and raised it to his lips before clicking his heels, bowing and introducing himself as Jiri Zellek.

--Fräulein Treichler; now that I have met a real live authoress, I cannot let you go. Would you permit me to take you for coffee at the Daisy?

Jiri paid for his selection of novels, which the stationer's clerk wrapped in brown paper; he whistled for Otto and they left the shop.

He was not sorry to sit down for a while; he had the walk home before him, so some refreshment was a good idea.

In the Daisy, everyone seemed to know Jiri and Otto and have something to say to them; it took a while for them to do the rounds of polite conversation and find a quiet table.

--Tell me, asked Ilse, when they had ordered coffee and made their selection of pastries, when did you start reading the Edelweiss books?

--In the army, was the surprising answer.

Quite a few of us in the Ulans used to exchange them from time to time. And then, I have been convalescing… for some months, and at night, when one is not quite well…

Ilse now noticed Jiri's air of fragility; he was so lively, suntanned and, well, somehow entrancing, that his extreme thinness and slight awkwardness of movement were not immediately apparent.

--Herr Zellek, she mused. Is that – forgive me for I am new to Pallin – is that Zellek and Co?

--Yes, at least I am Zellek if not Co. It is a family firm. And... forgive me in your turn, Fräulein Treichler, perhaps you can help me. Let us think of your readers...

--You mean other than convalescing Ulan officers? For I am sure you have been an officer.

--Well, yes. Perhaps I mean your more typical readers. Now, Fräulein, suppose one of your readers wished to buy some inexpensive but pretty glassware, what kind of designs do you think she might prefer? Floral? Or something more *moderne*, or even kitsch? My designer has produced some bear motifs which are rather *süss*.

--Do you know, Herr Zellek, that is a most interesting question. And I in turn have one to ask. I have seen your advertisement for a manager.

--Oh! I am currently doing my best to run things myself, but it would be much more efficient to have a full-time factory and business manager; that way, in time I might be able to have other activities, even to travel. But, Fräulein, you already have a profession, do you not, as Irma Fendl?

--It is not for me, although thank you for thinking of it! It is for my brother.

--Fräulein, I see that we must meet for a longer discussion. I regret that tomorrow I must be at the factory all day, and on Wednesday I shall have to write business letters in the morning; in the afternoon I am visiting some neighbours to rehearse a piano duet. I don't suppose you play?

--No, I am afraid not; although I would like to hear you and your friends some day; and my brother is very musical.

--Indeed! So, shall we say Thursday morning at about this time, and here at the Daisy?

On Thursday Ilse was at the Daisy in good time, but no Jiri appeared.

She was about to feel hurt and annoyed when a smartly dressed pageboy approached her, asking politely whether she was Fräulein Treichler.

--Herr Leutnant Zellek presents his compliments, Gnädiges Fräulein. He regrets that he is indisposed and unable to meet you here, but, if you would do him the honour of visiting him at home, and if you will be so good as to overlook his receiving you informally, our pony trap is outside.

Ilse took the opportunity to ask the lad about Jiri's 'indisposition'; it was his back again, she learned; he had been much better lately, but last night he had been Taken Bad again.

When she entered the salon of the Zellek villa, Ilse realised what 'informally' meant. Jiri was lying flat on a couch near the open French windows. He was wearing silk pyjamas and a very smart, obviously expensive dressing gown with a pattern of black and orange geometric shapes.

--How very good of you to come, Fräulein! I humbly apologise for receiving you like this; although I hope I am presentable. I have a new dressing gown; it is quite *moderne*, as you see.

--It is most elegant.

Because of his suntan and rather dark complexion, Jiri could not be described as looking pale. But he was drawn and tired.

--Fritz, he called to the page boy. Please move this table, and bring us coffee and cake. Dear Fräulein, please be seated.

Ilse sat down; the page returned very briskly with the refreshments.

--Please help yourself, Fräulein.

--Are you not having coffee?

--To do that I should have to sit up.

--Shall I call Ernst? asked the page.

--No. I have had enough of Ernst. And as I had him up for most of the night, I have told him to sleep this morning.

--Can we not help you?

Jiri looked at her doubtfully.

She continued,

--Fritz, is it? Surely we can help Mr Zellek between us.

--Well, madam, I have done it with Ernst: one person has to hold Mr Zellek up and the other one gets the cushions, those over there, into position behind him.

--Which did you do, Fritz?

--The cushions.

--Well then.

--Fräulein, interposed Jiri, I am afraid I shall be too heavy for you.

--I think that is unlikely.

Suddenly he asked,

--Do you understand Hungarian?

--No, but what has that to do with...

--I am likely to use strong language. But if I swear in Hungarian, that will be all right, will it not?

--Ah. I see. Fritz, bring the cushions over here. Mr Zellek, please hold me like this with your hands on my shoulders.

Ilse put her arms around Jiri. She knew that at all costs a sudden jerk must be avoided: slowly, steadily... He smelled of rather nice soap; evidently Ernst had given him a wash before retiring to his bed, and he was, as she had suspected, frighteningly thin. He gave a gasp and let out several expressions that, she presumed, were Hungarian expletives.

Fritz moved into place with the cushions, and she lowered Jiri back onto them, now in a semi-upright position. His eyes were closed and his mouth firmly set. Then he opened his eyes and grinned.

--Oh, thank you. That is so much better! I am sure this bout is not going to last so long, and now I can have some breakfast!

--Have you had nothing this morning?

--No, I did not manage it. So this will be breakfast for me. Although perhaps I shall have some chocolates instead. Please, could you hand me the box? I think it is on the buffet over there. Thank you!

It was a prettily decorated box of expensive sweets. Jiri selected one.

Ilse looked around the room. It was dominated by a portrait of a woman, probably a few years older than Jiri, and strikingly like him. She wore the plain gold ring with the tiny lapis cameo seal, which Jiri now had on his third finger.

--My mother.

--She is rather lovely.

--Yes. Everyone says I am very like her.

There was no answer to this; Ilse's gaze shifted to the vase beneath the picture, into which some roses and springs of fern had been rather inexpertly stuffed.

--I'm afraid I don't have the knack, and, though I dare not tell her, my housekeeper Frau Anna is not much better.

--Let me; I'll need some scissors.

--In the drawer.

--Fräulein, you are so clever! Now I see why your heroines are always so good at arranging flowers: you know all about it.

--Actually, I describe it because it is a traditional female accomplishment. It shows how womanly they are.

--Well, I am very fond of flowers, but I am no gardener and no flower arranger. I just like to look at them.

There was short silence while Ilse sipped her coffee and Jiri helped himself to another chocolate, before assuming a businesslike air.

--Now, Fräulein Treichler, please tell me something about your brother, and why he may wish to apply for the post I advertised. Of course, we should have to meet, we must be sure of suiting each other.

Ilse took a breath.

--My brother Sigmund Treichler was training to be an accountant, and was also assisting in our father's woodworking business before the war. He can return to neither of these occupations. Our business no longer exists. And his accountancy employer will not take him back. Mr Zellek, have you heard of shell shock?

--I suppose we all have it, more or less. But in severe form... yes. You should know that I spent some time, eighteen months in fact, having treatment in Switzerland for the injuries I got on the Russian Front. There were many fellows there who were being treated for shell shock, as well as some who were badly disfigured or had lost the means of... well, let us say that I have learned to think myself fortunate to be as I am, especially as I have every prospect of further recovery. I am sorry; we should not be speaking about me. But I intended only to say that, yes indeed, I am familiar with that terrible condition.

But, Fräulein, let me say now that I am not sure that the factory would be the best place for your brother. I have grown up with it; there are inevitably noises, flashes of light, heat... the business side, perhaps, might suit him, but the actual day-to-day management of the factory itself would, I fear, be extremely trying for him.

--You do not find it so?

--No, but, as I said, I have grown up with it, and with me any after-effects of battle have been quite different. I might perhaps consider separating the two roles, but that would mean paying two salaries, and with Austria's economic situation as it is...

Jiri shrugged as only the Viennese can do.

Ilse looked around the room. It struck her that Jiri Zellek probably employed a cook–housekeeper, two maids, a valet, a pageboy, an outside man and a boot and stable boy, all occupied in looking after one small, slight person around whom their world revolved. This probably accounted for his air of supreme confidence.

--Mr Zellek, would it be possible for me to see the factory?

--I would be delighted! Only, I am afraid I shall need to be a little more active than I am at present! In a very few days... It is Thursday today, shall we say Monday? If you would be good enough to come here at, let us say, nine o'clock.

By the time Ilse got back to the inn where she was staying, the entire staff and customers knew that she had been seen having coffee with Jiri, and that she had visited him at the Villa Zellek.

According to the age and status of her informants, Jiri was known as Master Jiri, Young Herr Zellek or the Herr Leutnant. But known to all he was, and soon she knew more of his antecedents than perhaps she wished.

He had been born here in Pallin. His father, Old Herr Zellek or Herr Anton, had married Gisela von Tarnheim, a very great lady but in very frail health. Shortly after her son's birth, she had gone to Switzerland for treatment and had never returned; the poor lady was buried over there, not with all the Zelleks in the Pallin churchyard or even in the vault at Tarnheim. She had been cared for by Grethe, a companion/nurse apparently recommended by Herr Anton's sister, who lived somewhere in north Germany. Not long after Gisela's death, Anton and Grethe had married; with no children of the marriage, Jiri had been their cherished child. He had been educated at the parish school, where he was still remembered as one of the naughtiest children ever, and, briefly, at the Oberschule. By the time he had either been expelled, or hastily withdrawn by his parents (accounts varied), his musical talents had gained him entry to the Pallin Conservatoire. All agreed that he sang like an angel and that he had few rivals as a pianist; he was wasted here at Pallin, and after Herr Anton died – that was about ten years ago – he went to board with a friend of Frau Grethe in Vienna to study there.

Master Jiri had always been small and thin, and everyone feared that, like his mother, he was destined for early death. So he had always spent as much time as possible in the mountain air at Tarnheim; his uncle Karel Graf von

Tarnheim took a great interest in him, and of course he was the last of the male von Tarnheims, Karel's only child being Jiri's cousin Christa.

When Jiri was seventeen, Karel had persuaded Grethe that Master Jiri should join the army, in his own old Ulan regiment, and it was clear to anyone with half an eye that the cousins were likely to marry.

Meanwhile, Grethe had managed the glass business with great success; a wonderful head for business, she had, poor lady.

Poor lady?

Yes, she saw the war through and then got that Spanish flu. By then, of course...

By then the Herr Leutnant had been terribly wounded on the Eastern Front. Despite his slight physique he had always been daring and fearless; many tales were told of his plucky exploits. He had been decorated by the Emperor, not the old Emperor, no, the new one, with all the children, who was now in exile in Madeira or somewhere. Anyway, the Herr Leutnant had spent months in a military hospital and then at Tarnheim, and then went off to Switzerland for some operations. No one knows quite what happened there. Gräfin Christa went with him, but then she disappeared; they say she ran off with some American army doctor.

Mind you, her mother was like that.

Now, now, the young lady doesn't want to hear all about that.

Ilse was thinking that there might be some useful copy in this, and resolved to ask later.

Next thing, the Herr Leutnant turns up here with an English lady, Frau Loudon, who'd been Madame Christa's governess, and I suppose Master Jiri's when he'd been at Tarnheim. If you think he looks bad now, you should have seen him then.

Well, all of them at the villa say he's getting much better, and look at him out and about in the town. And he's down at the factory a lot.

Looks to me like he's made up his mind to settle down here in Pallin. Maybe find himself a wife, now that Madam Christa's out of the picture.

According to that young fellow Ernst, there's nothing wrong with his tackle, wherever else he was wounded.

Quiet! Ladies present!

Sorry…

Some further background was added later by Jiri himself.

--The Zellek family, he said, had come originally from Bohemia, traditionally a centre of glass making. The founder of the dynasty had recognised that the raw materials, the work force, and the distribution channels around Pallin made the place ideal to start a new industry, and the family firm had never looked back, with extensive international investments, although these had been badly affected by the war.

So I am originally a Czech; the name Jaroslav was my great-grandfather's. There were quite a few Czech fellows, troopers, in the army, and I was able to learn some of my ancestral language; although of course it is not my mother tongue, that is what is spoken in the Principality, and Christi… my cousin and I spoke it as children at Tarnheim.

--So… you speak German, of course, and I know you can swear in Hungarian! And I believe you shared an English governess.

--Languages are rather an interest of mine… and it is useful as a musician, and in business, as it was in the army, to speak several… although I am constantly told that I have an appalling accent in all of them, except of course when I sing!

--Do you sing now?

--I am beginning to be able to do so again; I think the voice is still functioning.

He leaned back in the pony trap and sang a few bars from a popular song.

--Forgive me, Fräulein Ilse, but has your brother received any treatment for his condition?

--Yes; it was terrible, and we begged them to stop it. If he had been in the German army, he might have been sent to a farm, to work on the land, and maybe recover in his own time; as it was, he was given electrical treatment; it made him worse.

--Dear Fräulein, I am sorry, please do not distress yourself; it is just that, when I was in Switzerland, as I told you, there were certainly cases of Kriegshysterie, as it is called here, and they were being treated by a talking cure. Professor Alte had studied with a Swiss practitioner; he said that a terrible experience imprints itself on the mind and that the only way to gain release is to revisit it, to go where it hurts the most, and come to terms, as it were. I fear I do not express this correctly.

--It sounds, Herr Zellek, as if you have experienced this yourself. I thought that you said that your war injuries were merely physical. I am sorry! 'Merely' is a cruel expression, since I see that you have endured a great deal, and, if I may say so, endured it very bravely.

--Thank you. As you have so acutely discerned, I have had that experience, but it was not related to my war years. Something happened while I was being treated at the institute, and although I still think that my reaction to it was quite normal and understandable, others were not of that opinion, and it was recommended that I did not leave until it was to an extent resolved. In fact, once one knows what those alienists are expecting to hear it is quite easy to satisfy them. But, Fräulein, we are speaking of your brother. He must be missing you. Although I cannot at present see my way to offering employment, perhaps I can offer you both something of a holiday, a chance to reassess your prospects. Would you consent to be my guests here for a few weeks? It would really be doing me a favour, you know!

Ilse spoke to the housekeeper, Frau Anna; she feared that the sudden arrival of two guests might place unacceptable burdens on the household. In fact, the housekeeper, who had been a parlourmaid with the late Frau Zellek, was quite pleased, especially when Ilse offered to undertake any suitable tasks about the house, stressing that she and Sigmund would not need a maid or valet.

--It will be good for the master to have young company. And you may be able to get him to eat properly. You must see that he is far too thin. When he has had a good night, and thank God, he has more often than not, he makes quite a good breakfast. Then he just nibbles sweets and chocolates though the morning, and says he doesn't want luncheon, or only a slice of ham and bread. Then in the afternoon we might get him to have a piece of cake; by evening he says he is starving hungry, he wolfs down half of his dinner, then starts playing with Otto, or reading some storybook, and leaves the rest.

Once she had started, Frau Anna seemed keen to talk about Jiri. Old Frau Schmidt, who had been housekeeper when he was born, was still in place when Frau Anna joined the household, and she had many stories to tell. He'd been a delicate baby; the usual childhood illnesses had almost carried him off, and for that reason he was rather spoiled. Yes, Frau Zellek had sometimes to give him a good smack, and then the howling and wailing nearly brought the house down! Surely, Master Jiri, Frau Schmidt would say, it can't have hurt you that much. Oh no, he'd pipe up, I'm crying because Mutti is cross with me! And of course after that it would be a kiss and cuddle and he'd run off back to whatever mischief he was up to! She was a real mother to him, better than his own would have been, I dare say, and they always showed him that picture, the one that hangs in the salon, so he knew that was his birth mother. He used to get a bit confused at times, though; they explained that Madam Gisela was in Heaven, as of course was quite right; but he must have overheard people talking about how she went to Switzerland for treatment, and never came back, poor lady. So Frau Schmidt heard him saying to some visitor, That's my mother. She's in Heaven. Or maybe in Switzerland. Anyway, she's not here except in the picture.

--Poor little boy! exclaimed Ilse.

--Oh no! As I said, Frau Zellek was as good as a mother to him. And the master's always had a happy nature, unless he gets one of his tempers. And they blow over soon enough. He'll tell you himself, what a wonderful childhood he had.

Ilse returned with Sigmund about a week later.

During the journey, people stared at Sigmund and of course that made him worse. It had been difficult to persuade him to come; but the prospect of possible employment, however doubtful, was impossible to ignore.

The pony trap collected them at the station and they arrived at the Villa Zellek late in the summer afternoon; the garden was colourful and sunlit; the housekeeper stood at the open door.

-- Fräulein Treichler, how good to see you again! Herr Treichler, welcome! We are expecting you! Please come in; Fritz, take the luggage upstairs. I will show you your rooms later; the master has been very particular about them. Please come into the salon and take some refreshment. I will tell the master that you are here. He is in the garden, bathing Otto; the dog has rolled in… something nasty… we could not have him in the house, let alone on the master's bed, and he hates being bathed, the master is the only one who can do anything with him.

Ilse looked out at the garden. Jiri, wearing a straw hat and a huge sacking apron, was kneeling beside a tin bath, rinsing the protesting dog. His sleeves were rolled up; the sun glinted on the dark hairs of his wet, skinny arms. As she watched, the housekeeper approached him; he looked towards the windows and waved.

Then he lifted the dog out of the water; Otto shook himself, scattering sparkling drops; Jiri and the housekeeper both backed away laughing; Jiri caught the dog and wrapped him in a towel.

The housekeeper returned.

--The master apologises, Fräulein; he will be here in a moment. Meanwhile please take some coffee and cakes.

Jiri ran in through the French windows, removing his hat and running his hand through his mop of curly hair.

--Welcome! I humbly apologise! It is unpardonable. In fact I have been at the door several times... but Otto rolled in something unmentionable... he had to be bathed before your arrival. Sigmund! I am delighted to meet you.

He held out his hand English fashion and grasped Sigmund's shaking fingers.

Ilse found that she was unexpectedly happy to see him; he seemed to be able to brighten her mood; but Sigmund's reaction was less favourable. Naturally he had asked his sister about their host and possible future employer. Ilse had found it rather difficult to describe Jiri, and also she wanted Sigmund to form his own impressions; she had merely said that Jiri was young, perhaps a couple of years their junior; in appearance he was short, slight and dark; he had been seriously injured on the Eastern Front and was still recovering, which might account for some volatility and wilfulness.

Jiri, Sigmund now recognised, was officer caste. Absolutely at ease, polite, considerate but also absolutely in command.

The morning after their installation at the villa, Ilse looked out into the garden. It seemed that a huge tortoiseshell butterfly fluttered onto the lawn; it was Jiri wearing his '*moderne*' dressing gown, which he took off and draped over a statue of a gnome. In his vest and drawers, it was clear that although he was far too thin, his body was quite well proportioned, apart from rather unexpectedly large feet. Ilse could not help looking at his left leg, which showed a mass of scarring. He began a series of physical exercises, some of which he clearly found easier than others. Suddenly he looked up and saw Ilse; he waved and adopted a mock strongman pose before continuing with his movements. Rather ostentatiously, Ilse closed her shutters.

The first evening had been difficult. Jiri had not really succeeded in putting Sigmund at ease, and the meal had been excruciating because of Sigmund's shaking hands, with conversation inhibited by his stammer. Only when they went into the salon and Jiri began to play the piano did things improve; Siggi lay back and gradually as he became absorbed in the music he seemed to relax, the shaking ceased, his face no longer twitched. Ilse gazed at him and wished the music could go on for ever: at the piano Jiri was not wilful, arrogant or affected; Siggi looked almost as he had done before the war. At last Jiri rose, excused himself and said goodnight; he wished them a peaceful night's rest and would see them in the morning.

In the following days, Jiri took Sigmund into the music room. He was not, he admitted to himself, willing for his guest to touch the Bösendorfer but the other piano, the one on which Jiri had learned to play, was Herr Treichler's to use whenever he wished. And he was free to select from the collection of scores and sheet music, although Jiri would be greatly obliged if anything moved could be replaced exactly where it had been found; things were organised according to Jiri's personal system, which, in fact, Sigmund never succeeded in fathoming, but which allowed Jiri to find any item within seconds. Jiri sat beside Sigmund on the piano seat and began to play a few chords, encouraging Siggi to join in; he was able to do so, his fingers automatically remembering the pieces he had played as a boy. They began to play together each evening, which was actually easier than talking, and all three of them would often take their coffee into the music room. One night Jiri took some music, and asked Siggi if he could play this; after a few attempts, it was clear that he could; suddenly Jiri said, Strong bass line, Siggi, and stood up. Ilse had never heard him sing more than a few bars or, lately, some practice exercises, and it was a revelation as he began,

Du holde Kunst, in wieviel grauen Stunden,
Wo mich des Lebens wilder Kreis umstrickt,

Hast du mein Herz zu warmer Lieb' entzunden,
Hast mich in eine beßre Welt entrückt,
In eine beßre Welt entrückt!

Oft hat ein Seufzer, deiner Harf' entfloßen,
Ein süßer, heiliger Akkord von dir,

Den Himmel beßrer Zeiten mir erschloßen,
Du holde Kunst, ich danke dir dafür,
Du holde Kunst, ich danke dir!

There was silence.

--Jiri, that was beautiful, said Ilse.

--Yes; it is a lovely song. And it is true too, isn't it, Siggi? Although I am not sure about the grey hours, it has helped me in some very different coloured ones.

--Siggi, said Jiri the next morning, I want to ask you a very great favour. Of course, if you would rather not do it, you have only to say, and of course I shall pay you the current accountancy rates for your time. It is this.

He led him into Anton Zellek's study. The desk, table, chairs and floor were heaped with ledgers, files and papers.

I have arranged for all the financial records from the company to be brought here, and I have begun to arrange them in what seems to me a logical system, so that I can begin to make sense of them. But I am not an accountant, and perhaps you might be able to guide me through them more quickly.

Siggi looked at the material.

--What system have you used? he asked.

Jiri told him, only to lose his hearer very early on. Siggi's was a trained analytical approach to figures, which failed to comprehend Jiri's vision of the colours, shapes and sounds by which the universe was organised. Finally, he announced, after a deep breath and with very little hesitation:

--Accountants and actuaries have a set format for these things. I think it would be best for me to apply that to your records. It will be different from your system, but when I have applied it I am sure I can explain it to you.

Jiri looked delighted.

--Oh Siggi! Would you really be willing to do that? It's not that I find it boring – indeed, it has its own fascination – but it does seem to be taking me a long time and I have so many other things to attend to. And I will take you into my confidence. It seems to me that the firm's international investments have been very badly affected by the war. Of course, before I left Switzerland I was well enough to make some transfers and arrangements in that country; my late father opened an account while my mother was being treated there. And now that the war is over, we should be able to gain access to our London assets. Even so, I would like to know what else we can salvage from the wreckage; I would like an overview of the firm's current situation, if you feel able to provide one.

This Sigmund had promised to do almost before he knew it; at least, he thought, he could keep an accurate account of the hours it would take.

Ilse was also fully occupied. She was now writing a new Edelweiss story; Jiri had suggested that it would be nice to include a dog in this one, which she thought rather a good idea. She got into the habit of accompanying him to the factory, where he arranged for her to use one of the typewriting machines to type up her manuscript. While doing this, she noticed a row of leather notebooks; these turned out to be the late Frau Zellek's records, with meticulous accounts of the day-to-day running of the company. At the end of the war, Grethe Zellek had intended to invest in some new equipment, and to find a replacement for the elderly general manager. Neither of these things had been done. Ilse also saw the dining room and crèche for the factory employees; she learned that soon after his first visit to the factory, Jiri had appeared with a box of toys for the children and that he spent time with them whenever he could. I had to check that I had bought the right things, he explained; it was such fun choosing them, and of course the children tell me if they want anything else.

The weather became hotter. Ilse thought that Jiri found it trying; he spent more time on his reclining chair in the garden, with a book in his hand but with his eyes closed. Otto, who sat around with his tongue hanging out, did not attempt to jump onto his lap. At the suggestion of the housekeeper, Ilse took out a cool drink and some biscuits; these Jiri ignored, but he thanked her and gratefully sipped the cordial.

--It seems so airless here, he complained. Last summer I was in Switzerland; of course I was not well, but the air was so... so... and of course I miss the mountains... I used to spend every summer up at Tarnheim, with my uncle... and cousin... I suppose I could visit my uncle still; it would be lovely to be there, with the bathing pool... Ah! Here at Pallin there is a men's bathing place on the river; it will be open now. Siggi! Siggi! Would you like to come and swim?

--Are you able to swim? asked Ilse.

--Oh yes. It was one of the first things I could do; there was a swimming bath at the institute. It was wonderful! The water supports one, you know, so it does not hurt at all, and it is so good for the muscles! Siggi! I can lend you a bathing costume, I have three, although perhaps they would not fit you...

--Three bathing costumes!

--Yes; one I bought to use in Switzerland, and I brought it with me; there is one which I left here, I had it before the war, although I hate that one, it is so itchy, and I have a new one, it is very chic indeed. And, although it is woollen, it is made specially for sensitive skins. I am hoping that when I wear it, it will distract attention from my leg. I think you have seen that, Ilse, and it is rather a mess, I am afraid; the scars will fade a bit more, but even so; still, I have made up my mind not to worry about that. After all, I am not vain.

Ilse smiled, but decided not to contradict him.

--What do you think, Siggi? Shall we? Even if none of my costumes fit you, perhaps that will not matter. Most fellows don't bother about them. I sometimes wear one; there is a certain amount of waterweed and some fish, which... anyway, I want to show off my new one.

The prospect seemed to have given him fresh life. Sigmund was reluctant; Jiri did not persist, but suggested that Siggi find a spare pair of drawers and a towel, and come with him to the bathing place. He would see that it was just a collection of local blokes splashing around and keeping cool, and if he did not like the look of it he could come straight home. This Sigmund agreed to do. They collected their things and went off in the pony trap. Fritz might like to bathe too; by agreement the lower classes bathed a little further down the river, and as none of them possessed bathing costumes, often girls tended to peep out from the bushes for viewing. Fritz could take Siggi back, if that was what he preferred, or he could go for a swim there and return for them later.

The bathing place was a section of the riverbank that had been strengthened and paved; there was a tumbledown hut for changing, but few bathers used this, stripping off either in full view or behind some undergrowth. Jiri emerged in his new costume: the top half was red and white stripes, the lower half black. It was the latest thing, and drew some cries of admiration and amusement; almost everyone there seemed to know him, encouraging Otto when he raced into the water; there was a great deal of splashing and badinage. Someone shouted to Jiri that now they had all had seen his bathing suit, he could take it off like everyone else: cries of Get it off, Zellek! resulted in his stripping naked and plunging in. Jiri swam with the neatness, competence and daring that characterised all his physical actions. Perhaps deliberately, he did not look at Sigmund.

Sigmund stood on the bank. Suddenly the sight of men naked or scarcely clothed brought back visions of medical inspections, hospitals, doctors... he closed his eyes and began to shake, regretting that he had told Fritz to go; he had not liked to spoil the boy's anticipation of a swim. He looked at the water. Beyond the crowd of bathers, the river wound under a band of willow trees; it got even deeper, it was brown, with golden lights, and a little mist of midges... fish leaped at these, returning to the water with a sound between a plop and a splash... a couple of ducks, offended by the noise upstream (and now, downstream also, as Fritz and his fellow bathers shouted and laughed) took flight. Sigmund was now the only person on the bank. He took off his clothing, leaving it in a heap; Jiri's was, predictably, neatly folded.

Blast him. How could he be like this, after all that he must have seen and done, all that he had undoubtedly gone through. Sigmund had seen Jiri's injured leg, but only now did he realise that actually someone had cut his back open. The scar, unlike the ones on his leg, was a neat surgical incision, and had Jiri's spine been less knobbly and prominent might hardly have been noticeable, but it was there. The problem was not, Sigmund now realised, that Jiri was privileged, wealthy, an officer; he had seen officers in worse plight than himself, devastated by the same hideous memories and experiences. Sigmund hated the thought that skinny, fragile, vain, ridiculous Jiri was in any way superior to himself. And he was definitely flirting with Ilse. At times he had wondered whether Jiri was one of those who preferred other men; there was still something about him that suggested a certain ambivalence, but his reactions to women seemed normal, even enthusiastic. One evening he had even hinted at a place in Pallin where the prices were reasonable and the girls clean, should Siggi desire an introduction. And Siggi had nearly caught him with the girl who came on Tuesdays to help with the ironing; she had been smoothing down her skirt while Jiri buttoned his trousers, afterward slipping something into her hand.

Sigmund slipped into the water. It was cool but not cold; the sun had been on it all day. It swiftly became deep. He struck out towards the other bank; it had been months since he had swum and it felt good; as Jiri had said, the water supported you, and he experienced no involuntary movements; in fact, he felt fully in command of his body, regaining control in the same way that perhaps, Jiri had done with a body far more broken and damaged than his had ever been.

All this time, Jiri and Sigmund had never spoken of their army experiences. Then, as luck would have it, one evening the talk turned apparently innocuously to foreign languages and the difficulties of translation; it may have arisen through discussion of foreign sales for the company. Suddenly Jiri began to laugh.

--What is it?

--Oh, I'm just reminded of something really funny that happened in the army! It was in 1916; we'd been dismounted by then although some of us were kept for reconnaissance, messages and orderly duty, and finding remounts and draught horses for the artillery and supplies. So Bruno (he was my horse) and I were doing that. One day I'd been out since early morning trying to get a look at the Russian lines, and it was bloody cold... snow everywhere... by the time we got back I'd been in the saddle for hours and practically lost the feeling in my legs. Well, no sooner had I handed dear old Bruno over to the stable orderly and staggered into the mess for a mug of soup or anything hot I could get than I'm told the Colonel wants you now, just get your greatcoat off and move yourself! He's sitting there with a couple of troopers, a German general that everyone hated as he was always berating us for 'Austrian sloppiness' and a Russian; he'd been captured lurking around our trenches.

--Leutnant Zellek, snaps the Colonel, do you speak Russian?

--Humbly report sir, only basic.

--Do you or do you not?

--Not nearly so well as Captain Restov, sir. He's been teaching me, as I thought it might be of interest. The Captain is your man for this job, sir.

--Zellek, when I want your opinion I will request it. And I have not done so, nor am I likely to do so at any point in the future. Restov is not available.

There was a whole other story behind that, of course; one day I will tell you what happened to poor Restov.

--Well, Zellek, goes on the Colonel, you will have to do your best. Speak to the prisoner and ask if he can understand you.

So I do.

--Right, says the Colonel, what did he say?

--Actually he'd said that mine was the worst accent he'd ever heard and I was obviously speaking through some... other orifice... than my mouth.

So I told the Colonel, Yes, he does understand me but he thinks my accent could be improved.

--That wasn't all the fellow said, though, was it? says the General, who was probably brighter than he looked.

--No, sir.

--Well then, come on, man.

--He passed some comments, sir.

--About what?

--About yourself, sir.

I'd had enough by then. So I told the General exactly what the prisoner had said about him; of course, it wasn't nearly as good as it was in Russian but even so it was pretty colourful... if Ilse wasn't here, I'd give you some examples, but...

There I stood to attention, telling the General that he was, well, you can imagine, and it was perfect, because I was absolutely straight-faced and under orders.

The two lads on guard were falling over themselves and even the Colonel – who had no love for the General, I can tell you – was trying not to grin.

Anyway, they tell me to ask the Russian a few obvious questions to which I get the obvious answers, then they get me to threaten him a bit, which has no effect. By now the General has somehow taken a dislike to me and tells the Colonel to get rid of that upstart little officer, which meant that I could finally go get a glass of something.

--What happened to the Russian? asked Ilse.

--Oh, they shot him. But it was war, and that is what happens. But it was so funny, wasn't it?

His hand shook slightly as he put down his coffee cup.

That night Sigmund underwent a series of dreams and flashbacks, taking him back to his worst days at the military hospital for shell-shock cases. He became aware of someone at his bedside; it was Jiri, who began to soothe him as he might have done a frightened horse or dog.

--Siggi, I couldn't sleep either. I should not have spoken about the war. It is my fault.

He slipped under the covers. I'll hold you, Siggi. It will be all right. Otto will keep our feet warm.

When Sigmund woke, he was alone.

What was that? he wondered. Trust Zellek. Fancied a bit of mutual wanking and brought his bloody dog with him. But it had been the answer; he must have slept for hours.

As the autumn progressed, Sigmund began to get the company finances in order, and slowly Ilse began to take over the role of Grethe Zellek. Jiri worked with Gestner, and corresponded with prospective customers, securing visits from a German, and an English, firm of distributors.

For a couple of days Jiri had seemed tired and out of sorts, but Ilse attributed this to the increased preparations for the German sales rep. Then she came into the salon to find him lying on the couch. As he struggled to rise, she asked him if his back was troubling him,

--No, yes… I don't know, only I have a headache… and it seems so hot…

She put her hand on his forehead.

--Oh… that is lovely… thank you.

--Jiri, I think you have a fever. Get up, and I will ask Ernst to help you to bed.

233

With this, a convulsive shiver shook him.

Jiri grew worse, but refused have a doctor, saying he would only hurt him and give him medicine that would make him sick. He seemed to have some pain and swelling among the scars under his knee and the area looked red and hot. At night he moaned, sweated, and was tormented by dreams; he seemed terrified that a doctor would give him injections. Sigmund and Ernst took turns to sit with him. Frau Anna sent for the local nurse, who applied poultices to his leg.

--What day is it?

--Jiri, it's Tuesday.

--The German! I can't get up! Oh Siggi…

--Look Jiri, we know what to say.

--Frau Anna, whatever the master says, you must get him a doctor, I don't think he really knows what is happening, and I will take the responsibility.

The Treichlers could hardly believe how well things had gone. They sat back in the pony trap, occasionally exchanging looks of surprise, exaltation and amazement.

It was only as they approached the villa that they began to wonder what had been happening in their absence.

Frau Anna ran to meet them.

--How is he? asked Ilse.

--Better! Oh, Fräulein, what a day!

She explained that the doctor had seen at once that there was an abscess under Jiri's knee that could be lanced and drained. In the course of this, a small piece of shrapnel had emerged; it must have been so deeply embedded that the Swiss surgeon had missed it, and it had now worked its way out.

The master was wonderful; he had asked only that he might hold her hand (and he had nearly crushed it) but had made hardly a murmur. Ernst, though, had fainted when the incision was made, and Otto, sensing that something was going on, had howled miserably outside the door for hours.

The doctor had given Jiri something to make him sleep; he was still sleeping now, but it was clear that his temperature had gone down and the doctor had said that when he woke he should be given some nourishment – she had some clear soup ready – and then he should be encouraged to sleep again. He must be kept in bed until there was no further risk of the wound becoming reinfected as blood poisoning was a real danger; after that, he could gradually begin to get about; in fact, since the trouble had been brewing for some time, they might even expect an improvement in his general health. The scar would be negligible compared with all the others.

--Can we see him?

--Ilse! Siggi!

--Jiri, it went well. We have a signed contract; we'll tell you all about it when you're well enough.

--Wonderful! Oh, you two are so clever! I see that you do not need me.

--Oh, yes we do! The London rep is coming in three weeks' time and as we don't speak a word of English; you have to be on your feet by then.

Ilse took his hand.

--Jiri, does your leg hurt?

--Yes, but not like before. It hurts like things do when they are beginning to get better.

He closed his eyes but did not let go of her hand. She signed to her brother to leave the room.

Ilse noticed that Sigmund had changed. For several days, Jiri was confined to bed while the abscess continued to discharge and gradually healed; now that his fever had abated, and the pain lessened, he actually felt quite well, and played endless games of tarok with Sigmund and Ernst. They had shared some quite intimate nursing during Jiri's illness, and the three young men seemed to enjoy banter, jokes and even horseplay; when Jiri became impossible, demanding a change of scene, the other two volunteered to carry him downstairs, while Otto yapped around their feet threatening to send all three of them tumbling in a heap.

Eventually Jiri was dumped on the couch in the salon.

--There you are! Now let's have no more grumbling!

Ilse realised that she had heard her brother's laugh more often in the last few days than before he had left for the Front. He was physically able to help lift Jiri; his stammer had been barely noticeably in the business meeting with the German rep, although she had done most of the talking.

Three weeks later, Jiri was able to meet the English sales team. It was not as easy as they had hoped; there was still prejudice against German and Austrian goods, and the English drove a hard bargain; they were eventually won round by Jiri's suggestion that they might like a new range of glass animals to supplement the Wolfi set, based on Otto. I know the English, he said; they can never resist a dog.

Towards the end of November, a large, ornately decorated invitation card arrived.

It was from the Pallin Chamber of Commerce, inviting Jiri and a partner to the annual dinner and dance at the rathaus, a few days before Christmas.

It will be very boring, Jiri announced. But I had better go, in the way of business. It would not be good to suggest that we are struggling. Fräulein Ilse, will you do me the honour of accompanying me? I will introduce you, quite correctly, as my colleague. I'm afraid that we shall be, as the English say, quite low down in the pecking order. I am a member, but unlike my late father I have never held office, and I do not attend their meetings, although of course I do have an excuse for that. It is evening dress, of course; decorations will be worn so we shall all look like Christmas trees.

--Jiri, thank you. But I do not have, I mean my dinner dress is not...

A silence followed, then Jiri jumped up.

--Frau Anna, he shouted, come at once. Stop whatever you are doing; I am sure it is not important.

Frau Anna appeared wearing a What Is It Now? expression.

--Frau Anna, Frau Anna, what was done with Mutti's things, I mean her dresses, her furs?

--Well, sir. During the war she gave a lot of it away. People were in need. She helped everyone she could.

--Of course; Mutti would do that, but...

--And, Jiri, said Ilse, I suppose those things are rather... old... and perhaps Frau Zellek was not...

--Not your size? No, no you are right, she was not, but surely...

--We could have look, sir. And I can always get a pattern with the new silhouette. Because you're right sir, if you are thinking that it's too late to get a dressmaker in the town. They will all be booked up by now. We shall have to do

237

something ourselves. I'll find some of the neighbours' maids and I have a sewing machine.

Finally they selected an ample, formal gown in a blue green shimmering silk that would provide enough material for an evening dress in the new slim style. On a shelf, wrapped in special paper, was a bundle:

--Oh! This is beautiful. It was silver lace, unused, obviously handmade and very expensive.

--I remember that, said Frau Anna. Sir, it was your mother's, not your late stepmother's.

--But I thought all her things, with all the important jewels, went back to Tarnheim?

--So they did, sir; this must have been overlooked. It is perfect with the silk.

--Ah, added Jiri. Jewels. Let us look at those.

Most of Grethe Zellek's jewellery had been bought during the period when design was prioritised over intrinsic value. Semi-precious stones, silver, even copper and enamel, in pre-war settings that were lovely but now looking rather old-fashioned.

--These... he held up a set of moonstone and silver necklace, bracelet and earrings...

The necklace would suit you. And the bracelet; would it make one of those bandeaux I see in all the magazines?

They also needed to practise dancing.

--I hope I can still dance. I have not done so since... well, for some time. But I am hoping it will be like skating (Jiri had experimented successfully with this earlier that month). I mean, one only needs to adjust one's balance a little, strap up the leg and ankle and get used to it.

He took a few steps. Siggi, Siggi, play some dance music, you must know some and if not... Oh and surely you know a tango? Or a foxtrot?

On the night of the dinner, Ilse came out of her room and walked down the stairs. As well as a beautiful shimmering dress with silver lace and a moonstone necklace and bandeau, she had silver dancing shoes, which Jiri had been horrified to learn had been bought in a shop rather than specially made, with a matching bag.

Frau Anna stood below, holding out a magnificent silver fox wrap.

There was Jiri. His evening dress, which must have dated from before he joined the army, fitted him perfectly; his current fragility meant that he was the same size that he had been at seventeen. He was convinced that he had grown at least an inch after that, and had taken the suit to his tailor in the city for minor adjustments; at all events, the fit could not now be faulted. He was wearing his medals, which Ilse and Sigmund had never seen.

--One from Serbia, the other two from Galicia, said Ernst, who had pinned them on. That different one round the neck is really something. Not many get those; I had a look at the citation, it was with the box, he told Siggi as Ilse and Jiri drove off in a motor taxi.

In the cloakroom, Ilse saw that people were staring at her fur, which must be recognised as the property of the late Frau Zellek. Probably the moonstones would also be identified. Jiri, she thought, had put her in something of a false position; had he done this unthinkingly, in deliberate mischief, or for some other reason? Fortunately attention was now focussed on a newcomer, one who like herself was not a native of the city. Ilse had been rather pleased with her own appearance; Siggi had no idea about female dress, Jiri's taste veered towards kitsch, but Frau Anna had some grasp of what was acceptable in Pallin society, and she had been more than satisfied. Now she felt fat, frumpish and provincial in contrast to the fashionably flat figure, bobbed hair, sleeveless drop-waisted dress and geometric jewellery of a young woman, perhaps Jiri's age, who flung off her wrap and swayed out into the arms of a tall, heavy-set, clumsy-looking fellow, who obviously regarded her as a trophy.

--Don't spend more time primping, Biki, you're painted and powdered enough already, he noted.

Jiri appeared at exactly the right moment. Ilse was not sorry to take the arm of such a trim, dapper, elegant figure, with those medals.

As they waited to be called in to dinner, they were approached by a young couple. He was of muscular middle height with light brown hair and blue eyes; she was shorter, very fair, and about five months pregnant.

--Wilhelm, Inge!

--Jiri!

--You are back in Pallin! May I introduce my colleague, Fräulein Treichler?

The story was soon told. Wilhelm and Inge were natives of Pallin. They had married immediately after the war, and subsequently spent some months in Bremen, where he had employment. But now the opportunity has arisen, they were back here, near their families, looking for a house and as you see, hoping to start a family.

--So you have all known each other for a long time?

--Oh yes. We started school together. Jiri and I have been friends ever since he emptied a flowerpot of geraniums over my head.

--That was only because you threw my exercise book out of the window.

--You threw mine first.

--Jiri was really sticking up for me, Fräulein Treichler; Willi was pulling my plaits like he always did.

--Anyway, Sister Imelda lost her temper and gave Jiri a good whack with the ruler, then he hid behind a cupboard until the headmistress persuaded him out.

--Well, I didn't want another smack, did I? But dear Mother Jerome was very kind to me after that.

Suddenly he remembered that day; the headmistress had told him that she was thinking seriously of asking his parents to remove him from school. He had burst into tears and the nun had taken the overtired, overwrought child on her knee and comforted him.

--Frau Brume, perhaps you should sit down?

--Inge, please... and it's Ilse, isn't it? Yes, thank you.

They found two chairs.

--We shan't stay late, but as I'm feeling so much better after being so sick for the first few months, and as it's good for business, we thought we'd come just for part of the evening.

--What is your husband's business?

--Willi is in automobiles! He studied engineering and was in the artillery; it's the next big thing. We are lagging behind France and the US, you know. Willi says we must build up our industry if we are to recover from the war. I hear Jiri is working hard at the glass factory. It's wonderful to see him looking so well. We heard that he'd been dreadfully crushed; it was terrible to think of that, he was always such an imp, so full of life and so deliciously naughty. At lunchtime he always used to tell everyone how to behave: I can hear him now! *No, no, one does not grab the serving spoon. That is not correct. One waits until the footman approaches one, so, and then instructs. Only do not be too long about it, as others are waiting, and their soup will grow cold while you are arguing and dithering.* And of course all the children would look around for the footman! I'm sure, looking back, he must have heard that when he stayed with his uncle at Tarnheim. And then his engagement seemed to come to nothing, although I've always thought that was one of those arrangements those old families make, rather than a love match. He doesn't look like someone with a broken heart, does he?

No, thought Ilse. Jiri was more likely to suffer from backache than heartache, and tomorrow he probably would.

Inge broke off as Jiri himself approached them, accompanied by a rotund man in his fifties, not much taller than Jiri, and wearing a pointed beard.

--This is the Herr Editor of the *Pallin Beobachter*! He has had the most wonderful idea! Beginning in the New Year, he will print a weekly column for ladies; of course, there will be material on fashion and cookery, ladies are always interested in that, but it is to be from the viewpoint of a modern, independent, yet hardworking and respectable young woman, one of those whose efforts will construct the new Austrian Republic and bring us into the 1920s! Someone like you, Fräulein Ilse! Oh how I wish I had thought of something like that! The Herr Editor is really a brilliant man!

I gather it will be paid on a weekly basis, with extra for any additional work the writer is asked to undertake.

The editor cleared his throat as Jiri paused for breath.

--Well, yes. Herr Zellek has summed it up very well. He suggested that perhaps you might be interested in the position, depending of course on your many other journalistic commitments...

--Yes. Yes. I might well consider it.

--Perhaps then, Fräulein, you might call at the newspaper offices between now and Christmas? The New Year edition would be an excellent moment to begin the new venture.

At dinner, Jiri and Ilse were seated at the same table, although not together. As Jiri had foretold, they were among the younger and less distinguished guests, who were possibly somewhat less boring than the older contingent. Even so, the conversation ran mainly on matters of business, gossip about Pallin residents about whom Ilse knew nothing, and the doings of the young families of those who had children. Glancing down the ranks, she saw that Jiri kept up a stream of chatter, turning meticulously from one neighbour to the next, and having lost interest in the food at an early stage, drinking as much as he could get.

She had the first two dances with him. He was, as she had realised, an excellent dancer, firmly guiding her, absolutely in time, as neat, elegant and economical as he was in all physical activities.

He was also surprisingly sensible, pacing himself by not dancing every number; periodically he sat out, chatting to anyone who would listen. Even so, he managed to dance with all the most attractive ladies who were not actually six feet tall, and flirted with absolutely everyone. Or nearly; the only couple he avoided was the young woman Ilse had noticed in the cloakroom, and her escort. Biki flitted around from partner to partner, earning dark looks from him; Ilse saw that she often glanced at Jiri with interest. The medals, the impeccable evening dress, the undoubtedly aristocratic, slightly arrogant air, together with his clear popularity and evident dancing skills obviously interested her, especially as he did not come near her.

It was towards early morning when Jiri led Ilse to an anteroom where there were more refreshments. He eagerly helped them both to ice creams, and ordered champagne.

--Oh, if it isn't little Jiri Zellek!

This was not Jiri's favourite mode of address, but he kept a polite expression.

What a surprise! I thought you were killed, or at least crippled.

--I am sorry to disappoint you, Konrad, but as you see I am not dead and not entirely crippled. I have scars, but I acquired them honourably, not while bullying a fourteen-year-old boy.

He gestured towards Konrad's cheek, which showed a distinct mark, as of an old knife cut.

Konrad turned to Ilse.

--Be careful, Fräulein, even if you have got your hands on Mutti's moonstones and furs. He's got a nasty temper, this little rat, and some crazy relatives.

--Konrad, these things are mine to lend as I see fit. I would rather see my stepmother's jewels on a valued colleague than adorning a little whore hired for the evening, like your cheap ill-fitting suit.

Konrad clenched his fists... Jiri stepped forward.

--Jiri, don't!

Ilse held him back, horrified at the expression on his face.

--Ah, Konrad! Here you are! Excuse me for interrupting, but I've been wanting to talk to you about the donations to the orphans' Christmas party... Can we step outside, and maybe share a glass?

It was the treasurer of the Chamber of Commerce.

Whether it was sheer chance or a masterpiece of timely tact, it took Konrad from the scene. With a furious glance at Jiri, he followed the older man from the room.

Jiri sat down.

--Who was that? I saw him earlier with that rather lovely girl, the one with the make-up... Biki, I think.

--Konrad Schrank. He got me thrown out of Oberschule.

--What?

--Yes. After I gave him that cut on the cheek. It's an old story. He and his gang of friends were the school bullies and one day they decided to set on me. I won't tell you what they were trying to do, but it was shaming and insulting. I did my best, kneed two of them in the groin and brained one with my history textbook, but Konrad kept on coming... I used to take my hunting knife to school; somehow I seemed to get into quite a lot of fights in those days... and... well, to be honest, I missed his throat and got his cheek, as you see.

--Jiri, how old were you?

--Fourteen. And I was quite a puny little chap in those days.

Ilse did not make the obvious answer. Jiri did not need reminding that Konrad was still at least seven inches, and several kilos, larger than he was.

Jiri got to his feet.

--Your leg's tired.

--Yes. But I'm not going to let that bastard know it.

Some more champagne. He beckoned the waiter, took the proffered glass and, drawing a Fabergé pill box from an inner pocket, took a small white tablet, washing it down with champagne.

--Jiri, what's that?

--We had them in the army. They stop the pain and give one a bit of energy. Now, Fräulein Ilse, do something kind; look, Alois Gruber has been gazing at you ever since you danced with him earlier. If you go in his direction, he will ask you again, and you will make the poor fellow ecstatically happy... please do!

He was right; Gruber was all too keen to whisk Ilse away for the next dance; meanwhile Jiri went over to the band and spoke to the leader; several musicians rearranged their positions. The waltz ended and the dancers moved aside. Head high, the picture of elegance, his medals in full evidence, Jiri crossed the empty dance floor. He stopped in front of Konrad and Biki. Bowing, he took her hand and whispered something. The band struck up 'La Cumparasita'.

The tango that followed was unforgettable. Its South American origins as a means of seduction and display of male sensuality were fully manifested to the Pallin business community. As a climax, Jiri bent his partner backwards and gave her a long, passionate kiss on the mouth before handing her over to Konrad as if she were a bag of groceries. If he had copulated with her in public, his meaning could not have been clearer.

--Fräulein Ilse! We have finished here! Jiri held out his hand and, to her shame, Ilse came meekly forward, took it and let him lead her to the cloakrooms, where they reclaimed their things in silence before taking one of the taxicabs waiting in line before the rathaus.

Ilse managed not to speak until they reached the villa. Then she faced him.

--Jiri Zellek, you're either an arrogant, vain, stuck-up, condescending snob or a foul-mouthed, vindictive guttersnipe show-off, and I'm not sure which I dislike more.

--Oh, Fräulein Ilse! Don't be so cross! I'm very tired, my leg really hurts, and that ice cream and champagne... I'm going to throw up.

He did so, noisily, into a flower bed.

--It serves you right. It is your own fault.

Ilse strode past him and hammered on the door, rousing Ernst, who was supposed to be waiting up for them and who was dozing on Jiri's couch.

--Mr Jiri is being sick in the garden. It is utterly disgusting, but I suppose we cannot leave him outside all night.

Ilse marched upstairs, threw her fur in a heap, kicked off her shoes and sat down on the bed. In a rage, she then ripped off her dress and jewellery, lay down and pulled the covers over her head so that she should not hear the sounds from downstairs.

She did not get up until almost lunchtime. Sigmund, who was waiting for her in the dining room, told her that Jiri was still in bed, having sent word that his leg was so stiff that he could not move, let alone come out of his room.

--Well, said Sigmund. According to Frau Anna, all Pallin is talking about Jiri.

--I don't suppose it's the first time.

--Illa, are you going to tell me what happened?

--I'm furious with him. He behaved appallingly. Although perhaps he was provoked.

--He didn't try anything with you, did he? Because if he did, in spite of everything…

--No, no. In fact he was the perfect escort until…

Suddenly Ilse realised that she would not have minded if Jiri had tried something; actually, she had almost expected it, perhaps wanted it. Oh dear.

Fritz appeared in the doorway, carrying a huge bunch of hothouse flowers, lavishly wrapped and tied with ribbon.

--Who on earth are those from?

Ilse took the card.

To Fräulein Ilse, with fond thoughts of two wonderful dances, and hoping we shall meet again, often, during the festive season… With deep respects, Alois Gruber.

--Who the hell is he?

--Gruber, corn merchants, millers, bakers and distributors…

--That Gruber?

--Yes.

--Well, Illa, if you play it right, we can say goodbye to Jiri and move into that big house on Helderstrasse.

For a moment she took him seriously, then they both grinned.

But, of course, he may be handsome and charming as well as quite rich.

--Actually he looks like a toad. Of course that would not matter if he was amusing, intelligent and a good dancer. But he is not.

Actually, she thought, Jiri was all of those things. And, in his own way physically attractive, yes.

Fritz reappeared.

--Something else was delivered, Fräulein Ilse. This came for the master. I was going to take it up, but Frau Anna said he wasn't to be disturbed. I thought you would know what to do with it.

It was a single red rose, in an elaborate wrapping, with a card.

--I will put it in water, Fritz. Thank you.

As Ilse prepared to put the flower in a small vase, she could not help moving the card. It featured drawings of cute puppies, wearing Christmassy bows and party hats.

--He's going to love that.

--Yes. I'm afraid he is.

Darling Jiri, for your buttonhole. Look me up whenever you like, kisses, Biki.

--Biki?

Ilse turned the card over.

Biki Schramm, 130a, Hofstrasse, Brunstadt.

--Illa, I think you had better begin at the beginning.

Over a light luncheon, Ilse told her brother almost everything that had happened the previous evening.

Sigmund seemed to think most of it quite funny, but then he became more serious.

--There are a couple of things that worry me, Ilse. That Konrad bloke: I'm afraid he'll harm Zellek and Co if he gets the chance. We have to be careful. The other thing: those pills. What did Jiri say about them?

--He said they had them in the army, to 'stop the pain and give one a bit of energy'. Why? Did you?

--Yes. They work. But they... they... well, too many of them and they change you. Look, I know why Jiri won't have morphine, and hates injections. He didn't spell it out, but he must have had a lot of the stuff while he was in hospital, and then when he was having those operations. It must have been hell coming off it and he doesn't want to go through that again. That's why he puts up with a lot more than he lets on. We'll need to watch him, that's all. And I hope the idiot hasn't set off another abscess in his leg; I think Ernst will give notice if we have to go through another week like that.

Jiri came down for dinner. He looked pale, and was leaning on his stick, but greeted them cheerfully.

--How's your head, Jiri? asked Sigmund. I heard it was quite a heavy night.

--Thank you. It is not too bad. You know, I threw up when we got home. Although that is unpleasant, sometimes it means that after a sleep one is quite *in Ordnung*. It was my own fault; I adore champagne and ice cream, but if one has too much... Really, it's my leg that's the problem. But I expect it will be better tomorrow. Ilse, what lovely flowers! Who has sent them?

--Herr Gruber.

--Oh *ho*! Fräulein Ilse, I knew you had made a conquest there, and it is partly my doing, you know.

--Jiri, you have something too.

She directed him to the rose and its card.

--Oh, how pretty. (I knew it, groaned Sigmund.) And how sweet of her. I do hope she won't get into trouble with Konrad. But really, she would be much better off without him. I'm sure there are lots of fellows who would be glad to take her on. I wonder what she charges. Do you know, I am quite hungry; I suppose the last thing I ate was that ice cream, which, of course... And, Siggi, do you think we can afford a motor? I'm sure Willi Brume could get us one on special terms; we could all learn to drive it, so we would not need to engage a chauffeur, although Ernst might like it. Fräulein Ilse, you could be the first lady driver in Pallin! And wouldn't it be a nice idea for one of your stories?

From all over Pallin, church bells were ringing in the New Year of 1921. In the salon of the Villa Zellek, glowing with its Christmas tree, decorations and candles, the singing, kissing and clinking of glasses gradually quietened as Jiri stepped into the centre of the room. The entire household, several employees from the factory, Wilhelm and Inge, the parish priest and various neighbours looked at him as he raised his champagne glass. Karel von Tarnheim was not among them. Ilse had asked Jiri whether he should invite his uncle for Christmas. His look of dismay had been answer enough, although Jiri had said, No, that would not be necessary, his uncle would likely be in Prague, where 'he had somebody'.

--Friends, began Jiri. Many of you will already know much of what I have to say. But I want to include you all, who have helped me, and the company, so much over the past months, in our plans for 1921. Herr and Fräulein Treichler, Siggi and Ilse, have agreed to live permanently here at Villa Zellek. Siggi is to handle all the financial affairs of the company, of course with full reference to myself. Fräulein Ilse, who has of course her own eminent career, will also assist me in the management of the factory, where we shall be promoting young Herr Kramm here to trainee manager. This arrangement should, in due course, allow me the means and time to travel and to pursue other interests. We have arrived at a most satisfactory financial arrangement, (he did not go into details, but he had offset the Treichlers' board and lodging against one and a half salaries, which, considering the improved situation of the company, was really not too bad). Now! To 1921! To Zellek and Co! To life, to laughter, and to music!

As he drank his champagne, Jiri's eyes met Ilse's. He experienced a strange sensation; his real life had been taken away from him, so that in a sense he did not exist, but there was the chance of an alternative existence. At that moment it seemed entirely attractive. Pallin, the factory, Ilse… but of course that was not real either. And in his pocket was his Christmas letter from Heinrich.

BERLIN, MUNICH
(AND LUNCH IN BUDAPEST)

In the freezing March of 1924, Sister Magdalena Kowaleska was completing her nursing training and improving her German at the Berlin house of her order. Although she had not yet made her Solemn Profession, the Mother Superior in Kracow had been willing to let her go; and she was proving valuable in Berlin. A long winter of icy temperatures, food shortages and sickness had affected everyone in Berlin; the sisters were relying on the younger, fitter nuns to take over the duties of the household as well as sick visiting and so on. While the general rule was that the sisters operate in pairs, under these conditions sometimes they had to go out singly and so it was that Magdalena was by herself in the bread queue that morning. Somewhere in the line ahead she heard a baby crying, then a very sweet male voice singing softly. The crying ceased, and the young nun noticed that the singer was, as she thought, a teenage boy probably caring for his younger brother. The pair reached the head of the queue, and came back, the boy triumphantly placing the loaf into a shopping basket already containing a load of potatoes, two turnips and half a cabbage. But as he reached her he began to waver and sway, his steps unsteady.

She knew what would happen. He would slide to the ground, people would cluster around him and within seconds his precious provisions would have melted away. He knew it too. Please, sister, he murmured, please, hold him just for a minute, and he thrust the baby into her arms.

Sister Magdalena abandoned her place in the queue. Taking the baby on one arm (it was very warmly wrapped up and surprisingly heavy), she supported the youngster over to the steps of a nearby building, where he sank down, his arms crossed over the basket of food, and dropped his head onto it. She was able to notice that he too was very warmly dressed, in a good-quality overcoat with a cap and scarf as well as woollen gloves. When after a few minutes he looked up, she realised with a shock that he was not a boy at all; he was a man probably in his late twenties, in fact a few years older than herself.

--Thank you, thank you, sister, he was saying. His German was cultured and refined, with an accent that showed that he was not a Berliner. I knew when I saw your habit that you would help us. But I am afraid you have lost your place in the queue.

--Never mind that now. I do not think you are fit to walk far. Where do you live?

He told her and they set off, the nun still carrying the baby and her companion hauling the shopping.

--You have hurt yourself? she asked, noticing that he limped.

--No; it is a war injury. Usually it is all right, only today the weather is rather cold. Is Pauli warm enough?

--Pauli! His name is Paul? And yes, he is quite snug.

--Yes, Paul. My son's name is Paul. And I must introduce myself: Jiri Zellek.

His son? Ah then, there must be someone at home to look after them.

--I hope your wife will not be worried about you, Herr Zellek.

--My wife? Oh... no... Paul... Paul's mother has been gone for nearly three months now.

--Then who looks after the baby?

--I do! And there's Heini, the friend I share a flat with; and the landlady minds him sometimes; and for feeding, there's poor Frau Keller. Her baby died, it was so sad, and no one knows where her husband is, only I am pretty sure he is in prison, but I do not mention it, of course; sometimes she is not well, or she does not have enough milk, and then we have to give him formula. One has to be sure that it is good quality and not adulterated, so I have to go to the expensive pharmacies in the city centre.

Jiri, even in a weakened state, could never resist a captive listener.

As they drew nearer to the address he had given she noticed that everyone seemed to know him.

--Hi, Jiri, got yourself a girlfriend?

--Love the outfit, darling!

(Take no notice, sister, they are quite nice girls really.)

--How's young Pauli? Teething yet?

--Come by tomorrow, my little dandy, and I'll save you a buttonhole, called the flower seller.

--Sister, sister, I am sorry but we must stop for moment.

They were a passing a one-legged beggar, dressed in faded

Waffenrock, sitting in a doorway close to a grating exuding warm air. Jiri acknowledged the man's salute.

--Good morning, Corporal! Where is Richard this morning?

--He's at the vegetable market, earning a few pfennigs sweeping up, and he can always pick up a few leftovers.

--What a very good idea! Jiri's tone made it sound as though he might well do the same himself.

He is a very good boy, isn't he?

--Yes, Herr Leutnant. He is.

Jiri now drew a knife from his pocket. The young nun had seen one like it: the Polish aristocrat who owned the land her family farmed carried one very similar. With it Jiri cut a chunk from the loaf in his basket.

--Here. This will keep you going till he gets back. I'm sorry I cannot stop longer, Corporal, but it is very cold for Pauli to be out, and I am not quite well this morning.

--Take care of the Herr Leutnant, said the old soldier. He's a real good officer, even if he was with the sloppy Austrians!

When Heinrich opened the door of the flat, he was met by warmth and the smell of cooking. A young nun sat by the stove feeding Paul.

Heinrich felt himself turning pale.

Where's Jiri? he croaked.

--He is quite all right. He is sleeping; he has no fever, and he has had some tea and bread and jam. He left the butter for you, and says you must save some soup for Frau Keller, in case she is well enough to come and feed Paul later. As it is, I have found Paul's formula and bottle, and I have changed his nappy. I have started the soup; it will be ready before long.

Heinrich said nothing, but ran to the small bedroom where Jiri and Paul generally slept. Jiri was as Sister Magdalena had said, fast asleep, his dark head and delicate, irregular features snuggled into the pillow. Heinrich breathed deeply.

--Thank you, he said. I'm sorry, it was just for a moment that I thought…

--I understand. He became a little faint after getting the bread from the bakery. So I brought him home; he was very tired, and cold, and perhaps had not eaten.

--Stupid little idiot! Heinrich, having been deadly anxious, was now annoyed. I told him not to go out, but I suppose he decided to go to look for something to eat.

He held out his hand.

Heinrich Rheinrose. He had, she thought, the most beautiful hands she had ever seen. And, in fact, he was a remarkably good-looking man. Early thirties, perhaps, dark, with the most riveting brown eyes, just under six feet tall, probably Jewish. Jiri, she knew, must be a Catholic. There was a rosary hanging on Paul's cradle, and Jiri had made the sign of the cross when she had finally rolled him into bed, dressed only in his long winter underwear and warm socks.

--Thank you, sister, for looking after my friend and Pauli. May I escort you home, when you have settled the child?

Heinrich clearly did not wish to have anything more to do with her, and she might never have seen any of them again. But late one night a few weeks later she was roused by the sister on door duty.

--Sister Magdalena! There is a man here asking for you; he is carrying a baby and they both seem very distressed.

It was Jiri, holding Paul, who was screaming at the top of his powerful lungs. One side of his face was fiery red.

--Sister, sister! Please! I don't know what to do! What is wrong with him? I think he is teething and I believe it is very dangerous! Heini is playing in a concert and going out afterwards... Pauli, oh Pauli... I can't bear...

Magdalena took Paul and Jiri sank down on a bench. He looked exhausted and almost in tears.

Do we need a doctor? he queried. I have some money, or at least I can go out and find some.

--No, no, Herr Zellek. You are quite right. The poor child is cutting some teeth. It is painful for him but really it is quite normal. I am sure you must have driven your parents distracted when you were producing teeth!

--Why yes, so I have been told. Apparently I was a very sickly infant, and was lucky to grow up at all; perhaps that is why I am so worried about Pauli. He does seem a little quieter now.

--Yes. And I think we can find something to rub on his gums which will soothe him, too. Come with me to the infirmary. And by the way, Herr Zellek, I do not think anyone could call your son sickly.

He followed her meekly though the corridors.

--Herr Zellek... How did you manage to find me? You know my name, of course, but...

--Oh, that was easy! After Mass I asked our priest where I could find a beautiful Polish nun dressed... *so*... with a beautiful name... and of course he directed me here. Your name is beautiful, Magdalena. But where I come from, we always use little names. Mine as you know is Jiri; that is for Jaroslav; and I shall call you Magda. Yes, you are my Magda.

1928

Magda was supervising Paul's breakfast in the kitchen. Heinrich was trying something out on the piano.

There was a step on the stairs, a key in the lock, and the sound of a stick and hat on the hallstand.

--Pa!

Jiri came into the kitchen. He was carrying a loaf of bread, a newspaper and the mail, all of which he dropped onto the table before kissing Magda lightly and stroking Paul's fair hair.

--Pauli! What a good boy! I can see you have eaten a good breakfast.

--Yes. I've eaten yours too, Pa.

--You are most welcome to it! But I would like some coffee, please, darling.

Magda moved the bread and the newspaper before pouring him a cup.

--Thank you, ah, yes…

Jiri reached into his inside pocket and brought out a wad of notes. Devaluation was less than it had been, but there was still a discrepancy between the impressive wad and what it actually represented.

Magda, though, was pleased as she counted it.

--So much?

--Yes. The new girl didn't turn up last night, so I sang all the evening. So, Pauli, who was Pa?

--Little Tommy Tucker.

--And what did little Tommy Tucker do?

--He sang for his supper, said Paul in English.

Magda had queried the usefulness of teaching Paul English, but Jiri persisted; if they moved to England, or even America, he said, it would be useful for the boy; and besides, whoever spoke only one language?

Jiri continued,

--It's as well I don't have a voice class this morning, I don't think I have much left!

--What time did you get in?

--About four; I didn't want to disturb you and Paul so I went in with Heini.

--And you are going to work again tonight? When will you sleep?

--Well, I may have a nap this afternoon, when Pauli has his. I'm at the *Kino* later, and I don't want to fall asleep at the piano… it's happened before and the management don't like it. Oh, I forgot; if you are going to be a darling and brush my evening jacket, it must stink of smoke, if you look in the pocket there are some cigars and ciggies for you and Heini.

Jiri did not smoke, having realised that his voice did not like it, but if anyone offered him a cigarette or cigar he 'took it for later'. Magda and Heinrich never had to buy any and there were often enough to offer to guests.

Jiri drank his coffee and took up the letters. One was to Jiri as Heinrich's agent, offering a cello recital date; a bill from the conservatoire for Jiri's lessons; a cheque, for no great amount, from the Treichlers at the glass factory, and one from Budapest.

--Ferzi Balinkay. He wants me to visit... he has someone coming from England about translating his books, and wants me to act as, well, a sort of interpreter. Heini! Heini!

Heinrich appeared in the doorway.

--Heini, is there anything I can do for us in Budapest? Anyone I can see? And I might take a few glass samples there.

--I'll be thinking. Where will you stay?

--Ferzi invites me to their home.

Silence. Jiri was wondering whether he could bear to stay at the Balinkays'. The last time he had been there had been for Mikki Balinkay's funeral.

He and Flora Loudon had not long been back in the Pallin villa after his discharge from the Mühlethurnen Institute; she was staying with him until he was well enough to be independent. One morning he had wondered why the newspaper had not been brought in. Flora came into the salon; together they had read the brief news item 'Intrepid Young Hungarian Aviator Dies in Freak Crash'. Jiri had insisted on going to the funeral; it was the least he could do for the best comrade he ever had. He had been literally supported by Flora and his new valet, Ernst. The Balinkays had been shocked by his appearance, and as he had worn his Ulan uniform and medals in tribute to Mikki, who was so proud of his friend's decorations, he had acquired a reputation as a wounded war hero.

But that had been eight years ago and much had happened to Jiri since then. Holding Ferzi's letter, suddenly Jiri thought how nice it would be to go to a large, comfortable house, away from this cramped Berlin apartment where he was constantly reminded that meals, clean shirts and polished shoes did not silently appear when wanted. Both Ferzi and Mr Balinkay would have a valet; one of them would doubtless be assigned to help him dress, bathe, shave…

--It will save a great deal of money if I stay with them, he announced.

Ferzi was still living with his parents. They had both aged; Mr Balinkay's moustache was as black as ever, but possibly he now had some cosmetic help; Madame Balinkay was grey-haired. She shed tears when Jiri embraced her; he had been so fond of Mikki… it was wonderful to see him so much better, though still very thin, and you must be tired after your journey… and Ferzi tells me that you are a father? To think of little Jiri having a son! His mother… a tragedy?

--Sadly, Madame Mama, we lost her, but Paul is being very well looked after. He is a fine boy.

--Not a little shrimp like you were, Master Jiri? grinned Mr Balinkay.

--No, sir; he is very like my late father, who was twice the man I am.

--Well, well. Mr Balinkay clapped him heartily on the shoulder, something Jiri had learned to put up with from many similarly large men over the years. You have done your duty to the empire and the King Emperor, Jiri. You have always had plenty of pluck, like poor Mikki.

Jiri basked in the comforts of the Balinkay household. The food was wonderful, and he thought that he must be gaining weight; he slept long and well. He and Ferzi visited the newly extended Gellert Turkish baths; as they relaxed in the steam room,

Ferzi explained the situation. He had now published three novels. Jiri hoped fervently that he would not wish to discuss these in detail as he, Jiri, had been unable to finish reading any of them. At first he had told himself that he was still convalescent, so not up to serious reading. Then he had tried again, only to suffer from headaches, although there appeared to be nothing wrong with his vision. Finally he had made it about two-thirds of the way through the second novel, and was beginning to think that he had grasped the gist of the story, such as it was, only to find that meaning had somehow slipped away. He was well able to read other things in Hungarian: newspapers, magazines, he even enjoyed the novels of Lajos Zilahy, which Ferzi regarded with scorn, but which Jiri thought truly heartrending, but somehow Ferzi's style escaped him.

So he merely nodded sagely when Ferzi discoursed at length about these works. Somehow, an English publisher had got word of them, but they would need to be translated as there were sadly few readers of Hungarian in England. The intermediary was a lady called Zarah FitzHay; apparently she had met some charming Hungarians in London, and was learning the language. With the help of these contacts, she hoped to produce English versions of at least one of Ferzi's novels. The possibility of this, and the decision as to which text would be selected, hung upon the success of her visit. The problem was, Ferzi continued, that this lady actually seemed to know very little Hungarian, while Ferzi's English was rather limited. Who better than Jiri, with his language skills and Viennese charm, to work some magic? Ferzi knew his friend well enough to have learned that Jiri, small, apparently ingenuous and vulnerable, yet strangely attractive, could usually get results.

They were to have lunch, Ferzi explained, at a very smart Budapest restaurant, where discussions would be opened.

Jiri got off to a slightly rocky start by being a few minutes late. He had been shopping; in general he kept his gambling profits as private pocket money, and as he had been doing quite well recently he decided to visit an excellent Hungarian tailor and to purchase some new shirts, ties and socks. He was also contemplating some lovely pyjamas. Meanwhile he was wearing a rather old-fashioned grey suit of excellent quality, with violets in his buttonhole.

As he entered the foyer of the restaurant, he saw at once that Ferzi was finding Miss FitzHay hard going. She was probably about their age, with bobbed hair, fashionable make-up and festoons of beads, scarves and bags. After her rather laboured Hungarian greeting, Ferzi had taken heart and launched into enthusiastic descriptions of current trends in European fiction, which had clearly left her behind. Jiri ran up to them, apologising profusely in his accented, but fluent English.

--Forgive me, Gnädiges Fräulein, should I rather say, gracious lady, I am unpardonable! I beg forgiveness: with which he bowed, clicked his heels, kissed her hand and introduced himself as Jaroslav Felix von Tarnheim Zellek.

This seemed to break the ice.

--I fear my friend Ferzi has neglected to offer you a cocktail; he is of course an artist, a poet, one who thinks only of higher matters, but for myself, I would welcome refreshment while we contemplate lunch.

After all, he thought, Ferzi is paying for this.

Things were improving; before long they were seated at a table, with a waiter hovering beside them.

Ferzi advised on the choice of food, with guidance from the waiter about wine... the more the better, thought Jiri, who knew that alcohol always helped matters along.

--Ferzi here tells me that you live in Berlin, Mr Zellek?

--Oh, do please call me Jiri! Yes, indeed, that is so.

--Berlin is becoming quite popular with English writers, although perhaps you are not in those intellectual circles?

--Indeed, I am no intellectual! But I have met some English writers.

--Really? I don't suppose you know young Wystan Auden?

There surely could not be two English poets in Berlin called Wystan Auden, thought Jiri.

--Well actually, yes, I have met him; is he not about twenty-one, with a longish face and hair, so...

Jiri indicated Auden's hairstyle.

--Why yes, that's him! She was obviously impressed. Do tell me, Jiri, how did you meet?

Jiri thought frantically.

--It was at an evening entertainment.

That should cover it, he thought. The Cozy Corner was certainly entertaining, and continued to be so throughout the evening and indeed, night. Jiri had been standing in for the regular pianist when Wystan had got into conversation and bought him several drinks; fortunately Jiri had realised that firstly he must stop drinking and secondly he must not

265

play or sing anything too provocative. Certainly not 'Das Lila Lied'. He did not want to end up in bed with Wystan Auden or any of his friends.

Next she asked him about Ferzi's novels, which was hardly less dangerous ground. Which was his favourite?

--It is hard to say… they are all… equally… Perhaps the most recent one.

Jiri had quite liked the cover design, which was in what he called *moderne* style, rather like his favourite dressing gown.

--I was thinking that *Unanchored Vessels* might appeal more to an English reader, she continued. Squinting at Jiri, she added, I wonder whether perhaps you were the inspiration for Tomas…

On opening *Unanchored Vessels*, Jiri had rather hoped that it would be a tale of seafaring life. But this was not so. Which one of the characters was Tomas, and what had happened to him, in as far as anything happened to anyone in Ferzi's novels…?

It was at this point that Ferzi was called away to a telephone call, which proved to be from his publisher.

Zarah lit a cigarette in her long, amber holder. By now they had all had a reasonable amount to drink.

--Ah! I so love the Hungarian language, she cried: I recall the very first lines I learned from the wonderful poet…

And with this she began to declaim from the works of the national poet Sandor Petofi.

--Tell me, Jiri darling, what was the very first piece of Hungarian you learned?

It was unfortunate that just then the gypsy band went for their lunch break. Apart from a hum of polite conversation, the room was silent as Jiri's resonant, clear and rather high-pitched voice told her,

--Stop doing that or I'll smack your bottom.

This warning had come from Mikki Balinkay's nanny and was, for good reason, the first complete Hungarian sentence that Jiri had learned.

Ferzi re-entered the dining room to find most of the diners and all the waiters convulsed with ill-suppressed laughter, Zarah FitzHay looking extremely embarrassed and confused (had she heard aright, and did he mean it?) and Jiri wearing an expression of complete innocence.

--Why do we not order dessert? he suggested. I will have ice cream, any flavour except pistachio.

--Why, sir, do you not care for that flavour? asked the waiter.

--No. I had it once and it made me throw up.

This did for any measure of self-control in the dining room.

--Vanilla with chocolate sauce, sir. With the compliments of the manager.

--How delightful. See, Ferzi, I have a free dessert! So perhaps you could run to some champagne, to celebrate dear Madam Zarah's decision to recommend your novels to her firm. How very perspicacious of you, dear lady!

The fact that he could pronounce perspicacious gave Jiri immense pleasure; he felt that he was doing extremely well. Rising to his feet, he repeated his remarks in Hungarian, adding the information that Ferzi's great contribution to modern European fiction, *Unanchored Vessels*, was about to reach an Anglophone readership. The restaurant exploded into applause. The gypsy band, returning, struck up a czardas. Miss FitzHay was congratulated on all sides for being the means of bringing a Hungarian masterpiece to a wider public. Ferzi was congratulated on being a literary genius and a true Magyar. As for Jiri, several clients had drifted over, wishing him well for his stay in Budapest, and adding that they were sure he still had a sweet little bottom that one would be happy to smack any time.

I have to get him out while we are winning, and before he starts singing, was Ferzi's surprisingly practical thought. But the champagne had appeared; backed by the gypsy band, Jiri brought the house down with some wild Hungarian folk songs and a selection from Franz Lehar, followed by a couple of smokily seductive Berlin cabaret numbers. Budapest appeared to be full of aspiring authors, most of whom were propositioning Zarah FitzHay. In fact it was some time before he could summon a taxi to return Zarah to her hotel... he hoped she would be able to get as far as the lift... Jiri put his head on Ferzi's shoulder and appeared to be ready to go to sleep.

--Just remember, Ferzi, he said as he dropped off. Be sure to send her a note in the morning saying how delighted you are to accept the offer of British publication, and that you have instructed your solicitor to draw up the contract.

Later Jiri rather hazily recalled that he had had a wonderful luncheon. It was a pity that he had thrown up so violently at the Balinkays' but he had made it to the lavatory, his new tie was undamaged, Mr Balinkay's valet had put him to bed, and the next morning he had been pretty much *in Ordnung*.

He thought that, overall, Ferzi was quite pleased with the way things had gone.

The morning after Jiri's return from Budapest, Magda looked at him as she poured his coffee. Last night he had insisted on seeing Paul, leaving the presents he had bought him beside the bed; he had given Magda and Heinrich their gifts, and, saying that the long train journeys had made his back tired, although the thermal baths in Budapest had done it a world of good, he went to bed and instantly to sleep.

She had rarely seen him look so well; or at least, he looked much better than when he had left two weeks ago. Food and sleep had done him good; he had a new haircut and was wearing a new tie.

--Jiri, called Heinrich, have you been singing in Budapest?

--Only in the evenings at the Balinkays'. I think the rest has done my voice good; I believe I have a class this afternoon with Professor Weissenborn.

--I'd like to hear you.

They moved to the piano, which dominated the single living room.

--What shall it be, Jiri?

--This one; I have been singing it, it makes me think of Mikki, although I don't suppose the Aviation Corps got as far as the Ganges.

He pulled out 'On Wings of Song'. Heinrich played a few bars, then they began in earnest.

Auf Flügeln des Gesanges,
Herzliebchen, trag' ich dich fort,
Fort nach den Fluren des Ganges,
Dort weiß ich den schönsten Ort.

So, as Vernon Dakins climbed the stairs to the apartment, he heard Mendelssohn's setting of Heine's poem. Jiri's voice always came as a surprise; in a confined space it was an almost palpable entity, and as he was of the 'stand still and just sing' style of performer (except when he had to double as a nightclub singer) it often seemed quite separate from his persona.

Magda opened the door to him and they waited in silence until the final notes.

--Jiri, Heinrich was saying, that was much more like it! Singing in the clubs was ruining it. You will have to stop.

--Yes, said Vernon. You will. I need to speak to you alone, Jiri. You have been having far too much fun at the Cozy Corner.

--Take me out for coffee and ice cream, Vernon. As long as I am at the conservatoire in time.

Paul ran up to his godfather.

--Look, Herr Verni. Pa brought me this.

It was a model motor car, which wound up and ran across the floor.

--Oh, I would like one of those! You are a lucky boy, Paul.

Vernon and Jiri were walking in the park.

--I need a private chat with you, Jiri, before you get your coffee and ice cream.

--Very well… do you know, spring has come? It is lovely, even here in the city.

--I meant that Jiri, about the clubs, and not just what they do to your voice, although that is your own concern.

--Verni, you know that it is in the line of business, although I am sure that none of the gossip is really of interest to your embassy. I have a family to support; Magda is a wonderful housekeeper, and Heini does earn something from recitals and orchestra work, but I am trying to put any profits back into the glass business, and somehow we do seem always to need extra income.

--That, Jiri, may be because the aristocratic and prosperous bourgeois tastes of your youth aren't likely to be eradicated. Only the best for Jiri von Tarnheim Zellek.

Jiri shrugged.

--Actually, he said, one does have fun, although of course one does have to be careful. And Heini is right about the voice. If I could just go as a customer, now and then, and not have to be there all night, or sing.

--Jiri, you don't have to be there all night. But there is more. How is my godson doing? I must say he seems a fine lad.

If Jiri was surprised at the change of subject, he was always ready to talk about Paul.

--Indeed he is, Verni! I cannot believe how well he eats, and he has so much energy, he runs Magda off her feet! And I am sure he is quite intelligent; I am teaching him English.

--What about music?

--Ah well. He seems easily bored.

Jiri recalled how, when he was even younger than Paul, his father would sit him on his lap, and help him to pick out tunes on the piano; and surely Paul, although certainly noisy, did not sing much, and if he did, it was hardly tuneful. Perhaps it would come in time. He fell silent.

--The thing is, Jiri, do you think that apartment and that neighbourhood is going to be quite the best place for Paul to grow up?

--He is too young for school.

--But when he is old enough? I am Paul's godfather, and of course I would wish him to have a Catholic education, as I'm sure do you and Magda. What, really, is there to keep you in Berlin?

There was a short silence, then Jiri mused aloud…

--Well… that audition with Berlin Radio came to nothing; and people prefer the talkies now, so *Kino* work is beginning to drop off; and I have been with Professor Weissenborn almost since we got here, and I have learned a great deal… and, between ourselves, Heini has been applying for positions in Munich.

--Munich! Jiri that would be perfect. There are things you could do for me there too.

--It would be more like home for us both.

--I thought Magda was Polish.

--I meant me and Heini. I'd need to go to Pallin, just to see about the factory finances… and perhaps I could get the piano and some furniture. But, Verni, I should be sorry not to see you so often; you are a good friend and comrade to us all.

Vernon looked at his companion. Yes; besides the business angle, that was clearly how Jiri saw him. Apart perhaps from his relationship with Heinrich, poor fickle, flirtatious Jiri really preferred women. Anything further between them would just give him a hold over Vernon that he might, under certain circumstances, decide to use.

--Just one more thing… perhaps it might be as well for you and Magda to get married.

Jiri and Vernon had met in church. Not leaving the cabaret until it was light, Jiri had attended early Mass before going home. He was still wearing his make-up; he used very little, just enough to make him look better under the lights, but, combined with his evening dress, the traces gave him a more inviting appearance than his actual tastes warranted. Vernon had approached him by the holy water stoup, found that he spoke fluent English, bought him breakfast, was intrigued and began seeing him often, finally recruiting him for occasional verbal reports to the British embassy. Somehow, Jiri persuaded him to become Paul's godfather; practising Catholics with useful influence were hard to come by in a working-class district of Berlin. Jiri explained that he had himself baptised Paul shortly after the boy's birth; his views on limbo and baptismal regeneration being absolutely traditional. But, he added, although it was said that anyone could perform a valid baptism, perhaps it might be as well to make sure, and anyway, Paul would need a baptismal certificate later on. So Paul became Paul Vernon Zellek; after all, the V could always be converted to von Tarnheim.

MUNICH

So, by 1929/30, the Zelleks were living in a fairly spacious apartment in a good middle-class district of Munich. They had a maid, and a girl to clean the flat and their shoes; Jiri had arranged for the pick of his parents' furniture to be removed from Pallin, including his piano. His income from the factory greatly increased in the general economic upturn. The art glass of Anton Zellek's time had been replaced by cheaper, more mass-produced household items and ornaments. The Wolfi and Otto ranges had been supplemented by Florianware, with its stylised floral motifs in Art Deco style. Jiri's taste, which Christa had characterised as that of a provincial hausfrau, hit exactly the right note for their customers and the 10% he had always taken from the profits now became a useful sum. In addition he was acting as an agent and tour manager for various musicians, thanks to his language skills and European and English contacts; Vernon Dakins continued to employ him on a casual basis. Heinrich now had a flat of his own and, it seemed, a life of his own.

Paul started school and got on well. He remembered little of their life in Berlin, and later it seemed to him that these years in Munich were the happiest of his childhood. The city was beautiful; there was a marvellous flower and vegetable market; his parents went constantly to the theatre, the opera, and to concerts; his father gave a few recitals accompanied by Heinrich, who was almost as brilliant a pianist as he was cellist; sometimes for the second half, they would change places and Jiri would accompany Heinrich's cello.

Perhaps during these years in Munich there was only one disappointment, which affected Magda considerably, Jiri to some extent and Paul not at all.

In the spring of 1932, when Jiri was due to leave for England, escorting a group of musicians on a series of recitals in London, Manchester and Birmingham, Magda told him that she suspected that she might be pregnant. He was delighted; he was sure it would be a little girl, and they would call her Valerie, and she would have Magda's looks and sing like an angel...

Three weeks later he returned, with a list of useful contacts, various invitations to stay any time he was in England, a suitcase full of dirty washing and a grinding backache. He looked as though he had gone the entire time without food or sleep; neither was a high priority with him, and the tour had presented all the challenges of artistic temperaments, missing luggage, inappropriate halls and impossible digs, as well as accidents and emergencies. Jiri had even performed at Wigmore Hall himself, getting quite nice reviews, although these mostly centred on his plucky ability to step in at the last moment. He'd also taken every opportunity to see and hear theatre, opera and music, catching a matinee performance of *The Dubarry* at His Majesty's Theatre. He was entranced by Anny Ahlers, whom he had seen performing in Germany, and very struck by the voice of the leading man, tenor Heddle Nash; in fact he bought the sheet music of Nash's big number, 'If I Am Dreaming', which he thought might suit his own voice quite well.

He had been looking forward to some cosseting and perhaps even a couple of days in bed. Instead he found Magda recovering from a miscarriage, the maid run off her feet, and Paul demanding attention. Jiri had coped, mainly by asking Heinrich to Come At Once; but somewhere, perhaps unconsciously, he realised that an addition to the family would mean that he would get much less of Magda's time and attention. It would have been fun to have a daughter, but he came to terms with the disappointment extremely quickly.

Jiri continued to regard Paul with something like awe. He was so strong, sturdy and tall; he ate everything put before him, went to bed with little protest, and was generally independent and obedient. Although Jiri constantly referred to his own wonderful childhood, he seemed to recall that he had been nothing like that. At the same time, he seemed unable to understand why anyone closely connected with him had no innate feeling for rhythm and pitch, or had any physical hesitation when faced with hazards… fast horses, high places, deep water, aggressive situations had never held any fear for Jiri and he had to remind himself that not everyone was like that. And of course, Paul was still very young.

At this time, Jiri was able to keep a horse, riding in the parks and woodlands around the city. In doing this he fell in with two German former Ulan officers, men only slightly older than himself. One had been given medical discharge after serious chest wounds had permanently affected his health; the other had resigned in order to marry and devote himself to family business interests. The former, Fritz, drove his own gleaming motor, and he would call for Jiri and Hermann. In their boots and breeches they would go off for a day of riding, bathing, talking, lunching and, towards evening, drinking. They indulged in horseplay and relived days on manoeuvres. It was soon 'du' between them.

One afternoon Fritz paid a duty call on his great aunt Adelheid. He mentioned, to make conversation, that he was well enough to ride these days, and that he had met a fellow called Jiri von Tarnheim Zellek, who was good company although an Austrian from some unknown corner of the former Habsburg empire.

--von Tarnheim? He must be a relative of Karel von Tarnheim; there were very few of them left. She ordered her companion to fetch down the Almanach de Gotha. If he is Karel's nephew, he must be the last male von Tarnheim.

--Ah, that, Auntie, is where you are wrong for once! Jiri has a son, a fine boy with blond hair.

--Then he is hardly a von Tarnheim. Who is the child's mother?

--I think Jiri said his wife is Polish.

While Jiri made no secret of the fact that Magda was not Paul's mother, he did not volunteer the information, so that it was not widely known.

--A nobody, I suppose. The blood must be sadly diluted. But this Jiri, what is he like?

--Nothing much of him; he's quite a small, thin fellow, though stronger than he looks.

--Hmm. Karel was, or is, tall. I suppose he is still alive. Dark?

--Oh yes. Jiri has dark hair, always wants cutting!

--And... the von Tarnheims have always thought a great deal of themselves. They are of course the oldest family in that Principality, but one would think that they were second only to the royal house. And they are notorious for violent tempers.

Fritz had actually heard Jiri described as a jumped-up, arsey little bastard with a nasty streak, but felt he had better rephrase this:

--Well, I have to say that our little Jiri fits what you say. He doesn't throw his weight around, not that there is much to throw, but he has that air about him... makes you want to thump him sometimes, but you know what I mean... and somehow he's not a person to provoke unless you have to.

--Yes, my boy. I think this is your friend. She pointed to the entry in the Almanach.

His mother was Gisela von Tarnheim; she married this Zellek person, whoever he might have been. So actually this Jiri is only half a von Tarnheim. Karel married his cousin Valerie von Tarnheim, although that ended badly.

--Sorry, Auntie, this is getting confusing.

--Gisela and Karel had a cousin called Valerie. She was also von Tarnheim; her father was Karel and Gisela's father's younger brother. Karel and Valerie had a daughter. Here she is: Christina Maria. It was said that Karel wished to repair the family line by getting Jiri, his fuller name is Jaroslav, and this Christa married. Clearly something has gone wrong. Ah, I remember, there was something about Christa running off to America while Jaroslav was recovering from his war injuries. Decorated by the Emperor Carl, I think.

--Well, Auntie, given what we know now about race and inheritance, perhaps it was as well that those cousins did not marry. Young Paul is clearly an excellent specimen of German boyhood.

Fritz, Hermann and Jiri inevitably discussed the political situation.

Jiri did not like Adolf Hitler.

--I'm afraid he is too like me: an arrogant little Austrian. Although I have a better singing voice.

The others laughed.

--And, Jiri, you did not start out as a house painter from Linz.

--True, Hermann. I have earned a living in several ways, but never with a ladder and paint brush. Do you think it is difficult?

Hermann now pictured Jiri perched on a ladder, wielding a brush and singing a selection from Viennese operetta...

--I don't advise you to try it, old man...

He and Jiri laughed again. But Fritz looked more serious.

--He has great public appeal, though. A strong leader with the right ideas is what this country needs.

--Perhaps... but what are the right ideas?

--I think he is right about the Jews. There are too many of them about; they are not our kind of people, and they have too much influence.

--I think many of my kind of people are Jews, said Jiri. I work with some wonderful musicians and I know they are from Jewish families. Of course they know I am a Catholic, and we have no need to discuss religion. And one can learn from some synagogue cantors; why, Joseph Schmidt, that one hears on the wireless so often, is a cantor. What a voice that is; we studied under the same singing teacher in Berlin; and do you know, another reason why I adore him... he makes me look like a giant!

--What?

--Oh, of course, don't you wonder why, with his marvellous command of Italian opera, he never appears on the stage? I will tell you: he is at least six inches shorter than me!

--Jiri, you're making it up!

--Hermann, no, I assure you, it is true.

--You're a liar.

--I am not.

A mock fight was about to start.

--For goodness' sake, you two are behaving like stupid kids. Stop it.

Jiri was inured to being told to shut up and stop whatever it was he was doing, as this had been happening to him since the age of two. Poor Fritz, he thought; I suppose he is not feeling too well today.

--What a shiner, Jiri! Magda been giving you what for... or was it a jealous husband?

--Bloody stupid... just got into a bit of an argument.

Jiri grimaced as he swung into the saddle.

--What? More?

--Bloody stupid. Got somebody's boot in my ribs.

--Are you sure you should be out today?

--It is better than yesterday. I have taken some aspirin. Fresh air will do me good.

Jiri was obviously not prepared to discuss his evident injuries further.

--Did you find out what happened to him, Hermann? I suspect one of those gangs of Jewish thugs picked on him.

--Well, as far as I can gather, it was a gang of thugs. But not Jewish ones. In fact, the opposite.

--What do you mean?

--Well, if you must have it, badge wearers picking on an elderly Jewish fellow and his grandson. Jiri gets involved... and... things got out of hand. Police broke it up before Jiri got even more than he did. And they gave him a warning...

--Quite right. A gentleman, which I suppose Jiri is, should not involve himself with such degenerate lowlife. If he was humiliated by a police warning, so much the better. Hermann, I know Jiri is good fellow at heart, and he certainly comes from an aristocratic family, but if he will associate with degenerates, he will inevitably get into trouble. And it is good that he understands what the consequences may be. I know he was in the Ulans, even if they were the Austrians, and there is no doubt that he has courage...

--I should think not!

--Even to a foolhardy degree...

Fritz began to cough.

--Don't get excited about it, old boy. Look, Jiri should be able to look after himself.

Even as he said this Hermann knew it was not true.

In the summer of 1933, Jiri was away from Munich, accompanying a group of Bavarian folksingers on an extended tour of Holland, Belgium and Northern France. At least to begin with, Dutch was not one of his languages but since none of the folksingers spoke anything except German, and that with a strong Bavarian accent, his skills were invaluable. He got all of them (bar one or two) back in time for Oktoberfest; he was predictably exhausted, but armed with a supply of risqué anecdotes that kept Fritz, Hermann, Heinrich and Vernon amused for weeks.

After an absence, Jiri noticed changes; one of them was that with the new government legislation people were being arrested and others losing their jobs. Heinrich was finding it more difficult to get work and had been dismissed from his post at the opera; together they planned and had almost finalised some prospects for Heinrich in Boston, where several of his colleagues had contacts.

Oktoberfest, the first one from which Jews had been excluded from the fairground, came and went. Jiri and his friends rode, joked and drank in the autumn woods. Magda was well; Paul was approaching his tenth birthday, and looking forward to joining the DJ, the junior branch of the Hitlerjugend. Neither Magda nor the boy could understand why Jiri insisted on postponing this until the following spring, and hoped that he would change his mind over the coming weeks. As the date of Heinrich's departure approached, Magda felt that Jiri was unusually tense and volatile, and it was at the beginning of November that she was startled by an urgent ringing at the downstairs door. Peering through the frosted glass, she saw four figures.

--Please, please… Frau Zellek? Quickly… please…

No coward, Magda opened the door, although not widely. Three young men stood panting outside, two of them supporting Jiri, who was almost unrecognisable, his clothing torn and his face covered with blood. One of the trio ran off; the other two brought Jiri inside and closed the door, against which they leaned, gasping. As they did so, running feet were heard passing in the street.

--We'll go as soon as they're round the corner, Frau Zellek. Rudi will lose them once they get to the bahnhof.

The speaker opened the door cautiously, looked around, and then motioned to his companion.

--Now.

--Thank you... thank you... I hope you will be all right... was all that Magda could say before turning to her husband. He lay curled up on the floor, clutching his ribs and moaning.

--I have to get him upstairs. Magda called to the maid and between them they got Jiri into the flat, where he collapsed on the salon carpet.

--Where is Paul? He must not see his father like this.

--Playing with the neighbour boy, Frau Zellek. I will go and see if they can keep him there for a while.

--Yes. Thank you. Please go.

Magda knew that she would need to establish what was wrong with Jiri before attempting to move him further; she might already have done damage by bringing him upstairs, but that had to be.

She fetched a cloth and wiped his face.

--Jiri, Jiri, liebling... it's me, darling, you are all right...

Jiri seemed to hear this, which was a good sign, and tried to answer, but broke into a series of cries and gasps. The maid had gone downstairs and must have admitted someone on her way out, as a knock now came at the door of the flat itself.

--Who is it?

--I am a doctor. Frau Zellek? Please let me in.

--I have not sent for a doctor.

--No, but I have heard that your husband needs one. I am Doctor Weisenthal; I live at number 39.

Magda opened the door. He was an elderly man in a dark coat and hat, carrying a doctor's bag. He knelt at once beside Jiri, then, removing his outer garments, he began to loosen Jiri's clothing and examine him.

--Do we need to get him to a hospital?

--I hope not, and I think moving him would do more harm than good. Are you used to nursing, madam?

--Yes. I have some nursing training.

--Good. Then I think we shall be able to manage, especially if you can get some help during the nights.

Some time later, Jiri was in bed and sleeping after a morphine injection. Magda had protested against this, explaining that after his war experiences Jiri was terrified of morphine addiction and hated needles.

--I will try to make sure that this is the only time, Frau Zellek. But he will have enough to put up with without enduring this initial night.

--What are his injuries, doctor?

--Perhaps he has been lucky. No ribs broken, although one at least is cracked. Cut on his cheek, but that will heal. I have stitched it, as you saw. It will hardly show. I am more concerned about possible internal injuries; for those we will have to wait and see, and I want him in bed for at least the next few days, while we watch, and, Frau Zellek, I would suppose that any... earlier... injuries he has may be affected. You mentioned the war?

--Yes. He was wounded on the Russian Front, but had some successful treatment afterwards. His leg hardly bothers him; in fact, he is able to ride, swim and even play tennis! Sometimes he says it aches after a long day, or it is stiff in the morning. But his back is perhaps more troublesome, although generally...

--I think we must be prepared for a bout of back pain after this. But the main thing is to watch him through the night. Call me if there is any change; and I will be here in the morning.

Doctor, thank you. Thank you. Your bill?

--No. Your husband was injured helping a member of our synagogue congregation. It is an honour to treat him. It is the least I can do.

The next few days were extremely anxious and unpleasant. Jiri ran a high temperature and was quite ill. He could not be left alone at night; Magda shared the nursing with Heinrich and, surprisingly, with Vernon Dakins, who turned up unexpectedly and proved most helpful. One night when Vernon was with Jiri, the doctor drew Magda discreetly aside.

--Forgive me, Frau Zellek, but your husband is calling for someone named Christi. If she, or perhaps he, is a relative or friend, could I suggest that she be sent for? It is piteous to hear him, and you know that it is important to keep him quiet and calm.

Magda flushed. The doctor clearly thought that Jiri had a mistress somewhere. Whatever he got up to on tour, she was pretty sure he had no one in Munich.

--I'm afraid that will not be possible, doctor. I think Christi is Jiri's cousin, Christa von Tarnheim. They were close as children, and I believe she nursed him for a while when he came out of hospital in 1918. They lost touch after the war; I think she is somewhere in America now. Jiri hardly ever mentions her.

--Ah, that accounts for it; often in these circumstances patients revert to earlier experiences of similar illness. Well, we must just do the best we can to reassure him.

Jiri gradually regained some sort of consciousness, his first thought being that all this was terribly inconvenient just as Heinrich was about to leave for America. Again, Vernon was able to be of assistance, undertaking some of the arrangements.

Jiri had begun to recover, but was still bedridden. Vernon was able to lift him and then lower him onto the pillows so that he was in an upright position. Jiri closed his eyes, and opened them again as the pain in his back and ribs slowly began to subside...

--Better?

--No. My arse hurts.

--So it bloody well should. It's all the colours of the rainbow, plus a good big graze from some bastard's toecap. Pity you can't see it. It's quite spectacular! We could charge ten pfennigs a look.

--Don't make me laugh, Verni... it's agony...

--How about some breakfast?

--No.

--Well, just try. Here.

--So much butter on the bread. It's greasy.

--Try it without.

--Too dry.

Magda appeared.

--Jiri, you have a visitor.

It was Hermann, carrying a huge bunch of hothouse flowers and a beribboned box of chocolates.

--I just thought these might cheer you up, Jiri. From me and Fritz. I know he likes sweets, Frau Zellek.

Hermann was actually horrified by what he saw, as Jiri did indeed look and feel terrible, although he brightened up at the sight of the flowers and bonbons.

--How lovely to see a fresh face! Thank you for coming, Hermann.

--That's typical Jiri, snorted Vernon. Here we've been bathing his head and wiping his bottom for five days, and what do we get? No thanks! Yet in you come with a box of chocs, which I'm sure the doc won't let you have, Jiri, and it's all sweetness and light! Well, I'm off.

I'll see you later, Magda, he added as he went out.

Hermann spent some time keeping Jiri company before sensing that he was tiring. He promised to come again and went to speak to Magda.

--Frau Zellek, Jiri is being seen by a doctor, isn't he?

--Yes, of course, although not our usual one.

--Oh?

--Yes; on the night Jiri was injured our neighbour, Doctor Weisenthal, got to hear of it and offered his services free of charge. He has been wonderful. Several times he has stayed with Jiri all night.

--I believe he is a very good man. And I think I understand why he feels he has to do what he can here. But, Frau Zellek, please be careful. You realise of course that Weisenthal is a Jew. Having a Jewish doctor at the moment may not be advisable, especially since Jiri is, well, a bit of a known troublemaker. Actually, Frau Zellek, Fritz asked me to warn you. Don't worry too much; that beating Jiri took when he foolishly waded into the synagogue row was probably meant to teach him a lesson, and if he stays out of trouble it will look as though it has worked; and from what Fritz tells me, he is not in the front line of undesirables...

--But... we are not Jews; we are Catholics, the Führer has signed a concordat with the Vatican; I am Polish, Jiri is Austrian, Paul was born here in Germany.

--Exactly. So as long as you don't... I mean, as long as you act like good German citizens, all will be well. It makes me so angry to see poor Jiri. If only he could learn to control his temper... You know as well as I do that he's one of the pluckiest fellows alive. May I come and see him again soon?

Jiri was convalescent, and still being very difficult and fractious by the time of Heinrich's departure. Magda's instinct had been to invite their old friend for a farewell supper, but Jiri's fragile state meant that this would certainly be a hugely emotional ordeal. So Heinrich came to the flat, went into Jiri's bedroom and shut the door. He was not there long. He came out in tears, embraced Magda and Paul, and left. Jiri literally turned his face to the wall. He said nothing, and ate nothing, for two days. He clearly cried for much of that time. Then he got up, shaved, announced that he wanted breakfast immediately, and began work on the letters that had accumulated during his illness. He did not mention Heinrich's name for several weeks.

Doctor Weisenthal quizzed Magda about Jiri's state of health under normal circumstances; he asked some rather strange questions, she thought.

Was Paul their only child? Well, actually Magda was

not Paul's mother; last year she had become pregnant, but miscarried.

--And, forgive the question, you do nothing to... prevent?

--No. We are Catholics.

--Ah well. There is still time... you are how old, Frau Zellek?

--I am five years younger than Jiri, so, thirty-three.

--It is nothing! And at that time, did your doctor give any explanation?

--Oh, said Magda bitterly, what they always say. It often happens, and sometimes it is because the child would not be as it should be.

--You and your husband are not related in any way?

--No, not at all! We are not even of the same nationality. Why do you ask?

--It does not matter, Frau Zellek. Paul is a very fine child. And let us hope that some time in the future, your husband, who is somewhat exceptional, will be lucky enough to beget a perfect son or daughter.

The doctor also said that, given the current state of legislation and anti-Jewish feeling, it would be better if he ceased treating Jiri, although before doing so he would like to give him a short course of vitamin injections, which should cure his remaining problem of recurrent dizziness and faintness. Even Jiri had to admit that, firstly, the doctor gave such painless injections that he hardly knew they were happening, and secondly that he was feeling better than he had for months.

So they entered the period of Christmas and New Year. Jiri seemed determined to make this time even more magical than usual: he enjoyed the Christmas tree as much as Paul did, he sang beautifully at midnight Mass, he skated on the municipal rink without complaining about his leg, he entered into the full round of entertainments, festivities, hospitality and concerts. In fact, Magda was able to enjoy his company, his lovemaking and his whimsicalities without anxiety, although he was sometimes in a strange, unusually nostalgic, mood. He told Magda and Paul about the Christmas traditions with which he had grown up, as these were rather different from those of either Poland or Bavaria. He described how the Krampus came around with Saint Nicolas on 6 December, admonishing naughty children to mend their ways if they wanted Christmas presents; Jiri had usually been warned, but somehow the Christ Child always relented and brought him lovely things on Christmas Eve. Then, in the mountains, where he had spent a few Christmasses, you had to watch out for the Perchten. Of course, in the daylight, he knew they were just Gustl and his friends dressed up, and he only pretended to be frightened, but at night he had thought about the real ones, the ones the boys had dressed up to frighten away. Grushenka said that for the rest of the year they were chained up inside big fir trees; sometimes you could hear them moaning and crying to be set free. But between Christmas and Epiphany they could roam about, trying to catch you, and if they did they would slit your stomach open and…

Magda gave him a warning glance.

--Oh, I was just a silly little boy, not a big sensible fellow like Pauli. I'm sure you are not scared by things of that sort, are you, Paul?

--No. They are not true.

Jiri was in a mischievous spirit. And he did, of course, believe in the Perchten.

--Well, you know... even if they are... we believe in our guardian angels, and the holy saints, so we have plenty of protection.

Paul said nothing. Some bigger boys, who were already in the Jung Volk, said that it was all nonsense, made up by parents and priests to make you do what they said. German boys must think for themselves; and Paul had already begun to doubt certain aspects of Catholic teaching.

One evening in the second week of January, his parents sat by the stove in the salon, Jiri leaning against Magda's knee. Outside the snow fell, the lamplight catching iridescent flakes. They were drinking coffee; Jiri had opened a box of his favourite chocolates.

--Darling, he said, we have been happy here, haven't we?

--Yes, Jiri... we are happy, especially now you are so much better.

--I mean, you like this flat, don't you?

--You know I do. I don't want to move anywhere.

--My darling, I am afraid that we may have to.

--What! Jiri, is it the rent? I am sure we could spend a little less, save more towards the rent?

He did not respond. She went on,

But, if we really have to, well, there are nice flats that would cost a bit less, and still be near to Paul's school...

--I mean, darling, that we have to leave Munich.

--What? You are not thinking of going back to Berlin?

--No, no, definitely not Berlin!

--Then Pallin, perhaps? That might be lovely; you own the villa there, Paul could go to the same school that you attended, we could come to some arrangement with the Treichlers...

--I had thought of that. I know you and Paul could be happy there. But Pallin is in Austria, and sometime soon there will be some sort of... I don't know... Anschluss. Magda, you do not think that I am a coward, do you?

--You, Jiri? Oh darling! My dearest, bravest boy!

This rather rare endearment from Magda was so like the things Christa had whispered to him during some of his worst nights after the war that Jiri felt that sickening lurch in the stomach that accompanied her recall, like a revenant. He went on,

--Well then, I can tell you that I do not want any more beatings in the street. I do not want Paul to grow into one of those young thugs who give such beatings. I do not want to see my friends taken to those camps, like the one they built just over in Dachau last year. I do not want to be taken to one myself.

--But Jiri, we are not Jews. We are Catholics. We are probably eligible for German citizenship.

--I do not want German citizenship. I do not want to be a citizen of a country which does the things I am witnessing, and I fear will do even worse before time is out. And make no mistake. I am a Slav. You are Polish. Who do you think will be declared undesirable after they have finished with the Jews? And I am already known as someone who disagrees with certain policies. Magda, I have arranged it. We are moving to London.

It never occurred to either of them that she might query the 'we'.

--But... your friends here... Heinrich, when he comes back?

--Magda, Heinrich will not come back. When his conducting engagement is over, he will find something else. A cellist of his calibre will always find an audience. I do not know when I shall see him again. I had thought... but never mind that now. Hermann, Fritz... they are German officers. They cannot change, although perhaps one day Hermann at least will become disillusioned with that Austrian house painter. Verni... ah, Magda, it is Verni who has been helping me. He has found us a flat in a part of London called Maida Vale. I have been there and it is really quite acceptable. I shall find work, and I am making some arrangements about selling the glass factory to the government, before they take it over by force; the proceeds will give us something to start on and in fact I have a bank account in London; my father opened it in 1902.

I shall need to travel over the next few months: to Pallin, to Tarnheim, and at least once to London; I shall make sure Paul continues with his English lessons. I expect us to be removed by Easter.

Jiri was standing facing her. His tone and expression were entirely unfamiliar. Magda had never met Karel von Tarnheim; if she had, she would have recognised their origin.

I am the head of this family and I am a von Tarnheim.

So Paul never got to join the DJ or the Hitlerjugend. Somehow the Maida Vale Catholic Scouts never matched up.

SUMMER 1936,
SHANKLIN, ISLE OF WIGHT

Paul woke, as so frequently, to the sound of his father's voice. Raised in song, protest or comment, it was rarely silent unless Pa was asleep or playing the piano, then he was really just making another kind of noise.

--Magda, he was saying, who has caused this? The landlady or the laundry? Feel it; it is starched! How can I wear this next to my skin? Do we not have another clean set while this is attended to?

Evidently Pa was complaining about his underwear. Mum's voice did not share the clear, carrying power of her husband's and her reply could not be heard from upstairs.

Paul got out of bed. The sun was coming between the rather flimsy curtains, much thinner than his at home, and he looked forward to another day on the beach, meeting up with the lads from the town, maybe tennis. In his pyjamas, he went into the kitchen. They had the ground floor and the first floor of the house, which included the bathroom, which was shared with the lodgers from the top floor, currently Presto the Prestidigitator and sisters Annie and Edie, a comedy duo.

Pa of course greatly disliked sharing the bathroom, and had particular rules and rituals connected with it; the Zelleks also had sole use of the outside lavatory. Mum had evidently persuaded Pa to sit down, still in his dressing gown, and eat some breakfast. He was staring moodily at a slice of toast and marmalade.

Paul glanced at the kitchen cabinet and his suspicions were alerted.

--Pa, you've been pinching my sherbet lemons.

--Only two, Pauli. And they were so delicious! But I shall make amends! I have to run over to the theatre first, but then I can find you on the beach and we can go to that *vunderful* sweet shop on the esplanade. I am thinking of some Edinburgh rock; they have such a tempting range of colours.

--Neither of you are dressed, noted Mum, serving Paul with a boiled egg and soldiers. But I suppose it IS Paul's holiday.

--I will get dressed as soon as I have a vest and drawers (Pa persisted in referring to underpants in this way) which will not scrape the skin from my body. Meanwhile, liebling, may I have another cup of tea?

If Pa goes to the theatre, thought Paul, he'll be gone at least an hour, which gives me time to meet the train from the Pier Head with the lads and their handcart.

Since Paul was here for the whole of the school holidays rather than the one or two weeks granted to most holidaymakers, or, as they were known on the island, 'visiters', he had been able to make friends with some local boys who earned a small but regular income by meeting the trains from the ferry and carrying the visiters' luggage to their boarding houses or hotels in a handcart, thus saving their clients from hiring expensive taxis. They were not popular with the taxi drivers, but otherwise it was not a difficult way of making money. Paul's father, who had been in Shanklin since the beginning of the summer season, was known to be with the theatricals, and Paul's possible ability to get tickets for the end-of-the-pier shows stood the boy in good stead.

After a reasonably profitable couple of handcart trips, he made for the beach, where his father joined him.

Jiri had been to see the theatre wardrobe. Esme, the dancer Esme Doran, was now three months' pregnant and it was beginning to show. At least she had stopped being sick all the time, and with a bit of costume adjustment she should make it to the end of the season. After that she might pick up a couple of weeks' chorus work, then fortunately her sister in Bakewell had come to the rescue, offering to put Esme up for the crucial period and even to take on the child. Jiri had asked Esme about the father; a few words from the right person might encourage him to step up to his responsibilities. Jiri knew Esme to be a Catholic; he had seen her lighting a candle in the Sacred Heart Church and this gave force to her bitter comment that the only help 'he' had been prepared to give was the cost of 'getting rid of it', which she would never do. So little was to be expected there. But for now, Jiri felt that things were under control and that he could enjoy a morning on the beach.

Paul saw that his father carried a rolled towel, containing his bathing costume. He had an understanding with the owner of the hired beach huts, who hung a striped towel across a gap between two of them especially for Jiri and Paul. Behind this Jiri stripped off and changed, before running down the sand towards Paul.

--Coming in, Pauli?

He raced into the sea, plunging in as soon as he reached water deep enough, and appeared about to swim across the Solent, all before Paul had made up his mind whether to paddle. He was not a keen swimmer. His father had insisted on taking him to the local London swimming baths, where he struggled in the shallow end while Pa dived gracefully from the top diving board, a sight that made Paul's stomach churn and a strange feeling creep up the back of his legs. He knew that Pa would expect him to do the same before long. There were all sorts of things that Pa did and which he expected Paul to do.

One thing which had made Pa proud, though, was Paul's success in the entrance exam to the Cardinal Vaughan School, where he was due to start in September. His new uniform, satchel and textbooks awaited him back in London, all purchased before he and Mum had come down to join Pa on the island, as they had done for the past two years, in fact every summer since they had come to England. Paul was now twelve; he would be thirteen in November. The headmaster of the Vaughan had said that Pa had done right in keeping him at the parish school a little longer, to allow his written English to catch up with his speaking and reading; his arithmetic and maths results were outstanding already. Pa was insistent that Paul should have a Real English Education; reticent about his own schooling, he had let fall that he'd been expelled from Austrian Oberschule at fourteen, and never returned to formal education.

Pa emerged from the water and came up the beach in search of his towel. Few people looked at his leg, and fewer did more than glance at it. Many men of his age and older carried war scars, and much of the time it didn't greatly inhibit him. Drying himself, he suggested that they join a communal game with a beach ball, which took them through the rest of the morning. Although Paul hated contact sports, he had a good eye for the ball and good aim; he was a promising cricketer, and enjoyed tennis; he might ask Pa for the hire price of one of the courts this afternoon and invite that boy who was staying at the Badminton Hotel in Sandown.

They just had time for the sweet shop before returning for what Jiri and Magda called lunch and everyone else called dinner. By now Pa was complaining that the sand Got Everywhere; that was the only drawback with these *vunderful* beaches. He would change when they got home, adding to the pile of garments for Magda to wash specially, using Lifebuoy soap.

That morning Magda had done some cleaning, helped by the charlady; she then handwashed Jiri's unfortunate set of underwear before going shopping. The range of fresh fish was wonderful, the locally grown vegetables almost up to German standards and the bread and pastries most acceptable.

Magda was thrifty by training, and she and Jiri had experienced some changes of fortune. At present, he seemed able to come up with pretty well all that was needed, although she wondered whether Vernon Dakins was still helping with the rent of the London flat. Jiri was doing occasional translation work, going into a city office for this; but his main income was from managing and arranging theatrical and musical events, as he had in Munich though now on a humbler scale. He had, too, a few professional engagements especially as a singer; tenors were hard to come by. And,

Magda was pretty sure, he was gambling. When Paul asked for anything, his father would usually provide it, saying he had been lucky on the horses, or had won a few pounds playing cards. Vernon had left Jiri the keys of his Chelsea flat while he was on a two-year secondment to Washington; how Jiri made use of these Magda did not ask. At the very least, he might stay there after leaving a poker club in the small hours. Actually, he was better off on the Isle of Wight. And he seemed well and happy.

Back at their lodgings, Paul and his father found that the post had come.

--This must be from Uncle Verni. Can I have the stamps, Pa? Paul already had several American stamps from his godfather's letters, but they were always good for swaps.

--Yes, of course, Pauli. I will cut them off for you.

For some reason Pa never gave him the envelopes Uncle Verni's letters came in, but it wasn't difficult to steam or soak the stamps off. As well as stamps, Paul collected cigarette cards, particularly cricketers; his father did not smoke, but everyone in the theatre companies did and most of them saved cards for him.

The Zelleks were having fried, fresh mackerel with mashed potatoes and runner beans. Pa was letting his get cold, as usual, while he opened the letter.

--What has Vernon to say, Jiri? asked Mum.

Pa read out accounts of Vernon Dakins's visits to Texas and New York.

--What's he say on that last page, Pa?

--Oh, just some things he wants me to do for him.

--You won't have to go up to London, will you, Jiri? asked

Magda. It's so expensive and inconvenient with the paddle steamer and everything.

--No, no, darling. I can do it all from here. He folded up the letter and put it into the top pocket of his shirt.

Without enthusiasm he pushed his lunch around his plate.

--This has bones in it, Magda.

--Yes, darling. It's a fish.

--I'll eat it, Pa, if you don't want it.

Paul knew that his father had already consumed an ice cream cornet and several chunks of Edinburgh rock; he had said it was necessary to try all the flavours. Jiri looked at him gratefully and pushed his plate in Paul's direction, under Magda's disapproving gaze.

In the afternoon, as there was no matinee, Jiri went round to Esme's digs. The landlady told him that Miss Doran had popped out for a couple of bits, but he was welcome to wait; she would not be long.

She had realised of course that the poor girl was expecting. For a moment she wondered whether this skinny little fellow, holding a bunch of carnations (five, as he was wearing the sixth in his buttonhole) and a paper bag from Clarkson's bakery, could be responsible. But somehow she doubted it, and she recognised him as a member of the theatricals.

When Esme returned, she found Jerry sitting by the window, doing some of her knitting. He put it down and kissed her on both cheeks.

--Esme, darling! You are looking so well!

--I see you've made yourself at home, Jerry.

--I always do! Look, I've put the kettle on (he indicated

the gas ring) and perhaps you might give me a cup of tea? I have bought us a Bath bun each.

These were arranged on a plate, lightly but neatly covered by the bag.

--The flowers are in the sink; I'm afraid I've left those for you, as I never was any good at floral arrangements!

Esme looked at the buns. She was starving; since she'd stopped being sick, she seemed to be hungry all the time.

She also looked at the knitting.

--I didn't know you could knit, Jerry.

--Oh, lots of us learned it in the military hospital. Only Magda doesn't like me to touch hers, as she says our tensions are different, and she can always tell. I can do cross-stitch too. I learned that in Switzerland. I did a lovely set of table napkins with gentians and edelweiss.

These had been left behind in one of his moves, and he often regretted them.

He went on, I've been to see wardrobe, and Miss Sprigg is letting out your costumes. They should see us through to the end of the season.

Perhaps I should not have bought the buns, he thought, especially as he suspected that Esme would eat his too: but it was too late now.

--So, darling… May I ask you something?

She nodded; she was pouring boiling water into the teapot.

--Didn't you once say that you knew shorthand and typing?

--Yes, Jerry. Mum and Dad made me do a course before I joined Sammy's dance troupe, so I had 'something to fall back on'. My heart wasn't in it, but I knew I had to get it out of the way, and in the end I did pretty well.

--You've got one of my agency cards? He handed her an attractive card featuring a suave black and white male figure leaning on a cane and holding a topper. This read,

Tommy Tucker Theatrical Enterprises.
Manager, agent, vocalist and accompanist
For all your Variety needs.
L.T. Tucker, registered office 1013b, Streatham Hill.

--Why Tommy Tucker, I've often wondered.

--Yes. It is rather silly, I know, but Paul, when he was quite a baby, used to call me little Tommy Tucker, because of the nursery rhyme, you know, and because at that time, in Berlin, I often used to do just that, sing for our supper! So when I wanted a business name, L.T. Tucker it was... and of course people might think I was English, too! Anyway, I was thinking that Mrs Melmot who runs the office could do with a bit of help, especially as business is likely to pick up before the Christmas season. She's getting on a bit, as they say.

Mrs Melmot was over seventy. She had been one of the *grandes horizontales* of the belle époque and in that position had known many of the great men of the day, but during the Depression she had fallen on hard times. She and Jiri had a mutually helpful relationship. Learning that it was her birthday (although not which one) he had brought in some caviar and a bottle of good champagne; as they worked through this, he asked her the question that had perplexed him since the age of fifteen. Her answer had transformed his sex life.

--She is a most interesting woman, and one can learn much from her, Jerry continued. I am afraid I cannot pay you a high salary, but while you are resting it might just help you out until... he paused... until you visit your sister in the New Year.

Esme felt a rush of affection for him. Somehow she knew that if he had been the father of her child, he would have carried the can; he might have been, too: there had been that fling with him last year before his wife and kid came down to the island, but no consequences from that, which had been sheer luck, luck that had run out with... Sometimes when you looked at Jerry, you wondered if he was a queer, and blokes often gave him the eye, but that little fling had proved something, and of course he was married, and idolised that kid Paul.

In the end, Esme did eat Jerry's bun as well as her own, but managed to find him two rather stale garibaldis. He drank some tea, looked briefly and wistfully towards the bed, told her to get some rest before the evening's show, and trotted off.

Next day there was a rehearsal. Jerry accompanied the Portuguese banjo player for a run-through of a couple of new numbers while his sister, the usual pianist, was having her hair permed. He timed his entry with the props for the Bashful Brothers' sketch, and then stood watching the company finale, a song and dance routine accompanied by Stan, the resident pianist.

The producer also stood at the back.

--Sounds a bit thin from here, he said. Jerry, could you get in the wings and sing along, just to give it a bit of oomph?

Jerry did not move.

--*A bit of oomph?* Was it for this that I studied for years with Professor Weissenborn, while my wife and child tramped the streets of Berlin to save money on tram fares? To stand concealed in the wings giving a bit of oomph to this... this... *Gurkentruppe?*

--Five bob at the end of the week.

--Seven and six.

--Six bob.

Jerry shrugged. Very well.

--Right. Get up there, Jerry. Now, Stan... Positions everyone.

Birds do it, bees do it... Let's fall in love...

There was an unexpected gap in that evening's programme, so Stan and Jiri filled in with some numbers they had in readiness.

Jiri started with 'When the Bloom is on the Rye'. Stan was always amazed by what Jerry could do with this apparently simple song. Certainly he was showing off a bit at the end (maybe taking his cue from the virtuoso Heddle Nash recording) but it appeared absolutely natural and effortless. An English summer evening, a full moon, a pretty girl, a young man in love, an invitation to the woods... Jerry conveyed all the piece's nostalgia, and romance with a slight spiciness, striking a chord with almost everyone in the audience, and they loved it. He followed with a couple of standards and ended with 'The Road to the Isles'; he had no idea what most of it meant, but his attempt at a Scottish accent was perfectly acceptable on the Isle of Wight. At the beginning of the final refrain he began to walk slowly off, singing the last line pianissimo over his shoulder. He came out of the wings to take a bow, making sure that Stan got adequate acknowledgement.

--Sounded good tonight, Jerry, said Stan later.

--Thank you, Stan. I'm always good, but some nights I am better.

That's tenors for you, thought the veteran pianist.

On Sunday after Mass, Pa suggested that they take a boat out, perhaps around the coast to Ventnor and Luccombe. Paul had been rather surprised to find that Pa could handle a sailing boat; he'd said that he hadn't seen the sea until a trip to London when he was about eight. But when asked, he explained that for several summers he had stayed with a family on Lake Balaton in Hungary, where everyone swam and sailed. Once started, he began to reminisce about the Balinkay family. Ferzi, he said, was a little older than himself, and was now quite a famous writer; he and Pa were good friends, but Pa had also enjoyed playing with Ferzi's brother, Mikki.

--He was about four years younger than me, which I know is quite a lot with children, but I suppose I was rather silly and backward, not at all like you, Pauli. Anyway, we used to have a lovely time, we made up lots of games and got into all sorts of trouble; I suppose really Mikki was the best friend I've ever had. Barátom, we called it in Hungary, a sort of brother friend.

--What did he do when he grew up, Pa?

--He became an airman. Like Biggles, only Hungarian.

One of the few interests Paul and his father shared was an enthusiasm for the adventure stories of W.E. Johns.

--Where is he now? Still in Hungary?

--I don't know... one day he got into his aeroplane and flew away, and never came back.

There was a brief silence.

--Do you think you'll see him again, Pa?

--Oh yes. I expect I shall. But it might be a long time.

Although Paul knew that any expedition with Pa meant excitement and unpredictability, the boat trip was actually enjoyable. Pa was able to give Paul clear, timely instructions; it was lovely weather, the sea was calm with just enough breeze. Pa had his binoculars, and looked at the various caves and inlets around the point, telling Paul stories he'd heard of the pirates and smugglers who used to frequent the island and perhaps still did. Ventnor, he added, was often shrouded in mist even when the rest of the coast was clear.

--Do you mean people could secretly come over from France in their own boats, Pa? On special missions, and things like that?

--Oh yes, Pauli. Although I don't suppose that really happens nowadays.

They landed in Ventnor, where they ate the sandwiches they'd brought, before sailing back to Shanklin. By the time they had returned the boat and walked home, both had worked up an appetite for the cooked tea waiting for them. Paul spent the evening sorting his cigarette cards while his parents listened to the wireless; it had been one of their more successful days.

The next morning at the theatre, Jiri learned the reason for the empty slot in the Saturday evening programme. Harry, the ventriloquist, and his dummy Hubert, had done a flit, taking their belongings and leaving the week's rent unpaid. They weren't one of Jiri's acts; they were regulars who came every year and had done so for decades.

--Wonderful what that bloke could do in his prime, explained Stan. But he wasn't the same after he had his teeth out; his false ones never fitted right.

--Well, said the manager, Jerry and Stan can fill in for a few shows; Jerry's a class act, but it does make for too many musical items. We are short of variety turns. Trouble is, anybody any good is already working this far into the season. Jerry, we'll both look though our books.

A couple of days later, Paul was wakened by sounds from the kitchen. Looking at his alarm clock, he saw that it was still only 6am; lured by the smell of toast, he went down to find his father pouring a cup of tea and proudly surveying a slice of toast.

--Look, Pauli! I have made some tea and toast! And I have not burned it at all! Shall I make you a slice?

--Yes please, Pa, but what are you doing at this time of the morning?

--Oh, I could not sleep. It gets light so early these days. So I have been for a bicycle ride, and a swim and I have bought some lovely fish from the fishermen.

He indicated a parcel wrapped in newspaper beside the sink. Pa looked somehow odd: excited, perhaps or thinking about something. Still, it was amazing that he had actually started getting breakfast. Paul looked out of the window and saw the rather antiquated bike propped against the fence. It actually belonged to Mr Battrill, who was one of the oldest people Paul had ever seen; he and Mrs Battrill lived in a tiny cottage in Fort Street, Sandown. Apparently Pa knew them by some complicated means involving 'our nipper Ralph that went to Canada'.

--Pauli, continued Pa. You are a Boy Scout and perhaps you know about such things. Could you help me to fry some eggs and perhaps a rasher of bacon? I am very hungry.

There was no matinee performance that day, so the Zelleks planned a leisurely tea before Pa left for the theatre.

--Are you writing to Uncle Verni, Pa?

307

--Yes. Any messages for him? It will be good to see him again, won't it?

--Did you do those jobs he wanted?

--Oh yes.

Magda called though the door.

--Darling, in some ways I shall be glad to be back in my own kitchen. This knife is useless; I have these lovely fresh fish you brought back from the beach, but I have to prepare them myself and one needs a good knife. I expect you have your old hunting knife somewhere? I know you don't like anyone but yourself to use it, but if I do not have it for a few minutes none of us will have any supper. And I promise I will clean it properly.

--Oh very well, liebling. It is quite suitable for cutting up offal. I will fetch it.

--I know it's ready to use, Mum. I saw Pa cleaning it this morning.

On the following morning, Magda was preparing breakfast by herself.

--Pa is sleeping, Paul; try not to disturb him. He had a wakeful night. His back was troubling him although I can't think that he has lifted anything heavy lately, and when he did drop off, he had some of his dreams.

Paul thought he had heard Pa shouting, in the language neither he nor Mum could understand. This happened from time to time; Mum said that Paul should not worry about it; it was because Pa had been in the war, and that was all in the past now. Paul knew that people who'd been in the war sometimes acted strangely, although they never talked about it and most of the time they seemed quite normal. When they'd lived in Germany, there were lots of men missing an arm or a leg. Pa said they should help them whenever they could, as he was lucky not to have ended up like that himself.

Anyway by the afternoon Pa was up and about, leaving for the theatre where the management and company were still discussing the lack of variety turns.

At this point, the foyer doors opened to admit the biggest man any of them had ever seen. He was huge and wore a black beard.

--Theatre? he asked.

Had he been normal size, someone would have answered, What does it look like? The bleedin' Houses of Parliament? But as it was, everyone nodded.

Jiri spoke up.

--Yes, my friend. You are in Shanklin Theatre.

The newcomer grunted, reached into his packet and pulled out a folded poster:

SERGEI STROGONOV THE SIBERIAN STRONGMAN.
Bends iron bars, lifts ton weights, will wrestle any
contenders. Never before seen in this country.

--Sergei, he announced.

--Anyone speak Russian?

--Mine is rather basic, but I can try.

--All right, Jerry. But if I were you, I'd be careful not to annoy him.

Jiri approached the Siberian and greeted him courteously, then they exchanged a few questions and answers.

--Well?

--He's been working with a circus in Portsmouth but seems to have fallen out with them. I could not quite ascertain why; he speaks a dialect with which I am not familiar. He is looking for work.

--Where is he staying?

Jiri again spoke to the strongman.

--He says, as the weather is warm, he will sleep on the beach for the time being. I think he will be safe enough as long as he takes notice of the tides.

--Right. Offer him two quid a week; no, wait, let's see what he can do first.

--I do not see any iron bars immediately to hand.

Sergei obviously got the gist of this and gave a demonstration by picking Jiri up in one hand and Stan in the other. He then juggled with them. When they had recovered they both refused to form part of Sergei's regular act. Two of the chorus girls could do it; Stan and Jerry were classical musicians and needed to preserve their dignity. Sergei was hired with a down payment.

The next ten days or so passed swiftly; Sergei was quite a hit, although no one came forward to test his wrestling skills. Esme grew fatter. Jiri's voice augmented the group numbers. Then one evening Sergei failed to appear and had apparently left the island. His disappearance was talked of for a day or two; he was gone as suddenly as he had come, but these things happened, especially with foreigners (not you, of course, Jerry), and by good fortune Jerry was contacted by a troupe of acrobats who had been out of circulation due to injury, but were now on top form again and keenly seeking work.

Another successful season drew to an end; Jiri returned the bike to Alf Battrill, promising to see them again next year.

--You do that, Mr Zellek, and bring that nipper of yours with you; he don't take much after you, do he?

To this Jiri replied as he always did,

--I am pleased to say that he does not! Paul is very like his mother, and he also reminds me greatly of my late father.

Back in London, the papers were full of the liaison between the new King Edward and the American divorcee Mrs Simpson, and in December came the abdication crisis. Instead of King Edward VIII, there would be King George VI and Queen Elizabeth, with a coronation planned for May 1937.

Jiri remarked that his acquaintance with the crowned heads of Europe led him to the conclusion that there was sadly little correlation between royal blood, good looks and intelligence; possible exceptions were dear Queen Alexandra, so sad that she had died in 1925, and the Duke of Kent, who was really quite a cultured and attractive person. Jiri did not say where he had met him.

As 1937 progressed, little was talked of but the coronation, the ceremony, the route, the role of the two little princesses and their grandmother Queen Mary, whether the new king would be able to conquer his stammer, the street parties, the society parties... Jiri said he had missed the coronation of the Austrian Emperor Carl as he had been serving in Galicia in 1916, but they had celebrated as best they could, and there had been film footage of the young monarch wearing St Stephen's crown, in which unfortunately anybody would look an idiot.

There was little space in the newspapers for a report from

the Isle of Wight, where it had been a wet and windy spring. Landslips were not uncommon there, especially in the Ventnor and Luccombe area whose cliffs were notoriously unstable. One such fall had exposed a cave revealing human remains that must have been there for almost a year; it was hard to tell, given the work of rodents, crabs and seagulls. A suitcase was also found, containing a British passport, a rather large sum of money, and clothing evidently purchased in France.

The Isle of Wight Constabulary followed up the passport; the address within it did not exist. Dating the death to the summer of 1936, they made enquiries about anything or anyone unusual seen in the area at that time. Of course, it being in holiday season, with hundreds of 'visiters' coming and going, made things even more difficult, but a breakthrough came when several locals recalled a Siberian strongman's mysterious appearance and disappearance. Yes, he had been seen roaming the cliffs and beaches; yes, he looked capable of violence and yes, he had been on the spot at an appropriate time. Given his distinctive appearance, it ought not to have been too difficult to track down this obvious suspect. Not so; the manager of the theatre had no idea where he might have gone, and a sighting on the Southampton-bound ferry was the last that had been reported. In all probability, he had gone back to Russia having completed his grisly task, which was likely connected with some Bolshevik intrigue.

No more was heard of the case.

1937–39

At Christmas 1937, Vernon Dakins returned from his two-year Washington posting. En route to Devon to stay with his sister for the holiday he spent a day with Jiri, Magda and Paul, bringing them presents from the States: cowboy boots (filled with Hershey bars) for Jiri, a fur cape for Magda and a camera for Paul, who had turned fourteen in November.

Vernon and Jiri walked beside the Regents Canal while Magda prepared lunch and Paul inspected the workings of his new camera. They had missed each other. Jiri thought Vernon was looking the worse for wear; he had put on weight and his face appeared more florid.

--That business on the island, Jiri.

--Yes. Shame about the landslip; he'd still be there if that hadn't happened. But, you know, it is interesting that the cliffs there are most unstable. The Isle of Wight has a fascinating geological structure. Perhaps I should have thought of that. But one cannot be prepared for everything.

--Use the good old family hunting knife?

--Oh yes. Shooting would have attracted attention, and he was too big for anything else.

--Mess, though?

--Well, yes.

--What did you do about stains on your togs?

--No stains. No togs, actually.

--You mean you did it in the nude?

--Yes. I know that the major problem with using the knife is, well, as you say, blood on one's clothing. It is almost unavoidable. So, what then is the solution? Dispense with clothing. It was in the summer.

I had bicycled to Luccombe. It was easy to remain concealed and partially dressed. Once he had landed I removed the rest of my clothing, advanced on him and well, the world is much better off without him. Verni, I know what that man did and what he was planning to do in England. There will be a war and one does not want the likes of him making it worse. And, my dear friend, I could not have you endangered. Then I made sure that he and his suitcase were in one of the caves, and I blocked the entrance. That was really the only difficult part; those rocks are quite heavy. Then I went for a dip.

By the time the local fishing boat turned up I was getting dressed; we had a cheerful conversation and I told them I'd been advised that their fish was the best on the island, so I had come early in order to secure some, found I had time to spare and had gone for a swim. In fact I went back several times; their fish was indeed good, and the water was delightful; it became deep much more readily than at Shanklin or Sandown, where one has to wade in for some considerable distance before swimming.

Of course, the Russian fellow was the contact; he gave up after a few days, assumed his man had never made it across the Channel, and fortunately for us, the Island Constabulary see him as the prime suspect.

Jiri's delicate irregular features were outlined beneath his hat against the frosty mist. Vernon leaned towards him.

--Verni, I think Magda will have lunch ready by now. We do not want to make her cross.

When Vernon was back in London at New Year, he and Jiri resumed their close companionship, drinking, playing poker and going to the races. He had already introduced Jiri to a government office specialising in translation from central European languages; a good deal of regular work now came Jiri's way, which was most welcome after the pantomime season ended, and he made weekly visits to the office to collect and return assignments. At times, he was told that the material was 'sensitive' and must be handled on the premises; in this way he became quite friendly with a few colleagues, notably Cyril Bowes Barnard, like himself a keen bridge player.

With the Anschluss in March 1938, Jiri became preoccupied; he reminded Magda that he had foretold this; he did not like the way things were going in Hitler's Germany and he suggested that they might all apply for British citizenship. This, however, was not likely to be easy and could take some time; Magda, too, was reluctant to surrender her Polish nationality.

That summer was spent not on the Isle of Wight but in Great Yarmouth on the Norfolk coast.

Over tea and biscuits in the Streatham office, Jiri explained how this came about.

--To begin with, last year on the island I was able to help three ladies in distress. Or more accurately, one was not in distress, in fact very far from it, but the other two were, in a manner, desperate. The Riviera Ladies Trio. Piano, violin and cello. They were regularly engaged at the Winter Gardens in Ventnor. But one Saturday there were only two, and myself. I should explain that over the weeks I had become quite intimate – in a friendly manner only, of course – with Miss Gwendolyn Powell, Miss Agatha Forbes-Bennet and Mrs Wheeler (she is a widow). It appears that many years ago, Miss Powell formed an attachment to a military man, a Major Rodney Recketts. Now returned from India, the Major sought out his lost love (it is so romantic, is it not? Quite like an opera, or a really nice novel) and, in brief, tracked her down in Ventnor. Bursting upon the scene (oh, one can quite imagine it!), he declared his intentions of taking Miss Powell to an hotel, at once, then and there, to make up for lost time. Thirty years of it should, I imagine, take some doing, especially with a man of the Major's age, but at all events his actual words were, I understand, Damn it, Gwen, I've waited nearly forty years for this and I'm not going to let the confounded Winter Gardens get in my way.

So, Mrs Wheeler telephoned me in haste. As a result, I was the pianist for the afternoon. It was a little embarrassing as we were advertised as three ladies, but I was partially concealed behind a large palm tree in a pot. The afternoon was entirely successful; in fact, I played a couple of solo pieces, for which the manager was good enough to pay me extra.

Well, to continue: once Miss Powell had embarked on a new life in Eastbourne as Mrs Recketts (the Major, of course, made an honest woman of her), the Riviera Ladies Trio seemed doomed and indeed the other two ladies were already contemplating retirement. Then came an offer they could not refuse: to pass one last season playing at a very prestigious hotel in Great Yarmouth. I would join them and we would rename ourselves as simply The Riviera Trio; in fact, I believe all three ladies originally hailed from Accrington, which I assume to be at some distance from the South of France…

--Get on with it, Jerry!

--There is little more to tell.

He went on to explain that the hotel had offered accommodation for himself, Magda and Paul at a very advantageous rate. In its early days the hotel had catered for guests bringing their own maids and valets, who would stay in smaller rooms with less attractive views. Increasingly these were less in demand, and two such rooms with facilities were occupied by the Zelleks; the two ladies stayed in a boarding house run by a friend. Jiri was basically the hotel's resident musician, playing in the trio during the afternoons, but also at the piano bar and occasionally singing with the dance band employed in the evenings. At this time Viennese operetta was extremely popular; Jiri had great success with a couple of Tauber songs and 'If I Am Dreaming' from *The Dubarry*. He also took requests and in this way broadened his repertoire to include anything from 'Come Into the Garden Maud' to 'Alexander's Ragtime Band' and 'Begin the Beguine'. Really, he said later when Casablanca came out, I was like Sam, only white and in Great Yarmouth.

Paul now had a bike and was able to bring it down by train so that he could explore the flat neighbouring countryside. At fifteen, he was beginning to outgrow the delights of Shanklin and Sandown and appreciated the slightly racier atmosphere of the Norfolk resort. Released from cooking and cleaning,

Magda readily found bridge partners or relaxed with her knitting or a library book. Earlier that summer she had been rather concerned about Jiri, who seemed alternately silent and thoughtful, and frenetically voluble. Great Yarmouth and the constant but agreeable musical activity, the fresh air and the changing social scene, seemed to do him good; and there was also a racecourse.

In July they heard that a four-man Austrian and German team had scaled the north face of the Eiger. This sparked a series of reminiscences from Jiri about how much he had loved climbing and skiing when he'd been Paul's age; if only they had not had to leave Munich, they could have joined the Deutscher und Osterreichischer Alpenverrein and enjoyed these pursuits together in the Bavarian Alps. This was one of the few occasions when Paul was not sorry that they had come to England. The thought of hurtling down a mountainside or inching his way up a sheer rock face, especially in the company of his father, did not appeal to him.

Shortly after they had settled back in Maida Vale, came the catastrophic news that Vernon Dakins had been killed in a car accident in the New Forest; his sports car had been found burned out near Lymington; a charred body, identified as Vernon through papers and clothing, was pulled from the wreck. It transpired that he had left his godson Paul Zellek a useful amount of money.

Magda had expected Jiri to experience one of his periodic collapses, but in fact he kept on his feet, although looking terrible. He insisted that they attend Vernon's requiem; he stayed on at the wake and was brought home, disastrously drunk, by a younger colleague of Vernon. He spent several hours vomiting and shaking but made it to the translation office the next day. After this he seemed determined to pursue the course of naturalisation for the three of them; this went through surprisingly quickly after all, and in addition, Jiri, as a British citizen, was offered full-time employment at the office.

And so Jiri became a civil servant. He had a three-piece suit made, with an extra pair of trousers, so that he could alternate them to avoid wear while sitting at a desk; he bought a selection of sober but expensive ties, he was issued with an HMG briefcase, which usually contained sandwiches prepared by Magda. Each morning he set off for the Tube station, arriving at the translation office promptly at nine. At five, he locked away the documents he was working on. Once a week he played bridge at the Civil Service Club; on other days sometimes he stopped off for a drink with colleagues, but more often he went straight home.

A regular salary with increments and a guaranteed pension was a novelty for the Zelleks. Of course, Jiri still had other, largely undiscussed, sources of income. The payments from Vernon Dakins had ceased with his death, but the theatrical agency that Jiri had founded under his 'other name' continued to function in a small way under the direction of Mrs Melmot and Esme Doran. He had some investments based on the funds raised from the sale of the Pallin factory, or what was left of them after the expenses of the Zelleks' settlement in London and the months when Jiri had been earning very little from performance or management. He was certainly still gambling; he had always kept this separate from his other finances and continued to do so, although it was becoming increasingly difficult since it had become almost his only source of excitement, apart perhaps from a few activities connected with the O'Reilly family, whom he'd met when Paul was at the parish school. And there was still the bank vault container and its contents, which he was reluctant to sell, mainly for sentimental reasons, while the bank account in Switzerland must remain untouched for as long as possible. Often he mentally thanked Sigmund Treichler for his financial skill and foresight.

Sigmund was enthusiastic about the Anschluss. Under the Führer the economy had been improving; it was a pity Jiri had decided to sell out when he did, but as manager of a government-owned enterprise Sigmund was well placed. Things could only get better; people had suggested that another war was on the cards, but Siggi doubted it. And if worst came to worst, the factory could turn to military utensils, as it had in 1914. When Siggi married, Ilse finally yielded to the persuasions of Alois Gruber. He gave her a comfortable home, and she continued her work in journalism after the birth of her twins. Sigmund also had a young family.

Jiri had not been to Pallin since early 1934. He had never taken Magda and Paul there, partly because he suspected that Magda would fall in love with the place, so that he would have been tempted to settle there with his family despite his misgivings about the future of Austrian politics. As it was, he rarely thought of Pallin; Tarnheim was more often in his mind, although he tried constantly to push away his memories and his *heimweh* for the Alpine landscape. Particularly in London, he felt stifled, and believed that his voice longed for lungfuls of mountain air. He had, too, anxieties about his uncle, while there were things he needed to take away from Tarnheim. As an Austrian citizen he had been wary of travelling through

Germany but with a British passport he should be able to do so in the assurance of returning to London.

So in the spring of 1939 he applied for two weeks' holiday. He had wondered about taking Paul with him, but two factors prevented this; firstly, Paul was studying for his school certificate and more significantly, Jiri's superiors at the office became most interested in his proposed route through Europe. Hitler had just seized control of Czechoslovakia; the international situation was highly unstable. Zellek, it was suggested, might still enjoy two weeks' summer holiday later in the year if he would, in exchange, be prepared to take a rather circuitous path to Tarnheim; it would be part of a, well, not exactly a mission, more like a delivery service for messages and documents too sensitive to be sent by post or even through diplomatic channels. A fifteen-year-old boy might well provide a measure of camouflage, but Jiri drew the line at this and thus Paul never got to meet his great uncle Karel.

So Jiri spent some convivial evenings in the British embassy in Berlin (of course, he was there to look up old friends); in Munich he met some extremely interesting people, remarking later that Hitler suffered from terrible flatulence, although he had excellent taste in cream cakes and a delightful dog, while Goering was no gentlemen and SO fat. His last stop was Vienna, where he arrived very early in the morning, having taken an overnight train from Munich. Driving through the streets, he felt joy and excitement at returning to the city in which so much had happened to him. At his hotel he had a bath, shaved, took a leisurely breakfast and went out to stroll around before his morning appointment at the embassy. He became increasingly distressed by the same signs of Nazi dominance and anti-Semitism that he'd seen in the other two cities. Somehow he had imagined that things would be better in Vienna. Clearly they were not.

Debriefing went fairly well; he was reminded that his last task would be to send a picture postcard to Magda (he thought he would choose one of the Karlskirche) with an agreed greeting in English; after a few days Cyril would telephone her casually to ask if she had heard from her husband; of course she would innocently remark that she had received a card. Then Cyril would know that Jiri was spending his allotted time at Tarnheim and would be back in the office as arranged. As he was about to leave the building, an attaché hailed him.

--Zellek! good to see you again! Don't you remember me? McCormack, from the Berlin days!

It had been ten years, and McCormack had broadened from a gangly red-haired recruit to the diplomatic service into a rather distinguished smooth-faced individual.

--Of course! Jiri shook hands with him, English fashion.

--How long are you in Vienna?

--Only until tomorrow evening; I am on my way to visit my uncle in the Principality.

--Then strike while the iron's hot! Lunch today? I'll ring and book a table at (he named a well-known restaurant). One o'clock suit you?

Jiri hesitated. The man had been familiar with Vernon Dakins. Jiri suspected that the invitation was a means of finding out more about Vernon's death and he did not want to talk about Vernon. On the other hand lunch would be nice, and to refuse would look awkward.

He arrived at the restaurant a few minutes late; this was not on purpose, but in fact meant that he made an entrance, with people noticing his impeccably tailored English suit and arrogant bearing. One or two even thought that he looked familiar.

It took McCormack a while to work around to the subject of Dakins. They covered the European situation, McCormack's recent marriage, the progress of Jiri's son (involving a photograph of Paul with the school cricket team) and some general reminiscences of Berlin in the Twenties. Eventually,

--Terrible about old Dakins, wasn't it?

--Yes. It was a great shock. He was a good friend to me and my family. You know he was Paul's godfather.

--Yes, of course! I expect you saw a lot of him after you moved to London and he came back from Washington?

--Indeed. Jiri took the last mouthful of his schnitzel. You must know, he added, (getting ahead of the game) that Vernon asked me to undertake various tasks for him, and it was Vernon who found me employment at the translation office.

McCormack did of course know this and more.

--Yes. You're doing good work there, I hear.

--Thank you.

McCormack took a gulp of wine.

--Look, he said, you and I both knew quite a lot about Dakins.

Jiri nodded.

Well, the younger man continued, of course it's clear that these days you are a happily married family man.

--Indeed.

--But anyone close to Dakins must have known that he was a queer. It's just that, did it ever occur to you that he was being blackmailed?

Jiri considered.

--It would not have surprised me. But Vernon never talked to me about it; and I think he might have done so had he wanted me to… to take any action in the matter.

McCormack recalled some of the rumours he'd heard about Zellek. He hadn't just been Dakins's informant; he'd reputedly done some dirty work for him, which partly accounted for Dakins's role in getting the Zelleks out of Germany and settled in Maida Vale. The little man opposite him was perhaps not as harmless as he looked.

Right now Jiri was studying the dessert menu.

--I think perhaps… What do you favour, McCormack? Ah, I will consult the waiter.

Instantly the man was beside them and Jiri engaged him in prolonged discussion.

Suddenly McCormack thought of a way forward.

--I believe it was Dakins who taught you to play bridge?

--Yes indeed. My dear wife also; she proved an apt pupil.

--Fancy a game this evening? Come round to our flat after dinner? (A relaxed atmosphere, a few more drinks…)

--How tempting! That would have been delightful. But I have been fortunate enough to secure a ticket at the Staatsoper; that is why I was so unpardonably late for lunch: I was reluctant to surrender my place in the queue for returned tickets.

--What is the work?

--*The Magic Flute*; the conductor is new to me, von Karajan.

--Ah yes! There's a row between him and Furtwängler... You've just missed a wonderful *Tristan and Isolde*, though.

--Ah, perhaps I am not sorry. I am not in the frame of mind for anything too sad, and though Tamino and Pamina have to face dangers, toils and snares, they win through, do they not? And *The Magic Flute* has wonderful memories for me; do you know, I saw Director Mahler conduct?

--When was that? Surely you aren't old enough.

--It was in 1907, just before he left for America. I was a boy of twelve. My father had come to Vienna on business and took me with him. My cousin was at school here, and he obtained permission for her to come with us. Of course, the philosophical aspects of the work were beyond me, and I fear still are, and I have seen the opera performed many times since then, but it was a formative experience and has always meant a great deal to me.

That evening, immaculately dressed, Jiri sat in the audience. Of course, in his boyhood and youth, it had been the Hofoper but the magnificent auditorium was unchanged. He opened his programme.

The Magic Flute: Wolfgang Amadeus Mozart.

Was it a true memory, or one superimposed by being frequently retold? He was very little, perhaps three. He had come into the music room at Pallin:

--Papa what's that?

--That, my boy, is music by Wolfgang Amadeus Mozart.

The name enchanted him; he sang it, repeated it, dancing around. That same day; surely not, it would be too much of a coincidence... he had been given Wolfi.

--Jiri, what's your bear's name?

--He is Wolfgang Amadeus Mozart Bear, but I shall call him Wolfi.

Act One, Scene One, a rough, rocky landscape. He and Christa sat close together. In the dark they held hands, both aware that the other was completely entranced. How hard it had been to take her back to the convent, that horse-drawn cab clattering through the dark streets. Afterwards he had lain awake in the hotel bedroom, his head full of the music; in his broken dreams, he and Christa roamed the rocky landscape above Tarnheim in search of something important.

In the interval, he went in search of champagne. Two elegantly dressed ladies, evidently a mother and daughter, stood near him, opening a box of wonderful Viennese chocolates. He must buy some tomorrow to take to Tarnheim.

--Excuse me, sir, I know you will think us most unmannerly... but your hungry look... would you accept one of our bonbons?

It was the elder, a carefully made up, beautifully coiffured woman of Jiri's age, maybe slightly older.

He smiled and bowed.

--How delightful! And how very rude of me to stare at them! But yes indeed, I would love one!

As he selected his favourite, the daughter laughed.

--Ah, Mother, you see he has fallen for it! Now we can get into conversation and ask him what you really wanted to know...

--Which is?

--Whether you are Jiri Zellek, Jiri von Tarnheim Zellek.

Jiri bowed, clicked his heels and introduced himself, kissing the hands of both mother and daughter.

--I am of course flattered to be so well known. But, dear ladies, may I ask how it is that you know me? Perhaps that somewhat flattering publicity photograph from my years in Munich?

--Ah, no! I must put you out of your anguish, Herr Zellek. I am or was, Gerda von Wichsel und Wachsel; I am now Frau Director Havensbruck; this is my younger daughter, Klara. Seeing that he still looked bewildered, she clarified.

I was at school with your cousin Christa; we were great friends. In fact, she travelled with us to Italy and Paris before the war.

Of course! Gerda's family had stood in a similar relation to Christa as the Balinkays had to the boy Jiri.

It was almost time to return to their seats.

--Herr Zellek, how long are you to be in Vienna?

--Alas! I leave for Tarnheim tomorrow evening.

She drew out her card case.

--Then perhaps we may have the pleasure of giving you tea tomorrow at four? At our apartment.

Jiri slept badly. He was excited by the music and he was disturbed by the meeting with Gerda and Klara. If they had news of Christa? No, no, he would not think about it. But of course he did, and by the morning he was tired, headachy and suffering from the delayed effects of the long train journeys of the last couple of weeks. He really could not cope with a bout of back pain just now.

The hotel valet recommended a Turkish bath (no Jews admitted, but of course Herr Zellek would be accepted; the man had glanced discreetly at Jiri's foreskin while helping him dress), where there was an excellent masseur. He would go there, and then have a shave and a haircut; the valet would do his packing and send it to the station for the Strelitz train; he would go shopping, buy some flowers and appear at the Havensbruck apartment, which had, he noted, a very smart address.

All of this worked fairly well. Certainly the Turkish bath did wonders for his back; unfortunately the place was full of party officials, just as obnoxious naked as they were clothed; one or two of them seemed keen to pick him up, but they were eminently resistible and the only remotely attractive fellows were obviously paired up already.

Promptly at four he rang the bell for his tea date.

At first it was, as he might have predicted, quite delightful. He learned that the aristocratic Gerda had married into money; her husband headed an armaments firm. Klara had an elder sister who was already married, and a younger brother who was still at school and an enthusiastic member of the Hitler Youth. The selection of cakes was obviously from Demels.

At last came the moment when Jiri, moistening his dry mouth with a sip of tea, asked whether they had ever heard from Christa?

--You mean after she left for America?

Gerda looked very closely at Jiri. She dearly longed to learn the whole story of Christa's broken engagement to Jiri and her subsequent marriage to the American doctor. Looking at Jiri's hands, she noted that he wore a wedding ring; indeed he had mentioned his wife and son. On the little finger of his other hand, he wore a plain gold band with a tiny lapis cameo; it had the look of a von Tarnheim piece.

--Yes. You see, dear lady, I was most unwell at the time and we have not been able to keep in touch.

She took pity on him. He was really rather a sweet little man with a certain air of, well, attractive naughtiness about him, perhaps the sort of person who would be quite innovative in bed, which as one grew older was a change from those young studs who thought they were doing you a favour.

--I did not hear anything until, well, let me see, it must have been 1922. She sent me a Christmas card, perhaps I still have it somewhere, although of course one cannot keep everything like that, and she said she had a son, his name was Charlton – Carl, they called him – who was a few months old.

--Was there an address on the envelope?

--Yes, it was a hotel in Washington, not a private address.

--So you could not write back?

--Well, no. And the only other thing was, would you believe, about two years ago, an invitation to a private viewing of her paintings, somewhere else... do you know where Houston might be?

--I think it is in Texas, said Jiri with a sudden impression of John Wayne, cows, prairies, lassoes and gambling joints.

--Oh. Anyway, this, I mean, however did she think I could attend, it came from the gallery itself. I must admit I do not now recall the name of the gallery and I threw the card away; I was rather annoyed: just like Christa to think one could go all that way for a few of her pictures!

Jiri felt that he liked Gerda less than he had anticipated. Just now, too, he wanted to be by himself, until his train left and he had to prepare himself mentally for Tarnheim.

Thanking the ladies courteously, he took his leave and went to sit in the Karlskirche, gazing up at Rottmeyer's exuberant dome fresco, where God the Father loomed out with much of the menace of the painted window in Tarnheim village church as he had seen it in childhood.

--Miss Drake, Miss Drake, my tooth is going to come out! It's coming out NOW! I shall swallow it and CHOKE TO DEATH!

Jiri's penetrating whisper reached throughout the silent church. Every child in the building turned expectantly towards him.

Karel sank his head in his hands, apparently deep in prayer. Flora removed her glove, inserted her thumb and finger into Jiri's mouth and produced the tooth. She knew which one to go for as it had been the focus of drama for several days. Wrapping it in her handkerchief, she dropped it into her handbag.

--I want my tooth!

--Hush, Jiri! You shall have it when we get home. Now be quiet, remember you are in a church.

Jiri looked up at the accusing figure of God the Father in the painted window, and fell silent, exploring the gap with his tongue.

Perhaps the Tarnheim window is a copy of the Viennese fresco, thought Jiri more than thirty years later. After a while he felt able to say a few decades of the rosary, light a candle for the souls of his father and stepmother, and set off for the Eastern station. As he did so, he passed the lighted windows of shops and cafes; catching a glimpse of himself, he was rather pleased by his neat, upright figure; Klara had been a very pretty young woman and her mother, also attractive, perhaps available, but approaching the point of being 'well-preserved'; she must be, what? Forty-five or six? He would be forty-four in June; Christa, he realised with a jolt, must already be forty-six, and twenty years of their life had passed in separation.

Eventually he got off the train at Strelitz. He had last been there in 1934 and then as now he experienced a conviction that the nineteenth-century railway buildings, the posters on the walls, even the station master and porters, were totally unchanged since about 1902. He had considered spending a night in a hotel so that he would arrive at Tarnheim in the morning, fresh and with his wits about him, but now he longed only to be there, and as he left the station his uncle's car was waiting. Karel had finally parted with the Austro Daimler and now had a Steyr, still driven by Gregor. How many times Jiri had been driven along this road? He recalled the pony trap that had collected him each summer and returned him in early autumn, the rare shopping trips with Christa and Miss Drake, a few Christmas holidays, with the town brightly lit.

When they arrived at Tarnheim, it was late and dark. Jiri no longer felt tired as he saw his uncle's tall figure standing in the doorway.

--Uncle! Here I am, like a bad penny, as the English say, or the prodigal son!

He took Karel's outstretched hands, which he noticed were crooked and bony, with protuberant veins.

--Come in, come in, my boy! Gregor, Sepp, Mister Jiri's luggage; to his usual bedroom.

A footman took Jiri's hat, gloves, stick and travelling coat.

Karel looked at him. With the light from the hall lantern falling on his dark, curly hair, delicate yet masculine features and dapper figure, he was, Karel thought, quite a good-looking man; in his prime, really; he could not be far into his forties.

--I have dined, Jiri, but come into my study and I will order something for you. Have you eaten anything?

Jiri thought. He remembered asking for a roll and coffee in his hotel room that morning. Perhaps he had eaten some of that? Lunch? No, he had been too occupied, but he had done full justice to Gerda's pastries.

--Thank you, Uncle; that would be most welcome.

--In you go, then; make yourself comfortable. I will be with you presently.

Jiri sat down and looked at his uncle's desk. There, in a silver and enamelled frame, stood a photograph that he could not recall having seen before, although of course he must have done so.

It was evidently taken in the late 1860s or early 70s, as it showed Karel and his sister Gisela as children of about ten and seven; a little younger than Jiri and Christa in the picture that Flora Drake had commissioned in 1906, but like them, formally dressed and holding hands before a painted Alpine backdrop. For some reason, it sparked a memory of Jiri's boyhood. He was probably about seven or eight, certainly no older. Karel must have decided to visit the schoolroom to see how the children were progressing; perhaps he had warned Miss Drake of this, as when he arrived they were prepared to stand to attention, hands behind their backs, and recite.

Firstly, English poems. 'Daffodils' for Christa, and 'I Have a Little Shadow' for Jiri (oh, he could remember it now: I have a little shadow that goes in and out with me, and what can be the use of him is more than I can see. Really, it was rather delightful). Then Christa had declaimed 'Le Corbeau et le Renard'. Jiri was so impressed that he burst into applause and after a moment Karel and Miss Drake laughed and joined in. Then Jiri had piped up,

--Uncle, I am so sorry that I do not know a French poem yet, even a little one (of course this was because he had been too inattentive), but I can sing you a song instead.

It was in their native language and it was the sort of folk song common to many European cultures: 'Goodbye to My Homeland', the lilting farewell of a soldier to his mother, his sweetheart, the fields he had tilled, and the mountains of his homeland.

When he had finished, Uncle Karel had looked very odd. Jiri was afraid he had not liked the song. Then, clearing his throat, he said,

--Thank you, my boy. That is a lovely song. Your mother used to sing it when she was a girl and, Jiri, she had a sweet voice just like yours. Thank you, Miss Drake. The children do you credit. Christa, I congratulate you, my dear, on your good memory and excellent French accent. I will leave you now. At ease! As you were!

Looking back, Jiri thought that the only impressions the scene had made on him at the time were his awestruck admiration of Christa's prowess in French, and the fact that Miss Drake had been very pleased with them both; she had allowed them each to choose a sweet from the box she kept to reward exceptionally good work.

Jiri then looked up and saw the portrait of Gisela that hung above the fireplace; she was rather younger than in the Pallin picture, and wore a white dress with her single ring. Jiri recalled the first time he had seen it.

He was barely seven. He was walking with Miss Drake when Karel had called them into his study; there was something he wished to discuss with Miss Drake; it would not take long, and surely the boy could stand quietly for a few minutes. Jiri gazed around the room.

--I know who that is!

--Hush, Jiri. You know that you should not speak to your uncle unless he speaks to you first.

--I know, I know! But why is she here and why has she changed her dress?

There was a silence.

Then Flora had a moment of intuition. Of course! There must be a similar portrait at Pallin and from babyhood Jiri had been told, That is your mother. He was still very young and in some ways rather backward. It was easy to see how confusion might arise.

--Come, Jiri. I am sure you understand that there can be different pictures of the same person. Why, here is a portrait of the Emperor; we have one in the schoolroom and there is another one in the big dining room.

--Oh, yes! How silly of me! Of course! There are two pictures of her, but she is somewhere else.

Flora glanced at Karel and was horrified by the look on his face. Swallowing her scruples, she sought to make things better by saying,

--That is right, Jiri. I am sure your father has told you that your mother is in Heaven. That is why you have Mutti to look after you.

Jiri nodded. This seemed to satisfy him, and he began hopping from one foot to the other as he looked at the other features of the unfamiliar room.

--We can conclude this another time, Miss Drake. I find Jiri's presence rather distracting. He must be trained to stand to attention unless otherwise instructed. I will begin tomorrow, but for now you might both return to the schoolroom. Door!

He clapped his hands and the door was swiftly opened. As it was now, to admit first Karel, and then two maids with Jiri's supper.

Jiri's previous visit to Tarnheim, in the early months of 1934, had been brief and in wintry weather. Now it was an unusually warm spring; next morning he stepped onto the terrace to see sunshine, greening meadows, alpine flowers. Suddenly he thought of the bathing pool; surely later in the day, when the sun had been on the water, it might not be too cold. He longed to be there; and that afternoon set out with a towel.

The pool was smaller than he remembered. But the sense of intense quiet, so often broken by their shouting and splashing, was still there, as were the antique statues, the inscribed stone, and the ribbons and bunches of herbs tied to the bushes. Jiri decided not to feel the temperature of the water. He was here now, and was going in anyway. It was none too warm as he stripped off, but he did not hesitate, and plunged in.

It was icy!

He swam vigorously, managing to warm up with an exhilarating sense of clarity; he disappeared behind the waterfall, came out, jumped up and down, plunged under the water and came up; the spring breeze felt chilly on his wet shoulders, and he heard a voice:

--You'd better come out! You're getting cold!

Looking to the side of the pool, he saw a woman holding out his towel; he swam towards her, scrambled out and was enfolded in the towel, with which she was soon rubbing him dry.

--That's good! Just open your legs a bit... There! Now you can get some clothes on, and sit down somewhere while I find your socks and dry your feet.

Jiri stamped his feet to warm them, then the stamping turned into one of the dances of the region; he seized her as he sang the music and they whirled and stamped around the pool. He ended by pressing her to him and sharing a long kiss.

--Not now! You've only just got dressed again. We'll find somewhere warmer for another time.

She was wearing a dirndl in the traditional Tarnheim village print, with a warm shawl; not a girl, she was perhaps in her mid-thirties, strongly built, brown-haired and blue-eyed.

--You don't know who I am, Mister Jiri?

--I am sorry, but no.

--Remember Grushenka? She was my great grandmother; I have the same name as her, Hertha.

Jiri had never known the old nurse's given name; she'd always been just Grushenka.

--Hertha! I thought Grushenka's family all lived down in the village now.

--We do. But I come up here from time to time to keep an eye on things.

They were walking down the mountain path towards the castle.

--Baba Hertha taught me a lot of things.

--She was very wise. But she got some things wrong.

--Oh?

--Yes. Did she tell you about my Waking Up Drink? She made me have that for years, telling me that it would make me grow as tall as my uncle, and at last, I had to admit, it didn't work.

--Of course not! Anyone with a grain of sense could see that! She just told you that to make sure you'd drink it! She only wanted to build you up a bit as you were such a scrawny little thing. You still are. Though you've got a nice bottom.

--So I have been told.

Hertha laughed, a deep, warm, infectious laugh in which Jiri joined.

--How are you going to get home?

--Someone will be waiting to take me. But don't worry, little Master Jiri. I'll come to see you before you go back. If you do go.

Karel had ordered a fire to be lit in the Jaegerzimmer, the small room, hung with tapestries and decorated with antlers and mounted deer heads, where he usually went after dinner. Sitting opposite each other the two men looked strikingly alike. Both wore dinner jackets; seated, the difference in height was less appreciable, and the dim light obscured their difference in age. They had glasses of cognac; Karel was smoking a cigar, while Jiri held a cigarette; he rarely smoked as he said the voice did not like it, but when he did so he preferred Russian cigarettes. Now he had a Balkan Sobranie, its black paper and golden tip fitting the sophistication of his clothing.

337

--Jiri, his uncle was saying, can you assure me that the items you took with you to England five years ago are safely in a bank?

--Yes, sir. I promised you that I would draw on them only if my family was in absolute want, and that has not happened.

In fact, Jiri had kept back some of the jewellery. Magda now had two brooches and a hinged bangle; sometimes acquaintances, noting Mrs Zellek's sensibly subdued dress style, wondered why she wore such flashy costume jewellery; it could surely not be real. Jiri's grandmother's pearl choker had been restrung into two single-strand necklaces; Magda had one and often wore it since Jiri assured her that in England one wore pearls with everything, and pearls needed to be kept close to the skin rather than in a drawer. The other he had given to Flora Loudon.

Finally, there were the rings and bracelet which he kept on hand in case he needed to pawn anything. Paul's entry to the Vaughan School had required an expensive uniform, new satchel and a Conway Stewart fountain pen. A gratifying run of professional engagements meant that Jiri had the outlay of new evening clothes from a good tailor plus the expense of hiring a regular accompanist. But, at present, everything could be accounted for. He took up the conversation.

--Sir, in two days the courier from the Swiss bank will be here to take the other things to Geneva; they will be safe in the strongbox my father established. When things settle down politically, we can recall them at any time. I will also, as we discussed, take a few additional items with me to London; I have had my larger suitcase specially adapted and I am sure there will be no difficulty, especially if I remove the tiara from its case.

--Ah, yes, the tiara... strictly speaking, your wife could have worn it at your wedding, as did your mother, and Christa's mother.

Jiri smiled inwardly at the thought of the Tarnheim tiara at the very quiet wedding he and Magda had in Berlin; she wore a pale blue costume with a rose corsage, and a rather smart hat. But of course, Paul would marry; he would make a wonderfully handsome bridegroom and any woman would be lucky to have him. The tiara would come in handy then.

--Really, Uncle, he continued, this is for the best. You will be safe here, and if there is war, which I am sadly certain there will be, you can sit it out and I will return when I can.

--Huh! If the Führer declares war, then, however much I disapprove of some of his policies, it is my duty to do what I can. I was a reserve officer until relatively recently.

--Uncle, neither of us is at all likely to be called to active service. Thank God you are fit and healthy, but you are... of advancing years... and I would not pass any medical entry to the British army.

--The British army? I had forgotten: you are now a British citizen, Jiri, why? Why?

--Uncle, I have explained this. When I came here in 1934, I told you that it was not safe for me, nor my family, to remain in Germany or Austria. By great good fortune, I have obtained citizenship for us all, so we are not subject to internment or deportation.

For a moment he hesitated, and then found himself saying,

--Uncle, if... if... you felt it in your best interests, we could manage, I mean, you could come to us in London. We could make room for you and I doubt whether a man of your age would be subject to internment.

It was a huge relief when his uncle, though visibly touched, refused the offer. Then in his turn the older man said something surprising.

Refilling Jiri's glass, he asked suddenly,

--My boy, are you happy?

The von Tarnheims spoke so rarely of emotions as distinct from concepts of duty, honour and family loyalty. Karel had never asked his nephew whether he had wanted to join the Ulans, or what his hopes and plans might be. Before he knew it, Jiri answered him sincerely.

--No, Uncle. No I am not happy.

It was true. He did not like going to the office each day, all day; the work itself was actually most interesting and his colleagues at least a fascinating study, but when was he to do the important things, the piano, singing, riding, poker, roulette, the occasional fling with someone attractive? While he did not dislike their flat in Maida Vale, where he had the best furniture from Pallin and of course the Bösendorfer, and where Magda made things so comfortable, how often he suffered a dreadful *heimweh* for the mountains. And there was something else: Vernon. Although nothing could now be done about that.

--Don't go back, my dear boy. You belong here. You are all I have, unless Christa is returned to us, and then she would be returning to you as much as to me. This woman you have married does not matter to us.

Jiri covered his face. Christi. He must be here if she does come back. He thought of the afternoon's meeting at the bathing pool. What had Hertha said?

He could write to Magda. He could tell her that he had been detained. Then he could write again and again, putting off his return. He would see the next Alpine summer and the next. The autumns when the sunsets coloured the mountains. The winters... he would be safe and warm here, he would play the piano, he would care for his uncle and at last lay him honourably in the von Tarnheim vault; he would live here alone as his uncle had done until one day, one night, while the snowflakes fell outside, he would lie in his carved bedstead and fall asleep...

--Jiri! Be careful, my boy! You are still tired from your journey!

His uncle was taking the cigarette from his fingers and stubbing it out.

--Uncle! I humbly apologise! But listen: I have a son. If I bring him here, and there is war, he will be interned once he is eighteen. Or, if he relinquished British citizenship, he will be in the Nazi war effort, which is exactly what I wish to avoid. I must go back for his sake.

--You have never brought him here. He is, what, fifteen years old? And, from what you tell me, I suspect born out of wedlock. I cannot accept him as my heir. You and this... Magda... have no children; I suppose it is too late?

--Sir. Paul is my son. It was not possible to marry his mother, although I would gladly have done so. You do not know, Uncle, what it was like in Berlin at the time. As for Magda, even if we had been blessed with children, and at one time we had hopes, Paul would remain my eldest son and will inherit anything I have.

He showed Karel a small photograph of Paul. His uncle considered it.

--He is not like you, Jiri.

--No. He is very like my own father, and also takes after his mother. He is a wonderfully strong, healthy fellow.

--That boy is not a von Tarnheim.

Jiri did not argue. Suddenly he felt very tired.

--Uncle, there is something I must tell you, something I have only just learned. Christa: she has a son, I think he must now be seventeen or eighteen. And two years ago she may have been living in Texas. You have a grandson as well as a great-nephew. Those boys are both von Tarnheims. Uncle, when the coming war is over, why do I not try to reunite us? I could travel to America; I could track them down.

--Yes, Jiri. You would do that and you would do something that you would regret.

--I should not regret killing Bruce Westenberger.

There was silence.

--Jiri. You must give this up. I have no daughter. And I do not accept your wife and this boy. You know that I have never approved of your way of life; I do not approve of your present actions. But you are all I have and I will not have you endangering yourself by committing a capital crime. Jiri, I had to accept something worse: we must both try to realise that both Christa and her mother rejected us. They were not lured away or kidnapped; they made the decision to go. And, Jiri, there is in turn something I must tell you. You have a right to know. Jiri, your mother is dead.

Was Karel losing his mind?

Jiri spoke gently and calmly.

--Yes, Uncle. Of course. I have always known that. My father and stepmother never hid that from me; I never knew her, but of course from time to time I have thought about her. I did try to find her grave before I left Switzerland; you may recall that I wrote to you, asking its whereabouts, but I suppose you never received the letter, as there was no answer; after that I went back to Pallin and have never visited Switzerland since.

Karel covered his face with his hands.

--Dear Uncle, do not distress yourself. I see now that her death must have been worse for you than for anyone. Of course my father mourned her, but he had me, and my stepmother made him very happy. I know you never liked Mutti, but she was a wonderful woman; after all, she took on a child who by all accounts was no easy task! While you, at that time, well, it must have been rather soon after Aunt Valerie left you, and the loss of your beloved sister, coming when it did...

--Yes. Yes. You are right. Now, please leave me, my boy.

--Very well, sir. I will ask Hans to come to you; perhaps you are not quite well.

Jiri rose and went obediently to the door. He did not see Karel opening a drawer and replacing a letter he had taken from it, a letter headed with a Swiss address.

I am an old coward. But the boy was so full of consideration; he thought I was becoming senile. Well, let him think so; it may keep him here.

For the next couple of days, Jiri was fully occupied with the Swiss courier and various other arrangements. He went into Strelitz to send telegrams: to Magda, to the translation office, to Mrs Melmot.

He played chess with his uncle and attempted to tune the sadly neglected piano that he'd so often played in the past, and which seemed an old friend under his fingers. As always, for such a slight person, Jiri seemed to take up a lot of space, singing, naming the dogs, teasing the servants, asking his uncle questions, calling for his boots, demanding his old chamois Austrian hat; it must surely be somewhere about? He swam in the pool again; this time Hertha was not there, so he had to get dried and dressed by himself. As there was no one to dance with, he warmed his feet by stepping briskly down the mountain path. Karel saw and heard him coming, glowing from his swim, in his English flannels and Fair Isle sweater, his unmistakeably pitched and accented voice calling for the dogs.

Then, one evening, he was preparing for bed when he heard a gentle but firm knock at his door; he assumed it was one of the servants, coming to check the fire, to see if he needed anything.

--*Komm*!

He was standing in his shirt, bare-legged, wearing his slippers. Hertha stared at his scars.

--Those Russians hurt you, didn't they?

--Yes. Yes, they did.

--And Gräfin Christa. She hurt you too. Although perhaps that was for the best.

--I don't think about it.

--They say you've got a wife and boy.

--They say correctly.

--Not bringing them here?

--No. It's not safe.

--I don't know about that. But anyway, the honoured Graf wouldn't like it.

--No; that's why I have stayed away. Partly, at least. I didn't see him for fourteen years. He didn't approve of the way I lived, and I would not subject my wife to his contempt and condescension. Then five years ago I came back for a few days, just before we moved to London. But I expect you know about that. We made peace, and I have kept in touch with him since.

--He's an old man now.

--Yes. I am rather concerned about his health but he will be safe up here. I have told him that once the world has settled down, I will come back. And perhaps I will bring Magda and Paul; if he met them he might accept them and we will all live here and...

He buried his face in his hands. I have been so homesick.

--Come now. Baba Hertha told me that you don't like being alone at night.

--This will make it harder for me to leave.

--I know. That's why I'm here.

Jiri left Tarnheim so early that it was still dawn. Sunrise on the mountains showed its daily wanton useless and uncaring beauty. By now, he had a feeling of inexorability: *quand le vin est tiré, il faut le boire.* One could endure almost anything if one set one's mind to it. Also perhaps none of this was real.

Gregor was to drive him to Strelitz, where he would begin what he must think of as his homeward journey. His luggage was loaded into the Steyr. Slowly his uncle came down the staircase; he said nothing but approached Jiri and embraced him. He had never done this before; he had patted the boy on the head, clapped him on the shoulder, clasped his hands but never until now had he held him in his arms. Jiri let his head rest on the old man's shoulder, then he disengaged himself and got into the car.

I will not look back. But he did. His uncle stood in the doorway, his hand raised in farewell, or was it a salute? Jiri's tears made it impossible to tell.

After his return to London, Jiri announced that this year they would have a proper summer holiday. Magda deserved to be waited on; they would spend two weeks at an excellent hotel in Torquay. There would be swimming, sailing, tennis, dancing and lots of bridge. There would be a theatre and cinema. Jiri would take his riding things and find the stables. Magda must have at least two new frocks, a summer hat and something elegant for the evening. Paul must have a new tennis racquet. It would all be delightful.

Actually it was. And it was especially memorable as it was the last summer the three Zelleks were to spend together; they had not long been back in Maida Vale when Magda was stricken by the news of Hitler's invasion of Poland, and two days later war with Germany was declared.

1941

The spring of 1941 had not begun well for Jiri Zellek.

He had just returned from a rather disastrous mission to occupied France.

Cyril, anyone with a grain of sense would have realised that smuggling Jerry Zellek into Normandy was bound to end badly. The minute he opened his mouth the French would take him for German and have him shot, or the Germans would look at him and assume he was non-Aryan scum and should be shot, or he would get entangled with some local woman whose husband would want him shot. Sometimes I've wondered whether that wasn't actually the object of the exercise, in which case it failed doubly in that he got out and took that French priest with him; the only redeeming feature, that, since Armand Sentier has been able to fill in a lot about the Resistance. But of course they managed to derail the wrong train.

How did he account for that?

Cyril turned back to the typed transcript of Jiri's debriefing.

'I was tired and confused. And anyone could misread a train timetable. I have often thought that they should be differently organised. And at least I was quite successful in

placing the exploding rat so that the fireman would shovel it into the firebox.'

True. It was just that he was supposed to do it with the German munitions train. Instead he got a train transporting forced labourers; with no munitions on board, the train carriages didn't blow up and Zellek and some of the Resistance released all the prisoners, hundreds of them, swarming all over the region, keeping the Germans occupied for weeks. Probably most of them got away or were hidden by the locals.

Did Zellek say anything else?

Not really.

'It was an honour to have met Father Sentier, and it was delightful to be back in France, I have not been there since before the war, but actually I do not think that being a special agent is my metier. Are not ENSA short of pianists at the moment?'

No, we're not going to let him get away with that. But I think it's time to move Zellek. Especially as Captain Treven is being invalided back from North Africa.

Treven?

Yes, husband of Rosamund Treven, the local lady that Zellek's been carrying on with. Goes over to help her with the horses; takes him all night sometimes.

Jiri's affair with Rosamund Treven had begun in autumn 1940. He'd been at Felden Hall for a few weeks by then. He had soon found his niche in the eclectic collection of eccentrically wired brains occupied in translating and decoding wireless messages. The group was almost entirely male; there was one married couple, both mathematicians, though with different specialisms, and one female polyglot Cambridge librarian with multiple degrees in Middle Eastern languages. Sexual interest, at least for those focussed on women, centred on the secretarial staff, who somehow found time for shorthand and typing in between. There were several excellent musicians (flute, violin, viola and two or three good pianists: one had to reserve practice time on the instrument), and many fanatical chess and bridge players. Jiri was not the only Catholic. He learned that a number of bikes were available for use, and that on Sunday mornings the RCs usually rode over to Mass at a nearby village. It was a few years since he had ridden a bike, and the choice was between a very old, heavy machine that he could hardly shift and a lighter ladies' one. Between discomfort and humiliation Jerry opted for the latter and was soon riding around the countryside whenever possible; it cleared his mind, helped him with problem-solving and, he was convinced, strengthened his left leg wonderfully. Thus he had turned up in Rosamund Treven's stable yard one frosty morning.

--What's your name?

--Jerry.

--You're joking! You mean you've been parachuted into the yard as a spy?

--No. It's my name; at least English people call me Jerry, maybe because they can't pronounce my real name, and maybe because I sound like one. But I assure you I'm not.

--Well, what is your real name then?

--In the family my name is Jiri. But, as you are so inquisitive...

Jerry clicked his heels and bowed. Jaroslav Felix von Tarnheim Zellek.

--Pleased to meet you. I think I'll try Jiri. Have you worked with horses?

--Yes.

In fact Rosamond and Jiri meant something rather different; he had grown up in a world where mucking out, tacking and untacking were done by others. But he was making friend with the horses, particularly a beautiful mare who reminded him of Grazia.

--I can't let you try Rowena until I've seen you ride. Maybe you could try Sultan?

--I would like to but... he indicated his flannels and brogues.

--Stable boy's been called up. His things are in the tack room. They should fit.

Jiri emerged from the tack room, leaving his trousers and jacket neatly folded on a bale of straw, and his shoes and bicycle clips parked beside it.

He was wearing the stable boy's breeches and jacket, plus his boots, which fitted well.

--Up you go. He may be a bit fresh.

Sultan was something of a test. He was a massive hunter of over seventeen hands, raring to go and in need of exercise.

Jiri controlled the horse and walked him into the paddock; he trotted, cantered, walked again, getting the feel of the horse. Rosamond watched. Very neat, very confident, very happy to be in the saddle, she thought. Jerry and Sultan jumped a low pole, turned, cantered back.

--He really wants to go; could I take him out for half an hour? I'll be in trouble if I stay longer.

--You're up at the Hall, aren't you? No need to answer; I know they're all hush-hush. But yes. You know what you're doing. Take the bridle path over that field, then back by the lane.

Rosamund's husband had been away for some time, and when a few days later she accidentally came upon Jerry changing in the tack room she made little resistance, although it was cold in there and not very romantic to do it against the wall. Also Jerry was notoriously fast in action.

They were drinking tea in the kitchen one day when Rosamund finally said,

--We could go to bed. I mean really.

--Rose... he had removed his shirt and vest... Rose, I have scars.

As he stepped out of his trousers, she saw what he meant.

--Jiri, it's... you must have been smashed up. I'd noticed something; thought it must have been hunting or point to pointing.

--No. It was the war, the last one.

Another thing, or rather one among many things, that Rosamond noticed about Jiri was that he sang. When he was happy, which he was oddly and constantly during that autumn and winter, he sang all the time: popular songs, songs from the shows, folk songs in several languages, hymns, some of them in Latin, and stuff that she later, over many years, occasionally heard on the wireless and identified as opera or classical music. Neither Rosamond nor her husband, Roddy, had any knowledge at all of music apart from dance music, and she had never heard anything like this voice at close quarters. There was a German song that he seemed to associate with her particularly... what does it mean, Jiri? Ah, that! Rose, it's you, Rose, rose among the heather. Once years later she heard it sung at one of the boys' school concerts, heard it with a weird lurch of emotion. Jiri, oh Jiri, what

351

happened to you, are you still living and no, no, I will never try to find you... the war was another life, wasn't it?

Christmas came; there were festive activities at Felden Hall, and Rosamund had been invited to a neighbouring farm, but he came to her after midnight Mass. She gave him a box of chocolates: Rose! You must have spent all your sweet coupons on this! It is delightful! And a pair of socks that she had knitted for him, an oblique reference to his large, cold feet. He produced a long flat box wrapped in expensive paper. Inside on a bed of tissue was a silk and lace nightdress.

--Jiri! HOW did you come by this... you little blackmarketeer!

--I hope it is the correct size. I must ask you to try it on now, just in case.

At the end of January, he disappeared for some weeks. Rosamund knew better than to ask what was going on; it was widely known that Felden Hall's activities were secret and unpredictable. She received a postcard, which he must have broken all the rules to send; it was posted from somewhere in Kent and said only, See you soon, darling, JXXX

After checking the horses for the night, Rosamund locked the kitchen door and prepared to make herself some cocoa.

She heard knocking, unlocked the door cautiously and saw Jiri, wearing his tweed cap, overcoat and gumboots. His face was haggard.

--Jiri! You look as if you've been to Hell and back.

--Not quite. May I come in, Rose?

She drew him inside and relocked the door.

--I'm sorry... I don't think I can get my boots off. He seemed strangely distressed by this.

--It's all right. I'll help you. Let's get your coat off, sit down...

She began to pull his boots off.

--My ankle hurts.

--All right, I'll be careful.

Not knowing which ankle he meant, she pulled slowly, discovering that his left ankle was tightly wrapped in a crepe bandage.

--Here.

He needed the cocoa more than she did. Gradually he began to look slightly better.

--Rose, I wanted you.

--All right. But right now, I'll get you upstairs.

--I don't know if I can...

--Then I'll just hold you.

In bed, Jiri fell asleep almost instantly. He was never a comfortable bedfellow, all bones and angles, with icy feet. Rosamund dozed, until he woke towards dawn. They made love, and he went back to sleep.

--Tea. And a couple of shortbreads.

--Thank you. My back feels so much better after last night! Perhaps, Rose...

He pulled her towards him.

--No, Jiri. I need to talk to you. While you were... away... and I know you can't tell me anything about that... I had some news.

--Roddy? Jiri's sharp features were thinner than ever.

--Yes. He's on his way home.

--Wounded?

--No, in a horrible sort of way, he's been lucky. He got some illness, and while he was in hospital, almost the whole of his unit were killed...

--Never underestimate the Afrika Korps, muttered Jiri.

--So everyone and everything is being regrouped. Roddy's being sent back to England to advise on that, and I think he's going to be based in York, so he'll come and go between here and there.

--You'll still need someone to exercise the horses.

--I'd thought of that, but it wouldn't work, Jiri. Roddy's bright, and... So I've found a couple of girls locally. They were keen to come before, but I put them off because you and I... well anyway... Jiri, it's...

--One last time, my beautiful, beautiful Rose...

Making his way back to Felden Hall, Jiri had taken to his bed for two days. By now the powers in charge had decided that he would be of more use back in London, where a special translation unit was being set up in Vauxhall to deal with random material from the capital's foreign refugees, resistance groups and displaced persons. Still, the resident doctor had pronounced that he needed time somewhere out of the way before facing the bomb-torn city. He was pretty useless as he was.

One of the clerks travelled with him to Kings Cross and then on to Victoria. He had given Jiri his ticket, put his suitcase up onto the rack for him and left him on the train to his final destination. As they progressed the carriage emptied and he became preoccupied with the problem of how he was going to get his suitcase down. He was past feeling any pride, and would have asked one of the departing passengers to do it for him, had he thought of this in time. But he had not. Eventually he formed a strategy of inching the case towards the edge of the rack so that it tipped over and fell to the floor.

He was, then, ready to open the door and get out when the guard announced the name of his station, and with difficulty he hauled the case onto the platform. In gathering twilight, the train steamed off. Jiri sighted a bench and thought he would just stay there, but someone was coming towards him.

--Mr Zellek?

--Yes.

--You're for the convent. I'm Williams; the pony trap is outside.

Thank God, Williams picked up the suitcase, then led the way, making allowances for Jiri's relatively slow progress and helping him up into the vehicle.

--Thank you. That is a good-looking pony... is he... Dartmoor?

--No, sir! Bryn here is a Welsh pony; they're all like that, honey-coloured with the cream mane and tail. What with the petrol shortage and all, the sisters have been using him in the pony trap for getting about generally, not that they get about much, of course, seeing what their vows are.

The convent gates were imposing, but little of the grounds could be seen at this time of the evening.

--You're in the guestrooms, Mr Zellek. Here's your room and the bathroom opens here.

Jiri sat down in the single armchair.

--I reckon you might need a bit of help, sir.

Williams helped him off with his overcoat.

--Yes. Thank you. The bathroom? Would it be possible to take a bath?

The thought of sinking into warm water was irresistible.

--Well, the geyser does need a bit of a knack. I'll explain it to you tomorrow. But perhaps for now I could run you a bath and then come back with your bit of supper.

In the end, Williams helped Jiri undress, got him into the bath, got him out of the bath and helped him into his pyjamas.

Hot tea, and sandwiches, some of which Jiri ate before getting into bed.

--Mother Superior will see you in the morning, Mr Zellek. I'll come round to make sure you are up and doing.

--Good evening, Mr Williams. How did you find our guest?

--Dog tired, Mother, and maybe not well. But a night's sleep might make all the difference. What time shall I tell him to come to see you?

The next morning, Mr Williams found Jiri out of bed, and staring bemusedly at the geyser.

--Good morning, Williams! I thought I had better shave before meeting Mother Superior, but I am not sure how to obtain hot water.

--I'll get it going for you in a minute, sir, but first how about some breakfast before it gets cold?

Breakfast was often Jiri's best meal and he looked eagerly at the large tray. It was lined with an embroidered tray cloth; the teapot was covered by a knitted cosy in the shape of a country cottage, with its features carefully worked. The boiled egg, fresh from Mrs Williams's hens, was kept warm by an egg cosy, also knitted, in the shape of a chicken.

Jiri knew that as a boy he would have been enchanted by these items, and as it was he still appreciated their charm.

--How delightfully Mrs Williams has prepared this! Do please thank her for me.

He sat down and made an excellent breakfast while Mr Williams persuaded the geyser to produce Jiri's shaving water. Mr Zellek was rising in his estimation: interested in horses, showing proper respect for Mother Superior, and knowing a good tea cosy when he saw one.

--Ah, Mr Zellek.

--Mother Superior. Jiri bowed.

--I trust Mr Williams has made you comfortable?

--He has been very kind.

--Good. Please sit down. I hope your stay here will be of benefit. Tomorrow Dr Logan comes to see Sister Marie, one of our older sisters, as he does each week. I will ask him to look at you also.

--I would rather not, thank you.

--Oh? Why is that?

--These examinations are usually unpleasant, and they tell me only what I know already.

--Which is?

--That I have an old back injury; that much of the time it is quite well, and sometimes it is not.

--Forgive me, Mr Zellek, but I have to say that, apart from any back trouble, you are very thin, and I believe you suffer from spells of dizziness; perhaps Dr Logan might concentrate on that. At all events I will send him to you. In the meantime, one of the sisters will show you round. Mass is at eleven each morning and you are welcome to attend; you are also welcome at our other offices, although I must ask you to sit in the gallery, as we do not allow men to be present otherwise. You may enjoy the grounds, apart from our enclosure. The gardens are just beginning to look springlike.

Indeed they were. It was as different from Yorkshire as it was from London; this was Jiri's first experience of spring in the south of England, and to be able to observe it quietly and at leisure was a revelation. Willows were a particular short-lived crisp yellow/green that sounded to him like a harpsichord. There were daffodils, primroses and celandines all varying in their shades of gold; birds ranging from rooks building in the tall trees around the convent, to tiny tits and wrens doing what birds need to do in spring and making quite a noise doing it. Jiri stood and watched, or walked slowly along the paths, into the walled garden with its central fountain, and sat on one of the surrounding seats. He began to recognise individual nuns, and Williams entertained him with stories of their idiosyncrasies including stories of Sister Marie, the elderly nun whom Dr Logan visited regularly. Sister Marie, who had indeed numerous physical infirmities to contend with, made sure that those around her were as miserable as she was. Far from 'offering it up' as a penance, she inflicted her grievances on her sisters, who silently considered an hour spent with Sister Marie sufficient atonement for a fair number of sins. Sister Marie sat in her wheelchair on a glassed-in terrace, sheltered from the wind and attracting the sun, where Jiri also sometimes rested. One of the novices was reading to her, and the younger woman was close to tears.

--Sister, suggested Jiri, perhaps I might read to Sister Marie for a while; we could change places, or you might sit in the garden, or in the chapel perhaps… I'm sure the novice mistress would not object, and if she does, well, of course I shall be to blame.

Mother Superior was walking with Sister Scholastica, the choirmistress…

--Do you see that, Mother?

Jiri was reading to Sister Marie. Every now and again she tapped him sharply on the wrist; he would stop reading, say something, and resume.

--What is happening?

--Ah! She is correcting his pronunciation.

--Sister Marie says that she can hear a man's voice better than the novices' as they all mumble. But why, she asks, does she have to have a foreigner? At least she can do the poor fellow a good turn by pointing out his mistakes.

By now, Jiri was spending quite a bit of time with the Williamses. Rather than have Mrs Williams bring his supper from their cottage to the guestrooms, he would go and eat it with them; there was no wireless in the guest accommodation, but here he was able to listen to the news, and sometimes other broadcasts. A social distance was observed; he was Mr Zellek, whatever they called him behind his back, and they were Williams and Mrs Williams. This distinction had perhaps made it easier for the Williams's help to be offered and accepted on Jiri's first evening; for half his life, he had been accustomed to the services of a nanny, valet, body servant or batman. Williams, for his part, was naturally kind and gentle, used to handling animals and drawn to the vulnerable.

--Bart, said Mrs Williams one evening, I reckon our Mr Zed isn't taking that tonic Dr Logan gave him. I'm sure he pours some down the lavatory every day to make it look as though he's taking it.

--Devious little sod! He's worse'n a kid! But I don't see what we can do about it.

--Well, Mother Superior did ask us to look after him.

--That's what we're doing, Em.

Jiri stood in a flowerbed beneath an open window.

Sister Scholastica was leading choir practice. Jiri listened to the Latin responses and after while he joined in; Sister Scholastica put her head out of the window.

--Mr Zellek?

--Yes? Am I doing this incorrectly?

--No, but the sisters have stopped singing to listen to you. Perhaps you could sing something else, somewhere else.

--What would you like? Jiri tried to think of suitable hymns, and the one that came into his head was not a Latin one at all; it was an Anglican hymn he had heard often on the wireless and at some Church of England services that he had attended, mainly to listen to the organ.

So David Lomax heard Jiri before he saw him. *(I fell in love with the voice. I only discovered later that it came with a rather annoying person.)* Someone was singing 'Morning Has Broken'; the voice was a light yet resonantly powerful tenor, the sort sometimes called *tenore di grazia*. It was somehow different from an English tone, yet certainly not robustly Italian. It was a moment of absolute magic, the spring garden, the feeling and clarity of the performance...

He saw a short, skinny man with dark curly hair, evidently

completely absorbed in singing. The hymn was quite a short one. Silence fell. David felt his eyes prick.

--Good morning, sister, he called, dispelling the atmosphere. Shall I take this nuisance away, whoever he is, and let you get on with your choir practice?

--He is not a nuisance, Mr Lomax, but he is something of a distraction.

The singer turned towards him and smiled. His was a mobile, mischievous face, not young… perhaps forty? Forty-five?

--I'm David Lomax. He was wearing khaki, he was a tall young man, broad-shouldered but rather gaunt. I'm on my way to the chapel to have a go on the organ; I'm stationed near here and the sisters have kindly allowed me in…

Jiri clicked his heels and bowed. Jerry Zellek.

--Jerry? You're joking?

--No, I am not. In the family my name is Jiri… and in England, well, I'm Jerry, although I assure you I am not a Jerry as it is commonly understood here.

(Of course, he's Austrian, or something like it… that explains…)

David gave Jiri an organ lesson, then suggested a pint at the local pub.

--Are you allowed out?

--I have not taken vows of obedience to Mother Superior. And she has not expressly forbidden the occasional pint.

Williams came into the stable to find Jiri talking to Bryn.

--Williams, he asked, does anyone ride Bryn?

--Not now; when he was with the Rector's family, they all rode him as well as using him in the pony trap. When they left, the sisters had him and put him out to grass, but, as I told you, with the petrol shortage, he's earned his keep.

--Do you think he would take my weight?

Williams had seen Jiri naked.

--No question. Do you ride, sir?

--Yes.

--And you wouldn't be going far, or fast, would you?

--No, no, not far.

--Forgive me asking, but is your back up to it?

--Yes, I think it is; it has been much better for the last couple of days, and sometimes a gentle ride actually does it good.

--Tell you what. I'll look over the tack this afternoon, try to find you a pair of breeches, and we might give it a go tomorrow...

--I'll need a mounting block, unless you can give me a leg up? Perfect!

Bryn seemed pleased; perhaps he recalled the days when he was the pet of a large family; Jerry walked him round the yard and into the paddock, where he was persuaded to offer a sedate trot.

--Where did you learn, Mr Zellek?

--As a child, and then in the army.

Most of Jiri's stay so far had of course been in Lent. As Easter approached, he recalled that when the priest from the neighbouring village came to say Mass, he heard the sisters' confessions; would he have time, asked Jiri, to fit me in?

So he was able to go to confession before celebrating the Triduum with the sisters. It meant little sleep between Good

Friday and Easter Sunday, but he was not one to worry about that, and in fact characteristically from time to time he fell asleep in chapel, woke up fully alert, and went back to sleep…

On Easter Sunday the sisters celebrated, and Jiri celebrated with them. That evening he sang to them, and they sang too.

--David, I think I shall be going to London quite soon.

--What?

--Yes, we live there, and I am being sent to do some war work.

--What about the bombing?

--Well, our flat has been unharmed so far. Although naturally I have been worried about the piano. And my dear wife, of course.

The last time David caught sight of Jerry (as he called him) was unexpected. He was crossing the meadows one morning when a horse and rider appeared out of the mist. It was Bryn, achieving a stately canter, and David realised that the rider was Jerry; he had never seen his friend on horseback before. Slowing to a trot, Jerry raised his hand and waved.

The next day he had left the convent.

David did not see his friend again until the winter of 1943.

He was on leave, and decided to attend one of the lunchtime concerts at the National Gallery, joining the huge queue that wound its way through Trafalgar Square. There was something familiar about the person marshalling the orderly crowd, handing out programmes and ensuring that as many as possible had the correct change. *(That is always a problem, David.)* As David drew nearer, he recognised Jerry, wearing a dark overcoat with a fur collar, and a black hat.

Mutual delight.

--What are you doing here, Jerry? Stupid question as it was obvious, but Jerry answered good-naturedly that Myra was always short-handed and had asked him to help out when possible.

--So you know Myra Hess?

--Well, I have worked with her... excuse me, David... enjoy the concert!

--Wait, Jerry... can we go for a drink afterwards?

--See you on the portico!

On the way to the pub David noticed that Jerry was using his stick even more than when they had last met.

--A little adventure with some bomb damage. It is much better already; I have had a *v/wunderful* doctor.

Jerry led the way to a pub in Villiers Street, where he was evidently well known to the publican and other regulars.

--Afternoon, Mr Zed, let me know if there's anything I can do for you, one or two lucky accidents, I'll see you later...

The speaker winked and sauntered off.

--Who was that? David had suspected the typical wide boy/black market operator.

--He was my bookie before the war. But of course he has had to extend his activities; it is shocking that so many people have been denied the chance of making an honest living, poor fellow!

David decided not to attempt to decode this, and asked after Jerry's family, not that he was particularly interested as he had as yet met none of them. Magda, it appeared, was driving an ambulance. She had teamed up with several exiled Polish compatriots: 'Here come the Poles!' signalled their arrival at bomb sites. Saint Cecilia still seemed to be looking after the piano, as the flat had sustained no, or very little, bomb damage. Paul, to the amazement of his parents, had opted to join the navy on call-up. Neither of them had any connections with seafaring. But it had been a wise decision (so like Paul) and his ability with numbers and systems, plus the excellent knowledge of German which he was usually at pains to conceal, ensured him a place as a wireless operator.

--You see, David, Paul is actually a native speaker, and his accent is purer than mine or Magda's! We lived in Berlin, and then Munich, until he was ten. He is on a destroyer protecting the Atlantic shipping. It is dangerous because of the U-boats, but you know, David, I would rather he was there than involved in hand-to-hand, or perhaps I should say tank to tank, fighting.

As they moved towards Embankment Tube station, they heard a newsboy's cryptic cry:

Star News 'n' Stannard! Star News 'n' Stannard! [*Star, (Evening) News* and *(Evening) Standard*].

American liner torpedoed! Huge loss of life! Hundreds drowned!

Jerry bought a paper. The SS *Floritania* had been sunk in the mid-Atlantic. There was little hope for any of her passengers and crew.

David saw with horror that Jerry was swaying, his knees buckling. As David grabbed him, he muttered,

--I am sorry, David. Suddenly I am not well. Would it be

too much to ask for your help? I do not think I can manage the escalators but there should be a bus.

Taxis were out of the question in the petrol shortage but it was possible to get to Maida Vale, where Jerry said he lived, by bus and David managed to get him aboard; neither of them spoke on the journey.

So David got to meet Magda Zellek for the first time. Her demeanour as she opened the door somehow indicated that she was not unfamiliar with her husband being brought home in state of collapse. In the hallway, an Ambulance Service jacket hung next to Jerry's tin hat, stirrup pump and Wellingtons, standard issue for air raid wardens. David recalled that Magda was an ambulance driver. Together they got Jerry to bed; for the first time David saw the scarring on his friend's leg.

--Thank you for helping me, David. No, I do not want anything.

Magda made tea and they chatted before the young man left, promising to telephone the next day.

As had happened a few times before, Jiri lay for two days without eating and apparently without sleeping, saying nothing. On the third morning, he asked if Magda had kept the newspapers for the last couple of days; she brought them to him. Half an hour later, he got up, shaved, demanded breakfast and left for the translation office.

Over the following days and nights they saw little of each other; they both had periods on duty, snatching sleep when they could; Magda was also occupied in finding adequate food and Jiri was at the office much of the day.

When he was around, he was either silent or boisterous, taking nothing seriously and drinking a fair amount. From his fellow wardens she learned that he was taking risks far beyond what could be expected of a man of his age and physique; he had also lost his temper with a couple of looters, and had nearly killed one of them with a brick.

This strange mood changed magically when Paul came home on leave. Jiri's devotion to Paul was one of the redeeming aspects of his character, and Magda was now convinced that his behaviour stemmed from anxiety for his son's safety; she remembered that it had started with the sinking of the *Floritania*, which had probably reminded Jiri of the dangers of the Atlantic crossing. Paul brought with him the news that for the time being, he was being deployed to wireless operations in Portsmouth: not the safest place in the UK but certainly less perilous than the high seas.

Jiri seemed to settle back into his usual persona, which was difficult enough but at least what Magda was accustomed to. As for David, once Jerry seemed more or less himself again, he forgot the episode; it was almost forty years before he was reminded of it.

Mrs Melmot died during the war; Jiri suspected that she had taken her own life and he felt guiltily that he should have taken better care of her. When he had closed down the L.T. Tucker Agency in 1940, Esme Doran had joined the Wrens. Posted to Malta, she met and married a Valletta restaurant owner; her son was being brought up by her sister in Bakewell as one of her own children. He was a bright boy and in due course he passed the scholarship examination for the local grammar school. As a teenager, he enjoyed holidays in Malta with Auntie Esme and Uncle Mario; perhaps at some point he would learn the truth.

In 1946, Jiri received letters from Hertha and from Ilse Gruber, geb. Treichler. Hertha's contained a pamphlet extolling the deeds of the Red Army. Tucked inside was a thin sheet of paper, with a message in their native language. At this point, Britain and Russia were still allies, both having fought Hitler in the Great Patriotic War, so there was little obstacle to the passage of post. Jiri knew that in 1945 the Russians had invaded the Principality along with much of eastern Germany and Austria.

Hertha said that as the Russian advance became inevitable, the villagers of Tarnheim had taken what precautions they could; even so, women had been raped and men shot, animals slaughtered and houses burned. She said nothing of her own situation. Karel had sent his few servants to hide as best they could. Only Hans, now in his nineties, remained. Karel had put on his reserve officer's uniform. Hans had found his formal evening household livery. They went onto the terrace, where there was a fine view of the mountains. Karel poured them each a glass of his best French cognac and they toasted the House of Tarnheim. After this Karel had shot first Hans and then himself.

Ilse's letter took longer to arrive. She had given it to a member of the International Red Cross, who had taken it to Geneva and posted it from there.

As Jiri had realised, Sigmund Treichler and Alois Gruber were both enthusiastic members of the Nazi Party, and although neither was initially fitted for active service, they were members of the Landsturm; in this capacity Alois had finally been drafted to the Front in the last desperate days of the war, when anyone who could hold a rifle was called to the defence of the Fatherland. Ilse did not, at the time of writing, know what had become of him. Sigmund, along with other party members, had been shot by the Russians. Both the Villa Zellek and the Gruber mansion were occupied by Russian officers, who left them in a sad condition; the factory had been bombed by the Allies in 1943. Ilse, Sigmund's wife Helga, Ilse's twins and the three Treichler children were all living, although the children were in poor health because of food shortages and lack of warmth and shelter. If Jiri could get any food parcels to them, that would be much appreciated, although Ilse doubted that such items would get through. She thought often of him; she was using his London address as the last she had for him.

PART THREE

WINCHESTER, 1948

Early October: golden autumn sunlight, a clear blue sky over the cathedral and the college, with St Catherine's Hill green behind the Norman buildings of St Cross. David Lomax drove the Morris Minor down Kingsgate Street, passing college boys in twos and threes wearing straw boaters and carrying lesson books. The car was one of the last produced before the war, and of course had not been much used since; he'd bought her soon after being demobbed, borrowing money from his father with the argument that his profession meant travelling to out-of-the-way churches at awkward times, increasingly possible now that more petrol was available. Even if he ran dry, whichever vicar he was helping out usually came up with a can or two; anything rather than do without a relief organist on a Sunday.

Heading out towards Southampton, David was making for the Woodlow Valley: Upper, Middle and Lower Woodlow, with the hamlet of Woodlow Green tucked somewhere in between. There was little traffic on the country roads, apart from a few trucks heading for local markets, the odd carload of shoppers and an occasional Hants and Dorset bus. So David made very good time and arrived early at the Middle Woodlow Livery Stables; he leaned against the car and smoked a Woodbine, the smoke curling into the frosty air. In the yard he was greeted monosyllabically by a tallish, wiry fellow in breeches, his long, weather-beaten face resembling one of the horses among whom his life was obviously spent.

--Waiting for Mr Zellek? They'll be back presently.

And as he spoke, a leggy bay gelding clattered in, ridden by a neat, upright figure in a tweed jacket.

--David!

--Jerry… good to see you!

--How did he go, Mr Zellek?

--Wonderful, Jack, wonderful! (As always, the W was not quite a V, but not quite an English W either.) Natural jumper!

--Did you take him over a couple of fences?

--I did indeed! We were right about him.

Jiri Zellek had now dismounted and was patting the horse's neck affectionately. Now in his early fifties, he was still a slightly built man, significantly shorter than either Jack Andrewes or lanky, broad-shouldered David.

--Can you untack him, Jack? Mr Lomax and I have rather a busy day ahead… although, David, he added as Jack led the horse away, we should have time for a very quick one at the Red Lion.

Jiri followed David to the car.

--No stick today, Jerry?

--No; if I don't need it I leave it at home! And I strap my knee up to ride.

In the Red Lion, publican Harry greeted Jiri cordially

and nodded at his companion. With two pints of Courage Best, they settled in a quiet corner.

--Well what do you think of Eddy, David?

--Eddy?

--Yes, Edelweiss Lad, by Mountain Peak out of Jungfrau. What a bargain! He is a WONDERFUL jumper...

Many as were the interests David shared with his friend, horses were not one of them. But he couldn't help remarking that if Eddy was really such a bargain, there must be a good reason.

--Well... he is... perhaps... just a little... nervous... but when he is used to me, he will settle down.

--Incidentally, does Magda know how *vunderful* (David parodied Jiri's accent) a jumper he is...? I thought not. What does it take to keep my mouth shut?

--David, you are cruel and you have no respect. I could be your father.

--Yes... although you would have needed to be quite an active youth.

--How do you know that I was not?

To avoid further discussion, David asked about Beech Cottage, which Jiri was now renting from the Fellowes Estate, or what was left of it.

--Somehow I never saw you as a village dweller, Jerry; a bit boring for you?

--Not at all, David! According to Agatha Christie, an English village is far more dangerous than Maida Vale. I expect a murder mystery at any moment! David, we shall be like Poirot and Hastings. Although one would not wish to be Belgian, and you are much more intelligent than Hastings.

Also he does not play the organ. So perhaps the analogy does not hold.

--I'd forgotten you and Magda are Christie fans.

--Yes of course! We are enjoying *Taken at the Flood*... Magda has it from the library.

--How did you manage to jump the queue? Christies are always in high demand.

--Magda has a friend who works at the library. She supplies her with biscuits for the staff tea break.

--Ah. And the cottage?

--Magda has been spending time there making it comfortable. She will be here this evening, and we will return to London on Sunday afternoon. I have to be at work on Monday, of course. Although Cyril Bowes Barnard has been very accommodating, in fact it was Cyril who put me onto the cottage, when I told him at the bridge club that Magda and I were getting a little middle-aged – what did he call it? Getting into a rut (although when he said that I misunderstood it as a crude reference to our married life). Apparently he knows Sir William Fellowes, who is a bit hard up at present; who is not?

--Well, you don't seem to be, Jerry, what with renting a cottage, buying a horse, and now splashing out on a piano, although I see that you must have one in the cottage.

--Oh well, I have been quite lucky on the horses lately. And since Paul has been independent, our expenses are less. But yes, David, we need to get into Winchester to try out the pianos.

--Who was that then? asked one of the Red Lion drinkers.

--Dunno about the tall one. The other fellow's Jerry Zellek, the chap who's renting Beech Cottage.

--Jerry by name and Jerry by nature, from the sound of him.

--I'm not so sure; the wife's Polish and they don't have much time for the Germans.

Mary Kingsley's doing for them and her old man's keeping an eye on the garden. She says the wife's all right, speaks her mind, doesn't stand any nonsense, but pretty straight. They're DPs, if you ask me, although they seem to have done quite well for themselves. The wife's been doing quite a bit at the cottage, she's having the phone put in.

--What do they want that for? There's a phone box ten minutes away.

--Says her husband needs it for his work.

Before the Zelleks took full possession of Beech Cottage, Magda Zellek had spent a few days there on her own, leaving her husband at their flat in London; he was capable of getting tea and toast in the morning, and she had organised everything else with their helper Mrs Chancellor, even the refreshments for Reggie and Isolde after the Wednesday evening chamber music session. And she and Jiri spoke on the telephone every day; having a line installed at the cottage was one of her tasks and, meanwhile, there was the phone box outside the village post office. Mrs Kingsley was a great help and also a source of information, which flowed both ways. One morning they had decided that all the kitchen cupboards needed a thorough clean before anything could be placed in them. At eleven o'clock they paused for a cup of tea and some of the cake that Magda had made while experimenting with the kitchen range; she had not yet decided whether they could afford to replace it with a gas cooker, especially as the cottage did not actually belong to them.

--What, she asked, was their landlord like?

So far all correspondence had been through someone called Rathbone Fellowes.

--Poor young Mr Rathbone (that's Sir William's son), he's out now and is Sir William's agent. They had to put him away for a while, you know. Mr Richmond (that's the gamekeeper) found him in a terrible state up in the woods.

Magda looked slightly confused then asked,

--You mean this person has been placed in a lunatic asylum? And is now released?

Mrs Kingsley, while taken aback by this plain speaking, was beginning to realise that Magda Did Not Mince Her Words.

--Yes. Poor young man. It was what he went through in the war that did it, they say.

Although tempted to relate what she knew, or had been told, of these horrors, Mrs Kingsley saw an opportunity to probe the Zelleks' own past. There was of course speculation about them in the village. Magda made no secret of her Polish origins, and the general consensus was that they were displaced persons.

--I've noticed your husband sometimes uses a walking stick, Mrs Zellek. I expect he was in the war?

--My husband was injured in the first war. He was shot by the Russians.

Mrs Kingsley felt that she had been close to finding out whose side Mr Zellek had fought on, and now at least she knew in which war. She was clear that the Russians had been on our side last time, although Mr Churchill was beginning to have his doubts about them now. But she could not quite recall what part they had played in 1914–18, although she thought that they had had a revolution. Perhaps Mr Zellek had been shot by the Bolsheviks, or maybe the commies? At all events, you couldn't trust the Russkis and it was looking increasingly unlikely that Jerry Zellek was, well, an actual Jerry.

Back at Beech Cottage, Jiri went upstairs to change.

--Mrs Kingsley has left some sandwiches. Meat paste, I think. You had better eat them for an early lunch, David, if you can bear to. I see some apples; I will have one in the car. Oh, and while we are in Winchester do you know of anywhere to buy furniture? I must replace THAT, and he indicated a sagging settee.

--Yes, looks a bit past its best.

--Worse! It's an instrument of torture. Last evening I needed a rest after the journey and I fell asleep on it; when I woke up I felt worse than I did when I lay down. I shall tell Mrs Kingsley to get rid of it.

As they left the village, Jiri bit happily into the apple, which tasted like the clear, golden light on the Woodlow Valley.

--It is lovely here, in its own way. I think Magda likes it. You see, David, since Paul left home, and Magda's ambulance and resettlement work has come to an end, perhaps she needs more…

--Jerry, the fact that you can imagine that she might need more than looking after you gives me hope for you. And how is Paul?

--Thank you, David, he is doing well. You know, he was one of the best in the country in his latest accountancy exams. And he has a wonderful head for business; I always see so much of my father in him.

David said nothing, although he was aware of much that lay behind these statements. Paul Zellek was as unlike his father as it was possible for two human beings to be. He was amazingly handsome, tall and blond, completely unmusical and totally averse to anything connected with horses. Nor did he play bridge or show any flair for language translation despite his good command of German. However, Jerry frequently stressed Paul's likeness to his own father, Anton Zellek.

In Winchester, they parked in the High Street and went straight to Whitwams music shop near the Westgate. The manager was expecting them and showed Jiri the three instruments he had for sale.

--I had a quick look yesterday, said David. Don't bother with that one.

Jiri surveyed the other two, chose one, removed his jacket and sat down to play. He tried a Chopin etude he had been working on, then the introduction to a Schubert piano trio. Then he moved to the second piano.

--Is Mr Zellek a professional, Mr Lomax?

--No; not now, at any rate. But you can see that he needs a suitable instrument.

Jiri invited David to try the second piano; clearly David was equally at home with it.

--That is the one I prefer, said Jiri eventually. I see it is less expensive; perhaps because the case is not in quite such good condition? And perhaps, if you have had it in stock for some time, you might consider…?

He wrote the cheque, made some music purchases while delivery was being arranged, and finally asked for the address of a piano tuner in the Middle Woodlow area.

--I thought you could do that yourself, Jerry: one of the skills you learned while you were on the road?

--As you say, I am capable, but I do not like to take employment from someone who needs a living. Thank you; I see, Mr Charles Armitage, Upper Woodlow. David, I must have something to eat, all this has made me ravenous; isn't there a Cadena in Winchester?

There was, and they had a pot of tea for two, toasted teacakes and coffee walnut cake.

--Now, the couch.

--Habels, I think. They have good second-hand furniture, much better than that utility rubbish.

Jiri tried several settees, eventually selecting one and arranging delivery before the following weekend.

--Mrs Kingsley can take it in, I am sure. The piano must wait until I am there. David, are you not wanted soon at St Lawrence's?

--Actually, Jerry, time's getting on; I will walk to the station with you; are you sure you'll be all right on the train?

--Yes, yes… it stops quite a lot, but it gets to Upper Woodlow, and then I can get the bus… or the station taxi driver knows me by now… at this rate he may have to take an IOU, though!

Jiri had brought his stick, just in case, and he was glad of it as they hurried up the hill to the station.

--David, can you please get me an evening paper while I

buy my ticket? I want to see the racing results.

As David turned back towards the city, he felt rather deflated. When Jerry left, things always seemed less lively, if rather more peaceful.

By the time Jiri arrived back at Beech Cottage, it was dark and the welcoming lights from the downstairs windows showed that Magda was already there; in fact, their Austin 7 was parked in the lane. As the train was a slow one, it had been twilight, and cold, when it reached Upper Woodlow station, and he had missed the bus. He was lucky, though, with the station taxi.

--Thanks, Harold, he said, searching his pockets for change. I'm afraid there's not much of a tip, but I'll make it up to you next time. I should be getting a cheque from my bookie.

--Think nothing of it, Mr Zed. Got any hot tips for the races, though?

--There's a few good French horses coming up. And I hear Airborne's gone to stud; I had a good win on him a couple of years ago, but I'm not sure I'd recommend any of his offspring. Meanwhile, try Barrow Boy for the 2.30 at Doncaster next Saturday.

Magda appeared in the doorway.

--Jiri, you are tired.

--Perhaps a little, but, my darling, I have had a very satisfying day... and it is not over yet! he said as he held her in his arms.

On Sunday morning they were up in time for Mass.

This had originally posed a problem. In Humboldt

Avenue, Maida Vale, it was a short walk to St Aloysius Renwell Hill, where Father ffoukes-Fenton presided over a flock of expatriate Hungarians, Poles, Czechs and others, like Jiri, of disparate origins. Early on Magda had asked her husband why their priest had two small ffs and a little dash, to which he replied that he did not know, but perhaps it was a matter of rank similar to um und zu. In Middle Woodlow, the nearest Catholic church was several miles away. This did not matter so much if they had enough petrol coupons to bring the car; otherwise, there was a bus which got them there in time. The return journey timetable meant that they had half an hour to wait after the end of Mass, but in fact this was quite an advantage. Magda found that she liked St Bernadette's. Although a tin chapel deserted by some Baptist sect, it had a garden with several statues and grottoes, enabling mini processions, floral decorations and outside rosary all reminding her of her childhood in Poland. Father Sullivan and many of the congregation were Irish, and when Jiri joined in such hymns as 'Faith of Our Fathers', 'I'll Sing a Hymn to Mary' and even 'Hail Glorious St Patrick' the priest commented, *I've not heard the like since Count John McCormack, God rest his soul.* Although Jiri viewed this as a compliment, he also realised that Fr Sullivan could not have heard too many Austrian-trained tenors, since he did not in fact sound at all like the late great Irishman. Fasting from midnight was not too difficult for Magda; Jiri could manage it at Humboldt Avenue, but the first time he tried it in conjunction with the bus journey he nearly passed out, so that Magda made sure he had something before they left Beech Cottage, and he had to forego communion. There was, fortunately, a chance of refreshment after Mass and before the bus home. The Felperham pub was run by a couple from London. The licensee's father had moved down to be with them after his wife's death; for years he had run a successful coffee stall on the Embankment, and seeing the Massgoers streaming out of St Bernadette's he seized the opportunity to set up a stand selling coffee, tea, buns, homemade biscuits… and of course it was a chance to get to know fellow parishioners.

It wasn't only St Bernadette's that appealed to Magda. Nor was it just that Jiri looked so well. For, although she was happy enough at Humboldt Avenue, she took readily to country life. It would be wonderful to have a garden; she planned a vegetable patch, what flowers she would grow, what herbs for cooking… she made friends in the village, particularly among the women, where the approval of District Nurse Baines and Mrs Kingsley meant much. That autumn she particularly impressed the Kingsleys with her knowledge of mushrooms; so many types of edible fungi, she explained, were wasted in England, while in Poland they were used in soups, stews and many other savoury dishes.

It was while gathering fungi in the woods near Garrods Lane that she encountered Ron Staples.

It was a lovely morning. Magda was by herself and had just bent down to examine a mushroom when she heard heavy footsteps and became aware of a pair of large black boots close to her face. She straightened up, glad that she held her mushroom knife, a special tool that Jiri had brought her back from a rather unsuccessful tour he had managed in northern France. Although she had little use for it in Maida Vale, down here it might well come in handy.

--D'you know you're trespassing?

The speaker was a very heavily built man, at least six feet in height, ruddy-faced, wearing a tweed jacket and carrying a rifle.

Magda gave him a direct look from her green eyes. A good-looking woman of middle height, she wore a well-cut tweed jacket and skirt, unusual calf-length boots, and a pre-war but evidently expensive French silk headscarf over thick, wavy honey-blonde hair.

--You are Sir William Fellowes? she asked, or perhaps his gamekeeper, Mr Richmond?

--Neither. I've bought this land from the Fellowes Estate, and Richmond works for me as well as for the Fellowes.

--I was not aware. I will leave if one is not permitted here.

--Where are you from? The question was clearly loaded.

--Beech Cottage, replied Magda, and we also live in London.

--I mean before. You're German?

--No, I am not. My husband and I are British citizens. May I ask your name?

--It's Staples. You'd better remember it. Wait: is your husband the jumped-up little nuisance who rides that brown horse? If he is, just tell him to stay off my land.

Staples eyed her insolently, although Magda returned his gaze.

--Can't think what a woman like you is doing with that sort. He's not wanted on my land. In fact, scum like him's not wanted in our country.

Staples then turned away, leaving Magda holding tightly to the mushroom knife.

As she did every year, in November Magda arranged to attend a three-day retreat at a convent in Sussex. Since it was deep in the countryside, she needed the car, so it was fortunate that David Lomax had work in Romsey that weekend; he said he could take Jerry down to Middle Woodlow on Friday morning if he could get time off work, and bring him back to London on Sunday night.

When David and Jiri entered the Red Lion that Friday, the locals were wetting the head of Princess Elizabeth's baby. Publican Harry Breen was running a book on the new prince's name.

--I reckon George after his grandad.

--Well, I don't fancy Edward. They won't want anything to do with the Dook of Winser!

--You never know, they might let bygones be bygones...

--They say he and Wallis were in with the Nazis, though.

--What about Henry?

--Him with the wives? Or William, there's been a couple of them.

--What about you, Mr Zellek? Fancy betting on the royals?

--Yes indeed, Harry. I'm putting two shillings on Charles.

--Not a hope sir! A hundred to one... Thanks, Mr Zellek, I reckon that's two bob you won't be seeing again.

--Why did you choose that, Jerry? asked David, who had not joined in the betting.

--Oh, because that is the only truly royal person I have ever met. One hardly counts the Windsors really since the Duke of Kent was killed; the Duke of Gloucester is a cretin and the current monarchs are so bourgeois. The British royal family have gone down sadly since dear Queen Alexandra's day. One is almost ashamed to be related to them; at least it is distantly. No, I mean the Emperor Carl, poor fellow.

David thought.

--Ah, the last Habsburg? Did you really meet him?

--Let's say, the last ruling Habsburg. There are still many of them around. He had eight children. But yes. It was in the military hospital. He came round pinning medals to our shirts. So it was not truly a fruitful conversation. But he was the Emperor.

David was not back at the Red Lion until late on the Sunday morning, when he stopped in for a quick one before going round to Beech Cottage. He was rather surprised not to see Jerry in the pub, but assumed that his friend was still over in Felperham attending Mass, and perhaps waiting for the bus. But what he heard in the saloon bar sent him driving hastily to the cottage, where he noticed Paul Zellek's two-seater parked in the lane.

David knocked urgently at the door.

--Paul!

--David! Have you heard about Pa's accident?

--No; what accident?

--He fell off Eddy trying to jump some bloody great hedge on Saturday morning. I had a call from the almoner at the cottage hospital early today telling me I could collect him. No bones broken and probably doesn't have concussion, but they said if he throws up, passes out or sees double, call an ambulance. You'd better come in.

--Thanks. Actually I'm here to warn Jerry that the police are on their way. He seems to be a prime suspect in a murder, some bloke found dead yesterday evening, killed sometime that afternoon.

--Why's Pa a suspect?

--Because he was seen having a blazing row with the victim on Friday afternoon, and probably because he's a foreigner.

--Hang on… this fellow was topped Saturday pm? When Pa was in the cottage hospital with suspected concussion? I know it seems a pretty extreme method of getting an alibi but, as alibis go, none better I'd say!

--So when the coppers turn up we can send them away discontented…

--Come and have a look at Pa.

--Is he all right?

--No, not really, but as he hasn't shown any of the three dreaded signs I suppose he'll survive, he usually does. But he could have broken his neck.

David looked at Jerry with horror. He had a black eye, one side of his face was bruised and discoloured; his left wrist was in a support, and his left ankle looked badly swollen.

--His wrist? he asked anxiously.

--Not even a bad sprain; they put on the support to make it more comfortable.

At this point, there was knocking at the door.

--Detective Inspector Romney and Detective Sergeant Trowbridge. Mr Zellek?

--I am Paul Zellek. I expect you want my father. Come in. This is Mr David Lomax, a family friend. Inspector, I must ask you not to trouble my father too much. He has just come out of the cottage hospital.

This statement had the effect Paul and David had been looking forward to.

--When was that, sir?

--This morning. My father was there overnight following an accident yesterday morning; he was admitted at about eleven o'clock that morning. With suspected concussion following a fall from his horse.

--Right. We can probably keep this short, then. Mr Zellek, I'm sorry to intrude and I won't ask you more than a couple of questions. Can you just confirm when you last saw Mr Ron Staples?

--Ron Staples? Has he sent the police after me? He has no right.

--Don't get agitated, Mr Zellek. No, Mr Staples has not sent us here... in fact... now, sir, can you just answer my question?

--Friday, Friday afternoon, murmured Jiri after an obvious effort at recollection. We had, what is it... a slanging match. But I did not actually hit him, as Richmond...

--Just one more question sir, and then we will leave you in peace. Are you sure that you did not see Mr Staples again after your... slanging match on Friday afternoon?

--Yes, I'm sure. No, I didn't see him. And I never want to see the bastard again.

David interposed.

--Please, Inspector. I'm sure you can see the state Mr Zellek is in.

--Yes Mr... Lomax...? we may just need to speak to him later, but for now...

Paul stepped forward.

--My father lives in London for most of the week, and as soon as he is able to travel we will take him home. I'll give you his London address.

Paul took one of Jerry's cards from the dresser.

Soon after the police had left, Mrs Kingsley arrived with Jiri's Sunday dinner, which David put in the oven to keep warm. He and Paul looked at each other.

--We'd better eat that, suggested Paul.

--Jerry, are you all right? asked David anxiously.

--No. I want to go to the lavatory and I can't get up.

--Can we get him to the outside one?

--Christ, I could do with a drink.

--There may be some beer in the larder. There's a bottle of whisky in the sideboard, although it looks like Pa's been hitting it a bit lately.

--We could open a tin of soup for Jerry.

--What are you doing with that toast?

--I'm cutting it into very small pieces. It's what Mum always does when Pa's not too good. Buck up, Pa! We're going to try some soup with little squares!

After they had shared the congealed dinner and some bread and cheese, Paul began to make it clear that he needed, or wanted, to return to London that evening.

--Dave *(DON'T CALL ME DAVE)*, you were going to take Pa home anyway, so couldn't you stay with him overnight and take him in the morning? Mum will be back on Monday.

--Hell, what's Magda going to say about this?

--Oh he'll get the *du arme kind* treatment and be spoiled rotten. We'll get it in the neck for not keeping an eye on him, and poor old Eddy will be lucky to escape the knacker's yard.

--We'll never get him upstairs, said David, putting off his inevitable reply.

--Why don't we get the mattress off the spare bed, try to make him comfortable on that, and you can have their bed?

David knew that he would pass the night on the settee, watching Jerry for loss of consciousness, vomiting or double vision…

Eventually Paul left with every sign of relief. Soon afterwards came yet another knock at the door. It was the doctor. He confirmed that Jerry had no bones broken, that he might indeed have broken his neck, that he should be watched for signs of… Yes, I think I know, sighed David. More usefully, Dr Grand reassured him that Jerry would be better off at home with his wife, and that Nurse Baines would come round first thing in the morning to help David get Jerry up, dressed and into the car, a process that David had been dreading.

--Jerry, I'm going to take you home in the morning, so try to get some rest now.

--Yes. I want Magda, was the only response.

However, on Monday morning their departure was delayed by Jerry refusing to leave until David had telephoned the stables, spoken to Jack Andrewes and arranged for the vet to check Eddy for any signs of injury. This took a while, and after a journey, the details of which David tried hard to forget, they reached Humboldt Avenue. David, primed by Paul, had hoped to get Jerry home and installed before

Magda arrived back, but this did not happen. She opened the door, took a look at her husband and demanded, WHAT?

Fell off a horse, they both muttered.

--There are no bones broken, Mrs Zellek. But the hospital said that he had suspected concussion and that we had to watch out for loss of consciousness, vomiting, or…

--I have nursing training. Do not tell me my business. Thank you. David, you may go.

When he reached his Fulham bed-sit David hoped guiltily that he would never see any of the Zelleks ever again. But towards the end of the week he received a letter from Magda. She thanked him for what he had done for Jerry, and apologised for seeming ungrateful on Monday. Paul (*poor sod, under interrogation*) had told her the whole story and now she understood how very kind and helpful David had been. 'Jaroslav is unable to remember these things clearly but that is quite normal when one has had a blow on the head. The police came on Wednesday. When I told them that Jaroslav and I are British citizens and this is a free country thanks to Mr Churchill and King George, they told me not to worry. They said one of our neighbours in Middle Woodlow, an unpleasant fellow named Ron Staples, had died in suspicious circumstances and they were looking for people who had seen him the day before his death. Jaroslav was able to tell them that he had seen Mr Staples on Friday afternoon. Several others had seen him after that so the police, two quite polite young men, said that it was unlikely that they would need to talk to Jaroslav again. You will be pleased to hear that he is recovering. We must thank God he was not seriously injured. With again many thanks your grateful friend Magda Zellek.'

Since Jerry Zellek had slipped down, indeed off, the list of suspects, Inspector Romney had decided to send DS Trowbridge to London with DC Brand to wrap up his statement. While he still harboured suspicions that Zellek was involved with, or at least knew something about, the murder of Ron Staples, clearly he could not have been the actual perpetrator, and finding him (almost certainly a him) was the first priority. Thus Trowbridge and Brand drove up to Maida Vale to be met by Magda's assertion of patriotism. When they gained entrance to the Zelleks' sitting room they found Jiri waiting for them.

--Good morning, Mr Zellek I'm glad to see you looking better than last time we met, began Trowbridge. Brand, noticing Jerry's luridly bruised face, blackened wrist and general air of misery, wondered briefly what he had looked like then.

--Now, sir, I'll try to keep this short so as not to tire you. Firstly, is it the case that you and Mr Staples were not on good terms, and that on the afternoon of last Friday you met at the stile by Garrods Lane, where you had what you later described as 'a slanging match'?

Jiri nodded.

--I'll just take you through the statement made by Mr and Mrs Richmond, and see whether it fits with your recollections, Mr Zellek. Just stop me if there is anything you disagree with or seems to have been left out. Brand?

The DC flicked open his notebook.

--Mr Richmond stated that as he was driving his vehicle down Garrods Lane, he saw you and Mr Staples 'facing up to each other'. He heard Mr Staples say, Out of my way, you rat-faced little yid (*which I am not*, interrupted Jiri, *although*

I would not hesitate to say so if I were) or I'll kick you into next week. At which, according to Mr Richmond, you replied, I'd like to see you try, you stinking fat filthy-minded arsehole, and at this point you raised your riding crop in a threatening manner. Staples responded, do that and I'll break your scrawny neck. Seeing things were getting nasty, Mr Richmond then stepped between you and laid his hand on your arm, saying to Mr Staples, Come on, sir, why don't you pick on someone your own size, and to you, Please, Mr Zellek, why don't you go home and calm down, to which you replied something that Mr Richmond could not understand, and Mr Staples replied, Who do you think you are, Richmond, telling me what to do? By now Mrs Richmond had let the dog out of the vehicle as it was barking and no doubt thinking Mr Richmond was under threat from Mr Staples, it ran towards him. Mr Staples then kicked the dog. Mr Richmond then spoke to him along the lines of, Now, nobody does that to my dog, and you also addressed words to Mr Staples, which again were not understood by those present. Mrs Richmond then joined the group, although Mr Richmond had told her to remain in the vehicle. Her words were, Leave them to it, George, it's not worth losing your job over it, and to you, Please, Mr Zellek, you just go home and let them settle things. She then took her husband's arm and urged him towards the vehicle, the dog following. Mr Richmond gave in to his wife's entreaties, you, in her words, turned on your heel and marched off, shouting some more language at Mr Staples.

Is that more or less correct, sir?

--Well, yes. I am very much ashamed of the things I said to Richmond and, I regret, even to Mrs Richmond. It was most fortunate, perhaps, that although English is a wonderful language, it is rather lacking range and variety of insults. So, as you said, most of my comments were not understood. All the same...

--Yes, yes, Mr Zellek. Although it seems to me that your command of English was more than sufficient for the occasion. Now can you tell us what you did after you had, as Mrs Richmond put it, marched off?

--Yes. I went home to Beech Cottage. I had a whisky and soda. Then I had a bath, and after that Mrs Kingsley, who looks after me when my dear wife is not at the cottage with me, brought my evening meal.

--I believe that after supper on such occasions you generally go down to the Red Lion?

--Yes, but that night I felt sure that I would meet either Staples or Richmond there. I knew that I needed to apologise to Richmond, and that it would be embarrassing for us both for me to do that in public. As for Staples, I could not answer for what I might do or say. I was still angry.

--So, sir, what did you do?

--I decided to sit down at the piano for a while. There was a piece I was practising and time passed rather quickly; it was soon too late to go to the Red Lion anyway, so I had another whisky and went to bed at about eleven.

--Just a moment, sir, would anyone have heard you playing the piano?

--There are no near neighbours, and as it was a chilly evening the windows were closed. I suppose someone passing in the lane might perhaps have heard something.

The next morning, I left for the stables in good time, in fact rather early; I often see Richmond on the way, and I thought it would be a good moment to apologise to him. But he was nowhere about. And I am afraid I have not been able to apologise to him yet. The rest you know about, Sergeant Trowbridge. Do help yourselves to some more of my wife's cake. By the way, is there absolutely no chance Staples's death could have been an accident? I have heard that it is 'suspicious' but surely that has a variety of interpretations.

Trowbridge and Brand looked at each other.

--No, sir, I'm afraid not. Mr Staples died as, er, a result of a frenzied attack. And there was some mutilation of the body. I suppose that under the circumstances no one has explained that to you.

--No. No one did. And so that is what your superior suspected me of, until he knew of my stay in hospital. I am not quite sure whether I am horrified or... he broke off as Magda entered offering more coffee, which the police officers declined, saying they must be on their way. Magda wrapped up the remains of the cake for them to take away with them.

Romney: Trowbridge? Brand? Anything new?

Trowbridge: No, sir, quite a bit of traffic going into London. Mrs Zellek sent this cake for the station.

Romney: Let's be having some, then. Any chance of a cuppa, WPC Evans?

Trowbridge: Well, guv, seeing Zellek was interesting but really doesn't add anything. I think he was genuinely surprised to hear how Staples died, not that we went into much detail. But mainly he seemed concerned about apologising to Richmond for shouting at him on Friday. Said he went to look for Richmond in his usual spot on the Saturday morning but couldn't find him. Then he went to the stables, saddled up that horse, Eddy, and the rest we know.

Romney: Staples does seem to have been very set against Zellek. By all accounts he's a cocky little bastard, not afraid of much, but even so I can't see why... unless, what did Staples call Zellek? A little yid?

Trowbridge: Which Zellek says he isn't, sir, and according to Mrs Kingsley their housekeeper at Beech Cottage, all the village knows that the Zelleks are RCs, never miss going to the RC church in Felperham when they're in the village, eat bacon and egg when they can get it, no worries about ham sandwiches... still, Staples did seem dead set against Zellek. Probably Zellek's being dark, foreign, and fond of music was enough to make Staples think he was Jewish... and evidently they just got on each other's wick. Just another thing, guv. Staples threatened to break Zellek's neck.

Anything fishy about Zellek's accident?

Enquiries failed to suggest this, however. Jiri himself remembered nothing between approaching the hedge and waking up in the ambulance, and that only dimly.

Andrewes, the groom at the stables, and Mr Richmond came up with very similar comments: Mr Zellek was a very experienced rider, had almost certainly served in a cavalry regiment at one time. But he was no longer a lad, had reduced strength in his left knee, and Eddy was notoriously temperamental. Falls happened to everybody, even if they'd been riding all their lives, as Mr Zellek evidently had; he had been lucky not to break his neck or anything else this time, and would probably be back in the saddle before long.

Romney: So all that gets us nowhere except proving what a sod Staples was. And perhaps raises a question as to where Richmond was on Saturday morning.

Brand: Phone call, guv, from the path lab. Doctor Alton has come up with something. It wasn't just a knife attack. Staples was shot. By someone who knew where to aim. The damage was done to the body at about the same time: impossible to tell which came first, the bullet or the knife, or axe. And the bullet came from one of Staples's own guns. Local PC has checked them, all in place and likely wiped clean of fingerprints.

Meanwhile at Humboldt Avenue Jiri sorted through a small pile of post, which included a card reminding him of an appointment with their dentist, Dr Frank Lawrence.

--Magda, darling, please could you call his surgery? I don't think I could manage to get there on Friday, but perhaps next week?

--Mrs Zellek! responded the receptionist. I've been meaning to call you. I'm so sorry! I have been telephoning all Dr Lawrence's patients, but I had not yet got to you.

--Of course. Z is at the end of the alphabet. But what is the difficulty?

--Dr Lawrence has been suddenly called away to his brother in the north of Scotland. I don't know how long he will be gone for, and, Mrs Zellek, although I wouldn't want this to get out to the other patients, recently he has been negotiating the sale of the practice. Of course, I will make sure that you and Mr Zellek are transferred to whoever takes his place.

--Jiri, did you know that Fritz Lorenz has a brother in the north of Scotland?

--Scotland? No, I thought the poor fellow told us that his family were all wiped out in Lithuania.

Jiri paused for a moment before ringing his place of work.

--Miss Silverstrom? This is Jerry Zellek.

--Mr Zellek! We were all so sorry to hear of your accident. You could have broken your neck!

--Yes indeed. So I have been told. Thank you for your concern, Miss Silverstrom. Now, please could you put me through to Mr Bowes Barnard?

--Of course. Which line would you require?

--Line B, I think. Thank you, Miss Silverstrom.

That afternoon, Cyril Bowes Barnard arrived at the Zelleks' flat.

--You are not going to see that man? I really do not like him, Jiri.

--Oh, he is quite a good fellow, Magda, as long as one does not trust him. Maybe some tea and biscuits? Jiri realised that Cyril did not merit cake.

--Cyril, I know you are busy with the Hebrew and Yiddish sections at present, and it is because of the activity of Mr Ben-Gurion and his agents that I wish to speak to you. I have sympathy with the decision of the new state of Israel to bring war criminals to justice. But it seems to me that someone is warning such men in time for them to flee the country. I am speaking of such people as Fritz Lorenz. Or, as he is called here, Frank Lawrence.

--Yes... how do you know him?

--He's my dentist.

--My God, Jerry! You're having your teeth looked at by the demon dentist of the concentration camps!

--Perhaps I have had a narrow escape. At all events, I was cancelling my appointment when I heard of his abrupt departure. I expect he is in South America by now. I am sure I can find an alternative dental practice; I believe there is an excellent Hungarian fellow near us in Maida Vale. But who, I wonder, may have, as the idiom has it, tipped him off?

--I can help you there, Jerry. Ron Staples, who has recently been killed, had a regrettable past, as a Moseleyite and a traitor, and an equally unfortunate present, as one of a group seeking to assist Nazi war criminals to escape.

--Ron Staples? Oh, Cyril. Surely there is no coincidence here.

--'Fraid not. Let's say, Jerry, that physically you can pass as Jewish, and it's no secret that you are an employee of the Civil Service Translation Office. So Staples would think that you were out to get him, he would tip off his contacts, some of whom we've been watching. Once we had him out in the open, we could get him and his contacts tried as war criminals. In other words, Jerry, we used you to flush him out.

--*Flush him out?* Cyril, I am not a lavatory cistern. And if I had been made aware of why my presence in Middle Woodlow was needed, I might perhaps have been of more use.

--No, Jerry, You wouldn't. We didn't need you to do anything. Staples just had to be tipped off that you might be, well, on to him.

--Cyril, I am offended.

--Too bad, old man. But actually, you can do something useful now, since you are on the spot, so to speak. Somehow, Staples's death doesn't have the trademark of Ben-Gurion's chaps. They do it neat and clean.

Jiri nodded approvingly.

--And in this case there seem to have been two different methods employed: the axe attack and the shot. No one seems able to say which came first. If there's someone else out there taking out Nazis, we need to know.

So, Jerry, you just find out who killed Ron Staples. And find it out before the Hampshire Constabulary.

Jiri was readily given sick leave, and was soon back at Beech Cottage. He and David went to the Red Lion to collect his winnings; the royal baby was to be christened Charles. Of course they celebrated with a pint, and joined in the animated discussion about Staples's murder. Apparently the body had been discovered by two hikers, legitimately walking the public footpath across Sir William's estate. They had done exactly the right thing: one had remained by the body while the other hurried back to the village to report the grisly find and summon the police. Despite speculation, there was little consensus on who had last seen Staples, where and when. Of course, no one had suspected Mr Zellek, no, not for one minute, absolutely not, and everyone was pleased to see him back after his accident (after all, he might have broken his neck) and glad he was doing so well.

As David left, Jiri said he would try to walk to the stables, to check on Eddy and have a chat with Jack Andrewes, although in fact he did not get that far. As he had hoped, he encountered George Richmond; after a moment's embarrassment on both sides, he shook the gamekeeper's hand and apologised to him for the foul language he had used towards him and Mrs Richmond.

--It was unforgivable, even if not all of it was, perhaps, understood. Please excuse me.

--Don't mention it, Mr Zellek. I could see you were angry. That Ron Staples was a nasty piece of work, the village is better off without him, and I give you credit for standing up to him. Shows guts, facing a fellow that size.

--Thank you, Richmond. But there were no guts involved. All bullies are cowards when challenged.

There was another silence, then Richmond resumed,

--If you and Mrs Zellek would like a brace of pheasants, there's couple in my lodge that you can have, if you've got a moment to come and get them?

Jiri said that Magda would be delighted.

The lodge was not far.

--Just wait here, sir, they're out the back…

Jiri looked around the lodge. It was impeccably neat, and over the desk hung a rack of keys. When Richmond returned with the pheasants, Jiri was watching a squirrel through the small window.

--Thank you so much; we shall enjoy these (Jiri had of course complete confidence that they would be plucked, drawn and cooked without any effort on his part). They are very cleanly shot, but of course that is part of your profession.

--Well, yes; though I say it myself, I'm a good shot. Won a few competitions in my time. My old dad taught me; he was gamekeeper here before me, and his father too.

--Indeed. Your family is commendably loyal to the Fellowes, is it not? Which reminds me, I need to discuss one or two matters concerning Beech Cottage with Mr Rathbone Fellowes, who I believe acts as his father's agent.

Richmond stiffened.

--He's none too well at the moment, Mr Zellek.

--I am sorry to hear that. Although when I met him previously, to arrange the rental of Beech Cottage, I realised that his health was uncertain. In my time I have known many ex-soldiers suffering from what in my army years was called shell shock.

Richmond, who had also served in the first war, although not on the same side as Jiri, nodded.

--Yes. Mr Rathbone had a very bad time after he was shot down over Germany. And when he got back home at last he had this idea that spies, traitors, Nazis, all that, were behind every hedge. He was always out looking for them, although we all told him that there was nothing like that in Middle Woodlow. He said if he ever got wind of one of those devils, he'd…

Richmond fell suddenly silent.

--Perhaps I will leave the meeting until later, said Jiri, picking up the pheasants. Thank you again, and I must be going. Just one thing, Richmond. If there is ever anything, such as, well, an axe, or stained clothing, I always recommend deep water for disposal. The lake over at Nesfield, for example.

Richmond had turned away towards the gun rack. When he again faced the door, with his rifle raised, he expected to see Jiri's departing back; instead, a revolver was pointed directly at him.

--Richmond… George… I really don't think we need to do each other harm, so…

He looked Richmond in the eye, and slowly both men lowered their weapons.

--Good. I believe we have some information to exchange. It seems to me that Staples's killer was the unfortunate Mr

Rathbone Fellowes. I now know that Staples was one of a group seeking to assist Nazi war criminals to escape. They are in increasing danger, as perhaps you know, from agents of the new state of Israel. Mr Fellowes learned this; for once, his suspicions were not the delusions of a war-torn mind and of course Staples was also hounding the Fellowes family over the sale of even more of their estates. As chance had it, Staples came upon Mr Fellowes chopping wood in the copse. Fellowes had an axe in his hand, anger in his heart and madness in his brain. When one is as angry as that, it is perhaps understandable.

Richmond groaned.

--And, continued Jiri, that was when you appeared… a crack shot, you despatched Staples, who must have been pretty far gone anyway, and took Mr Rathbone back to the manor. When the police began to make enquiries, it was convenient that you had witnessed my row with Staples… if suspicion had to fall on anyone, well, I am not a member of the Fellowes family, I am a foreigner and a relative stranger to the village… and at the very least my interrogation would buy time for you and Sir William to cover the tracks…

--I'm sorry, Mr Zellek, but, yes, that's about it. Then when you had your accident, everything was up in the air again… Between you and I, though, I've always thought there was something fishy about that accident. Staples had it in for you one way or another, and we know what a ruthless vindictive bastard he was.

--Well, if he was behind it, at least he provided me with an alibi… and it would be reassuring to know that it was not sheer incompetence as a rider… and wherever Staples is now, I suspect that he will be suffering more than I have done… and, in the end, I have absolutely no memory of what happened. It is often that way with falls: one moment you are approaching the fence, next you are on the ground hoping you are still in one piece. In fact, there's only one that I really recall in detail, and that one I would much rather not… but it makes nothing.

--Was that when… not hunting, was it Mr Zellek?

--No, George, it was not. But… one thing bothers me still… how was it that you were using Staples's gun?

--Staples asked me to bring the gun to him; said I'd find him in the copse.

--Which of course you did.

--I'd loaded it and was thinking that I'd like just one shot with it, lovely weapon it is… And when you came to the lodge to collect those pheasants, I knew you'd seen the row of keys and put two and two together… it was a mistake asking you over, but you'd been such a gent over the row with Staples. I'm used to animals, Mr Zellek. I know when they've sensed something… you're no different. And then you said about the lake. What are you going to do, Mr Zellek?

--Me? Nothing. This world is a better place without Staples; what befalls him in the next is not our concern. Poor Rathbone Fellowes is, I hope, being well cared for. And I gather that Miss Jane Fellowes has resigned her commission in the Wrens in order to return home and support her father. Inspector Romney will be discreetly informed that Staples was the target of Mr Ben-Gurion's agents bent on understandable revenge… although in fact they seek only to bring the criminals to justice, it would be easy to assume that one or two of them might get carried away, as it were.

The local press will be tipped off about an escaped lunatic… perhaps not so very far from the truth, I'm afraid. (*And,* thought Jiri, *Cyril will be quite satisfied with the information that Staples's murder was a one-off, rather than part of an organised campaign, and with the killer safely locked away.*) As for me, perhaps I may gain some advantages from all this.

They heard a car drawing up in the lane.

--Magda! said Jerry, thrusting the revolver back into his pocket, and with some amusement Richmond observed that he looked more apprehensive than when faced by a loaded rifle, or menaced by a bully twice his size. He recalled village gossip that Magda definitely kept her husband in order.

--Jiri! I thought I might find you here. Are those pheasants really for us? How very kind of you, Mr Richmond!

--My pleasure, Mrs Zellek. I'll send round some more when I can. I'd better be locking up here.

They paused on the threshold.

--That's it, then, Mr Zellek?

--Yes, that's it; *das ist das Ende, mein Freund.*

The winter of 1948–49 was phenomenally severe. Jiri and Magda had planned to spend a few days at Beech Cottage before returning to London for their usual hybrid Christmas celebration with its Polish, Austrian and English components, but deep snow covered the countryside, roads were impassable, trains were not running and the telephone wires collapsed under the weight of ice. They were snowed in and would have to spend Christmas in Middle Woodlow. Managing to send a telegram to Paul, they established that he would go to a colleague for Christmas dinner. Actually he was not sorry to face a solidly English Christmas without

Mum in tears over the fate of Poland and Pa singing 'O Tannenbaum'.

Magda and Jiri reviewed the situation. It was not so bad; since provisions were more plentiful in the country, they had obtained a chicken and supplies of vegetables to take back to Maida Vale; they would eat them here instead. Magda had been secretly knitting an intricate Fair Isle jumper for her husband; she'd brought it down to complete, so her gift was ready.

--But, said Jiri, we do not have a Christmas tree. We have always had one, even in the air raid shelter.

Magda had a sudden memory of the silence that had fallen on the crowded shelter as Jiri had sung 'Stille Nacht' in front of the spindly pine branch someone had smuggled in.

--I will obtain one. Jiri put on his overcoat, cap, scarf, gloves and Wellingtons. Taking the shovel that was propped against the back door, he dug his way to the shed, emerging with a spade and a saw. He then trudged off in the direction of the woods.

Two hours later he was back, with George Richmond and a fir tree.

They had probably paused at the back door of the Red Lion for a warming nip; at all events, they were very pleased with themselves as they placed the tree in a bucket of soil and brought it in through the kitchen, leaving a trail of mud, melted snow and pine needles.

--There! announced Richmond. That should do the trick. Can't help you with decorations, though.

--We can make some, Magda told him. Will you stay for a cup of tea and some of my Polish gingerbread, Mr Richmond?

When he had left, they set about the decorations. By the end of the day, Magda had found scraps of coloured knitting wool, which they plaited and tied into bows. She showed her husband how to make pompoms; he was delighted with this new skill and wondered how he had come to such a mature age without knowing of it.

Stars were cut from magazines and wrapping paper and on the top of the tree the star of Bethlehem was represented by an extra-large one made from back copies of the *Racing Post*.

As they stood back to admire it, Mrs Kingsley arrived with 'a couple of mince pies for you' and a promise to come round on Christmas afternoon, after the King's speech on the wireless, with a slice of Christmas cake; this year she had been able to make a proper one, though a bit short on the marzipan.

The Zelleks retained the tradition of exchanging presents on Christmas Eve, rather than on Christmas morning, as is usual in England. After putting on his new jumper, Jiri reached behind the settee and drew out a parcel bearing the name of an exclusive Bond Street shop. Magda unwrapped a beautifully made alligator handbag.

--I thought the old one had served its turn, said Jiri. You have had it since before the war.

Speechless, Magda opened the bag to admire the lining.

--What is this? The keys… you have had a new set cut.

--Yes, my darling. New keys for Beech Cottage. Because it is ours now. I have bought it from Sir William; he was willing to sell it for the going price, as he has some family medical expenses to defray. Happy Christmas, my Magda. *Frohe Weihnachten! Wesołych Świąt!*

RURAL HARMONY

Dein ist mein schönstes Lied

Gareth Bax Williams adjusted his cravat and tapped his music stand with his baton. The thirty members of the Woodlows Choral Society stopped chatting and turned to him expectantly.

--Ladies and gentlemen! After this evening's practice, I think we have finalised the first part of the concert. Now I have the news you have all been waiting for. I have here the printed scores of my composition for choir and piano, 'Green Willows'; when you take your copies, you will see that I have taken the decision to exclude solos, although I have included a duet section. Please take your copy as you leave, study it, and I look forward to seeing you all here this time next week.

Arthur, Jerry and Miss Sibthorp, can I ask you to stay behind for a few minutes?

--Arthur, Jerry, see you in the Warreners Arms, called Candace Drinkwater (alto), the choir secretary, as she and her husband Bernard (bass) left the hall of Felperham Girls' Grammar School.

Jiri Zellek and Arthur Broadhurst moved to the piano, where Miss Sibthorp, music mistress at the grammar school, was already opening her copy of Bax Williams's latest composition.

--Page fifteen, Gareth was saying. A passage for you, Miss Sibthorp, followed by a male voice duet for tenor and baritone.

Jiri, who was an instant sight reader, was already trying the opening notes of the tenor part. Arthur was slower.

--Permit me, Miss Sibthorp, said Jiri, reaching across to the keyboard. Here, Arthur, this is you... Gareth, thank you, this is lovely... I think you are a little influenced by Benjamin Britten, perhaps? Just here, I could go a little higher, if you think that would work, perhaps just transpose this, so that Arthur will be more of a contrast?

At this point the caretaker arrived, jangling his keys. The group separated and Arthur and Jiri walked over to the Warreners Arms, where several other members of the choir were enjoying the usual post-rehearsal drink.

They joined the Drinkwaters. Bernard, a churchwarden and choir treasurer, sipped his pint gloomily.

--It's all very well. Those printed scores are costing a pretty penny, and we agreed to stick to the decision not to ask people to pay for their music. Then there's Gareth's fee, and the hire of the hall for rehearsals, plus the cost of the Town Hall for final rehearsals and performance, then the programmes, and some publicity posters.

--We'll make some of it up from ticket sales, surely? asked Candace.

--Yes, dear, of course. But that won't be until much nearer the concert. And even if we fill the Town Hall, we're still in arrears from the Christmas catastrophe.

This had happened before Jiri had joined the choral society; he longed to know more, but decided not to revive what were evidently bad memories. Instead he attempted to look attentive while mentally running through what he had seen of the tenor part.

He returned to the conversation in time to hear Arthur Broadhurst's rather loud voice:

--What we need is a fundraiser.

--What, you mean a jumble sale or something?

--No, no, I'm thinking bigger than that. Another concert, more varied, less formal, cheap to organise.

--We can't expect people to do two concerts in six months.

--No, no, Candy! This wouldn't be all of us; we'd get some other items, short instrumental pieces.

--Like what?

--Well, if we want short, how about the 'Minute Waltz'? That's short.

--Which not even Chopin could play in one minute Arthur, interposed Jiri.

--Quite right! boomed Bernard. It's called Minute as in my-nute, small.

I thought it was something to do with a dog, mused Jiri, unheard by the others.

--Well then, Jerry, how long does it take you?

--Just under three minutes, last time I tried. But I expect I could shave off a few seconds with practice.

--Well Arthur, if you are thinking of a two-hour programme, with about twenty minutes of that for the interval, you have another one hour, thirty-eight minutes and say twenty seconds to fill, noted Bernard.

--Miss Sibthorp can call on a couple of her pupils; and young Kathy Armitage would play something. Candy, you and Bernard do folk songs, Fred Norris plays the accordion and... I've just thought... Jerry, you and I are already a double act, what about a duet... that one I heard on the wireless... from *The Pearl Fishers*.

--This one? Jiri sang the opening of the tenor part of 'Au fond du temple saint'.

--You see? He already knows it! Jerry, we'll knock their socks off!

Jiri had a brief vision of flying footwear before recognising this useful idiom.

--If you can learn it, Arthur, you would certainly sound exceptional, he added.

--Hold on, warned Bernard, where are we planning to hold this event?

Candace spoke up.

--How about Middle Woodlow Church Hall? That holds a reasonable number of people, the piano's OK thanks to Mr Armitage, we can make tea and coffee to sell in the interval, and if we offer to make an extra donation to the vicar, who is currently fundraising for his roof, we might get it cheap.

--There's quite a lot of organising to do.

--Well, perhaps I might undertake that. As you know, I am in Middle Woodlow most weekends, on the spot, so to speak, and Magda would be happy to help with the refreshments...

Jiri felt confident that he could easily manage so simple a task. After all, between the wars he had earned most of his income by organising and managing concerts, tours and recitals in both Germany and England; towards the end of the last war, while on war work in London, he had helped out with the National Gallery concerts; what he could do for Myra Hess he could surely do for Candace Drinkwater. This, of course, showed his complete ignorance of the politics of English village life; he was to learn.

It was now early May.

Once more, David waited at the stables to meet Jiri. He heard that clear rather high speaking voice calling as they approached, Jack! Jack! Did you know the bluebells are out? We have just come through Garrods Copse. David! It is *w/vunderful*! I have only seen them once before... do you remember Bryn, David? And the scent...

--Bryn?

--Oh, David, don't you remember where we met?

Of course he did; but, Bryn?

--That old Welsh pony... I couldn't ride much else then... but with Eddy... riding him through a bluebell wood... it is wonderful.

Jiri's face was radiant.

--What I don't understand, Jerry, said David a little later in the Red Lion, is what a pro like you is doing with a local choral society.

--That is a compliment; I hardly think a few recitals in Munich nearly twenty years ago, and various substitutions for singers and accompanists who were late, ill, drunk or, on at least one occasion, dead, really counts as a professional career, but, since you ask, it was because of Mr Armitage.

--Who?

--Surely you remember, David. Mr Charles Armitage, the piano tuner.

--Ah. Yes, when you bought the piano, Whitwams gave you his name.

--He is a remarkable man, David. The poor fellow was born blind, and sent to some special institution.

--The Sunshine Homes for Blind Babies.

--Yes, that is it. He then progressed to a school for the blind. It was there that he trained as a piano tuner. It was while visiting a client that he met his wife, who was at that time a housekeeper. I gather that her parents were not in favour of the marriage, and indeed I suppose all must have been anxious when Mrs Armitage became pregnant, but the twins, Kenn and Kathy, who are now about twenty, are not only healthy but quite musically gifted. Miss Kathy is a good pianist, taught by her father, and is in the choral society. Her brother is now doing National Service, but plans to sign up as a regular army musician. Mrs Armitage normally drives Mr Armitage to his clients, but Miss Kathy has obtained her licence and is able to share the driving. That is how I met her; she told me of the choral society, and that it was having some difficulties.

--I suppose she heard you sing.

--Yes, of course. Mr Armitage and I always spend some time together after he has finished with the piano. Then, naturally, I encountered Arthur Broadhurst. The baritone. It is remarkable. It reminds me of my father.

--Ah yes; your duet partner!

--Indeed. He is a loss to the concert platform. Why he took to soliciting instead of concentrating on the voice...

--Took to what?

--I told you. He is a solicitor.

--Not yours?

--Oh no; mine is a young fellow in Tunbridge Wells, just back from serving in India. He is most discreet. But Arthur is, as you say here, a Thoroughly Good Fellow. He has a charming wife, a charming house with a tennis court and three delightful daughters, the eldest of them at the girls' grammar school. We have visited them several times, and Magda has become friendly with Celia, Mrs Broadhurst. It was Arthur's idea that we have an informal fundraising evening at the Middle Woodlow Church Hall, the one which I am organising.

Suddenly Jiri's face clouded.

--I have to admit, David, that persuading the vicar was far more difficult than I had expected. Far more.

--Oh? I'd have thought he'd be glad of the chance to add a bit to the roof fund.

--Yes, one would assume that. In fact he wanted the whole proceeds to go to the roof, which of course contradicts the aim of the enterprise; it took much negotiation to secure a 75% to 25% cut, in our favour. And then only if we agree to provide the refreshments and programmes. But of course Bernard can keep separate accounts for those, with a bit of imagination. Then he wished to oversee and control the contents of the evening.

--Oh no! How did you get over that?

--I agreed to show him a draft list, but of course, as we all know, with these events, last-minute cancellations and changes are inevitable. Then he was difficult about dates. Apparently the church hall is in constant demand, although I must say that I had not noticed this... and, in short, he was most dubious about the whole undertaking.

--But he did agree in the end?

--Yes. I reminded him that the church we attend, St Bernadette's in Felperham, has a church hall.

--I didn't know that. Since when?

--Actually it hasn't. But he does not know that. Also, as thanks to you, David, I am becoming quite a competent organist, I told him that in an emergency I would help him out free of charge. In some ways I would quite like to do so, as it is a fine organ, a Willis, I believe, but on the other hand it would be complicated as we are not allowed to participate in Protestant acts of worship, so I would need to find time to go somewhere for confession afterwards...

Jiri sighed.

--Actually, Jerry, I think you'll need to go to confession anyway after all the whoppers you told the vicar. But look, Jerry, you don't really believe it all, do you?

--Why not? It is all quite logical. And if one is a Roman Catholic, one does not need to waste valuable time in pondering the meaning of life. That is an advantage in a German-speaking culture.

--Yes, I see that. But guardian angels, for example?

--Well, I did think mine faltered rather in 1917. But then I realised that they had all been a bit overworked at the time, and mine appointed a couple of deputies: Bruno and Miss Drake...

--Bruno?

--My cavalry mount. Surely, David, I have told you about Bruno.

David reckoned that Jerry almost certainly had, and at some length, but that it had been one of those horse conversations in which he let his attention wander. He changed the subject.

--Jerry, do you remember Janet Headland?

Yes; they had both met Miss Headland earlier that year, when they had been staying with David's father at his East Anglian vicarage. It was a long story but, in brief, she had fallen from her horse and they were on hand to assist her.

--What do you think of her?

Jiri did indeed think of Janet Headland. In fact, when confession required him to acknowledge Impure Thoughts, Janet came readily to mind. The Examination of Conscience in his prayer book asked if one had entertained Impure Thoughts but surely it was the other way around.

--In my opinion, Janet is one of the most beautiful women I have ever seen. You are making progress there, David?

This was not exactly the conversation David had envisaged. He realised too late that the mix of Jerry's Continental upbringing, his undoubted Catholic practice, his immersion in middle-class English mores and his evident interest in sex combined to make his reactions unpredictable.

--What do you mean by progress, Jerry?

--Well. Are you close to getting wherever you wish to be?

As he made this considered reply, Jiri tried not to be distracted by imagining exactly where he wished to be with Janet. A familiar fantasy image of her in black fishnets and suspender belt began to rise in his mind. No, he was a middle-aged man at least three inches shorter than the blonde goddess. With an effort, he refocussed his attention on David.

--That's just it. I'm not sure...

--I think, David, that you are sure of her attractions. And you can be sure, I feel, of her interest in you.

Evidently among young English people of this class, the natural outcome (as it were) was unnecessarily complicated.

He soldiered on. You mean that so far you have not…?

--Good heavens no! She's Colonel Headland's daughter.

Jiri could not picture David and the Colonel with swords or pistols at dawn, so let this aspect of the case pass him by.

Fortunately his friend took the initiative.

--You are happy with Magda, aren't you?

Jiri was taken aback. Marriage was evidently where this was going.

--But of course. Never for one moment have I regretted taking my dear wife, he declaimed. Remember, David, that Magda and I share many interests; we are both strangers in our adopted land, and we have Paul. Forgive me, David, but surely your present circumstances would not allow you to support a wife… and family?

--That's just it, Jerry. Right now, no, out of the question. But there's a chap I met at music college…

--You are lucky to have friends from your student days, David. Mine are all either dead or in America.

--And he's setting up an organ repair and installation business in Norfolk. So many instruments have been totally neglected during the war and now people are beginning to want them repaired, or even replaced. He'd do most of the technical workshop stuff, and I'd talk to customers, try out the organs, demonstrate what we could do. It would be a share in a business, houses are going there for next to nothing, I'd not be too far from my father…

Jiri did not want David to marry Miss Headland and move to Norfolk.

--I had seen you more in a cathedral post, David. You are a fine organist.

--That's as maybe. But it hasn't happened yet. And I'm

not sure it ever will. Meanwhile there's Janet. One of the few girls I've ever...

--All have their preferences. But, regarding Janet... perhaps she does not exactly... share...

--Look, she hasn't had much chance to learn about classical music; she enjoys listening, and after a while... and, well, Magda doesn't play an instrument, does she?

--Thank goodness, no! I would have liked Paul to show some talent, but perhaps one of us is enough. And she is happy for me to practise, to come to concerts, to have Reggie and Isolde at the flat every Wednesday...

--Still working on the Schubert piano trios?

--Yes, David. Although it is difficult for Isolde to bring her cello all the way from Palmers Green.

Both of them felt that an in-depth discussion of Reggie's approach to the violin part of Schubert's Piano Trio Number One might be a welcome escape route. Jiri went up to the bar and purchased two more pints.

By now the Zelleks were spending nearly every weekend at Beech Cottage. They followed much the same pattern. On Friday evening Jiri would probably ride Eddy for a short time, and again on Saturday morning, as he had started practising for the jumping competition at the hunt gymkhana. Jack Andrewes, groom at the livery stables, was very keen for him to enter this, as it would raise the profile of the stables and maybe give Jack one up against the groom from the manor. In the afternoons, there would be tennis at the Broadhursts, with time for Arthur and Jiri to rehearse their duet for the church hall concert as well as their piece for the choral society. Magda realised that her husband needed male friends.

She supposed all men did. He had never replaced Vernon Dakins, or even his Munich companions; she did not like Jiri's colleague and bridge partner Cyril, and David Lomax, although a personable young man, was at least eighteen years Jiri's junior. Arthur Broadhurst was good for him.

On Saturday evenings Jiri might have a quick pint at the Red Lion while Magda cooked dinner. With riding, tennis, singing and the Red Lion, he was usually tired out by bedtime and slept soundly until Magda roused him for Mass at Felperham. Occasionally, though, they went to the Odeon in Felperham, as well as to the local cinema in Maida Vale. Jiri adored the pictures; he was generally undiscriminating, but preferred action movies, including anything featuring John Wayne, and he had enjoyed *The Spanish Main*, a tale of piracy starring one of his favourite actors, fellow Austrian Paul Henreid. Magda knew that if anything promised to be sad or romantic, she needed to bring a supply of handkerchiefs, and given that Jiri needed to hear a tune only once to be able to sing it forever, musicals meant that she would be exposed to whatever numbers took his fancy for weeks to come.

These days Magda was greatly pleased with her husband. Physical exercise seemed to improve his health; he rarely used his stick, hardly ever complained of back pain and was now wiry rather than skinny.

Paul looked out of the window to see his father, racquet in hand, knocking a tennis ball against the shed wall.

--He hasn't taken up tennis again?

--Well, yes, Paul, he has. I know he gave it up when you got too good for him.

Paul recalled, with only a very slight feeling of guilt, how he had enjoyed making Pa run around the court almost to dropping point... but, Magda was continuing, he has teamed up with young Kathy Armitage for doubles: he hits the shots and she does the running around the court... they just play a few games at the Broadhursts' on a Saturday afternoon, they don't always lose and it doesn't seem to do him any harm.

--I see you've taken pity on poor old Jerry; not everyone would want to be his doubles partner, said Arthur Broadhurst, approaching Kathy Armitage, who was looking across the lawn. She could see Jiri sitting by a garden table; Magda came up to him with a cup of tea, and as she put it down, she placed her hand on her husband's arm. He had rolled up his shirt sleeve, and his muscular arm was sprinkled with curly black hair. Such a look passed between the two that Kathy felt that her casual glance was almost intrusive.

--I think Mr Zellek is a very happy person, she said. You can hear it when he sings.

--What about me? What do you hear about me when I sing, Kathy?

--Well, Mr Broadhurst...

--Arthur, please. We're both members of the choir, after all, and we're friends, aren't we?

--Yes of course, Arthur. You must be very happy too.

--Why's that?

--All this. She looked around at the large house with its wisteria and French windows, at the spacious garden and the groups of people relaxing.

--Don't be too sure, Kathy. Sometimes... it's just not

quite enough. Look, I need someone to talk to, someone who might really understand.

The first of the three planned local events was the choral society fundraising concert in Middle Woodlow. Jiri had worked with a wide variety of musicians, and in the Twenties and Thirties his voice teachers had introduced him to singers from the Berlin and Munich State Operas, so he thought he was familiar with outbursts of artistic temperament, including his own. All this was nothing, he discovered, to the grudges, rivalries and tantrums unleashed when the inhabitants of the Woodlows took to the stage. In addition, he knew that he would have to live with these people afterwards, at least at weekends. It took all his charm, ruthlessness, and carefully assumed ignorance of English idiom to arrive at the point where everyone had accepted his/her time slot, place on the programme, and agreed items of performance. He had hoped that the vicar would not attend the concert, but he seemed determined to do so, presumably to keep an eye on the takings. He had been given a draft programme, but it fell to Jiri to present him with a complimentary copy of the actual programme, explaining that the community hymn singing had been cancelled due to a sudden epidemic of tonsillitis, to be replaced by Fred Norris on the accordion. George Richmond would be singing 'The Foggy Foggy Dew' in place of 'Sheep May Safely Graze', and Harry and the staff of the Red Lion would be rendering 'Roll Out the Barrel' following the departure of the Felperham Savoyards on tour. When asked later when the next concert would be, Jiri was not forthcoming; he hoped it would not be for a long time.

As the doors opened and the performers gathered backstage, Magda felt that Jiri would be exhausted before he opened his mouth, especially as he had eaten nothing since breakfast except a bowl of soup and half a slice of toast; the voice apparently could not tolerate food before a performance. She need not have worried; he was already high on the nervous energy that had carried him through the last fifty years. She could see that at half time a great many cups of tea would be required and as she was by now familiar with the English habit of obsessive discrimination in the matter of tea, she prepared to serve with milk, without milk, with just a splash of milk, with plenty of milk, not too hot, not too cold, strong/weak, with one spoon, with two if you can spare it, no sugar for me, please, I haven't taken it since the war... The biscuits would need to be carefully watched, with not more than two per person. Celia Broadhurst was to be her helper, backed by Mrs Kingsley, and she was confident that they could cope as a team. Nurse Baines was on duty by the door lest anyone be overcome by the excitement.

Meanwhile Jiri was organising front of house.

--Ah, my important young ladies!

He advanced on the two younger Broadhurst girls, with a radiant expression that could convince anyone that they were the most important, if not the only, person in the room.

--Miss Sylvia, Miss Brenda! Your frocks are most elegant; and the hair ribbons! I am overcome. Here are the programmes, and your bags of change. (The programmes were most attractive; printed by Hallorans of Felperham, who produced the *Saint Bernadette's Magazine*; special rates for parishioners.)

--Now; you remember what we have rehearsed?

For several weeks, it had gone like this:

--Miss Sylvia, you will stand by the door. As each person comes in, you will ask if they would like a programme. If anyone is impolite enough to say no, you give them a look showing how very disappointing you find such incorrect behaviour: LIKE THIS.

Jiri then demonstrated an expression that had the girls smothering laughter.

--But, he continued, for the most part, they will reply, Yes please. You then say, That will be twopence. Do not give anyone a programme until he or she has handed over the money. There will be some who say, I have no change. Now, what will you reply?

You will say, We have plenty of change, or perhaps you would like to make a donation? That should complete the matter.

You, Miss Brenda, will stand a little further into the hall, so that if by chance anyone passes your sister by, you will be able to catch them.

We shall do this until five minutes before the performance starts. There is a large clock in the hall, so you will be aware of the time.

At this point, Miss Sylvia will stay by the door in case of any latecomers. Miss Brenda, you will slip in and out of the rows of chairs and if anyone has NOT yet bought a programme, you will be able to identify them and make sure that a sale is made.

Is that clear, ladies?

It was, and the girls took up their positions with appropriately, if deceptively, winning expressions.

Jiri had decided that the first items would be by the younger performers; they would have less time to be nervous, the audience would be eagerly attentive, and the youngsters would be able to go home after the interval. The eldest Broadhurst daughter, accompanied by Miss Sibthorp, played her grade five violin piece; the other two, released from their programme sales, played 'Shepherds Hey' on their recorders. A young bugler from the Scouts stepped forward; Jiri had been horrified to learn that until the previous week the lad had been unable to offer anything other than the Last Post, but he could now do 'Come to the Cookhouse Door', which might have been better scheduled immediately before the refreshment break.

Now came the first longer item.

Miss Sibthorp, angular in a long black dress with lace sleeves, strode towards the piano, followed by Kathy Armitage, carrying the music for the accompaniment. Kathy looked enchanting with her thick, curly brown hair and regular features; she wore a deep blue evening dress with a sweetheart neckline and a real rose, pink, pinned to her corsage. She was to play Für Elise a little later in the programme and was now about to be Miss Sibthorp's page turner. Silence fell as the two rather unlikely Pearl Fishers took centre stage. In evening dress they looked good: Jiri neat, Arthur, as was often commented, A Fine Figure of a Man. Miss Sibthorp's hands fell on the keys, fully prepared for the harp-like passages of the accompaniment. The men were singing in Bizet's original language as although Jiri contended that Tauber, Schmidt and Kiepura always sang everything in German whatever the original language, and that was how he was taught to sing, Arthur declined to utter any German, so

French it was. Fortunately the audience contained no native French speakers. As always when Jiri sang, his hearers were initially surprised that such a slight figure could produce such a sustained resonant sound. High notes were no problem for him, although he could never have attempted Wagner and was at his best in lieder and folk songs. 'Au fond du temple saint' was certainly ambitious, but he was in good voice these days and had a good deal of experience behind him. Arthur, though, was magnificent. As Jiri had said to David, it was a pity Arthur had taken to soliciting as a profession; more training, maybe more dedication and he could have earned an excellent living as a professional baritone. And as Gareth Bax Williams had spotted, the timbre of their voices was entirely complementary and, if Jiri had more technique, Arthur had considerable native force; by the time they reached the swearing of eternal friendship they had built up a satisfying volume of sound. They were not Björling and Merrill, but they were good enough to enchant and excite the audience in the church hall. Although David was aware of the faults in their performance (and he would tell Jerry about them later), and although really Bizet was not to his purist liking, he felt himself swept away by the blending of sound, mingled with a sudden feeling of affection for Jerry.

Their performance ended with them clapping each other on the shoulder, Arthur nearly flooring Jiri in his enthusiasm, and the audience applauding for a gratifyingly long time. Jiri moved to the piano, took Miss Sibthorp's hand and raised it to his lips with a bow and a heel click. Arthur went one further by embracing Kathy.

She remained at the piano for Für Elise, followed by Candace and Bernard's first selection of folk songs. The opening half concluded with Jiri's playing of the Minute Waltz, which he explained actually took a little over two minutes, a performance enlivened by Arthur's unexpected appearance with a stopwatch, offering to take bets on whether Jerry could do it in two and a half.

During the interval Jiri went into the gents' and took a slug from the hip flask he carried in his music case.

Meanwhile, the crowd queuing at the tea hatch was divided between the majority who cheerfully paid their threepence, those who felt strongly that the refreshments should have been included in the ticket price (these often lacked change) and a few generous souls who paid over the odds. They still only got the regulation two biscuits.

The second half was an undoubted success. Jiri had scheduled the more serious music for immediately before the interval, with the last part of the evening featuring more popular items, which the audience could join in. Perhaps the hit of the evening was the saxophonist from a Felperham dance band. Where the hell had Jerry found him? thought David, viewing the young man's Brylcreemed quiff and checked trousers. Then there was Fred Norris's accordion and songs from gamekeeper George Richmond, who had a good voice and a wide repertoire; this was to be followed by Candace and Bernard's second lot of folk songs. But, shortly after the saxophonist, Candace grabbed Jiri.

--Poor Bernard's been in the lavatory for ages; he's got a terrible stomach upset... it must be the sausages we had for lunch... we shall have to go home. Now, if he can make it...

--Do not worry, Candace! Miss Kathy and I have an emergency item that will fill the gap... Please wish Bernard well.

During the last few years, Richard Tauber, who had died only the previous January, had been extremely popular in England. On some Saturday afternoons at the Broadhursts, Kathy Armitage had played for Jiri while he sang a couple of Tauber's songs; the voice was very different, but in the Woodlows an Austrian tenor was an Austrian tenor, and when Jiri sang in English his accent was not dissimilar. He had brought their music just in case of emergencies, which his long experience had taught him to expect.

--Which one shall we have, Mr Zellek?

The choice was either 'You Are My Heart's Delight' or 'Girls Were Made to Love and Kiss'. Jiri did not really like the English version of 'Du Bist Mein Ganzes Herz', so, perhaps unfortunately, he went for option two. He waltzed across the stage:

Girls were made to love and kiss
And who am I to interfere with this?
Is it well? Who can tell?
But I know the good Lord made it so
Am I ashamed to follow nature's way?
Shall I be blamed if God has made me gay?
Does it pay? Who can say?
I'm a man and kiss her when I can

Yet I have suffered in love's great deeps
I know the passion that never sleeps
I know the longing and wronging of hearts
The hope that flatters and shatters and smarts
I suffer still but I sleep at nights
Man cannot always be on the heights

428

And when our aching and breaking is done
Flirting is jolly, it's folly, but fun!
Girls were made to love and kiss
And who am I to interfere with this?
Does it pay? Who can say?
I'm a man and kiss her when I can...

He took Kathy's hand and led her to the edge of the platform, where they bowed; he clicked his heels and kissed her hand, as he had done with Miss Sibthorp.

--Cheeky little bugger! commented George Richmond.

Finally Harry's lot had everyone singing along, by which time the vicar had left.

--Jerry, you really are a disgusting old show-off, said David as the party in the back room of the Red Lion warmed up. I've heard a worse two and a half minutes at Wigmore Hall. Although poor old Bizet must be turning in his urn after that assault on *The Pearl Fishers*. You and Arthur haven't even got the same terrible French accent.

--Come, David, it wasn't that bad! And Arthur has a remarkable voice.

David was looking at something over his friend's shoulder and, as he turned, Jiri saw Janet Headland coming towards them; every man, and most women, in the room followed her with their eyes.

--*C'est la déesse*, he sang softly. It is wonderful to see you again, Miss Headland. I hope Maisie is behaving herself.

--Oh yes, thank you Mr Zellek. I'm so ashamed to think I had to meet you and David like that.

--Miss Headland, if you had fallen off as many horses as I

have (Let's hope she doesn't, muttered David), you would feel no embarrassment.

--Oh, Mr Zellek (Jerry, please), I did enjoy your song with your friend. Although I'm afraid I couldn't quite make out what language you were singing in. The programme just said 'Duet from the Pearl Fishers by Bizet'. He was Spanish, wasn't he?

David dared not raise his eyes to meet Jerry's.

--Apologies, Miss Headland; I think I see my dear wife waving to me so do please excuse me for a moment.

Shoulders shaking, Jiri weaved his way across the room. Before he reached Magda, and just before he had regained control of his laughter, he encountered Kathy Armitage.

--Congratulations, Miss Kathy. That was charmingly played. And thank you so much for helping me out with the emergency song!

--Thank *you*, Mr Zellek, Dad's a good teacher.

--I am sorry not to see your father here tonight; I hope he is well.

--No, I'm afraid he isn't. Actually we are all really worried about him. We had the doctor yesterday and he was very, well, guarded about things and said he'd look in on Monday. Dad was so disappointed to miss this evening. He said he knew I'd be all right but he really wanted to hear you play the Chopin.

--Miss Kathy, we are going back to London tomorrow, but I shall be here later in the week for the choral society rehearsal. If it would please your father, I will gladly come to play the waltz to him at your home. And I may well do it better without the antics of Arthur Broadhurst and his stopwatch.

They both laughed.

--You didn't know that was going to happen?

--No, I did not! But I am trained to get on with the music whatever the circumstances. Kathy leaned forward and took his hand.

--Thank you. I know Dad would appreciate you coming. And, incidentally, I think you have made a conquest of Miss Sibthorp!

--I will go and speak with her now, and so he did.

--Thank you for all your help, Miss Sibthorp.

--And thank you for the Chopin, Mr Zellek... The audience liked our Bizet, didn't they? I wonder whether you ever sing lieder? I studied in Dresden before the war and sometimes I long to hear Schubert sung in perfect German.

--I have spent time in Dresden; it is, or, I fear we must now say, was a beautiful city. But if you have studied there, Miss Sibthorp, you may find that my German accent is not as pure as might be wished; it is not my mother tongue and my first teachers came from Austria.

--As did Schubert himself; he may have had a voice like yours in mind. Mr Zellek...

--Jerry, please.

--No, Mr Zellek, I do not wish to use that name for you or indeed anyone else.

--I am quite well aware of both pejorative (that was a word he had been wanting to try out for some time) meanings of the name, but I am quite willing to accept it as a short version of my Christian name.

Miss Sibthorp looked at him.

--If we are to be familiar—

--As friends should be, he interposed.

--Then may I call you by your full name?

--But of course, Jaroslav it shall be... but it cuts two ways, as the saying goes, so?

--Amanda. My Christian name is Amanda.

At last he turned towards Magda, who was standing near the doorway holding a plate of ham sandwiches.

--What an excellent idea! I am completely ravenous.

Into the warm summer night, the partygoers left the Red Lion. David walked Janet back to the Dog and Duck, where he had booked (separate) rooms for the night before the drive back to East Anglia. Others left in twos and threes.

Jiri and Magda turned down the lane towards their cottage. The air was fragrant with the scent of honeysuckle and they walked slowly, arms entwined. Jiri found himself leaning increasingly on Magda.

--Tired, liebling?

--Yes, yes, I think so but it is a pity that such a beautiful evening should end... when I was a boy I hated going to sleep. I thought what a waste of time it was, lying in bed instead of doing all the things I wanted to... and now, I feel I don't want the evening to end.

--Janet Headland is a very beautiful girl... what are you laughing about?

--Yes, yes, she is lovely, and David seems... well... but perhaps she is, as they say, more beauty than brain. Miss Armitage is almost as good-looking and she has more character.

--You mean that she can play the piano and is in the choral society. Her father was absent this evening?

--Yes. I think he is not at all well. I will visit them when we are here next week.

Later, he murmured: Magda, did you know that Miss Sibthorp's name is Amanda?

--It is a pretty name. It does not suit her. And now you are laughing again. Jiri, I think you need to be careful with Miss Sibthorp.

--Darling I think you are *ein bisschen eifersüchtig*, and I think I like it.

He reached over and began to unbutton her nightdress. Magda did not pursue the topic.

The concert evening brought in a satisfying amount of money, so much so that Father Sullivan, not wishing to be outdone by the Protestants, planned to do the same for St Bernadette's.

--David, he has asked me to sing. Perhaps something Irish?

--What? You mean Dennis the Dachsund sings 'Danny Boy'?

--David, surely I don't...?

--*Ja*, Jerry, *mein Freund*. Well perhaps not quite so bad as that. But do be careful, Jerry.

--What about 'Linden Lea', that beautiful Vaughan Williams?

--I'd stay off that too. It was written about Dorset, and no one is going to believe you have ever been much further west than Paddington Station.

Jiri changed the subject.

--David, I have not wanted to show my ignorance but I feel I can ask you. What does it mean when they say someone has a bit on the side?

--Well… it means he is playing away from home. Seeing that Jerry now looked completely bemused, David tried again: Well, what do you think it might have meant, Jerry?

--I wondered perhaps whether it signified that the person has an arrangement with someone, with or without the agreement of his wife?

--Not far off, old man, although you are putting a rather sophisticated interpretation on a rather sordid matter. Can I ask who you were talking to?

--It was Mrs Kingsley. I was chatting with her while she was preparing the vegetables. One can learn much from her.

--Yes, so it seems. Are you going to tell me who it is that she thinks has this bit on the side? And who the bit is?

--No, David. I think I will not do that. At least, I would rather not just now. As to the bit, no, she did not reveal that even if she knows, which I doubt.

--Why so?

--Because if she had known, she could not have resisted telling me, concluded Jiri, sidestepping the earlier question.

That Saturday, when David came to collect his friend at the stables, he found Jack Andrewes directing Jiri and Eddy over a series of challenging-looking jumps in the paddock. Although normally deferential towards Jiri, Jack was evidently in trainer mode.

--What are you, a suet pudding? Sit up! For God's sake, why go all around the houses to the fence… you can cut off a few seconds there… You're even slower than yesterday…

When they finally reached the yard and Jiri dismounted, he leaned against the wall as Jack continued…

--The one we've got to watch is Miss Fellowes's Orlando.

Real thoroughbred, but he's knocking on a bit now.

--Then he's like me, Jack. I've had enough for today and we were at it for hours yesterday. You're as bad as our riding master in the army, and I was a hell of a lot younger then.

--Cavalry's a good schooling, sir. You'll be all right. Maybe have a hot bath when you get home.

--Do you want to go straight back to Beech Cottage? asked David as Jiri lowered himself into the car.

--No. I'm going to be stiff anyway. Might as well have a few drinks first to dull the pain.

At the Red Lion Jiri grimaced as they took their usual seats.

David looked around and produced a cushion.

--Arse or back? You'll have to choose: I could only find one.

--Thank you. Jiri eased the cushion behind his lower back. I'll have a Scotch. Make it a double.

--You don't HAVE to do this, you know.

--David, I have agreed. Jack has put a lot of effort into this, and I think he is running a book on the competition. And I have paid the fee to join the Woodlow Valley Hunt, who are running the gymkhana.

David took the subject no further.

--You're not going to the Broadhursts' this afternoon, then?

--No. They are all going to a wedding. I think one of the girls is to be a bridesmaid. In any case, I would be too stiff to play tennis, and too tired to sing.

When some time later they reached Beech Cottage, David helped Jerry off with his boots and he lurched towards the stairs.

--I may be some time. David, you had better eat those...
he indicated a covered plate of paste sandwiches left by Mrs
Kingsley.

David ate them, conscientiously leaving one for Jerry,
and then moved to the piano. About an hour later, after a hot
bath with Epsom salts and a handful of aspirins, Jerry came
down looking much more cheerful and to David's surprise,
ravenously ate the remaining sandwich before looking
vaguely around the kitchen for more.

--Let's go into Felperham and I'll buy you tea at the
Copper Kettle, he suggested.

Felperham was quite lively on a Saturday afternoon.
The shops were open – no music shop; one had to go into
Winchester for that – but most other things were doing
business, including a department store, Woolers.

--Miss Armitage works there, said Jiri. She is a trainee
buyer in the fashion department. That is why she is always so
elegant and well turned out.

By now the Saturday market was beginning to run down,
with the fruit, veg and produce stalls selling their remaining
wares at bargain prices. David halted at a junk stall, piled
with bric-a-brac from house clearances and the leftover lots
from country auctions. This sort of browsing was far more
to David's taste than Jiri's, so David was surprised to see his
friend pulling a gilded frame from a stack at the back of the
stall.

--Look, David! I have to rescue him!

It was a coloured print of an elderly man with heavy
moustachios, dressed in military uniform with a double row
of medals.

--Who?

--It's dear old Franz Josef! We had that picture in my father's study. And my uncle's dining room. And the office at the glass factory. And we had it in every room at school, and in the conservatoire and of course in the officers' mess; he watched over every day of my life until... How much do they want for him? I could hang him up in Beech Cottage if Magda does not want him at the flat. So he can watch over me again. And, if I want to, I can turn his face to the wall.

The stallholder charged five shillings for the picture; as he said, the frame alone was worth that. Ignominiously wrapped in an old newspaper, the former Habsburg emperor was tucked under David's arm as they entered the Copper Kettle.

Hoping that the items on the menu were still available, they ordered Welsh rarebit (David), poached egg on toast (Jiri) and a pot of tea for two. They were in luck, and the proprietor looked pleased to have two hungry-looking men to feed. The Welsh rarebit was almost finished when David glanced up to see Jerry looking abstractedly out of the window, his poached egg forgotten.

--What is it, Jerry?

--I thought I saw... that's strange... but no... I expect...

--Jerry are you going to eat that?

--It's gone cold, his friend remarked without enthusiasm.

--You'll hurt their feelings if you leave all that. David indicated the waitress and proprietor at the till. Just try, Jerry.

Accustomed to this type of admonishment from Magda, Jiri picked up his knife and fork and did his best.

They were safely home before Magda drove up. David helped her to unload her suitcase and some bags of shopping from the car, and Jiri heaved himself up to greet her affectionately.

--Jaroslav, you are tired, she observed.

--Yes, a little. But *schatz*, see what I have here! He unwrapped Franz Josef.

--Where are we going to put him?

--I had thought of the outside lavatory, but one might not want him watching while one took a crap.

David realised that neither of the Zelleks saw this as other than acceptable English idiom. He would have to speak to Jerry later.

--So perhaps opposite Queen Victoria?

The photograph of the Queen in her jubilee costume of black dress, lace cap and diamonds, had been inherited as part of the cottage furnishings.

--Who is the old gentleman with the moustache? asked Mrs Kingsley later. Is he a relation?

--Well, not really, replied Magda (although with the Habsburgs one never knew). My husband bought the picture in Felperham market.

--Well, it's nice to have something opposite the old Queen. I don't remember her funeral, I was only tiny, but Mum always said we had black hair ribbons when she died.

The following week, David was to collect Jerry on Saturday morning and take him to the stables; Magda needed the car to get back to London in time for a meeting connected with their church in Maida Vale. When he knocked at the door, there was no answer; he pushed it open (it was ajar) and called up the stairs:

--Hello, it's me, David!

The Zelleks' bedroom was immediately above the kitchen.

--Good morning, David! Magda is just rubbing my back; we will be down in a minute.

Some English comments followed: Further to the left; Not so hard just there. Then a brief silence and the sound of movement. Magda's voice was heard speaking Polish, and his own name featured.

Jiri's voice, slightly muffled, called down,

--David, make yourself a pot of tea; you know where everything is.

As David busied himself with the teapot, the sounds from above became unmistakeable. A series of impressions passed through his mind, among them the thought that there could not be much wrong with Jerry's back… of course, Magda might be on top…

It did not last long. Soon Jiri appeared, almost fully dressed.

--Ah, good, you have made more tea!

--Yes.

David felt that, under the circumstances, any remark he made must appear a double entendre. He managed,

--How are you, Jerry?

--Very well, thank you! Although I must stink of embrocation.

--I will try to keep upwind of you; that way I may not get too excited.

Jiri was looking around the kitchen.

--Magda will be down soon. I wonder if she could get me a second breakfast.

--Jerry, I think Magda has already done enough for you this morning. I'll make you some toast.

--Oh. I would really like a scrambled egg.

The weeks passed.

Following a series of country lanes, David, who had been delayed, began to see improvised posters showing the way to the hunt gymkhana. Eventually he reached a field in which were parked a variety of vehicles ranging from a Rolls, through Austins and Morris Minors, to trucks, jeeps and vans. In one corner stood a row of horse boxes equally varied in design and repair. It wasn't difficult to find the paddock where the showjumping was in progress, and as he got there he spotted Paul Zellek waving to him. Paul looked unusually enthusiastic, as well as extremely handsome in tweed jacket, cravat and cap.

--This is getting exciting! Pa's in the last six, and I'm beginning to wish I'd backed him to win instead of both ways!

--I didn't think betting was allowed on these things.

--Officially no, but just about everyone here's got a couple of quid on someone. Half a crown on Pa getting in the first three? I've got a fiver riding on him so he'd better keep it up.

--Done. Where's Magda?

--Helping in the tea tent, and on hand for first aid. She says she can't bear to watch Pa over the jumps.

Next round! announced the fellow with the megaphone. Mr Allan on Manxman, Dr Smythe on Wrestler, Miss Fellowes on Orlando, Mr Zellek on Edelweiss Lad, Mr Browne on High Henry, Mr Harcourt on Marilda... Clear rounds go through; if no clear rounds, slowest times eliminated.

The fences had been raised, and the first two riders brought down a pole and two bricks, respectively. Fellowes was something else; daughter of the Big House, she was a brilliant rider on a thoroughbred horse. Clear round.

--Come on, Pa!

David held his breath.

--They're looking smart, aren't they?

Indeed they were. Eddy was gleaming, groomed to the ultimate shine. Jiri was impeccable in a dark hunting jacket, white stock and white breeches; his boots were polished and spotless. He'd done a good job on them, especially considering that he had never even thought of cleaning his own boots or shoes until he was well into his thirties. Suddenly Paul was struck by an early memory... his father was singing, well, he was always singing... *ein stoltzer reiter... ach reiter, lieber reiterman...* dear horseman... Oh, dear horseman!

Well done! Clear round.

The next two riders also had clear rounds, although Harcourt's horse brushed the top of the hedge.

Next round. Fellowes, Zellek, Browne, Harcourt.

Fellowes, clear round in great style. Zellek, near thing, Eddy clipped a top pole, which wobbled but remained in place so clear round. Browne, considerable drama as his horse first refused the gate, then cannoned into it and retired. After repairs to the gate, Harcourt had his round and knocked off the top pole of the second jump.

Fellowes, Zellek. Jane Fellowes did it again. Faultless. Watch that pole, Mr Zellek, warned Jack Andrewes. Just clipped it last round. Keep him straight for the jump, don't start turning till you're over.

--My God! Pa can certainly make that horse shift!

Clear round, and fast.

Last round. Miss Fellowes and Mr Zellek. If both clear rounds, faster time wins.

No surprise that Jane Fellowes got round clear and in impressive time.

--Pa's up against it... not much chance, Dave... *No one calls me Dave!*

Jiri was clearly going to give it a go and he and Eddy started off at a swift pace, getting over everything until they faced the last jump. Then it happened. What caused Eddy to spook was discussed later, but he certainly panicked: ears back, eyes rolling, sideways shuffle, followed by frantic bucking and rearing in an effort to get rid of his rider before galloping away, his genes as prey animal in full command.

--Christ, Paul, he's going to come off, he's lost a stirrup.

--Hang on, Pa! How did he manage that!

Jiri was calming the terrified horse; he leaned over and patted Eddy's neck, settled himself, walked Eddy back to the approach to the last fence, gathered him together and got him over.

That gets penalties as a refusal, although all the fences had been cleared.

--Bad luck, Pa, but you did well to stay on and get over that fence. Jerry, are you all right?

--Yes, yes, David, I am; it was just that as Eddy spooked, I thought I remembered something... but it's gone now, and it probably makes nothing. Good lad, Eddy, good lad!

Jiri dismounted.

--I must help Jack get him into the horse box.

--Nearly came off there, Mr Zellek, commented Jack dourly.

--Yes. I should have seen that coming.

--Never mind, sir. There's a lot of people here that didn't think you'd make it into the last three, so we may clean up, although not as good as if you'd won it.

--Thanks, Jack. We can settle up the book later... now I must congratulate Miss Fellowes.

In fact Miss Fellowes was coming towards them, as her

groom led her mount away. She admired Eddy – 'I can see he's a steeplechaser' – commended Jiri for staying on and ended by hoping that he would come out with the hounds that season. As she was turning away, her eyes met Paul's.

--May I introduce my son, Miss Fellowes? Paul Zellek.

David fought the impulse to say, He's a city accountant and he hates horses.

--Janey, that fellow Zellek gave you a close run!

--Yes, Farve; he's quite old too.

--Been in the army, I'd say. Though I wonder which side.

Later in the afternoon Miss Fellowes, Jiri and Mr Harcourt received awards and rosettes.

--Eddy has the rosette on his stable door, Jiri explained to Magda. We have to give this little shield back next year, but it will have my name and Eddy's on it and we can have it on the mantelpiece till then.

Magda's expression suggested that she did not think it had been worth the effort.

Much later, David and Paul left the Red Lion, where celebrations were continuing.

--I guess Pa will be sore at both ends tomorrow, grinned Paul. His arse took quite a pounding, and he's knocking the booze away this evening. And I doubt he'll get much sympathy from Mum.

Now rehearsals for the choral society event, which was scheduled for the end of July, just before the start of the school holidays, took centre stage.

While Gareth was pleased with overall progress, things did not always go smoothly, one reason being Jerry Zellek.

His voice was certainly a rare find, as was Arthur's; the atmosphere in the choir was quite buoyant, too, with a few useful new members, and the memories of the Christmas catastrophe overshadowed by the success of the recent impromptu fundraising concert. Jerry, though, had the irritating habit of offering helpful interpretative suggestions, in some of which he was backed by Miss Sibthorp. She had noticeably smartened up, at least to the extent of not always wearing the same bottle-green dress, and Gareth gathered that she and Jerry met regularly to rehearse lieder, with a planned pre-Christmas recital at the girls' grammar school. Finally Gareth told Jerry rather sharply, in front of the whole choir, that he, Gareth, had the final decision. This was taken in good part; Jerry shrugged, saying,

--Yes of course. One must obey the conductor, as is said on the bus.

For some reason this caused amusement and, unfortunately, set off a series of heavy-handed bus-themed jokes and repartee. Gareth had only to ask the choir to Take Your Places Please, for someone to comment Pass Right Down Along the Bus There, or, Mind the Step… it was even suggested that Gareth should be presented with a bus conductor's cap.

Occasionally a muttered remark that seemed to have come from Jerry set the tenor section laughing, but when Gareth glared in his direction, he was seen only to be checking his place in the score or waiting expectantly for the accompaniment.

--Jaroslav, began Miss Sibthorp. Jiri rather wished that he had not agreed that she might use his full name; uttered in that tone of voice, especially by a woman, it usually meant trouble. He looked as innocent and attentive as possible.

--This is rather difficult... I have something to say to you... you should know that...

A range of possibilities flashed through his mind, each more disastrous than the last... surely not...

--I would hate for your good name to be tarnished, she struggled on, of course it is obvious that you are a perfect gentleman, a churchgoer, and that you and Mrs Zellek... are... a devoted couple (which she felt was a very tactful way of putting things). But by association... well. It is rumoured that Arthur Broadhurst, your close friend, is... a philanderer.

This was a new one... was Arthur a member of an occult sect like the Masons? Did he collect some strange esoteric item: matchboxes, perhaps? Was he involved in illegal financial dealings? Did he practise some dangerous sport? Had he a concealed health condition?

Miss Sibthorp realised that her difficulties had been compounded by Jiri's complete lack of comprehension.

But, since they had been working together on the lieder, her fluency in German was returning.

I mean, she announced, that Arthur Broadhurst is *ein Schürzenjäger*.

--Magda, dear... Nurse Nancy Baines handed Magda a cup of tea. There's something I want to talk to you about. In strictest professional confidence of course. Your husband (what had Jiri been doing now?), your husband is a friend of Arthur Broadhurst, isn't he...?

--Yes. That is so. Jiri enjoys singing with Arthur. And we are often guests of Arthur and Celia Broadhurst.

--Well. It's being said, about Arthur Broadhurst, that he's taking advantage of someone, a young girl… mind you, she should know better but…

--Who is the young woman in question? asked Magda bluntly. Nancy leaned forward and whispered.

--So, dear, I thought that you might just have a word with your husband. Find out whether he knows about this, and if he can do anything about it. Perhaps when you have him to yourself. At bedtime, perhaps, have a serious word.

Magda felt that bedtime was not the most propitious moment for a serious conversation with Jiri, with whom there was generally one of three scenarios. Either he would fall asleep instantly, or they would make love and he would fall asleep instantly, or he would be suffering from some physical discomfort that demanded sympathy, massage, embrocation, aspirins or, at worst, help with going to the lavatory or turning over. However.

As she prepared for bed that night, Magda thought of Nancy Baines's advice. She would try.

By the time she got into bed, Jiri was half asleep. She patted his bottom.

--Hmm…

She patted more firmly.

--Mmm? He turned towards her.

--Jiri, she began, we need to…

--Yes, darling, so we do. His agile fingers began to unbutton her nightdress. This is pretty but it gets in the way.

Next morning Magda sat in the front room of the cottage, looking out over the garden. She was deeply troubled. From the kitchen came Jiri's voice:

*Dein ist mein ganzes Herz! Wo du nicht bist, kann ich
nicht sein,*

*so, wie die Blume welkt, wenn sie nicht küßt der
Sonnenschein!*

*Dein ist mein schönstes Lied, weil es allein aus der
Liebe erblüht.*

*Sag' mir noch einmal, mein einzig Lieb, o sag' noch
einmal mir:*

Ich hab' dich lieb!

and then, switching into English, 'You make my darkness
bright…'

That is a favourite with you, Mrs Kingsley?

--Well, it is, Mr Zellek. And I must say you sing it like
that Richard Tauber.

--Thank you; you have heard me sing another of his
songs, 'Girls Were Made to Love and Kiss'… it is better in
German but I know the English words…

Magda saw Nurse Baines leaving her bicycle against the
fence and went to open the door to her.

--Come in, Nancy; you have time for a cup of tea?

--Wish I could, dear; but I'm on my rounds and can only
stop a minute.

--I keep thinking of that poor girl, said Magda.

--Men! They only want one thing, snorted Nurse Baines.
At this point Jiri put his head around the door.

--Good morning, Nurse Baines. Mrs Kingsley and I
are having a sing-song in the kitchen. Any requests? And,
continuing with Lehar's anthem to flirtation, he disappeared.

--I'm sorry, said Magda.

Nurse Baines pursed her lips.

--Well, it's good to see somebody happy. And better than him riding around on that great horse, which you and I both know he shouldn't be doing at his age and with his war injuries.

--He is younger than Richard Tauber, blurted Magda, and not so fat.

Nurse Baines looked bemused, as well she might.

--Well, dear, what I really came about was to ask you to pop round for a cup of tea this afternoon. A patient has given me a Fuller's coffee walnut.

Magda set off to have tea with Nurse Baines.

--Enjoy yourself, *schatz*. My respects to Nurse Baines.

Pleasantly tired after the morning's ride, Jiri settled down with the *Racing Post*. He was perhaps just beginning to doze when there was a violent hammering at the door. Wondering why it was that no one ever seemed to knock at the door in a normal way, Jiri opened it to find a young man in khaki on the step. He was a male version of Kathy Armitage and was clearly very angry.

--I want a word with you, Zellek. I'm hearing filthy stuff about my sister and an older man, and it has to be either you or your mate Broadhurst.

--Private Armitage, if we are going to mention your sister's name, it is better to do so where the rest of the world cannot hear us. Come in. Won't you sit down?

--No. I want to have this out now.

Kenn Armitage stepped up close to Jiri, who did not back down.

It's all over the village that she's been taken advantage of. It's none of her colleagues at Woolers, there's no one else, it has to be from the choral society, and that's you or Broadhurst.

--Private Armitage, I can assure you that my relations with Miss Kathy are entirely innocent. I have a great regard for her, as I have for your parents, and I am glad to have the opportunity of singing with her, and she is good enough to be my tennis partner, but that is all. How is your father, may I enquire?

--Not too good. In fact that's why I'm here, on compassionate leave. I know he thinks a lot of you, Zellek, so that's why it would be even lower for you to...

--Truly. There's nothing.

--Do you swear to that?

--No. I am a Roman Catholic, and we do not swear in that way. But I have been in active service, and if you will accept the word of honour of an officer, I will give it. If not...

--Well, that may have to do. Now I look at you, I don't think... you aren't Kathy's type, I can't see you forcing yourself on her, she could stick up for herself against a bloke your size, you're old enough to be her father (not that that might stand in your way) and anyway all the village knows that your wife would string you up by the balls if you stepped out of line.

One section of Jiri's brain filed away some more useful English idioms, while another section attempted to take in the implications of Kenn's words.

The young soldier continued, If it's not you, what do you know about Broadhurst?

--I know he is a talented baritone, that he is a practising solicitor, that he has a charming wife and three young daughters, that he is a cheerful fellow and, as they say, good company. I am happy to call him my friend.

--So how often do you see him?

--At the choral society practice sessions and recently, at his home for tennis and when we were preparing for our duet at the concert; as you know, I am generally not in the village much during the week; my employment and main home are in London. But, Private Armitage, these are questions better addressed to Mr Broadhurst himself. I think I have satisfied you on my own behalf. Perhaps you might leave now.

Kenn paused, not exactly shamefaced but feeling that he had been slightly wrong-footed. As he did so, the door opened and Magda appeared.

Liebling… you are back early… This is Private Armitage.

Magda did not seem at all surprised to see Kenn, since she felt that the meeting was divinely arranged.

--Mr Armitage… Kenn… I have just come from Nurse Baines. She is on the way to your home. I am afraid your father is worse… I see you have your motor bike outside.

--Yes… yes… thank you, Mrs Zellek.

Among Jiri's conflicted responses to all this was a guilty feeling that somehow Arthur had a narrow escape. His personal dilemma was whether to warn him of Kenn's intended visit, but as this was now unlikely to take place in the immediate future, he put the matter aside. Miss Kathy was a lovely young woman; if she consented to a dalliance with some lucky fellow, it was not the business of village gossips.

The best way to remember expressions is to practise them.

--Magda, said Jiri that night in bed, are you aware that the whole village thinks that you would string me up by the balls if I stepped out of line? After a short silence, Magda's response was to slip her cool fingers between his legs.

Charles Armitage pulled back from the brink but he was now clearly mortally ill. Kenn returned to his unit but was told to expect bad news at any time. Jiri visited his friend whenever possible; Mr Armitage was confined to his bedroom, but his door was left open, as was the sitting room door, so he could clearly hear the piano and Jiri's voice. Jiri finished playing a Chopin Prelude and went upstairs.

--Your leg's better today, Mr Zellek.

--Yes.

--Thought so.

--Your hearing is still amazingly acute, Mr Armitage. You know my footsteps.

Jiri sat by the bed. Mr Armitage took his hand.

--They're not telling me anything. But I don't think I'll go on much longer.

Jiri said nothing.

--Thanks. I know I'll get no nonsense from you.

--It is not for me to... but let me say that... when the moment comes, it is quite all right. In fact, it is the only logical solution. And it does not hurt. What comes after, I cannot tell you. But the thing itself...

--How do you know, Mr Zellek?

--Perhaps you know that I am a Roman Catholic. In our Church, when a doctor or nurse thinks that one is... dying... a priest is called and we have a ceremony. It is called the last rites. So, if that is happening, one knows that one is about to die. So that is how I can tell you.

--Go on.

--Well. The pain grew less; then I did not feel it... I had been shot, you see, and then my horse fell on me... but that is not the point. I could not bear it anymore. Oh, how tired

I became of being brave! But again that is not the point. He anointed me…. that, Mr Armitage, is part of the ceremony, and he asked if I was sorry for my sins. I tried to answer, but I don't know if I did. Then, and this is what I am trying to tell you, it was very quiet, and I was not at all worried, or upset, or in pain, or… anything… it was just so… gentle, adagio… I was happy, and everything would have been quite, quite all right. That is how it is. Do not be afraid, dear Mr Armitage.

--But you came back.

--Yes. One of the nurses was rubbing my hands and slapping my face, and someone gave me an injection. Then it all started again. So I am here.

After a few minutes, Mr Armitage pulled Jiri towards him.

--I'm ready, he said. But there is something I want you to do for me. No one else has got the guts; maybe young Kenn, but he'd never get away with it; he'd be too obvious.

--Mr Armitage, I think I know what you want. And I understand your feelings as a father, of course. But Miss Kathy, she is a young woman of sense, she is nearly of age, and she is capable of making her own decisions, is she not?

--Yes. I'm not old-fashioned about these things any more than you are, Mr Zellek. But something she told me… she hasn't even told her mum; listen…

Jiri's face changed.

--I had not thought that Arthur… no gentleman would do that, to force himself… I must ask, are you sure of this, Mr Armitage?

--I'm a dying man. I swear to you. All right, she was a silly girl to get into that position, carrying on with a married man, but by all accounts he's a good-looking fellow, and spun her the old tale about his wife not understanding him. One night in his car it went, well, so far, and then she came to her senses and said no. She swore to me that she tried to stop him. Mr Zellek, he raped her.

Paul Zellek and David were in the Red Lion. They had been discussing the latest village gossip.

--I'll tell you what, Dave, if there is something fishy about Arthur Broadhurst, we're going to have to watch Pa.

--Why?

--Well, you may not have seen much of it, but he's got a temper. And he can be belligerent and aggressive in the way little blokes often are.

David thought of Jerry's run-in with Ron Staples, and nodded. Even so, what came next surprised him.

--That was one reason we left Germany, Paul was saying. You know, we lived there until I was ten. In fact, for years I held it against Pa that he moved us just as I was old enough to join the Jungvolk: somehow the Cub Scouts never measured up! Towards the end in Munich, things were complicated, and Pa got into some nasty street fights: wading in if a few roughs were beating up Jews, that kind of thing... and as Mum told me afterwards, often there'd be honest citizens hesitating, and seeing a little bastard like him taking action, they'd back him up and a right ruckus would get going. So, anyway, he got known to the authorities. We're not Jews, but Mum's Polish and Pa's – obviously – a Slav, so not high on the Nazi list of desirables.

David wondered how Paul's Aryan good looks and his ambivalence towards his father could have affected this situation had they remained in Munich, especially given

Paul's eagerness to join the junior branch of the Hitler Youth. All three Zelleks had probably had a narrow escape.

So, Paul was continuing, he moved us here, or at least to Maida Vale, the flat they're still in, actually.

--It must have been a bit difficult, Paul.

--Yes. I did a couple of years at the parish school before I went to the Vaughan, that's the Cardinal Vaughan Boys' Catholic Grammar School in Kensington. Pa had made sure I spoke a fair bit of English, and I was a big lad, able to look after myself, but there was one kid, name of Tom Swainson, who made my life a misery. Lived next door to the O'Reillys; I was pally with all of them, and it was Hughie O'Reilly who told me about the fight, as he and his brothers had a ringside view from an upstairs window, not that the tale lost much in the telling! Anyway, Pa goes round to have a word with Tom's father. He's already pretty fired up, and when Swainson comes to the door (six feet four and a good sixteen stone) and starts slagging Pa off, with hindsight he might have been threatening him with things he knew about Pa's activities (David was agog but decided to let Paul continue as he was in full flood of reminiscence), Pa hit him. Gave him a black eye in fact, never mind his precious pianist's hands. Swainson's gobsmacked, but he picks Pa up bodily and throws him against the garden fence in preparation to beat the shit out of him. That's when Mr O'Reilly comes over, stands up to Swainson and they're about to have, well, more than words, when Pa picks himself up, grabs a fence panel which he'd knocked out when he landed, and whacks Swainson over the head with it. Enter Mr O'Reilly's two brothers, and the police.

Swainson is the person in the worst shape, so the police

ask if he wants to prefer charges against anyone. The three O'Reillys give him a look, and he realises that firstly, no magistrate is going to believe that the skinny little guy with blood streaming down his face could be a threat to a man Swainson's size, and secondly, that the entire Irish community is on the case and on Pa's side. No charges, warnings all round and the police push off.

O'Reilly takes Pa home, where Mum gives him the talking-to of a lifetime, sorts him out and puts him to bed, where I remember he stayed for two days. Meanwhile word gets around that he's beaten Swainson to a pulp, and I'm a hero for the rest of my school career. The Swainsons moved away, and as far as I know, Pa's still friendly with the O'Reillys. Maybe more.

I know it's a good story, especially after sixteen-odd years, but the point is that Pa could have killed Swainson, been done for manslaughter, and all of us interned or deported as aliens. He got angry and he didn't think; in fact, claimed not to remember much of the evening, says he didn't feel a thing when he hit the fence… and there were other things… It's only recently I've been OK with going into the Maida Vale local with him; he built up a bit of a reputation there… *(The publican's exact words were: Zellek? You want to watch your old man. He's a fuckin' lunatic.)*

Dave, you may think my father's a likeable little fellow with a superb singing voice, nifty keyboard skills and a boring obsession with horses; actually, he's a spoiled, selfish, arrogant, ruthless little shit with a violent temper. So if he takes against Arthur Broadhurst, the one thing we can predict is trouble.

Amanda Sibthorp called at Beech Cottage to deliver a book of lieder; en route her bicycle chain had become loose, and her hands were covered with oil.

--Come upstairs, Miss Sibthorp, you can wash your hands in the bathroom. Jiri should be out of there by now, said Magda.

Miss Sibthorp went up the stairs, closely followed by Magda. As they reached the landing the bathroom door opened and there stood Jiri, completely naked.

--Liebchen, have we got a dry towel? This one is horribly damp.

Before she averted her eyes, Miss Sibthorp took in Jiri's small, wiry body, his hard muscular rider's thighs and buttocks, his dark curly body hair and the white scarring on his left leg. Jiri was the first to regain composure, and wrapped the damp towel around his waist.

--My apologies, Miss Sibthorp— Amanda... But may I offer my congratulations? You have joined a select circle, as you are now the third woman in the village to have seen me without my trousers.

With this he bowed and shut the door.

--Please don't worry, Miss Sibthorp, said Magda, putting her arm around the other woman. Take no notice of him. The other one is Nurse Baines. And he will have to manage without the dry towel.

It had been a very hot week in London. Amanda Sibthorp had spent all day Friday at an examiners' meeting; Jiri had suggested that they should travel down to the Woodlow Valley together when he finished work. Both were delayed by heavy traffic that affected buses and taxis, so when they boarded the train it was already crowded and stiflingly hot. It was clear that they would have to sit next to each other rather than opposite as there were only two seats remaining; Jiri asked her permission to remove his jacket, which he placed on the rack, and sat down in his shirtsleeves. This meant that Amanda felt him pressed against her from shoulder to waist and then from hip to knee. She was immensely conscious of his presence; she could catch the faint odour of the probably rather expensive soap he used. Conversation was impossible in the crowded compartment, and the book she had brought was in her bag, now also on the luggage rack. After a while she realised that Jiri was beginning to nod; he had been working all week, it was hot... he seemed most uncomfortable, she thought... after a while he really seemed asleep and suddenly she thought that she need never see any of the people around her ever again, and that just this once... she slid her arm around Jiri, who rested his head comfortably on her shoulder. His dark, crisply curly hair had the same smell as the soap but slightly stronger; he clearly didn't use anything like Brylcreem. They sat like that until the station before Felperham. Amanda withdrew her arm, which was in fact going numb, and Jiri jerked awake.

--Amanda! I apologise!

--Don't worry. I was just concerned that you would miss Upper Woodlow; we are near Felperham, where I get out. I will see you at the extra rehearsal tonight.

Charles Armitage died that hot afternoon. Kathy had been looking pale and ill for some time, due no doubt to the worry of her father's illness, and of course she did not appear at the rehearsal. Arthur Broadhurst's usual bonhomie was rather

457

forced, Miss Sibthorp seemed tired and preoccupied, and Jiri looked frequently at his watch. He had become irritated by the length of time rehearsals had dragged on; he was used to much shorter preparation periods, and would be glad to get the whole thing over with. Although he looked forward keenly to his duet with Arthur, the choir were really rather a *Gurkentruppe*.

It was only a couple of weeks now until the concert; then came the news that Kathy Armitage had been taken suddenly into Felperham General Hospital. Nurse Baines cycled over to Beech Cottage and she and Magda talked for some time in hushed voices, falling silent if Jiri came into earshot. But when he and Magda were alone, he asked her what she knew.

A few days later, there was another talking point in the Woodlows. DI Romney and DS Trowbridge sat in the Broadhursts' drawing room; WPC Evans was dispensing tea; Magda Zellek had taken the three girls into another room.

--These are definitely your husband's clothes, Mrs Broadhurst?

--Yes, yes, I'm sure.

--And have you any idea why they would have been found near the Woodlow Weir, or why Mr Broadhurst might have entered the water?

--Yes, Inspector, I'm very afraid I have... this morning... when I realised that he was missing... I found this note.

She handed it to Inspector Romney and he read it slowly; there seemed, sadly, little doubt.

--Had you noticed that he was at all worried, or concerned?

--Well. Yes. Things have not been going well with his practice. He always put up a brave face (she wiped her eyes) but, yes, he wasn't himself. He told me once that we... that's me and the girls... might be better off without him... we could go to stay with my mother in Liverpool... while he... sorted things out... and he wasn't sleeping well...

--Was there anyone he might have confided in?

--Well, I suppose perhaps Jerry Zellek.

(Oh, Christ, not him again)

You might speak to him. He and Arthur were certainly good friends.

--Mr Zellek.

--Yes, Inspector, Sergeant, how very nice to meet you again, although of course under sad, or at least difficult circumstances. Is it true that poor Arthur has taken his own life, and at such an inconvenient moment?

--Inconvenient?

--Yes; Arthur was due to take part in a choral concert the week after next; of course, the strain of preparation may have added to any anxieties he already had.

--To your knowledge, did Mr Broadhurst have any worries or concerns?

--You must understand, Inspector, that we were not what one calls confidants; I have noticed that in England men rarely confide in one another; but we saw each other frequently and I could not help noticing that lately he has seemed, well, preoccupied, and he told me that he had difficulty sleeping. In fact, I gave him some of the tablets prescribed for me by my doctor in London; perhaps that was unwise, but I saw no harm, and indeed I gave him only a very few. Inspector, this is playing on my mind; I hope I did not do wrong, and the whole situation is most distressing.

The Inspector noticed that Mr Zellek looked tired and upset. By all accounts he and Broadhurst had been good friends.

--Don't blame yourself, sir. I can tell you that in cases like this the, er, deceased's family and friends always worry about what they might have done to prevent the worst. I'm sure there is nothing to reproach yourself with.

--Dave, said Paul, this whole thing stinks. Arthur Broadhurst is the last person to commit suicide. Pa's in it up to his neck; either he's been having it away with Celia Broadhurst or more likely he's out for some sort of revenge. He's got a shine on Kathy Armitage, you realise. It's generally known that Pa's darling Miss Kathy is at death's door in hospital after, well, after some backstreet job. If he thinks Broadhurst is to blame for what's happened to her, he's likely to take action. I wouldn't put it past him to shove Broadhurst into the weir; you remember what I told you about Pa. It's not going to do my prospects any good to have a convicted murderer for a parent, let alone what it would do to Mum. I'm going to find out the truth, even if I have to beat it out of him.

--He's your father, Paul.

--Yes, that's the problem.

--What do you think happened?

--Don't know. Any ideas?

--Oh God. The boathook.

--What boathook?

--The one in the outside lavatory at Beech Cottage. I saw it last time I was there, and wondered what it was doing. I just thought it was something connected with Mr Kingsley; you know, the bog's mainly a bloke's preserve, just Kingsley when he's working in the garden, anyone doing jobs around the place, and Jerry when he doesn't want to walk upstairs.

--Jerry, said David.

Paul took over.

--Pa. Come into the kitchen. We have to talk to you. While Mum is out. Now.

Paul locked the door.

Sit down. Just tell us what has been going on with Arthur Broadhurst.

--Nothing, well nothing apart from his suicide.

--Sure? Come on, tell us…

--It's for your own good, Jerry, added David.

--When people say that, they always intend to subject one to something unpleasant. And, he continued bitterly, you two have certainly got your interrogation technique ready… one speaking kindly and one prepared to… My own son and my dear friend…

--Come on, Jerry, we're not in a Verdi opera. Just look at yourself; you're like death warmed up, you've crocked your leg, and what about the boathook?

--What boathook? There is no boathook. It is no longer there.

--Go and check, David.

--Right. Nothing.

--I told you.

--Pa, whose is it?

--George Richmond's. He was able to deliver and collect, using the outside lavatory.

--I'm not asking what it is that you've got on that poor sod, Pa, but at least that gets us a bit further.

By now Jiri seemed resigned to telling at least one version of his story.

--Arthur came to me for advice (Big mistake, muttered Paul) as he was having considerable difficulties; he was in trouble with the Law Society and in danger of being struck off; he had some problem with income tax, as do not we all, he was in debt and things at home... well, Arthur had an eye for the ladies, as well as something more serious going on. I suggested a solution. Under such circumstances, many a better man would have taken the honourable route of suicide. Of course, that is a mortal sin and I would never advise it; still, one can conveniently disappear without actual harm. I explained that it is possible to obtain a passport by various means... don't worry, Paul, ours are all genuine. Arthur would need to enlist the help of his wife; she could join him later, under his new identity, and start a new life, possibly in Canada or Australia, even Argentina, where there are some interesting people. It happens all the time.

David and Paul drew deep breaths. All this was dubiously legal, but it was not murder.

--I reminded Arthur that in these circumstances, the fewer people who may know anything, or be known to know anything, the better. I advised him not to tell Celia that the idea came from me, but unfortunately Arthur was something of a blabbermouth, so one cannot be sure. In fact, they really needed little help from me. All I would need to do would be to attest to Arthur's state of mind. Arthur would leave a note explaining his motives, he would hide a suitcase with a change of clothes, money and a few papers in the woods near the weir. He would write a suicide note. Early one morning, he would leave his garments folded on the riverbank, slip into the water and never be seen again; in fact, he would climb out above the weir – of course, there would be few footprints as he had swum downriver – retrieve his suitcase, dress, and make his way to Upper Woodlow in time for the milk train, which he would board unseen by the guard, and use his season ticket for part of an onward journey.

--So what went wrong?

--Ah. Has anything in fact gone wrong? Arthur is presumed to have committed suicide. After a while Celia and the girls will move away and the matter will be forgotten.

Neither David nor Paul was entirely satisfied by all this. For a start, the use of the boathook was still unaccounted for.

There was the sound of a motorcycle and a knock at the door.

David looked out.

--It's... I think it may be...

--Kenn Armitage! cried Jiri. You had better let him in.

--You all right, sir?

--Yes, thank you, Private Armitage. May I introduce my son, Paul Zellek, and Mr David Lomax? Paul, David, Private Kenn Armitage.

--Private Armitage, my father was just explaining to us the circumstances of Mr Broadhurst's disappearance.

Kenn and Jiri exchanged glances.

--Sure you're all right, squire? I just wanted to see if you were OK.

Kenn moved protectively towards Jiri. He was stocky and strongly built, only three or four inches taller than the older man, but of much more robust appearance.

463

--Better now you're here. Perhaps I should go on. I see that Paul and David are not quite satisfied with my account, and of course, now you are here, Private Armitage, they must realise that you are somehow implicated. As you all know, I was a friend of Arthur's. Otherwise I suppose he would not have come to me for advice, as I have explained. Looking back, I see that several ladies in the village felt that I might even be a good influence on him, as he was becoming known as...

--As a promiscuous bastard, broke in Kenn.

--Well, yes. Although at first, one knows, these things go on, sometimes it is as well to, as is said, turn the other eye; such affairs can be fun... although, of course, I would never... after all, I am told that in my case the whole village knows that Magda would string me up by the balls if I stepped out of line. *(Don't laugh, or he'll know he's won, thought Paul.)* I had of course suspected something: David, you remember the afternoon in Felperham, when you made me finish that cold poached egg, after I had rescued poor old Franz Josef?

Kenn looked bemused.

Jiri, amazed at the English ignorance of European history, began patiently to explain the rise, dominance and fall of the Austro-Hungarian Empire. David touched him gently on the arm.

--Not now, Jerry. You can explain all that to Kenn some other time.

--Yes. Right, agreed Kenn. We can have a drink in the Red Lion.

Jiri shrugged, used to such reactions, and resumed:

--I thought I saw Arthur and Kathy together, at a time when he was supposed to be at a wedding. Later I asked

Celia, out of politeness, how the event had gone, and she told me that Arthur had been called away to an emergency meeting with a client... eventually I realised that it was not a matter of mere dalliance but that he had, forgive me, Private Armitage... damaged... Miss Kathy. He had forced himself on her, with disastrous consequences. This altered my view of things; I was very angry, as I have the greatest respect and regard for her. Your dear father, Kenn, spoke to me in his last days, and asked something of me.

--He spoke to me too. Said he hadn't wanted to put me in any danger, but that he'd asked you... he said if anyone had the guts to do something about it, it was you. But he was worried about you, told me just to keep an eye on you in case you needed any help.

--So, went on Jiri, Private Armitage called on me; it was the second time he had done so, and he came in most gentlemanly fashion to apologise for suspecting me as the seducer of his sister. He now knew the truth and after discussion with me he sought an interview with Celia Broadhurst. He left her in no doubt that her husband had been unfaithful, and had acted most cruelly towards a young girl who had been their guest on many occasions. I allowed a few hours to elapse before visiting her myself. Of course I did not mention that I knew of Kenn's visit; I said that I had thought that it might be useful if I brought them a few of my... of those...

--Pa! You don't mean Dr Schweiz's knockout pills?

--What pills are these, Jerry? asked David.

Paul answered for him.

--I'm not sure what's in them, but Mum only ever gives Pa a quarter, and only if his back has kept them awake for three or four nights; once she was either desperate or completely knackered, maybe both, and gave him a half. He was asleep for fifteen hours and away with the fairies for another twelve. He'd be dead if he took more than that, although of course his body weight is relevant.

--Arthur was quite a large person, noted Jiri. Anyway, I thought that with the pills, one could not go wrong. At the very least, if Celia Broadhurst was still conniving with Arthur's faked suicide they could be used as evidence that Arthur was upset and had trouble sleeping. In the same circumstances, she might well innocently urge Arthur to take one, perhaps with a farewell drink, to calm his nerves before departure. I did not actually mention their strength. Or if, as I am beginning to suspect, she believed Kenn's account of what Arthur had done to Kathy, and decided to take matters into her own hands, they would help Arthur's despatch and if any residue was to be found in the, er, body, it would be further evidence of suicide, as he might be presumed to have made sure of things by taking a dose.

On Saturday evening I had a drink at the Red Lion as usual. I left at closing time and waited at home until about half past one, when I took the boathook from the outside lavatory and set off for the weir. It was a moonlit night, and I could take my time. I hid in the undergrowth; I had a hip flask but it became very cold; at last I heard a splash upstream, and I had expected Arthur to appear from the water in search of his suitcase. He was to swim a short distance to avoid leaving footprints. But I then saw him in the water, being carried by the current towards the weir; I had to run to the other side, and that's when my leg began to hurt; still, I got there in time to see him being washed over the weir into the pool below, where the river opens slightly. I took the boathook and pulled him to the bank.

--What else were you intending to do with the boathook, Pa?

--I did not have to do anything. I checked very carefully to make sure that he was dead. I made quite sure. There were no marks of violence on the body. He must have drowned either before or during his transit over the weir as he was not moving when he reached my side of it. So I pushed him back into the centre of the stream and he floated away. I expect he will turn up somewhere soon.

--And then?

--I set off home. I should have looked for the suitcase, but it was dark and I was getting very tired; I knew I had to get back with the boathook before dawn. I generally do not walk very long distances, Kenn. But it was still dark when I got here and returned the boathook to the outside lavatory for Richmond to collect. Of course, I wiped it carefully. Then I came inside... the stairs were impossible, so I lay down on the couch for while. When I felt able to go upstairs I took some aspirins with a whisky, and went to bed. I'm afraid I missed Mass, he added.

The others clearly felt that this was the least of his problems.

--I was woken by the telephone. I was very slow getting downstairs and the caller had rung off by the time I had managed. So I made some tea; the telephone rang again and this time it was Magda. Celia had rung her in London, telling her that she had tried to call me with no reply; they both assumed that I had gone to Mass in Felperham, and

Magda arranged to come straight down to be with Celia and the girls. I told her I would see her there in due course, which is when the police asked us both about Arthur's state of mind. I told Magda that I had wrenched my knee on the stairs after coming home from the Red Lion, and the next morning I rang my office explaining that I was not well, and that both of us were needed by a friend who had suffered a sudden bereavement. I am to be back to work by the end of the week. And my leg is beginning to feel much better.

--What about the suitcase with Arthur's getaway outfit? asked David.

--Ah, yes. I thought that, if it remained in place, that would suggest to me that Arthur's death was, in some sense, accidental and that Celia still believed her husband to be alive; she would then assume that he had removed it as planned. She would be unlikely to check on the suitcase for fear of being observed. If it had been removed it would suggest that Celia had made sure that her husband would not emerge from the weir, and the risk of being observed with the case was worth taking.

--So? Where is it?

--After speaking with the police, Magda wished to remain with Celia and the girls, so she said she would run me home to Beech Cottage before returning to them; she could see that I was tired, although I hope she did not perceive just how much; I asked her to drop me off at the Armitages', saying that I wished to enquire about Miss Kathy, and would make my own way home from there. I knew that I would not be able to get to the weir and back, even using my stick. As I had rather expected, Mrs Armitage was at the hospital with her daughter, but by great good fortune, Kenn was at home.

--So, sir, you turned up more dead than alive; seemed he hadn't eaten anything apart from a couple of biscuits at the Broadhursts' and he more or less passed out in the kitchen. I made him a good strong cuppa and left him with that and a slice of pork pie while I checked the woods around the weir. No sign of any suitcase, although someone had definitely been there. Smallish footprints in the mud; not Mr Zellek's nor Mr Broadhurst's, smaller than either of theirs.

I came back home and found Mr Zellek had perked up, so I took him to Beech Cottage on the back of the motor bike.

--Yes, it was *w/vunderful*... I would love to do that again. And now, do you think we might all have a drink, Paul? You know where everything is.

--Just a minute; what would you have done if the suitcase was still there?

--Oh, I expect we would have thought of something. Jiri and Kenn grinned at each other.

No one asked Jiri just how he had made sure that Arthur was dead, nor what exactly he had said to Celia about the strength of the pills. David thought of that moonlit scene, the white, naked body of Arthur Broadhurst, Jerry waiting shivering in the bushes, his struggle with the boathook and perhaps another, final struggle. Paul wondered just how his father had made sure that Arthur had taken those pills; perhaps, as a born, often a professional gambler, he had successfully calculated the odds on Celia's decision to do away with her husband. Or had he known of her decision, and arranged with her that he would be in waiting with the boathook? Whatever the level of his responsibility, it could never be proved in any court of law.

David and Paul left Magda, who arrived shortly afterwards, serving tea and cakes to Jiri and Kenn Armitage.

--Well, said David as they approached their relative cars, what did you make of all that?

--He's in the clear, which is the main thing. But if you ask me…

--And I am.

--Then I'm pretty sure Pa suspected quite early on that Kathy Armitage and Arthur Broadhurst were, in Pa's words, involved in a dalliance. Being the immoral bastard that he is, he probably wished Arthur good luck; I reckon he fancied Kathy himself. I think, though, he probably found out, either from village gossip or from Kenn Armitage, that it had gone too far and that Arthur had acted badly towards Kathy; certainly old Mr Armitage, on his deathbed, enlisted Pa as an agent of revenge, and Pa was angry with Broadhurst on his own account, given his feelings for Miss Kathy. Broadhurst, stupid sod, asks Pa for advice at about this time. I'm still not sure whether Pa already had other plans when he suggested Broadhurst's fake suicide, or whether he had suggested it earlier, as a way out of a friend's entanglements. Anyway, he had that second visit from young Kenn. As a result, Kenn calls on Mrs Broadhurst, leaving her in no doubt as to her husband's conduct. Pa then visits her, all innocence, as a partner in Broadhurst's fake suicide. He hands over the knockout pills; he can't lose: either Mrs B will give one or more to Arthur to calm his nerves before the fake suicide or, as Pa, gambler that he is, reckons, she sees them as a means of disposing of the poor fool by doping him before he enters the water. And I suspect that Pa may well have told her how strong they are. Just possibly, and I wouldn't put it past him,

Pa had something going with Celia Broadhurst, or maybe he just egged her on. Right. One way or another, Arthur is pretty well doped up before he folds his clothes and jumps into the river. The plan is that he swims down to just above the weir, climbs out, scrambles to the other side, finds the suitcase and makes off. But. One way or another, he goes over the weir, which he wasn't supposed to in the fake suicide scenario. Maybe he's doped. Maybe, although I devoutly hope not, he's helped by a boathook. By the time he gets to the other side, he's either dead or very near. And we heard that Pa made sure. Boathook marks accounted for.

The rest, I think, is pretty much as Pa told us. He makes his way home, by now in a bad way, which does indicate that he'd been exerting himself with that boathook. Next day he is all supportive at the Broadhursts, confirming that Arthur was in a suicidal state of mind. But he's worried about the suitcase; as he said, it was dark and he was near the end of his strength. If found, it might indicate that Arthur died accidentally in the course of a fake suicide; but much better for it to disappear: in a real suicide it would not have been there at all and, in the case of successful fake, Arthur would have taken it with him. That's where Kenn takes over. He found that the suitcase had already gone, evidently collected by Celia.

--So?

--Take your pick. At best, Pa's advised someone to stage a fake suicide which has ended badly. At worst, he's an accomplice or an actual murderer. And he's my father.

Arthur turned up some weeks later, in a decomposed state off the Isle of Wight. There were multiple marks on the body, some of which might have been made by a boathook, but were probably due to rocks, tides and flotsam. He was found to have ingested a considerable amount of barbiturates, and some alcohol. The coroner returned a verdict of suicide. Meanwhile Mrs Broadhurst and the girls had moved to be with her mother in Liverpool.

Gareth Bax Williams had been left in the lurch: not only was Kathy missing from the sopranos but, worse, he was without a partner for Jiri in the duet section.

--As I see it, Gareth, said Jiri, ever helpful, you have two options. Either you transpose it for Bernard Drinkwater, and I come down a bit but not too far, or we find a baritone who can learn it in time. If that is your preferred action, I suggest that we ask my friend David Lomax to approach one of the lay clerks from Winchester Cathedral or Romsey Abbey.

This happened; a very professional baritone not only partnered Jiri but, finding that much of the first part of the concert programme consisted of fairly well-known standard pieces, he stood in for most of these also.

Although overshadowed by the suicide of Arthur Broadhurst and the continued absence of Kathy Armitage, the concert was a highly successful end to the summer. Jiri rose to the challenge of singing with a new partner, and the days of frantic rehearsal renewed his interest in the piece, so that, as Gareth had intended, the duet was a focal point of the evening.

Kathy Armitage was ill for some time. Jiri visited her in hospital, sat with her, spent time with her when she was discharged. Whether at his suggestion, Kenn's, or of her own volition, she applied for jobs as a fashion buyer in some of the London stores, securing a traineeship at Selfridges and moving to a bedsit not unlike David's and within reach of the Zelleks in Humboldt Avenue.

Late one Saturday afternoon, David parked outside Beech Cottage, noticing that a lady's bicycle was already leaning against the fence. Magda was in the front garden, cutting orange and red dahlias. She was wearing a cotton frock, her arms brown in the September sun. As she was about to greet him, the piano accompaniment to 'Ständchen' came through the open window. *Leise flehen meine Lieder…* They both stood there, listening. In a few minutes the voice would cease, the piano die away; they would go in, they would make tea and eat cake with Jiri and Miss Sibthorp, the sun would set and another day would close. But for now, the autumn garden was filled with Jiri's voice.

> *They're philistines and drama queens,*
> *and rarely over five foot three…*
> *(Ben Moore, 'I'm Glad I'm Not a Tenor')*

Magda opened the door of the Maida Vale flat to admit David. Jiri would be with them soon, she explained. At the weekend he had been out with the Woodlow Valley Hounds, and was now treating his post-hunting aches to his usual remedy of a hot bath with Epsom salts, and aspirins washed down with whisky.

Jiri could be heard singing, which was a good sign, and he shortly appeared, looking very cheerful if moving rather cautiously.

--Yes, they had enjoyed a wonderful run. Eddy was one of the best horses he had ever had. True, he was suffering some after effects; in fact, yesterday he had been hardly able to move, but it would wear off, and he would toughen up as the season progressed; in the Ulans he had been in the saddle all day, although of course he had been much younger then and had not been through the war; of course, yes, he was being careful, no unnecessary risks, after all he had had enough falls in his time, but Eddy was really a superb jumper and it was a pity not to let him show his paces, why, on Saturday he had taken quite a difficult fence with no effort at all...

David realised that all this needed to be got through before what he viewed as a sensible conversation could take place.

Just as Jiri's hunting anecdotes slowed slightly, Magda reappeared, freshly made-up and wearing a becoming dress.

--David, you will stay for Abendessen? We expect another guest, we have plenty to share, and I can at once lay another place at the table.

--Please do, David, urged Jiri, it will be delightful to dine *a quatre*, unless of course you are wanted elsewhere?

David had to admit that he was not, although his chances of a quiet chat with Jerry were looking increasingly unlikely. Magda's cooking was never to be lightly refused, and he had agreed to stay, provoking gratifyingly delighted responses from both Zelleks, when the doorbell rang.

The other guest was Miss Sibthorp. She had been in London all day at a piano examiners' meeting; the Zelleks had persuaded her to come to dinner and catch a later train home.

--Come in, come in, Amanda! I am sure you need a glass of sherry after such a long and perhaps tedious day.

Jerry, David realised, was wearing a lounge suit and silk

474

tie; clearly he had considered a dinner jacket, but felt that Miss Sibthorp would not be able to change.

The first course was beetroot soup.

--It will make your piss turn pink, David, so do not worry about that, whispered Jerry.

The soup was followed by a central European treatment of... pheasant?

--This is just wonderful, Magda, gasped David.

--Jiri has shot them, she responded.

--In Maida Vale?

--No. Sir William has invited me to join a couple of shooting parties. Richmond has kindly lent me a gun, but I am in process of buying my own.

(That's very nice, Mr Zellek. Just about right for you, not too heavy and not too much recoil. Thank you, Richmond; I am glad you approve. He sensed George Richmond's thought, that must have cost a bit: I have been lucky on the horses recently. George was used to the gentry, which Mr Zellek undoubtedly was, although a foreigner, so you never quite knew... he'd turned up at the first shoot, suitably dressed but topped by a trachtenhut that he had worn for decades, which looked so right that after a moment no one had thought anything of it. That gun must have come from Chaplins' Winchester shop in Southgate Street, and George knew how much they cost. Either Mr Zellek was lying or he was quite a successful professional gambler.)

Given that Jiri had a hold over both George Richmond and Sir William, it may seem unwise of him to go out shooting with them; accidents happen. Of course, he had thought of this; Sir William and through him, Richmond, were quietly made aware that should any accident befall Zellek, some privileged information would be made public. Sir William, who was perhaps sharper than he looked, had also made enquiries through his solicitor; Zellek had been very much on the right side during the last war; at least on his mother's side he a had a pedigree longer than Sir William's own, he had contacts in important places, and actually he was quite good company.)

--I didn't know you could shoot, Jerry.

--But of course. My uncle Karel taught me. It is true that in the Ulans we had lances for parades and we used swords; in fact, I can still demonstrate cavalry sword drill, although I think I shall not do so this evening (David hoped that his expression managed to convey disappointment rather than relief) but we were not quite in the Middle Ages! How do you think we attacked the Russians?

Perhaps fortunately, Magda introduced the Linzertorte; she knew this was something that Jiri would eat, and it was not commonly served in England.

Dinner ended with strong coffee in porcelain cups so fine as to be almost transparent. Magda opened the box of expensive chocolates that Miss Sibthorp had brought; as guests, she and David were offered first pick. Magda then took the box and consulted the menu. Ah, these are the ones you like, Jiri, she said, and, selecting one, she popped it into his mouth, which he opened like a baby bird.

David and perhaps Miss Sibthorp felt that it was embarrassingly intrusive to witness this deliberately intimate gesture. Jiri, however, seemed unperturbed.

--Delicious! Thank you, Magda, and thank you, Amanda! Now... do we have time for a game of bridge?

David caught Miss Sibthorp's eye and shook his head slightly. He preferred not to play bridge with the Zelleks; whether they were partnering each other, or teamed with their guests, they were both frighteningly good players, especially Jerry, and although he never ventured criticism, it was clear that he registered any mistake.

--Or some music?

--Perhaps you might sing, Jaroslav? suggested Miss Sibthorp.

--I think not; the voice isn't at best this evening, and besides, which of my accompanists should I select? I would rather listen.

David always felt it a privilege to play Jerry's Bösendorfer. This instrument had belonged to Jerry's father, and had survived evacuation from Germany in the 1930s and subsequently the London Blitz. Jerry said, and perhaps believed, that Saint Cecilia had appointed its own guardian angel; he had certainly prayed constantly for the safety of his piano. Miss Sibthorp followed David and was marginally the better pianist; his main instrument was of course the organ.

With an eye to her guests' trains, Magda brought in more coffee and a plate of biscuits.

--Try one of these, David. Reggie brought them last Wednesday.

--Thanks. What does Reggie do when he's not playing the violin?

--He works in a bank. I think he likes it, but I think also that he is quite lonely. It would be nice for him to have a companion. His wife left him during the war, for an American airman.

--And Isolde?

--Isolde is like you, Amanda, a maiden lady. She has some income, but is finding things difficult at present. She has thought of giving some more lessons, but the cello is not a convenient instrument. I have suggested that she considers taking a lodger, as she has quite a large house in Palmers Green.

--Isolde... is she German?

--No. Her parents came from Yorkshire and were keen Wagnerians. They went always to Bayreuth.

--How is it you know so much, Magda?

--Jiri speaks to them only about music, but they stay behind for coffee and cakes. As I said, Reggie is lonely and Isolde has a long journey with her cello back to Palmers Green. She was most impressed, Amanda, to learn that Jiri had played with Heinrich Rheinrose; of course we knew him well in the Twenties and Thirties; in fact, we shared a flat with him for some time.

--Really? Jaroslav, you have never mentioned that.

--We met in our student days; we played trios and I was the pianist. Heinrich was of course the cellist, and the violinist was a fellow called Max Morgen; he became quite well known in the Thirties, but he did not survive the war.

David thought he would change the subject, and was helped by Amanda Sibthorp's eagerness to discover more about Jiri's association with the famous cellist. Magda reminded her of the time.

--Amanda, it has been a delightful evening, said Jiri. I will see you to the taxi rank and make sure that you are safely en route for Paddington, where you can change for the Felperham train. It is not far.

Outside, he hesitated at the top of the steps to the street.

--Amanda, might I take your arm? I am rather stiff this evening... Thank you. Ah, good, Sidney's taxi is here. Good evening, Sidney! This lady for Paddington Station, please!

He raised his hat as the vehicle pulled away, and turned towards home.

Meanwhile, David was helping Magda clear away the dinner things, and arrange them ready for Mrs Chancellor's attention in the morning, although of course Magda let no one but herself handle the porcelain.

--Well, Magda, is Jerry behaving himself?

--You heard; he is hunting this season.

--Yes, Paul has told me about that! Comes in covered with mud, absolutely knackered and totally full of himself, can't move for three days, then starts planning the next run.

--David, it is most unfair; everyone thinks that I am... am... what is it, a henpecker... but never, never in all these years have I been able to stop Jaroslav from doing anything he really wants to. And then there is this recital that he and Amanda Sibthorp are planning. Although that is at least less dangerous. In a way.

--Oh?

--You must see, David, how that woman feels about Jiri.

--Perhaps I do... but surely Jerry wouldn't...?

--You know he is – what is it? – a flirt, with anyone; but if I speak to him he says *es macht nichts.*

--I'm sure he's right. There are only a few things he takes seriously, Magda, and you know you are one of them.

--Also, I feel for her; it would be better if they had never met.

There was a short silence.

--Anyway, Magda, what was that about Isolde wanting to take a lodger?

--I'm hoping she will; it would be a great help to her. But it would not be suitable for you, David.

--Oh?

--Palmers Green is a long way from anywhere you might wish to be for your engagements, David. Are you no longer happy in Fulham?

--Well, as happy as I'm going to be, I suppose. I might look for somewhere bigger in the same area. And did Jerry mention that I'd thought about that business in Norfolk? But the Isolde place wouldn't be for me; I have a friend who may need digs soon. He wouldn't be able to pay much…

--A single gentleman?

--Yes.

--David, I will find one of Isolde's cards.

She did so. When David saw the fatal combination of consonants in Isolde's surname, Satterthwaite, he realised why the Zelleks always referred to her by her given name. He resolved that, next time he was particularly annoyed with Jerry, he would force him into a conversational situation where he would have to attempt the pronunciation.

The card also gave her music qualifications, her address and telephone number, adding that she was available for cello lessons.

At this point Jerry returned, and David wondered briefly whether he could keep him up a bit longer for the talk he had been wanting all evening. But although Jerry seemed quite inclined for a nightcap, Magda reminded him firmly that he needed to be at work the next morning. David, she said, would be welcome at any time: perhaps next week? And in fact, his chat with Magda seemed to have partially solved the problem he had come to talk about.

The pre-Christmas lieder recital that Magda had mentioned inaugurated a late flowering of Jiri's singing career.

Lieder were beginning once more to become fashionable with the cultured and those who hoped to be so categorised. Jaroslav Zellek and Amanda Sibthorp had a local reputation as performers; the headmistress of the girls' grammar school was eager to promote low-cost activities that would encourage parents to support the school. Although it was mainly a day school, there was a boarding house for girls from further away, and one of these was Cynthia Furness, daughter of the music master at a minor public school; he was deeply involved in organising and conducting concerts and oratorios in the south of England.

After the recital he approached Jiri, who, dapper in white tie and tails, was chatting politely to the headmistress.

--May I take a moment of your time, Mr Zellek? Let me congratulate you on this evening's performance. I particularly enjoyed that setting of 'Kennst du das Land'.

--Thank you, Mr…?

--I'm Donald Furness; my daughter is a pupil here.

The name meant something to Jiri, who was about to make intelligent comment on Furness's activities when he continued,

--The thing is, Mr Zellek, I'm looking for a Gerontius. I suppose you know the work, and perhaps you have sung the part previously?

--No, Mr Furness, I have not, although of course I am familiar with it.

--Well. What I want to ask you is to think about it, have a look at the score, and consider coming over to see me in the New Year. We could at least try out, see how it goes, how we both feel.

It was only as they parted that Furness realised that he had never heard Zellek sing in English, and that from what he had heard of his speaking voice, his accent was quite pronounced. Gerontius, of course, was an Everyman figure, who could indeed come from anywhere, but given that Elgar was so very English the Tauberesque accent might come as a shock.

Meanwhile over Christmas Jiri raided Whitwams for the score of *The Dream of Gerontius*, and a pile of recordings featuring different artists. By the time he stood beside Furness's piano in the second week of January, there was little doubt that in almost all respects he was as good a Gerontius as Furness was likely to find at low cost but with travel expenses paid. Everything Furness had noted at the recital was there: the easy top notes, the faultless breath control, the seamless change of register, the apparently effortless ability to fill a large space, the heartfelt yearning, the open, joyous attack... although...

The session ended with mutual congratulations; the performance in Cawley Abbey would feature the Southern Chamber Orchestra, and a chorus combined of singers from Furness's school and local choral societies, with soloists drawn from his wide circle of musical contacts. There would be three months for rehearsals. During that time, Furness suggested, would Jerry mind very much doing a little work with a voice coach who specialised in helping foreign singers with English language pronunciation?

--Ah, said Jiri. Heddle Nash.

--Er?

--I have the recording. Heddle Nash. He is *w/vunderful*. You want me to sound like him, *nicht wahr*?

--Well, his diction is unparalleled.

--Yes indeed! I saw him in an English version of *The Dubarry* before the war; the costumes were so romantic! And a couple of years ago in *Merrie England*... he was, sir... the sailor... but you know I am sure his tights were padded in that role. He is a little older than I am, although I think he pretends off a couple of years, and surely his legs... Jiri sensed that Mr Furness was losing track of his comments, so he concluded,

Mr Furness, I shall be most willing and interested to work with the teacher. I presume that the fees will be taken care of?

The performance was quite a big event. The abbey was huge, but every seat was sold.

David sat with Magda, Paul and Amanda Sibthorp.

--I suppose you have known Jaroslav for many years, David, she said. How did you meet him?

--Well, it was in 1941, then I didn't see anything of him till '43, when we met up again and have kept in touch. How did I meet him? He was standing in a flowerbed serenading a room full of nuns. I suppose I rather fell in love with the voice; it was later that I realised what an annoying little person came with it!

The orchestra and chorus were in place and the three soloists entered. The parts of the Priest and the Angel of the Agony were to be taken by the same singer, as is often done; he was the same lay clerk who had replaced Arthur Broadhurst at the choral society concert. The guardian Angel was a young singer called Pernel Staunton, at the very beginning of what was to be a most successful career.

Towards the end of the opening orchestral section, Jiri stood up, immaculate in evening dress: 'Jesu Maria, I am near to death...'

Jiri did not sound very much like the great contemporary English tenor Heddle Nash, but when singing in English his accent was certainly less noticeable than formerly; the wonderful passage beginning 'Take Me Away' survived its perilous consonant and was incredibly emotive and deeply felt. It seemed to David that his friend brought an unexpected maturity of interpretation to a voice enjoying renewed physical power together with undiminished clarity and resonance. After the performance, David could not stay in the abbey to hear the applause. He went outside and leaned against the stones of the abbey doorway, smoking a cigarette. How could anyone be unchanged after that performance? he thought. Yet Magda, who had been in silent tears for much of the hour and a half, would now be going round to the artists' entrance, and Jerry would be saying something like, How did it sound, my darling? And is not Pernel's voice a *w/vunder*... and can we not go for a drink somewhere?

He reminded himself that Jerry's voice had always been a separate entity from his personality but somehow tonight it had seemed... yet he was reluctant to accept Jerry's simple comment: *But of course. Elgar was a Catholic. That explains it all.*

Among the audience was, to Jiri's surprise, his colleague and bridge partner Cyril Bowes Barnard with his wife, whom Jiri had heard of but never seen. She was something of a revelation.

Evidently Bowes Barnard had been impressed. Shortly afterwards he came up with a proposition. Apparently the government was eager to bring culture and consolation into the dark places of prisons and hospitals for the criminally insane. If Jerry could find an accompanist, they would be sent on a tour of such institutions to give a series of recitals, not all in German, and not all religious, Cyril added firmly. The accompanist would be paid; accommodation and travelling expenses would be covered. No, the office would not fund a new dinner jacket; the one he had was quite good enough for the criminals and loonies.

Jiri was quite willing. Apart from anything else, since *Gerontius* he had been taking his religious obligations even more seriously, and here two of the corporal works of mercy would be covered in one three-week tour with expenses paid. His first thought of accompanist was Amanda, but the school term would get in the way, and the thought of sharing hotel rooms with her was… well… Anyway, he would ask David.

The prospect of three weeks' employment came at just the right moment for David. They plotted the route between the prescribed venues and checked the accommodation, which varied between hotels, pubs, digs, and the homes of prison governors; David undertook the driving. Jiri offered to share this. But having experienced his friend's driving, David said that, no, it would be too much for him; in fact, David felt safer with Magda, although, having learned her skills as an ambulance driver in the Blitz, she too had her moments.

So David spent three weeks of unadulterated Jerry Zellek. His admiration of Magda soon increased. While Jerry could be an amusing, stimulating and affectionate companion, he could also be demanding, irritable and fractious. Since part of David's job was to get him on stage in fit condition to sing, he had to be ready to supply him with sympathy, aspirins, massage and clean shirts; he had to stop at short notice for him to stretch his back, piss or, occasionally, throw up. David became familiar with the peculiarities of Jerry's bony body and surprisingly large, permanently icy feet. For the two Sundays involved, Catholic churches with accessible Mass times had to be found, as Jerry was convinced that it was a mortal sin to miss Sunday Mass. David also realised the truth of the accompanist's axiom that there is no such thing as a modest tenor. He could only respect Jerry's professionalism; for Jerry, performing for 'criminals and loonies' was as important as performing before royalty; his standards were absolute. He would not have a drink, or eat, before a performance, which posed its own problems, as David would have to explain to a hospitable governor's wife that her carefully prepared dinner was not required, and somehow find sandwiches, soup or the like after the performance, when Jerry would need an instant energy boost.

On arrival, Jerry would spend time with the head of the relevant institution; he explained that this was a lengthy bureaucratic procedure. David would check out the accommodation and the recital arrangements. Fortunately Jerry could speak to, and get on with, almost anyone; any conversational missteps, sometimes wickedly deliberate, could be passed over as ignorance of English idiom, and he could often iron out problems that had left David infuriated.

They tried to arrange the programme according to the venue and audience, plus how Jerry was feeling; some items were less demanding and if David thought Jerry was flagging, they could adjust accordingly. Still, Jerry tended to gain energy on stage, and quite often changed the programme in mid-performance without apparent reason.

His repertoire ranged from light-hearted Viennese charm, through poignant *heimweh*, yearning unrequited love, folk songs in several languages, songs from musical comedy, popular hits, to classical examples of profoundly musicianly interpretation.

The rapport with his audiences was unnerving; he seemed to sense when a particular song would have emotional impact, raise a laugh, have the audience singing along, or calm a turbulent atmosphere.

He in turn was badly affected by the prison and hospital conditions. He would often vomit when they got outside, complaining of the smell of the buildings, the smell of despair and cabbage, he called it. How can they, how can they live, whatever they have done? it does not... or he would clutch his rosary and cross himself.

Towards the end, at about the beginning of the third week, they performed in a secure unit in Yorkshire. The nature of the inmates was said to be particularly evil and troubled. That night they were staying in one of their better halts, a large, old-fashioned hotel where they had two bedrooms connected by a bathroom; Jerry had the larger room and when David came to check on him, Jerry was already in the double bed, waiflike in his crumpled pyjamas.

--Are you OK?

--Thank you. I... don't want... I'm glad you came.

David looked at him and saw the misery on his face. He wanted to hold Jerry's fragile bird body, to feel the weight of his head on his shoulder, and the crisp curls of his hair on his cheek.

Jerry pulled back the covers.

David took off his dressing gown.

--Poor old boy. It's all right. I'm here.

Magda saw David's car in the lane. He and Jiri got out, and David brought Jiri's suitcase inside. They both looked tired and dishevelled.

Jiri was enfolded in Magda's arms.

--You'll stay for lunch, David?

--Thanks, Magda. Yes; I'll need to get going soon afterwards, but thanks.

--Are you going back to Fulham?

--Actually no; I'm seeing someone in Palmers Green… you remember…

--Ah yes… Isolde has told me… your friend is settling into her spare room.

--Darling, have I got time for a bath?

--Yes, Jiri; go up now.

--Can you manage? asked David.

--I think so. He moved to the stairs and was gone.

--I'm afraid we've brought back a load of dirty washing, Magda.

--That will be done.

--And I'm afraid Jerry is very tired.

--That I can see.

--And he hasn't been eating too well.

--That I can see also. Drinking?

--No, hardly at all; we did have a couple of pints last night to celebrate the end of the tour, but you know he doesn't have a drink before a performance.

She nodded.

By the time lunch was ready, Jiri came back, looking quite spruce in a clean shirt, his hair slightly damp. It needed cutting; David wanted to touch it. Jiri ate quite well and enjoyed the Linzertorte that Magda had baked specially. She wrapped up a large section for David to take with him.

--The garden looks lovely, darling, said Jiri. Would you mind if I go and sit outside for a while?

From the kitchen window they could see him sinking into a garden chair.

--I'd better be on my way; thank you for lunch and the torte. Sorry to leave you with the washing-up. I'll just say goodbye to Jerry. Silly old boy, it's sunny and he hasn't got his hat.

David took the panama and went out.

Magda saw him bend over Jiri and kiss his forehead. Then he tilted Jiri's face and gave him a lingering kiss on the lips, before putting the hat in place and holding Jiri's hand against his cheek before leaving without looking back.

Magda's dishcloth fell with a splash into the sink.

Her perceptions took a shift, as when one steps unexpectedly off a kerb. David! She knew that some men found Jiri attractive, and that he... but... and, yes, something that Isolde had told her about David's friend, who was now her lodger... and, when David had looked at Jiri today, was it not like poor Amanda Sibthorp? Yet, Janet Headland?

For the next hour or so she was very, very angry.

Then she took a folding table into the garden, and placed on it a tray with tea and scones.

Gently she roused her husband.

His face was irradiated with delight.

--Darling! It is so... wonderful to be back with you, and here, it is so...

She saw that he was almost in tears.

--Here. She poured him a cup of tea, with exactly the amount of milk, and hint of sugar that his finicky taste demanded...

--Scones! They look lovely.

He made no move to take one. Magda buttered one, applied jam and cut it into small pieces.

--Come on. Here.

--It was so... those places, Magda... I can't begin... I know what Purgatory will be like...

Magda thought privately that English prisons and places for the criminally insane were probably far more comfortable than the Nazi death camps, and that Jiri ought to know this. But she began to imagine, perhaps, what had happened. Jiri had needed warmth, comfort and someone to hold him close in his distress. David had taken advantage, she thought; as for Jiri, well, whatever of a... sexual nature... might have taken place... he would have been half asleep and, as she knew, he was easily aroused and once aroused, he could not stop.

And to think she had given David most of the Linzertorte.

Magda had realised long ago that her husband's spiritual state had altered little since he had been prepared for first communion at the age of about eight. He had total confidence in all the ordinances of the Church; he prayed the rosary, fasted conscientiously and had dragged himself to Mass even in considerable discomfort. His comments about guardian angels were not made in jest. Deep thought or spiritual subtlety seemed, however, completely lacking. Magda had once mentioned this to a priest, to be told that, especially in these evil days, it was a wonderful thing to see such pure, childlike faith in a grown man. It was a grace from God and should not be disturbed on any account. She had acquiesced, but could not help thinking, as she did now, that this was all very convenient for Jiri; for him that side of things was completely taken care of, and if English Catholicism often fell short of the colour and ritual that had entranced him as a child in Austria–Hungary, well, there was always Westminster Cathedral. Did he, she wondered, have any real sense of sin? Evil, yes, he could recognise and fear, but as regards his own actions, his belief in the efficacy of confession and absolution verged on superstition. She must take him as he was.

That night Jiri fell asleep on Magda's shoulder. She looked at him; his hair was still thick and curly, but close up there were a few grey threads; there were lines around his mouth and across his forehead. Suddenly she thought of an English poem they had heard on the wireless: Jiri had said something about meeting the author in Berlin in the twenties; that must have been when they were sharing a flat with Heinrich.

Lay your sleeping head my love
Human on my faithless arm…

Strange that she should suddenly think of that; and if either of them was faithless, it was not her. Although she had not understood all of the poem, she recalled that the rest of it was an invocation of safety and peace for the sleeper. Strange too that the poet should know so much, and not notice that it becomes most uncomfortable to have another person, however beloved, weighing down one's arm. Gently she shifted Jiri, kissed his forehead and laid him back on the pillow. He remained fast asleep.

This was on Friday. The next day Jiri did not go to the stables. He had breakfast in bed, insisting that Magda stay with him while he ate. Later he went to see Mr Kingsley, saying that he needed to talk to him about the fence, and ask him to take a message to George Richmond. During the afternoon, he said he had work to do before Monday, and sat for some time with his notebook.

In the evening, they decided to listen to *Saturday Night Theatre* on the wireless; Jiri lay on the couch and went to sleep after five minutes.

On Sunday morning, Magda drove them both to Mass in Felperham, where several parishioners told Jiri that he was looking peaky, that he was skin and bone, that none of us is as young as we used to be, and other encouraging remarks not calculated to make him feel better.

Back at Beech Cottage, both Kingsleys, George Richmond (carrying his rifle) and the local police constable met them at the door.

--Sorry to have to tell you, but there's been a break in, sir. Good job we got your message yesterday about the shifty-looking bloke you saw hanging about; we've been keeping an eye on the place as you asked.

--That's right, Mr Zellek, added Mr Kingsley. After I went to the police station with your note, I called up George here, like you said, but I'm afraid the bloke got in through the French windows before we frightened him off... You'll need to get that pane replaced.

--Anything taken, sir, madam?

Magda did a hasty survey of the room.

--The corner cabinet; the lock is broken.

It was a Georgian oak cupboard. Guided by David's impeccable taste, Jiri had picked up several pieces of good country furniture for the cottage, which partially counteracted the Zelleks' central European addiction to handmade lace mats.

--Is anything missing from the cupboard, Mrs Zellek?

--Jiri! Your briefcase, but everything else looks as it should be.

--Ah well. It was time I was issued with another HMG briefcase; I have had that one since 1939.

--Anything valuable in it, Mr Zellek?

--Fortunately, no. The thief is the richer by five copies of the *Times*, which I have not had time to read, and a few crumbs from the sandwiches my dear wife makes for me to take to the office, which must be very stale by now, and by one handkerchief, badly stained with ink.

--Forgive me asking, sir, but why lock the briefcase away if that's all it had in it?

--Force of habit, officer.

Jiri drew the constable aside.

--You may know, officer, that I am employed by the government as a translator. Although nothing I handle has bearing on national security – I am not important enough for that – some of the material could cause distress or embarrassment should the contents become known.

Sometimes I bring work with me at the weekends and I make it a rule to lock my briefcase away whether its contents are sensitive or not; it is better that way than risking an oversight. Recently I have been occupied with a series of letters between a lady and a gentleman. Officer, I am a married man and I hope reasonably broadminded, but (here he shook his head sadly) let us say that a private detective, or, I am sorry to say, a blackmailer, would have been eager to catch sight of them. Possibly someone in my office may have been a little indiscreet, one cannot always vouch for one's colleagues, and it is easy to make a careless slip. It is most fortunate that on this occasion I did not bring any papers with me; they are securely locked up in the office safe. Now, I think my dear wife has made tea for us all; I am sure you are ready for a cup.

Back at Humboldt Avenue, Monday morning saw Jiri in his usual neat office attire, a three-piece suit.

--I am being taken to the office this morning, darling. Cyril does not want me to be travelling by Tube. Just keep a look out for the car.

The Bentley drew up. One moment… let me be sure that I recognise the driver… Ah, yes, it is Sutton! Good morning! Yes, I am ready.

--No briefcase, Mr Zellek?

--No, it has been mislaid. But I have my sandwiches safely in this paper bag.

And kissing Magda goodbye, he hopped into the car and was driven off.

--Cyril, I would ask you to put in a requisition for another briefcase. One in the new design, if you please.

--Well, as that's all you lost, I might manage. How was the tour?

--All here. Jiri handed over his notebook.

It has not been out of my possession at any time. I even took it to Mass on Sunday.

I got to see all but three of those named. One, sadly, hanged himself in his cell two days before the recital... perhaps he could not face the prospect of listening. But really I do not think David and I are quite so bad as to call for anything so extreme. The other... this one... well... I think some people know where he is. But I do not. And, Cyril, I would rather that you did not require me to find out. The Hungarian, it was not possible to see him privately, but he was in the audience; as I did not think anyone except the two of us would understand Hungarian, I changed the words of a couple of gypsy folk songs, and I think it was effective.

At this point, the telephone rang. Cyril answered: they were in his office.

--Miss Silverstrom? I told you that we did not wish to be disturbed. Oh? Yes, in that case, you have done the right thing. Put him through.

Right. Yes, I see.

--Well, Jerry, you certainly did succeed in communicating with him. He got out two days later, but someone found him between there and Dover. Kent Police pulled the body out of a reservoir.

--Poor fellow! I will pray for him, said Jiri simply.

This was not the sort of thing one said in a government office, but Cyril could not resist replying,

--An old sinner like you, Jerry?

--Well, yes; as you know, I sold my soul in 1938 for three British passports.

--Cheap at the price, Jerry!

--But we are told that the prayers of sinners are often more effective.

Cyril really did not wish to pursue this conversation. He was nominally a member of the Church of England.

Jiri had moved on.

--Then, Cyril, that particular group of people is no longer interested in me or my notes?

--Right. In fact, I needn't have sent the car for you this morning; you're back on the Tube tomorrow. Although, of course, you need to watch your back.

--I always do.

--Your accompanist, Lomax?

--Yes?

--I presume he didn't notice anything?

--I think not.

--Just in case, do we know anything useful about him?

--Yes, Cyril, I think we do. But for now I would rather keep it to myself.

--Very well. In any case, we have the Palmers Green address. Did you know about his actor friend, Denys Vigar? He's been there since he got out of prison for gross indecency.

Cyril glanced at Jerry's innocent, attentive face. Of course, he was so very much married to Magda, apart perhaps from a little dalliance with Miss Silverstrom. There were many other things that would be easier to pin on Jerry Zellek than deviant sexuality.

Jiri was thinking that he might manage to get over to the cathedral for confession at lunchtime. Priests were always so interested in the silly games one played in bed, especially with other men, the things that the Russians call gentlemen's mischief. Yes, he would get that done; now, what else?

--Ah, Cyril, I shall give Miss Silverstrom the bill for the repair of my French windows, and the lock of my antique cabinet. I expect the intruder was a hired petty thief, who was just paid to obtain the briefcase.

--Yes, as far as we know.

--Then I will get back to work. I am sure much has accumulated. Bridge club tomorrow, as usual?

It was not long before he needed to go to confession again.

David and Jiri were lying on the double bed in David's new flat. The window was open; sunlight and the sound of London traffic came through the waving curtain.

David lit a cigarette.

I shouldn't be doing this, and I'm not going to like what he says, he thought; but he went ahead anyway.

--Jerry...

--Hmm...?

--Wake up.

--I'm so comfortable...

--Jerry, have you ever been in love?

--Of course! Many times. I am very susceptible, as you know.

--I don't mean that. I mean really.

--Like you were with Janet Headland?

--One of these days I'm going to give you a good slap. No, not like that. Come on.

--Oh, well. I suppose we all have. You mean like you and Denys?

--More like that, yes. But I'm asking you, not talking about me and Denys.

Jiri seemed to reflect.

--Things that don't turn out well always seem more important somehow. So I suppose, once or twice. Paul's mother, although I'm not sure how that would have turned out in the long run. I can't see Mimi and Rudolpho settling down to a peaceful life in the suburbs, can you? Or Tosca and Cavaradosi? And there was someone in the war. There always is, of course. When I was in Yorkshire. Her husband came back. That was just before we met, you know. And, of course, Heini, dear, dear Heini... he used to call me *faygele*.

--What's that?

--It's a Yiddish word; it signifies quite a lot of things, including what we get up to, but the original means little bird.

--It suits you.

Jiri had fallen silent.

--Where's Heinrich now? You still hear from him, don't you?

--Yes, yes. He is very successful in Boston, and he has someone. I loved him deeply; I suppose I still do; but perhaps I wasn't in love with him. He was with me, though, and that goes a long way, doesn't it?

David noticed that Magda had not been mentioned. But they had always been strangely attuned, and his friend, his lover, now said,

--Magda. You know I cannot do without Magda.

--No. That woman is a saint. Jerry, I know you weren't

498

married to Paul's mother. But weren't you going to marry someone, before?

--Yes. Before. That wasn't being in love. It was serious. Have you finished your ciggie? Because if you have...

He raised his face towards David, who gave him a long kiss in the knowledge that he would get no further in the discussion for a while.

Later David lit another cigarette. Jiri reached over, took it, had a draw, something he rarely did, and replaced it between David's lips.

--You've made me feel all sentimental and nostalgic. Especially about Heini. You know, until I met him, I'd never felt that way about other boys, or men; in fact, I'd had a few explorations with girls my own age, and when I got to Vienna Max, Max Morgen – I must have told you about him – he took me to a brothel a couple of times... of course, I ended up having to pay for both of us, but that's another story. I met Heini, of course, and after the war I lived with him in Berlin.

--I've often wondered how you ended up there, Jerry.

--Partly because Heini had work there; partly because I realised that if I didn't leave Pallin then, I never would. I'd have been my father all over again. There was a girl I could have married. I was running the family business, I would have settled down as a good citizen and leading light in the musical society. Just like Papa. But mainly, I think, it was because of Hermann Weissenborn.

--I'm not sure...

--David, he's still alive and the best voice teacher of his generation. I was so fortunate to be able to study with him. It was Heini who got me the audition; I was going to sing 'Il

Mio Tesoro', and Heini talked me out of it; thank goodness he did, I thought I was so good and I was so very bad!

--What did you sing?

--It had to be one German piece and one in any other language; I sang 'Im Frühling' and Arlechino's serenade from *Pag*.

He sang a few bars very softly.

--Heini and I were a good team. Then, well, you know how it is in a marriage, you still get on well, you still love each other but some of the excitement goes. And remember, by then I was well into my twenties, ridiculously young as that seems to me now, and I'd been through the war. Heini really liked boys, quite young ones; I was sixteen when we first got together. I was getting a bit the worse for wear, I suppose!

--Never, said David loyally, though he imagined the lithe brown boy with hard muscles and tender, inviting crevices who had become the bony, scarred middle-aged man beside him.

--But what about you, what did you...?

--You don't know what Berlin was like in the twenties; there were all sorts of clubs, nightclubs, and there were things one was prepared to do for a box of chocolates, a bottle of cognac, once for some lovely toys for Pauli. That was the manager of the toy department at KaDeWe; he was quite sweet really. Heini and I did have a few rows about it, though; I think he was the only person who's ever hit me and got away with it!

--Really?

--Yes; he called me a little slut and hit me across the face. Of course, by then Paul's mother had come... and gone...

and then Magda... You know, David, I've never been quite like you, and Heini, and Vernon.

--You mean you're not a thorough-going queer, you perverted little hybrid... but who's Vernon?

--Someone I knew before the war, I mean this last one, but I don't want to talk about him now; I'm too hungry! He jumped off the bed.

--I want to try out that new restaurant, with the Italian owner! I want spaghetti, and a bottle of chianti and a HUGE gelato! Now, David! For goodness' sake get your clothes on!

I can no more; for now it comes again
That sense of ruin which is worse than pain,
That masterful negation and collapse
Of all that makes me man...
(The Dream of Gerontius, J.H. Newman)

When Paul Zellek invited David for a drink, they met in a pub in the City near the office where Paul worked. David arrived first and felt out of place among the dark suited types discussing business or downing a quick one before the commute home, but before long Paul appeared. Even in all-male company, several people could not take their eyes off him as he approached the bar and brought back two pints to the secluded table David had chosen.

--Well, Dave *(no one else calls me Dave)*, how are you getting on with the lovely Janet?

--All right, I suppose. David smiled to himself. Paul, he thought, if only you knew I'm fucking your father pretty regularly, but he continued,

What about you in that direction?

--Ah well, that's in a roundabout sort of way, what I wanted to talk to you about.

David said nothing.

--I'm seeing someone. Serious stuff. Could be.

Christ, is he asking me to be his best man? Or play Widor's Toccata at the wedding?

And... have you ever heard of the Cormer family?

--I think your father might have mentioned a racehorse trainer, but I'm not sure.

One of the few things David and Paul had in common was a complete lack of interest in horses; both of them mentally switched off when Jerry began on that subject.

--That's a cousin, I think. Thing is, they're a really old Catholic family, top notch, uncle lives in a castle.

--You can compete there, Paul! I quote, 'My uncle Karel had a castle in the mountains, but it was rather small and very inconveniently placed', and if it wasn't for a couple of wars, a revolution or two and some mountain landslides, it might be yours today.

--Much good that will do me! Not that Lucilla minds a damn.

(Lucilla?)

But if it goes any further I'll have to tell her father, and possibly a posse of lawyers, who I am and where I come from.

--So? Paul, no one need be ashamed of Jerry and Magda.

--Look, Dave, you know Magda's not my mother?

--Yes. Actually I do know. I nearly put my foot in it ages ago when I said that you took after Magda rather than Jerry. He just told me that she is your stepmother. That's all.

--He's my father all right, but Magda's not my mother. I've often wished it was the other way round.

Paul was now into his second pint.

I know you don't think I'm always fair to Pa. But I just got fed up with having a father who takes nothing seriously except music, horses and maybe bridge.

When David thought of the things his own father took very seriously, he felt that Paul had got off lightly. But he said nothing.

--And you know about some of the other stuff. I don't want to go into it all again now. I just wondered if Pa had ever told you anything more.

David thought quickly before replying:

--No, no, he hasn't. Sometimes he talks about the wonderful childhood he had, and about musicians he's worked with, but that's it.

--OK, thanks. Just one thing: any tips on getting him to open up a bit?

--I'd say invest in a bottle of Scotch. Make sure he has enough to start him talking but not so much that he starts singing.

--Will do. Although considering his size, Pa's got quite a good head for drink. The only thing that ever really gets to him is Polish potato vodka. There was the time he stripped naked and tried to jump in the Regents Canal; thought he was on military manoeuvres in 1913.

But Paul's careful plans were delayed. He soon heard that his father had gone down with a cold. The singer's nightmare: it came with a cough that hurt his back, and as always with Jiri, any indisposition led to a raised temperature and loss of appetite. He took to his bed, which was rather a relief since his tragic looks and constant complaints were at least behind a closed door.

Paul found his father sitting up in bed reading the *Racing Post*. He was wearing a knitted cardigan over his pyjamas and the room smelled of Vick.

--Don't come near me, he croaked dramatically. You will catch this terrible cold. It is the worst one I have ever had.

--Pa, you've said that about every cold you've had for at least the last twenty years.

--This time it is true.

--You've also said that for the last twenty years.

Jiri fell silent. Paul thought guiltily that his father looked like a small, crumpled bird huddled against winter storms.

Meanwhile Magda, blowing her nose, was preparing a tray.

--Is that all you're giving him? asked Mrs Chancellor. Feed a cold and starve a fever.

--He says he can't taste anything, that his throat is too bad to swallow solid food, and if he coughs he will be sick. So if he takes a couple of mouthfuls of soup or scrambled egg, we will be doing well.

--Pa, Paul continued, something's come up.

--Can you find me a dry handkerchief, Pauli? Try the drawer.

--Here. Pa, do you know anyone called Cormer?

--Cormer... yes, got a yard somewhere in Berkshire. Had a couple of winners at Doncaster. Why? Are you looking at form?

--No, not really Pa... er, there was something I wanted to ask you... about... when...

Jiri sneezed into the dry handkerchief.

--Pauli, you had better go. I do not wish to pass on these germs. And, on the way out, could you ask someone to refill my hot water bottle?

--Mum, said Paul, putting down his teacup. I need to ask you. About my... my other mother. And who I really am.

--Paul, of course you know who you are. You are Paul Vernon Zellek, you are Jiri's son and my stepson, you are a British citizen, and you are becoming a chartered accountant. When you were called up in 1942, we gave you all your papers as the War Office needed to see them. Your birth certificate, 1923 in Berlin (*that took some explaining*), your naturalisation papers (*God knows how Pa wangled that*), your school certificate, your vaccination forms...

--Yes, Mum. I've still got those, plus my demob papers, all safely filed. On my birth certificate, it says father, Jaroslav Felix von Tarnheim Zellek, mother, Rosa Seimel. There wasn't a marriage certificate, or a death certificate for Rosa Seimel.

--They were destroyed in the bombing.

--What bombing? Where?

--Paul, wait until your father is better. Then you can ask him. But please don't upset him while he is so unwell.

--Upset him? When was Pa ever upset? OK, if he loses on the horses or Reggie buggers up the violin part of the blasted piano trio.

--Paul, please...

--Sorry, Mum. I know you're having a hard time with him just now. Take it easy and don't overdo it. Look, I'll come back on Thursday as usual, but could you just do one thing for me, Mum?

--Of course, Paul.

--Get the old suitcase out of the Glory Hole.

Magda smiled. That was an English expression she liked. Having said that, the Zellek Glory Hole was meticulously organised and regularly dusted. The suitcase would be available.

Soon after Paul arrived on Thursday evening, Magda left to visit her friend Margery. As she reminded Paul, Margery worked at the library; Magda regularly baked cakes and biscuits for the library staff's tea break, and this, indirectly of course, ensured that the Zelleks never had to wait long for the newest titles.

Paul seated himself opposite his father and drew the bottle of Scotch from its paper bag.

--I thought we'd celebrate, Pa, as you are over your cold.

--Wonderful idea, Paul! I haven't had a drink since I've been laid up. I'll have mine neat.

As arranged, the suitcase was beside the table. It was really more like a trunk; Jerry had taken it with him on tour; it was large enough to hold his evening clothes, stage make-up, various changes of underwear, pyjamas and shirts, a quantity of sheet music and scores. The outside was plastered with stickers from stations and hotels all over the Continent and inside the UK. First out was a large, decorative photograph album kept by Jiri's stepmother. Paul had seen this before, and did not encourage his father to linger over the contents. A rare picture of Pa's mother, holding a beady-eyed infant in a frilly bonnet, already unmistakeably Pa; Pa aged about three, clutching a bear (Wolfi!); in a sailor suit with his father and stepmother; in an Eton collar beside a grand piano; in national costume with his cousin Christa; single portraits of his father, who did look very like Paul, his uncle Karel in hunting gear, and the cast of a student production of some operetta (I played the spirit of the woods: one good song and a lot of jumping about in tights); in military uniform:

--Pa, how did you manage the moustache, you can't have been more than about seventeen?

--It is easier when one is dark, Paul.

Paul turned to a few separate photographs.

--Who's this? He held up a *carte de visite* of a cabaret artiste. She looks like a relation; I didn't know we had anybody else on the stage.

Jiri was laughing.

--Oh, Paul, I made a great sacrifice for her... my moustache! Paul, don't you recognise... I had quite good legs in those days. Don't look so shocked. There were few women on the Galician Front, the evenings were long, we had to make our own amusements, and we did not have the benefit of ENSA.

Paul hastily fetched out some small leather boxes embossed with the Austro-Hungarian eagle.

--Gosh, Pa, you could wear these on Armistice Day.

--If I wore those, people would either think that I had bought them in Woolworths or have me shot as an enemy alien. Better in the suitcase. I got that one from the Emperor Carl when I was in the hospital. He came round pinning the medals to our pyjamas.

--What did you get it for? asked Paul, genuinely interested.

--For being an idiot, getting shot and lying under a dead horse for a long time. Now, Paul, what was it that you really wanted to ask me about?

Paul side-stepped.

--Pa... I suppose you don't remember your mother at all? I mean, your real mother, not your stepmother.

--Mutti Grethe was a real mother to me, as Magda is to you, Paul. But no, I have no recollection; after all, she left for

Switzerland when I was just a few months old, and she died there before I was two. She must have been very ill for some time, and of course having two children so close together was very unwise.

--TWO children?

--Yes. Florian was born about eighteen months before me. He lived only a few hours; they had him baptised so I expect he is all right.

Paul decided to avoid discussion of the Church's teachings on limbo and infant baptism.

--So did your parents never talk about him?

--Well, no; we had a Mass said on his anniversary, and there was a little memorial in the church: Florian Karel von Tarnheim Zellek, and, after all, they had me.

So obviously... but in truth, Paul, I did try to find my mother's grave. You know, I spent some months in Switzerland after the war, the first war, I mean. But I never found it; my uncle must not have received my letters, and then I was well enough to leave.

To his surprise, Paul covered his father's hand with his own.

--There, Pa. It was all a long time ago.

After a short silence, during which he poured out more Scotch, Paul resumed.

You see, Pa, I need to know about my mother. I asked Mum why there are no marriage or death certificates.

--There was a death certificate, but I tore it up and threw it in the river.

--What? Why did you do that?

--Because it was a lie. It said Rosa had died in a tram accident. That wasn't true.

--But she died?

--Yes. Yes. I couldn't change that. But I could get rid of the lies.

--Marriage certificate?

--Well, no, but of course that makes nothing.

--For Christ's sake, say it in German if you have to... *Es macht nichts*... But it does matter, if you're telling me I'm a bastard.

--Berlin in the twenties... Jiri emptied his glass and held it out for a refill... That's where I met poor Josef Schmidt... that beautiful song of his... it went so...

--No, Pa, I think you've had enough. But I need another one, sighed Paul as he recalled David Lomax's advice. He would get no further this evening.

Next, Jiri suffered a bout of acute back pain. In retrospect, he thought he knew what had triggered it. He had been riding Eddy when a decorator's van, unfortunately painted a bright yellow, came unexpectedly round a corner. Despite all that was said about horses being unable to perceive colours, he knew that Eddy was terrified of yellow objects, especially if they were large and moving. Not surprisingly, he shied; Jiri managed to stay on, but could not hold Eddy back from flight across a field, where he ran straight for a hedge, which he jumped. Still Jiri stayed on, but in landing he was in an awkward position; his backside hit the saddle with a jolt, which jarred his coccyx and lower back. As he had expected, he felt stiff and uncomfortable for a couple of days; just as this began to wear off, he was immobilised by the worst pain he had experienced for years.

--I had forgotten how bad it could be, he later confessed

to David. I am ashamed to think of how I have complained about a few twinges.

Magda too had almost forgotten the sheer hell involved for both of them. After two nights and three days without sleep she gave Jiri a quarter of one of the doctor's pills, only to be used as a last resort. As a result, she was able to sleep undisturbed for nearly twelve hours. Jiri did much the same, and with the aid of the district nurse she got him into a warm bath, which always helped. He was able to sit up and managed to eat something.

After a few days, he was back at work, but he seemed less active and cheerful than usual; he slept badly, and at last one morning announced that he needed to rest. Yet he was unable to go back to sleep.

There was no point in staying in bed any longer. He would get up, get dressed, go somewhere…

He felt dizzy, as he often did these days on getting up from lying or sitting. Black dots gathered before his eyes, and a sudden blinding crash of his worst back pain hit across him. Jiri slid sideways.

--Glad you're back with us, mate, commented one of the ambulance crew. Here we go.

Jiri realised that he was on a stretcher being carried somewhere. This suggested that he had fallen off a horse, but he had no recollection of doing so. He closed his eyes in an effort to remember, opening them when he heard a pleasant Irish voice above him.

--Good morning to you, Mr… Zellek, is it? You've had a little fainting spell and you're in St Mary's Hospital. I'm Dr

Hennessy and this is Nurse Grimshaw, who will be looking after you.

Despite her name, Nurse Grimshaw was a very pretty young woman.

Handy that you're in your pyjamas already! Just checking your blood pressure, and nurse here will be taking some blood from your arm... Let's just sit you up... easy, now! Some back trouble?

--An injury. It comes and goes.

--All right, nurse, lie him flat. I can see someone's done a good job on your leg sometime, Mr Zellek... tell me, now, you haven't been a jockey have you?

Jiri grinned.

--No, although I do ride.

--Ah, I had you down for a horseman!

--My wife will be anxious about me.

--Well, well, I'm sure she'll be on her way any minute.

--I should like to go home when she arrives.

--You'll be our guest for a little while. I'm just taking your blood pressure again... how's your appetite?

--Usually it is excellent.

Jiri actually believed this.

--Just ring the ward, nurse: men's medical.

--Mrs Chancellor! What is it? Where is my husband?

--The ambulance left a few minutes ago, Mrs Zellek; they are taking him to St Mary's... he was on the floor, it gave me quite a turn... no, he still hadn't come round when they came... I thought I'd better wait here until you came back.

Magda paid the taxi and ran into St Mary's Paddington. It is a very good hospital, she told herself.

--Then what, Mum? asked Paul later.

--I found him; the doctor told me that he has very low blood pressure, which is why he's been getting dizzy; they think he's anaemic; it's just possible he may be diabetic, and they are going to X-ray his back…

--So what can they do about it all?

--The blood pressure, nothing… with men of his age it's better low than high, and as he gains strength it may correct itself. The anaemia, they can give him some injections, and then iron tablets if he needs them. Tests for diabetes, just in case. His back, I told them about his 'Swiss exercises' but they have their own physiotherapist. I couldn't stay with him as it wasn't visiting time, but I'll go back and take him some fresh pyjamas and his shaving things.

On each visit, Jiri said little but clung to Magda's hand. She had to gently disengage it to put his things into his locker, and take some grapes from the beautiful bunch sent by Miss Silverstrom on behalf of the translation office.

--Yes, Magda, they look nice…

--Haven't you eaten any?

--No. There will be pips in them.

Magda silently removed the pips from a couple of grapes.

--Here.

Jiri had eaten nothing, and the taste of the grape exploded in his dry mouth. There, I knew you would like one. She fed him another, then two or three more; that's enough for now, but I'll ask the nurses about some more later.

--Yes, Mrs Zellek, we'll try to find time. It would be good if he could eat something. Perhaps you could speak to him.

--I will, but it would be better if I could come in at mealtimes to help him.

--No, I'm sorry, we can't allow that; visiting hours only, I'm afraid.

--Jiri, they say you aren't eating.

--No. The food smells horrible. And I'm not hungry. And my back hurts so much, I don't want to sit up.

--I thought they said the physiotherapist was seeing you?

--Yes, he did. That's why my back is hurting. It was horrible. Like the food.

--David, said Magda, what do you think is really going on with Jiri? He seems... he has no spirit... I have never seen him like this, and, you know, he has quite often been ill or in pain. It is as if he has no interest in anything, and if he grows weaker I'm afraid, so afraid, that he will get something bad, like pneumonia, which people can in those big hospitals... and...

--I'm glad you've asked me. Because I think it isn't just physical. He wouldn't speak to me when I visited him yesterday. I'd say he was depressed, I mean really unwell in that way.

--David, how can you say that? Jaroslav cannot be losing his mind.

--No, no, of course he isn't.

David, who had been seeing a practitioner for reasons of his own, decided that Magda would not be receptive to a discussion of the mid-life individuation process. She had been very guarded with David since the prison tour, and he guessed why, although she never referred to anything she had seen or suspected. And at the moment, their shared anxiety called for a truce. He continued,

--I mean that perhaps he has been anxious, or unhappy, and well, as we know, he is not robust (although a lot stronger than he looks, you know, Magda) and it's dragged him down. We all know Jerry works on nervous energy; that's why he suddenly needs to eat, or to go to sleep when he runs low. So maybe I've got it the wrong way around, and he is physically ill to start with, and that's making him depressed.

She shook her head.

--Perhaps. He's been saying for a while that he doesn't feel up to doing anything, can't get to Mass, and he won't have a visit from Father ffoukes-Fenton.

--Look, Magda, I wouldn't say refusing a visit from Father two-little-effs was a sign of mental instability or spiritual crisis. If anything the reverse. But, as we are being very frank with each other, if this isn't going to distress you, it's better you know that I don't believe in any of that... dimension... any more. So let's not pretend that I do.

Magda, as he suspected, was horrified.

--David, I realise that you are a Protestant, but... you are a church organist! How can you...

--There are probably more atheists in the Church of England than there are outside it!

Both of them were also thinking that there were probably more queers in the Anglican clergy than...

You get used to it, and feel all the better in the long run. And the organs aren't bothered.

Perhaps to distract her, David then asked Magda something he'd often wondered about.

--How did you two meet? Jerry always says you picked him up on the streets of Berlin.

Magda's rare smile rewarded him.

--Yes, that's what he tells people, and in a way it is true.

--He was sharing a flat with Heinrich Rheinrose, wasn't he?

How had Magda not known about Jerry and Heinrich? Even if, as Jerry had told him, their relationship was less passionate by then? But the story she was about to tell explained that, at least to a large degree.

Firstly she described how she had met Jiri and his subsequent visit to the convent with the teething baby. Then:

--Well, after that I visited them often, to make sure Paul was thriving and that Jiri was all right. After a while I asked him whether Paul had been baptised; I thought he must have, as it was clear that Jiri was a Catholic, but I needed to be sure, and Jiri said yes, he had baptised the baby himself, choosing the name of the child's grandfather. He said he knew a layperson could do that, and he had done it twice before. He never talked much about the war, I mean the Great War, but somehow then he seemed to want to. The first time was in Serbia.

It was a tiny baby; it had just been born, very early, I suppose; there wasn't any hope for either of them, we couldn't do anything for them, we had to move on; I couldn't bear to think of the poor little thing in limbo, and there was some water, so... I gave her the name Marie, I thought one couldn't go wrong with that, Our Lady would look after her.

The other one was just before he got wounded himself, so it must have been in Galicia, in 1917.

By then most of us had been dismounted, although I still had Bruno for reconnaissance, finding horses for the artillery, all that... but a lot of the fighting was in trenches, not as much as on the Western Front, but still, in the snow... The idea was to run at the Russian lines, do what you could, shoot a few and then run back. Some lads didn't get back to the trench; if they were dead, that was that. But I couldn't stand the… noise… of the ones that were out there, not able to… anyway, I knew that one of them was a fellow who'd been with us right from the beginning. I couldn't stand it. So I went to get him. When I got to him, I could see he was in a bad way but I thought maybe we could make it back. So off we went. He was quite a big chap, heavy, and we kept having to drop down to dodge the firing, but anyway at last we are back in the trench. It had taken a while and there was no one there, the trench had been evacuated. I told him we'd have a bit of a rest, then go and find the others. But he was worse than I'd thought. He asked me to say a prayer. I said what would he like, and he said, anything; his parents hadn't believed in all that, and he grew up without even being baptised. He said… what will happen to me afterwards? And I said, Well, it would be better if you were baptised. And I could do it. Go on then, Leutnant, says he; can't do any harm. There was plenty of water in the bottom of the trench but it was cleaner from his canteen so I used some of that. Then I said, Come on, my lad, I'll say a line from the Pater Noster (that's basic orders) and you say it after me. And if there's anything you're sorry for, that you wish you hadn't done, just say, Lord, I humbly apologise. Jawohl Herr Leutnant. We didn't actually get very far. I was holding his hand and I knew when… I wish I hadn't had to leave him in the trench for the rats, but I didn't get up until he was gone, and I had to rejoin the platoon.

I think that was one of the things Jiri was decorated for, Magda concluded. I mean, he often used to go and bring the wounded back. He said it was just that he couldn't stand hearing them crying out, anything was better than that, nothing brave about it.

--And Paul's mother? David resumed the conversation.

--Rosa? She had died before I met Jiri. I believed him about the death certificate: there had been one, but in his distress he destroyed it. He would never talk about her, but I was sure that they had never been legally married; Heinrich also swore to me that they were not married, and that Rosa had died; he said that she had been killed in a tram accident. And I am sure Jiri used to visit her grave. I learned that Heinrich was a wonderfully talented cellist and conductor, and that Jiri was also a musician. Heinrich was so fond of Jiri: treated him like a younger brother and looked after him. Then one evening when Heinrich was out, Jiri asked me to take off my headdress; he said Paul did not like it. I should not have done so, perhaps. But I did. And after that, well, David, eventually I left the order. I had not taken solemn vows, and it was not as difficult as I had imagined.

--And you got married?

--Actually, David, that was not for some while. I should judge no one. We lived in sin until just before we left Berlin; Jiri said that we should begin life in Munich as man and wife, and so we did; we were married in both church and state.

Of course, David realised, she had left out some of the most interesting bits. But she had obviously been totally innocent and naïve. Once Jiri had taken her to bed, and he accepted that he was unlikely to find out at what stage this had happened, or indeed whether Jerry had forced himself on her, as he was quite capable of doing. It was also evident that the Zelleks' married life was not unsuccessful in any sense.

There was still one question David longed to ask Magda when the right moment arose.

Who was Vernon Dakins?

Jiri was skating. The winter frost felt invigorating after the heavy atmosphere of the hospital ward. His balance was perfect; he had forgotten how he had loved this; he felt free, light, well and happy. Gradually the river along which he was skating ran between buildings, dark for the most part but with a few lighted windows. Jiri found himself in Trafalgar Square, just outside the church of St Martin in the Fields. He was no longer skating, and the London pavement was hard beneath his feet. Looking up he saw a figure standing on the plinth beside one of the four lions. It was a curly haired boy in a white hat and an old-fashioned sailor suit; Jiri recognised Prince Otto, although another area of his mind knew that Otto von Habsburg was now a man approaching his forties. Otto extended his arm and pointed to another plinth. Here stood a second boy, this one in grey flannel shorts, with a school blazer and satchel. It was Paul, and again Jiri registered that the real Paul was an adult. Now an air raid warning sounded and instantly the ground opened in a huge crater into which fell, soundlessly, the lions, the boys, Nelson and his column. Jiri looked into the crater and saw a writhing mass of bodies, severed limbs, entrails and decapitated heads, among them Vernon, and the head and torso of Colonel Buscevics, his old commanding officer. Jiri stood to attention and saluted, while at once a dreadful sound of screaming rose from the pit. The Irish doctor who had admitted him to St Mary's now stood by his side.

Do something, do something to help them, Jiri implored him.

Es tut mir leid, Herr Leutnant... we are running out of morphine, the Army Supply Unit has not sent any...

Jiri knew that he would have to go and fetch some.

There are no horses left; you will have to walk.

Jiri set off. He was now wearing his cavalry boots and, as often in dreams, his feet seemed to weigh heavily and his legs moved slowly and with difficulty.

Suddenly he was outside a building that he knew to be the Medical Supply Unit. He was able to move more quickly now, and found himself in a maze of rooms and passages. People were standing in some of these spaces and when he asked the way to the army supply dispensary they directed him to what turned out, again and again, to be a closed room, or an endless corridor. Finally he opened a door and hesitated on the edge of a sheer cliff that dropped away immediately outside. Across a deep ravine, he could see a hut that he knew held the things he was looking for. He would have to jump across the ravine. He was now riding Eddy. They collected themselves and jumped. Eddy's front hooves scraped the far edge of the further cliff, and could find no hold. They were falling, falling endlessly and Jiri knew that when they reached the bottom Eddy would be on top of him.

--Stop that noise! You've woken the whole ward.

--Pamela, get the duty doctor. We don't know if he's hurt himself. Mr Zellek, Mr Zellek...

Jiri was on the floor beside his bed. Two nurses, one clearly annoyed, the other more concerned and sympathetic, were kneeling beside him.

Jiri's first thought was that he was still alive, his second was that Eddy was, of course, not in the hospital, and finally that he must have had one of those dreams caused by the pills they were giving him. He closed his eyes and wished that everything would just go away.

David and Paul were in a pub near St Mary's Hospital. Its tobacco-stained walls and ceiling seemed to have absorbed the anxiety, boredom, grief, despair, and perhaps the hope and relief, of generations of drinkers after and before visiting hours on the wards.

--How did he seem, Paul?

--Much the same. Well, actually, not so good. It would be just like the awkward little bastard to kick the bucket before I've had the chance to find out.

--Look, I know you don't exactly see eye to eye with your father; I mean, I don't really get on with mine either, it's not unusual, but Jerry thinks the world of you, Paul, and, let's face it, he's made quite a few sacrifices for you and Magda.

--I'm not so sure about that. Pa expects to come first and last with the entire world.

--Oh, come on... you must have some good memories. As he spoke, David searched his mind for good memories of his own father.

--Well... it was pretty good in Munich, before Pa messed it all up.

--Don't you mean before Hitler messed it all up?

--I suppose I do. Pa did get us out in good time, although of course it suited him to do that.

--Well then. And things were bound to be a bit difficult, settling in a new country.

Suddenly Paul grinned. He could be quite breathtakingly handsome when his expression improved.

--There was one thing I had that none of the other fellows

did! Every summer we spent the whole of the holidays at the seaside, not just a week or two!

--Lucky you! We just had a fortnight when my father did an exchange with a seaside parish.

--I suppose it was much the same with Pa. He was involved with concert parties and artists at seaside theatres; he used to move around with them, and Mum and I would go with him; sometimes we'd go to three or four different places in the season, but sometimes we'd stay in the same place. And of course he knew everyone, so he'd be in with the end-of-the-pier entertainments. As he could play or sing almost anything at sight, (still can, added David) if anyone dropped out, fell ill or whatever, Pa could step in. Anyway, he earned a few extra quid, enough to keep me in ice creams and donkey rides. And he loved the beach! In fact he was more of a kid than I was; by the end I was starting to have an eye for the bathing beauties. Thinking about it, I suppose his *vunderful* childhood didn't include seaside holidays. In fact, he told me once that he didn't see the sea until he was eight, and that was the Channel when his parents took him with them on a business trip to London.

Paul had a sudden vision of his father, wearing a navy one-piece bathing suit, playing ball on the sands, building castles, splashing in the sea. Few people did more than glance at his scarred leg; lots of men of his age bore marks of conflict.

--Funny… it was while we were in Torquay in 1939 that we heard war declared…

--And he had managed to get citizenship for you all by then.

--I'll never know how he did that, and he'll never say.

He was already doing part-time translating work for the government and by 1939 he was full-time until he got sent to Yorkshire. I had a couple more years at the Vaughan before I got called up. While I was in the navy, Pa got sent back to London. When was it you met him, Dave?

--Nineteen forty-one.

David was seized by far too much recollection.

Yes. He was, I suppose, convalescing after, well, oddly, something like he has now... and then we didn't meet up until '43. And then again after the war.

--Do you think he's going to be all right?

The doctor sat down by Jiri's bed.

--Tell me, Mr Zellek, have you ever had an illness like this before?

--No... yes... the first time... I'd forgotten, it was so long ago, and of course it was before... so it was different from this... but...

--Go on.

--I was about seventeen. I was sent to my uncle's place in the mountains; I remember going for a walk with my cousin and passing out.

--Did you have any treatment?

--Well, they sent for a doctor. He gave me some horrible tonic, just the smell of it made me sick, then I suppose they fattened me up, because that was the summer my uncle decided to get me into officer training school.

--So you were quite fit?

--Yes, I was, until we were sent to the Front, and even then I did better than many until, of course...

--Ah, yes. We'll talk about your back tomorrow, when

I've had time to look again at your X-rays.

Jiri closed his eyes and immediately had a very distinct memory of his bedroom at Tarnheim. He saw the carved walnut bedstead with its crisp white linen, the tall windows admitting golden mountain sunlight; his uncle's valet Hans appeared carrying a tray, with a measuring glass, a spoon, a bottle of dark liquid and, wrapped in bright red and white paper, a peppermint. He realised that Hans intended to pop this into his mouth when he had taken the medicine. In retrospect Jiri felt touched by this act of kindness, although at the time he had accepted that all the servants treated him more like seven than seventeen.

Hans had given him a spoonful of the liquid... Quick, quick, the bowl! I'm going to be sick!

Hans was wiping his face, offering him a glass of water with instructions to rinse his mouth out... and then, yes, he did get the peppermint; he seemed to taste its sweetness and strong flavour... How odd that he should have forgotten this.

--Sit up, Mr Zellek. Here's a cup of tea for you.

The tea was not as Magda made it; it reminded Jiri of the stuff the Salvation Army brought round to the bomb sites; at the time one had been glad to get it, and it took away the taste of brick dust.

--Do you think you can get in there, Mr Zellek? You might be able to check the cellar.

--I can try; could one perhaps remove a brick or two?

--Better not; it's pretty unstable as it is.

--Very well. I will remove my Wellingtons and boiler suit.

Please ensure that no one makes away with them while I am down there.

Jiri did as he had said, then squeezed through the gap leading to the cellar of the bomb-shattered building; his colleague lowered him as gently as possible, passing his tin helmet after him. Jiri placed it on his head.

After a while, the watchers saw it moving below them; Jiri handed it up. He then pushed a struggling tabby cat, coated with dust, through the hole before raising his arms to be pulled free.

--Well?

--Cordon the area and call the bomb squad.

--Right. Now?

--Yes. It is quite large and it is making noises. I will replace my clothing when we are at a safe distance.

--Anyone down there, other than Tibbles here?

--Yes and no. I suppose they felt nothing.

Bomb Squad on its way.

--Who's seen it?

--I have. It is unexploded and it is in the cellar there.

--Can you identify it?

--No. I did not stop to examine it. But I could look at the recognition chart, or describe it.

--Go on.

This was not necessary.

After the flying masonry had settled, they all raised their heads.

--Well, that saved us the trouble. And all well, as the area was cordoned? Ah, here's the Sally Ally with the tea...

It must be Sunday morning. The wireless was on and the

usual noises in the ward were complicated by the sound of a broadcast church service. Jiri could hear the hymn:

Time like an ever rolling stream/Bears all its sons away…

He had never pictured time as a stream; for him it was more like differently coloured sequential blocks accompanied by appropriate chords. This was a new idea. He imagined being in a river, borne along towards the sea. If one scrambled out, one could walk or run along the riverbank. In fact, if one had a bicycle or a good horse, one might go faster than the flow of the water… so would that be going faster than time, he wondered? And if so, would one be in eternity?

Jiri had never fully grasped what was meant by eternity; it was the state one entered on death, but then Purgatory, where most of us fetch up, was certainly linked with time, for one could get some thousands of years off, if one played the cards correctly; hence time must have some relevance. With a start, he realised that he had fallen back into the habit of mind that accepted that the Four Last Things and all that he had been taught about them were absolutely unquestioned. He was outside that now. He was nowhere. His head ached. His back ached. Why wouldn't it all go away?

The Catholic chaplain is here to see you, Mr Zellek.

Sister McCarthy drew the curtains around Jiri's bed, leaving a gap to admit a little priest, of barely Jiri's stature, dressed in a soutane and a black beret, which he removed from a round head fringed with grey hair.

--Jiri, it is you! I thought there would not be another Jaroslav Zellek.

--Armand! What are you doing here?

As Sister Philomena McCarthy said, I am the Catholic

chaplain, at least for the next few weeks. I am sorry to see you in this state, Philomena tells me... but I am here not to minister to the patients' bodies but to their souls.

--Don't bother. It's too late for that. Jiri closed his eyes.

--Jiri, what has happened to you?

Father Armand Sentier seated himself beside the bed. He and Jiri had been fugitives together, cold, wet, tired and hungry; and in his own case, having once experienced Gestapo interrogation, deadly afraid of recapture. Not so Jiri; he had sung, joked, laughed and generally kept Armand going. Only once had he faltered. He had twisted his ankle in a rabbit hole the previous day, and now, resting halfway through the next morning and unable to get up, he told Armand to go on without him. It was not far to the next hiding place; he would be all right; Armand must go. The priest had reached in his pocket for the bar of chocolate he was keeping for emergencies. This was one. Breaking off a square, he placed it between Jiri's lips. It seemed to give him new energy; Armand helped him up, and together they had gone on. As for fear, Jiri seemed not to experience it. Thinking of some of the things he had done in France, Armand thought him among the bravest men he had ever met. One night, when they lay huddled together for warmth, he had asked Jiri if there was anything he was afraid of.

--Yes, he had replied. I am afraid of the Devil. But one would have to be very silly not to be afraid of him.

Now Jiri began to speak. He must try not to lapse into German, which he had tended to do lately, as it would bring bad memories to the former Resistance fighter.

--At first I thought I was in Purgatory, but there's still

526

hope if you're in there. But now that's gone too. It's because of the things I've done. I know you heard my confession in France. But I never told. Then I thought I would be damned. I kept thinking of Judas. What he felt like; what happened to him afterwards? I am so afraid of the Devil, you know, and I thought he'd got me. Perhaps he has. I don't know. I'm so tired. And there is nothing. I'm falling. Nothing is real. There's just nothing.

Father Armand took a deep breath.

--Jiri, listen to me. Thus far you have been granted the beautiful grace of a simple, childlike faith. I think it has carried you safely through many dangers of many kinds. But you are now well over fifty years old, and perhaps le Bon Dieu has decided that it is time for you to grow up. It seems to me that your faith has always been the rock on which your house is built, and, now the rock has crumbled or been taken away, you do not know who you are… now that it has gone, you can't stand up. You have collapsed as if struck down; perhaps you were already unwell or overtired, but in any case you were not physically able to bear the complete *bouleversement* of spirit.

Jiri gave him one look, and began to sob, tearing sobs that hurt his back and made his head feel ready to burst.

There, *mon fils*. Let it go.

Eventually he wiped Jiri's face with a clean white handkerchief and poured him a glass of water.

Jiri felt as if he had been sick after a night's drinking, or gone to the lavatory after eating contaminated food.

--How did you know?

--There is always someone who knows, replied Father Armand.

Placing his hands on Jiri's head, he recited two verses from Psalm 90:

Be with me O Lord in my distress.
He who dwells in the shelter of the Most High
And abides in the shade of the Almighty
Says to the Lord, 'my refuge
My stronghold, my God in whom I trust'.
Upon you shall no evil fall
No plague approach where you dwell
For you has he commanded his angels,
To keep you in all your ways.
Now I will hear your confession. A full one.
Bless me, Father, for I have sinned…

A couple of days later, Paul visited.

--Feeling a bit better, Pa?

--Yes, thank you, Paul. I've been asleep all the afternoon, then I got to the lavatory with a bit of help. And I'm hoping I've had the last of those horrible injections. You know I hate injections. And these hurt like hell. I have told them repeatedly that I do not require any more. But they take no notice. One is entirely at their mercy. I want to go home.

--Poor old Pa. It's been a tough time. Paul covered his father's hand in a rare sign of affection.

Jiri closed his eyes for a moment. Then he said firmly,

--Pauli, I know there is something you are wanting to ask me, to talk to me about. This is not the right time or place, but I promise you that when I am at home we will talk. And this time you need not bring a bottle of whisky with you, although that would be nice.

Pa's back, thought Paul, with an unexpected feeling of relief. A couple of days after Jiri was discharged from hospital, Paul visited him at home. He found his father up and dressed, although looking almost skeletal and evidently unable to cross the room unaided.

Magda would not let him stay long, nor give Jiri more than one glass of the whisky he had brought. Pa declared this did him more good than the horrible stuff prescribed by the hospital; he also had iron tablets, but was 'disposing' of these because they made him constipated.

--If she asks, tell her I'm taking them.

--All right, Pa. But couldn't you put up with...

--No. It is to be avoided if one has back trouble.

Predictably, Jiri was delighted by the news that Paul had fallen in love with, and wished to marry, a member of such an old Catholic family. It was so romantic, and so suitable! Oh, it made him feel better at once! Of course, he could quite understand why Paul needed the information he sought. If he could stall the solicitors for another week, and Jiri's health would be the ideal excuse, everything would be completely *in Ordnung*.

A week of Magda's care and Magda's cooking worked wonders. Pa was looking decidedly perky when Paul returned.

--Ah, Pauli! I have been in touch with my solicitor; as soon as I am well enough to take the train to Tunbridge Wells... it is a delightful town... I will be able to have the documents signed and witnessed. Oh, and I can readily call on the Cormers' solicitor in person, and, while I think of it, very soon we shall be able to invite your lovely Lucilla to dinner; we cannot wait to meet her.

But, of course, you want the details, my boy. Well. Your mother was born in Dresden in 1899. Unfortunately all records of births, deaths and so on were destroyed in the Allied bombing of the city... I have never been fully convinced that such carnage was necessary... but we have been able to locate a baptism certificate from the Lutheran Dreikönigskirche. Her father – that is your grandfather, Pauli – was a professor of mathematics at the university. That must be where you get your remarkable aptitude, and the university has provided copies of his records of tenure, degrees, honours and so on. Such an eminent man! Your mother had two brothers, both of whom sadly perished on the Western Front, in 1915 and 1917... which partly explains... but never mind that... Now we move to 1923; as you know, we have your birth certificate. It is well known that life in Berlin in the early twenties was difficult and chaotic if rather fun at times, and we were unable to marry until shortly after your birth, but we did so in a civil ceremony in early March 1924. Records were of course destroyed in the war. Yes, I did have a copy of the marriage certificate, but, as everyone must realise, my life has been one of hardship and disruption, fleeing Nazi persecution with just what we could carry.

--For goodness' sake, Pa, you arranged to ship over the bloody Bösendorfer!

--Well, perhaps one might amend that slightly; anyway, scraping a living, battling ill health... Jiri assumed a look of pathos... of course some things inevitably got mislaid. I can of course provide a signed affidavit that the marriage took place. Similarly, your mother's sudden death in a tram accident was sufficient to send me into a state of shock; after all, I had a tiny child to care for single-handed in difficult conditions. I do recall keeping her death certificate together with our marriage certificate, but...

--Hang on, Pa. You told me your tore up her death certificate and threw it in the river.

--Well, yes of course. Concentrate, my boy; I am telling you what my solicitor will prepare for me to sign. To continue: Rosa was buried in Berlin, but the cemetery and its records were totally annihilated in the bombing; we have a photograph of the cemetery taken in 1945 and it is a sorry sight: not a single grave could be positively identified, and I believe it is now in the Eastern Sector of the city. As for the years after 1930, we have all the papers to show that Magda and I are legally married, that all three of us have British citizenship, that you are fully vaccinated, absolutely everything *in Ordnung.*

And my side of the family is relatively straightforward. Zellek and Co was an internationally known firm; and as for the von Tarnheims, I am sure that the Cormers' solicitor is familiar with the Almanach de Gotha, and if not he can be referred to the relevant pages, and it is all there; actually, Pauli, if the Austrian government had not abolished titles of nobility in 1919, you would be in line to make your bride a countess.

Jiri ran out of breath, and sat back looking ridiculously pleased with himself.

You smug little bastard, thought Paul. What a load of bullshit! But there was enough verifiable fact, and enough likely conjecture, especially since Dresden and Berlin were among the cities most heavily attacked by the Allies. And his father was evidently prepared to swear to all of it.

--Of course, Pauli, he was saying, if you are really in a very great hurry, perhaps you might like to drive me down to

Tunbridge Wells. We could take Magda and have a delightful day, with lunch somewhere.

--But Pa, he began. That's not all, I mean, for a start how—

--Pauli, I have told you what you need to know. Let us not complicate matters. You must be quite confident if asked about this; really, just at present, I mean until you and Lucilla are safely married, my boy, just agree with what I propose. Now, why don't we have a drink on it?

--All right, Pa. Here. But Mum said you had to watch it.

--It is a hard life. Hardly anything to drink and no chocolate.

--Really?

--She says it spoils my appetite. I say, Pauli, you don't happen to have…

--No, Pa, I haven't got a bar of Cadbury's Dairy Milk in my pocket, and, if I had, you wouldn't get any. Anyway, you're too old for sweets.

He touched his father's hair, which showed a few distinctly grey streaks.

Jiri sighed.

--You too, Pauli! Everyone is teasing me about my grey hairs. It is good that I am not vain.

Paul snorted.

--Pa, you were in the Austro-Hungarian cavalry. That's vanity on horseback.

--So David is always telling me. But Amanda says it makes me look distinguished.

--She would.

--In the touring companies, some fellows touched up with black shoe polish. But it makes such a mess on the bedclothes. Thank God at least that the dark-haired men in my family do not go bald. I am afraid that will be your fate, Pauli, it always happens with fair hair.

Suddenly Paul felt deadly serious and greatly dissatisfied.

--Pa. What was she like, my mother? I know you're always telling me how much I look like your dad, but, well, I've never even seen a photograph of her.

--I did not have one.

--But, well, was she fair-haired?

--Yes. I have told you, she was from Saxony: blonde hair and blue eyes, just like you.

Paul knew too well that his father's taste in women favoured rather large blondes.

--How did you meet?

--I don't suppose you remember much about Berlin, Pauli, when we lived there?

--Not really; I must have been about five or six when we left. I do remember that we lived with Heini, and I remember Vernon, my godfather, but mainly I remember Munich.

--Do you remember little Tommy Tucker? That was me, wasn't it, when I used to sing at the clubs; there were lots of different ones in the twenties, different ones for people with different sorts of interests, and one night someone took me to the club where the Communists met. Actually he was a very interesting chap, a student of mathematics; we met at a club for poker, he agreed with me that there really cannot be such a thing as random numbers, and we had...

Paul realised that a typical digression was about to unfold.

--Yes, Pa. But about the communist place?

--It really wasn't my kind of thing, not at all chic and really rather serious, and of course we von Tarnheims were all so upset about what happened to the imperial family, they were such pretty girls, but that is where I met Rosa. You see, Pauli, your mother was a very brave woman; she was what one might call a political activist. And she did not believe in the institution of marriage. Not at all. It was an instrument of bourgeois oppression.

--Pa, if you don't mind me asking, what drew you together?

--Rosa was studying mathematics at the university and doing a bit of teaching for extra income. She was particularly interested in the study of probability and, as I have told you, I have often considered that there cannot be such a thing as random occurrences. We had some fascinating conversations and, well, we became close.

Jiri suddenly remembered Rosa's beautiful generous breasts, her white, curved buttocks, her...

He closed his eyes.

--Pa, are you all right?

--Yes, yes, my boy, quite all right. Jiri was experiencing the first erection he had had for weeks. With an effort, he continued,

--Rosa was known to the police, rather as I was in Munich towards the end, I suppose. She needed somewhere safe, so she moved in with us, I mean Heinrich and myself.

--Wasn't that a bit dangerous for you?

--Not particularly. Heini and I had no known communist connections, and we all three of us agreed that, if there were enquiries, we had just taken her in to help with the rent. Soon after that we knew that she was expecting you, and you were born, there in the Berlin flat. We had a midwife, and I baptised you – of course, I didn't let Rosa see that; she totally disapproved of the Church – and we called you Paul after her father. And, of course, it is Saint Paul. Rosa

534

was very fit and strong; you have inherited that too, my boy! And it was not long before she began attending meetings and demonstrations again. I did not accompany her; I found them so boring, and I had my musical studies and was still picking up work at the clubs, and then…

Jiri paused.

--Please, Pauli.

Paul refilled his glass.

--There was a huge gathering at a beer hall; it was broken up by the police on some excuse, and a number of the Communists were killed; shot, beaten, trampled…

--Where were you during all that, Pa?

--Actually I was at home looking after you. Heini was playing that night, and the landlady was busy, so I didn't go to work. She didn't come home. Of course, she did not have our address on her, that would have been most unwise, but she didn't come home, and when I heard about the killings, I went to the police and told them that my neighbour was missing. They took me to the morgue. They gave me a death certificate and told me to contact her family to make arrangements for burial. Of course they still thought I was just a neighbour. I told them I could do that. When I looked at the certificate I saw that it was lies. I was very, very angry. But Heini… he told me that I had to look after you. So we had a funeral, I threw away the certificate… So. Pauli, I did not mean to tell you any of this. It is between ourselves.

We will go to my solicitor, I will sign the affidavit, and we will invite Lucy to dinner. Ah yes. I shall need to get the tiara out of the bank vault; I wonder what Cartier will charge for cleaning?

MAY 1951: VERNON DAKINS I

Paul Zellek and Lucilla Cormer were married at the Brompton Oratory in May 1951. David Lomax played Widor's Toccata. The reception was held at the stately home of one of Lucilla's relatives. The honeymoon was to be in Scotland. Jiri bought a new morning suit; as he said, he would be using it at Ascot. Having reached the age when many of his contemporaries were growing paunchy, his skinny build was actually an advantage, and he, Magda and Lucilla all thought he looked wonderful in the role of the bridegroom's father.

Paul was paradoxically and privately rather annoyed by the way Lucy's family had taken to Pa. Jiri's Catholicism (without being Irish), his inclusion in the Almanach de Gotha, his ability to talk about horses for hours and parry tales of pig-sticking in India with accounts of boar hunts in the Black Forest and How I Shot a Bison in 1916 (*I had him stuffed and sent back to Tarnheim. I suppose the Russians have him now*) all worked in his favour, as did his Old World Viennese charm. Lucy herself adored him; he was 'beau' as in beau-père and, as she was decidedly musical, like many others she had fallen in love with the voice.

After the event, Jiri and Magda would really have liked to escape to Middle Woodlow for a few days, but there were obligations and arrangements that kept them in London for the following weekend. On the Saturday morning, Jiri had a phone call.

--It is Cyril. I know he said I would not be needed on Saturday mornings this month, but something urgent has cropped up and he wants me in the office.

Jiri thought of the document he had been working on; it was a phonetically transcribed interview with an informant who spoke only a Carpathian dialect with which the interviewer, who spoke little Hungarian anyway, had not been familiar. Jiri did recognise the dialect, as the Balinkays' cook, and several troopers in the Ulans had spoken it, but it was some time since he had needed it, and the phonetic angle posed some quite interesting puzzles; still, the information contained had not actually seemed especially vital, once one had worked out the gist of it.

--Good morning, Cyril. I am sorry if I have been rather slow with that interview work; I admit that we have all been somewhat distracted by Paul and Lucy's wedding.

--No, no, that's all right, Jerry. Wedding went well, I gather. Nice photos in the papers.

--Yes indeed! Jiri took a deep breath and Cyril realised that unless he moved quickly, he was in for a full minute-by-minute account of the event, plus various Zellek-style digressions. As it was, his colleague was explaining that, yes, Lucy had looked beautiful in the tiara, he had been so afraid that she would think it old-fashioned, indeed the setting was quite antique, but it had been in the bank vault ever since he had managed to get it over from Tarnheim, and he had always been reluctant to sell it, his mother had worn it at her wedding, and now how fully he had been justified, Cartiers had cleaned it up quite nicely, the only problem was that the insurance seemed suddenly to have gone up, it was quite iniquitous, was it not, that these firms took such advantage of ordinary citizens...

--Just let me stop you there, Jerry. It's just that... Look, something big is going to break in the next few days and I want to warn you not to speak to the press.

For the first time, Jiri noticed a faded buff folder on Cyril's desk. Reading the label upside down he noted a typed slip of paper, gummed on, with the words *Dakins/Zellek. 1938.*

Cyril locked the door of his office before explaining that two British diplomats who were suspected of espionage had fled the country via Southampton, and were believed to be headed for the Soviet Union. Very shortly it would be all over the papers, questions in the House and all that, but the point at issue was that there seemed to be a link with Vernon Dakins.

--Vernon? But, Cyril, Vernon has been dead for thirteen years.

--Well, actually no, Jerry. It seems he is alive and living in Moscow.

--You let me think... you... bastards...

Jiri rose to his feet. Cyril had never seen one of Jerry's famous outbursts but he experienced one now. A heavy brass pen tray and inkstand, a huge Victorian item presented to Cyril's grandfather for services to Agriculture and Fisheries, and outlawed from their home by Cyril's wife, lay near the folder. Seizing this, Jiri threw himself at Cyril, knocking him out of his chair; as he sprawled trying to recover his balance,

Jiri prepared to beat his head in with it. Although he knew French, German and some Russian, Cyril could not identify the language in which Jerry was screaming abuse; he hardly recognised his colleague, whose wiry frame seemed to embody sheer hatred and violence.

Cyril had no time to draw the revolver he kept in his desk drawer, but he had rather more recent combat training than Jerry, he was larger and stronger and, as he suddenly realised, several years younger; Jerry must now be well into his fifties. It was more difficult than he might have anticipated, but he eventually had Jerry face down on the floor, with one arm twisted behind him and Cyril's knee in the small of his back.

--You bloody idiot. (THUMP) We didn't know. (THUMP) Get that into your head. (THUMP) We didn't know. (THUMP) He banged Jiri's head rhythmically onto the (carpeted) floor. As he did so he realised that he had been wanting to do this for a very long time.

Jiri appeared to have gone limp. Very cautiously, Cyril released him, then heaved him up and threw him into a chair.

--Tidy yourself up. Here. He poured Jiri a large whisky and thrust it into his shaking hand.

--For thirteen years... for thirteen years, you let me think...

--No, Jerry. Do I have to knock it into your head again? Let's revisit this, just to get things clear. Everyone thought that Vernon Dakins was the body in the New Forest. After you, yes, let's have it, Jerry, after you shopped him to us (and I've wondered if, being the devious little operator you are, you might also have given him a warning) and the body was found in the burned-out car, with the papers.

--Was that you or the Soviets? Either way, I knew I'd killed him.

--Come now, Jerry, to all appearances it was clearly an accident, and everyone knew Dakins had been drinking heavily. We wouldn't have had him killed; he was one of us. That's not our style.

He opened the folder. Jiri suddenly thought that there must be another folder somewhere, labelled *Zellek 1925*.

--When you were interviewed in 1938, you told us that you met Dakins in Berlin in 1925. At the time, you thought it was a chance encounter, but later you realised that he must have known of your relations with Rosa Seimel, communist agitator and mother of your son, Paul. At no time was or is there any evidence to link you with communist activity: for once you're in the clear, Jerry. Your link with Rosa was purely (if that is the right word) personal. Dakins soon accepted this, but used you as a paid informant; he considered recruiting you as an intelligence agent, but realised that this would be disastrous, and may I say, this morning has once again proved how right he was in describing you as 'unpredictable and with a tendency to uncontrolled outbursts of violence'. You and Dakins maintained a professional and increasingly close personal relationship: you must have known that Dakins was homosexual?

--Yes. As far as I know, Vernon never wanted or had sex with a woman except maybe, perhaps in the course of business; anyway, he never approached me… or, well…

--OK, Jerry. He was too clever to let you get a hold over him.

--I came to see that. But when we were living in Munich he was very good to me. Then we heard he might be posted to Washington. By then I had made the decision to leave Germany.

--For once, Jerry, a very good decision.

--I could not stay there. And I could not let Paul be brought up under the Nazi regime. I considered taking my family to America; a good friend had already gone to Boston. But Verni thought we would be better off in London, where I had more chance of finding work, especially as I was quite familiar with the city.

(And Verni was one of the few people who I'd told about Christi. I'd drunk a bit too much, or, no, it was while he was looking after me when I was so ill in Munich. I talked about what I'd like to do to Westenberger, how I would find him and Christi one of these days. Oh, that would have made things complicated: better not take me to America.)

Vernon was wonderfully helpful. He found our flat, he helped with the removals; I was so worried about the piano, but *Gott sei Dank…*

--Yes, well, I think we know all that, and that when you arrived in 1934, and before he left for the States in 1935, Dakins put you in touch with us, recommending you for translation and decoding work.

(Zellek, an Austrian citizen, has been one of my informants since 1925, firstly in Berlin and for the past five years in Munich. He is a known opponent of the Nazi regime and cannot safely remain in Germany or Austria. In London, he should prove extremely useful to Caruthers's group. He knows a number of languages, including some minority central European languages and dialects; he is a musician and a synesthete. A what? Cyril had asked on first reading this. It means that he sees connections between colours, shapes, sounds and concepts;

it's not as rare as it sounds, though more common with women than men, and it often goes with some other kind of aptitude or abnormality He is also a useful bridge player; I taught him myself.)

Dakins came back to London in 1937, and you resumed your friendship. According to the interview you gave, it was then and only then that you began to suspect his communist sympathies, which we now know he had maintained since his days in Cambridge.

--That is correct. At that time I explained my reasons: the questions he asked about my work for Caruthers, the far more extensive knowledge of Russian than he claimed, some of the people he was meeting; some other things; it should be in the records.

--Jerry, when you were with Dakins at that time, did you ever meet a chap called Philby, Kim Philby?

Jiri thought for a moment.

--Yes, as a matter of fact. Vernon introduced us over dinner at his club.

Kim! My little friend is Jiri Zellek. He'll have a pink gin. Why?

--Never mind that now. What was your opinion of Philby?

--He was a charming young fellow, quite bit younger than either of us.

--What would you say was his relationship with Dakins?

--They seemed to be good friends. As I've said, he was younger; but he and Verni had a lot in common; as a drinker he was in the same league as Verni, and they were both English gentlemen.

--Which you are not.

542

--No. But I have my own code of honour as an Austrian officer. If all that had happened in 1913 instead of 1938, I could have challenged Verni to a duel. And I would probably have shot him; his aim wasn't too good after a heavy night. It would have been better to have done that.

--Did you see Philby again?

--A few times. He was at Verni's funeral; in fact, he took me home after the wake. I'm afraid I was very drunk. And then, a couple of times in passing, here.

--Here?

--Yes. At the office. I assumed he'd come to see Caruthers; it was during the war, before the old man retired. Where is Philby now, by the way?

--Based in Washington. But he's on his way back at the moment. Well; let's return to you and Dakins. As it happened, you got to the truth about him before we did. And it was not too difficult to read the signs of the times by then; once war broke out, you would have been interned as an enemy alien; your family would have suffered.

--Looking back, internment might not have been so bad. What I really dreaded was the possibility, which then seemed quite likely, of being sent back to Germany. And I hate communism. For personal reasons. And then I found that my closest friend had been working for them, had been lying to me for years, all along in fact. It has made it difficult for me to trust anyone since; I suppose I should never have done so in the first place.

(Remember, Birdie, however nice they are, we don't tell them things. We don't let them play. Not even Mikki? No, not even Mikki. He's too little, and he's not from Tarnheim. He doesn't know where things are. It's only us. Yes, it's just us, Christi.)

--So. Angry with Dakins for the way he'd deceived you, worried about the future for your family, you took a decision.

--Yes. I betrayed him.

--Well, you Romans are always supposed to believe that the End Justifies the Means. And you would not have been much use to anyone in an Internment Camp. As it was, Jerry, your war contribution, bar a couple of unfortunate episodes, was praiseworthy. After all, you got that civilian decoration for bravery in the Blitz, and you've done good work here since. Still, back to the point. Somehow and we won't go into that now, Dakins got wind of what lay in store for him, headed for Southampton, had an accident in the New Forest and what was left of the body was identified by the clothes and papers, and he wasn't heard of again; until now. Make no mistake, Jerry. Dakins was using you; he decided not to recruit you to British intelligence, but in getting you the translation job he still had a source of sensitive information; we had to believe you when you said you'd never passed anything important on to him, but we know you'd trusted him and been an informant for years, believing anything you told him was being used by the British against the Nazis and the Soviets. Jerry. I know you are a lot of things, but you are not a deliberate traitor to this country. Keep your mouth shut, and from your point of view the matter is at an end.

--Cyril, you are sure of what you are telling me? Verni is still alive?

It seemed to be taking him time to absorb this.

--Yes. There's no doubt of it. And, Jerry, although you tried to batter my head in, I really can assure you that everyone here thought he was dead. We reckoned on the Soviets, they let us go with that, and it could actually have been an accident, after all, Dakins was drinking heavily. Well, I don't know how he managed it, but it was convincing.

--Verni was very clever. I mean, he is.

When Cyril had banged Jiri's head into the floor, his thoughts became a jangle of coloured shards and discords; they were slowly coming together. He continued.

--Ah. Now I see.

--See what?

--Chris McColl.

--Who?

--The priest, Father McColl. He officiated at Verni's requiem. Then, and of course it looked a bit odd at the time, we were all told that Verni had left instructions that in the event of his death, after the requiem only a priest should attend the burial, no mourners. That's why we all went and got sozzled. Meanwhile I'll bet Chris and the coffin never made it to the cemetery; they probably headed for the North London Crematorium and Chris McColl later scattered the ashes. It would be just like him to choose the Solent at Lymington, where Verni used to go sailing; that way, if anyone enquired, it would look like some eccentric last wishes. Anyway, no evidence. Nothing that could be identified. Of course, Chris was the key. You know, Cyril, that we are not allowed to be cremated, although when I think of all the Catholics who have been smashed to smithereens or burned to cinders in the course of two wars, I somehow wonder...

--Jerry, try to keep to the point.

--I know you Protestants think the Church is full of secrets and plots. Well. Perhaps that is not so far from the truth. Of course, the Vatican has its own network and I think perhaps MI5 and MI6 could learn something from it. Perhaps Verni was, as they say, on the payroll. In which case he was... is... even cleverer than I thought. Chris knew quite a lot about Verni; perhaps he was his confessor. I know they were at Ampleforth together. For some reason, it was to his advantage that Verni's last wishes were carried out. Or perhaps he just cared more for Verni than I did.

--Where is this... this... McColl now?

--He was an army chaplain during the war. After that he had some kind of breakdown and he is now in a Trappist monastery in the north of Scotland. I hear from him from time to time.

Suddenly Jiri put his hands in front of his face and, to Cyril's horror, burst into tears.

Cyril took him by the shoulders.

--Pull yourself together, man.

--It was the worst thing I ever did. And now I know I didn't do it. I didn't kill Verni.

Jiri looked up. He was developing a black eye *(Thank goodness this has all happened after the wedding. Magda would have never forgiven me for turning up looking like this)* but his face was irradiated by immense relief.

--Imagine, Cyril, if Judas had suddenly been told it was all a mistake, no crucifixion, or at least some other fellow nailed up there by mistake, and of course if so I suppose one needs to give him a thought; I wonder who Verni used. But just assume that Jesus had buggered off to Egypt or somewhere? *Ego te absolvo*. Do you think he's happy in Moscow?

--Jerry, you're getting hysterical. Go back to your office and sit quietly for a bit. Take some aspirins; I'll see if Miss Silverstrom can get you a cup of tea. Go home at lunchtime;

maybe best take a taxi, and you can tell Magda that we had a few drinks and you fell down some stairs.

He had to lift Jiri bodily from the chair and help him towards the door. As he did so he felt his fragility; had he really been so, well, like someone possessed? Cyril felt guilty as he thought how roughly he had treated that skinny body, then he saw the brass inkstand as it lay on the floor. There was no doubt that Jerry had intended to kill him. He must call up the Zellek file and add some version of the morning's events.

FLORA'S STORY

Flora Loudon never found her husband's grave. But his name was inscribed on the Menin Gate, and on the war memorial in their Shropshire village. 'Their Name Liveth for Evermore' proclaimed this Celtic-style cross; Flora doubted it. While the older generation still remembered 'Doctor John' with respect and affection, by the early 1920s a new, and very efficient, GP catered to their medical needs, and many younger people had never known his predecessor. Mrs Loudon and Beatrice were now in their eighties. More like friends than employer and employee, they were company and support for each other and like Flora they gained local contacts over the years.

Their main sources of interest were letters from Anne. Although life in Canada had not always gone smoothly, it had worked out well, and the Battrills now had three children, a dark-haired, stocky trio with cheerful grins and intelligent eyes; Mrs Loudon was reconciled to the fact that she would never see them in person. Jiri wrote regular notes and postcards to dear Granny Loudon, with best respects to Beatrice, as he had always done; Flora had spared them the worst details of his war injuries, and they were happy that she had spent time with him during his recovery. In Mrs Loudon's heart he was still the mischievous little boy whose dark head and fragile body had nestled against her as she read to him from *The Arabian Nights*; it was not his fault that he had been born into an enemy nation, and of course he had fought the Russians, not the British.

Jiri also wrote to Flora. She still had the short missive he had sent her after her daughter Vera's death. It took months to reach her, having been opened and read by censors in Vienna and London, and by the time it arrived, John Loudon had been declared missing believed dead on the Somme, thankfully without knowing of the child's death. The letter was scribbled in pencil, on a page torn from an army notebook.

Dearest Frau Doktor Loudon,

I hold you in my arms. I have received your sad news. I have you and Doktor Jonni in my heart and soul and I reverence the pure spirit of your little Vera. Forgive this untidy letter. I am writing in the saddle. I send it quickly as we are advancing and I do not know when we shall be returned. I see an ambulance to go to the base. I will end now and give this letter to an orderly.

With greatest condolences and love,
Jiri.

His later letters, sent after their stay in Switzerland and Pallin, said nothing of his feelings, and not much about his health; by 1924 she knew that he was living in Berlin, studying singing and piano, sharing a flat with a friend from Vienna, and earning extra income as, yes, a *Kino* pianist! She knew too that he had a son, about whom he went into some enthusiastic description; the child's mother was dead but someone, a dear friend, was looking after him. Jiri left background details vague and Flora did not inquire.

Flora learned to drive and bought an Austin 7. She became active in the Women's Institute, helped at the village school and undertook some language lessons and translations.

Gradually she had brought herself to sort through John's things. First his clothes and personal possessions; everything she could bear to part with had gone by 1922. It had been terrible parting with her daughter's little clothes and toys; this was not quite so bad. His books and papers remained. Eventually the books went to the library of the research institute of which he had been a member; one of the directors contacted her to ask whether Dr Loudon had left any records of the research he had been undertaking before the war; he had published a number of influential papers on eugenics, genetics and inherited traits; his work could still be of value, and it was a pity to let it go unrecognised.

Flora and her mother-in-law were pleased by this thought. In that way, John's name could live on, if only as a footnote in a series of medical textbooks. A postgraduate researcher arranged to collect whatever Flora could find and was willing to donate.

Seeing so much of John's handwriting was a strange experience. It was now nearly ten years since his death in 1915; Flora no longer thought constantly of him, and when she did so it was often with pleasant, poignant reminiscence rather than tearing loss. Resolutely she sorted files, folders, envelopes and newspaper cuttings. They could all go to the institute. It was towards the end of a long afternoon that she came upon an envelope labelled *von Tarnheim (Flora: for use in certain circumstances)*. This was clearly intended for her; John had perhaps meant to hand it to her before he left for the Western Front, but had neglected to do so in the rush of preparation, and it had lain among his papers ever since. Flora sat down, opened the envelope and read the contents.

She knew that John had always urged her to prevent any marriage between Jiri Zellek and Christa von Tarnheim, on the grounds that they were first cousins within a family notorious for inbreeding. She also suspected that John had discovered, as she had done later in Switzerland, that they were even more closely related, since Jiri's mother Gisela and her brother Karel were first cousins of Karel's wife Valerie. Clearly, John had indeed found this out. There was more. Valerie's words at the Mühlethurnen Institute came back to her, as she read that John had strong grounds for believing that Jiri and Christa were in fact half-siblings. During the last summer that Flora had spent at Tarnheim, John took the opportunity to study eugenics at an institute in Vienna. There he met an older doctor, who asked him casually where he generally stayed in the empire; on hearing of Tarnheim, he said that he knew the place; it was very beautiful, with some good climbing, and as a young man he had holidayed there. Did John know the family? Yes; John's future wife was governess to young Christa von Tarnheim, and, in the summer months, to her cousin Jaroslav. His colleague immediately became interested and asked to see John privately. Over dinner, he explained that, while staying in the village – this would have been in the early 1890s – he was called to the castle to attend an emergency; no other doctor was available, or so it seemed. Karel von Tarnheim and his sister Gisela had been living alone in the castle; Karel had been posted to a remote base a few weeks previously, and Gisela had fallen seriously ill. It was a miscarriage. From what he could ascertain, the father was almost certainly Karel; the young doctor's advice to Gisela was that if she had any hopes of bearing a normal child, she should marry out of the von Tarnheim family altogether. He then knew no more until recently, when his developing research into eugenics led him to follow up some old cases. Gisela, he found, had followed his advice and married Anton Zellek in 1892, while her brother Karel was still away in the army. The following year, she had borne Anton a son, who lived only a few hours. Karel was now living at Tarnheim and Gisela went there to recuperate. She returned to Pallin in autumn 1894; Jaroslav was born in June 1895, an undersized but otherwise reasonably healthy infant who bore absolutely no resemblance to any member of the Zellek family. John sensed that the man would like to examine Jiri, as he asked several questions about the boy, but John urged him to let the matter rest; if the family ever featured in published research, their identity could be concealed.

John added that counter-indications were twofold. Firstly, Karel seemed genuinely convinced that Jiri was his nephew rather than his son, and sought the marriage between him and Christa; secondly, Jiri was always said to have inherited his musical talent from his father.

But: Karel could well have buried the memory of incest with his sister, and even if he admitted that, it was easy for him to believe that Jiri had been conceived after Gisela's return to Pallin. Indeed, he might have been, and there was no definite proof either way. If Karel had any doubts, he could have pushed them away, and perhaps somewhere deep in his mind was the thought that actually it did not much matter if Jiri and Christa were siblings... after all, he and Gisela...

Musical talent was certainly an inherited trait. But it was one that could resurface after several generations: there had, it seemed, actually been several gifted amateur musicians in the von Tarnheim family, no further back than the mid-eighteenth century. And such inherited talents flourish in a congenial atmosphere; Anton Zellek was the ideal person to spot, nurture and encourage the boy's gifts from an early age. Of course, too, in cases of dubious legitimacy, stress is often laid on the resemblances between the child and its supposed parent.

There was, he admitted, no way to definitely establish the truth. But, given the additional evidence of Karel's obviously obsessive relationship with his sister and with his ideal of the von Tarnheims as an exclusive house, together with the remarkably close yet volatile bond between Jiri and Christa, and Jiri's peculiar physique, personality and emotional patterning which (John went on) exhibited several marks of a child of sibling incest, well, the possibility could not be dismissed.

Therefore IF at any time marriage between Jiri and Christa seemed likely, Flora must in all conscience reveal this information to one or preferably both of them. Such knowledge would be a burden, and if they were to marry outside the von Tarnheim family it would be better for them to remain in ignorance. It was highly unlikely in any case that either of them was normally fertile; the von Tarnheim medical history suggested a low fertility rate at the best of times. A child of their union would be unlikely to be carried to term, and it would almost certainly be pathologically abnormal. They might well have difficulty in begetting or conceiving children with other partners, although Christa might be very slightly better off in this regard. John had considered keeping his thoughts and researches private. But this would, he ended, be contrary to the truth and might, just possibly, fail to prevent the eugenic disaster of a von Tarnheim marriage.

Flora sat holding the sheaf of papers. Folding them and replacing them in the envelope, she was about to drop it into the fire. And suddenly she wondered: did Jiri know? What had Valerie told him that day in Switzerland? Had he been sufficiently alert to take it in, and afterwards, would he perhaps attribute his memories to the effects of morphine? And on the other hand, which John could never know, Jiri had a son, Paul, who was said to look so very like Anton Zellek. She sat there for some time before placing the envelope in her desk drawer and locking it securely.

And there it stayed through the long, useful and often happy years of Flora's widowhood; through the deaths of Beatrice and Mrs Loudon, through her wonderful visit to the Battrills in Canada, through the Depression, the rise of fascism, the outbreak of war, the Blitz, the Battle of Britain; through Flora's tireless work with wartime evacuees; VE Day and postwar reconstruction. Through Jiri's periods in Berlin and Munich, and his move to England; his betrayal of Vernon Dakins and his meeting with David Lomax, his life with Magda and Paul, his purchase of Beech Cottage; through springtimes in Shropshire, Hampshire and Munich, through summer holidays, glorious autumns and the recurring magic nostalgia of Christmas, through many, many New Years greeted with hope, dread or relief.

After the war, Flora had regular meetings in town with Jiri, who would treat her to lunch or dinner and a show (he could always get tickets). In May 1946 Flora planned a day in London. As the train left the suburbs, and as the bus took her towards the Army and Navy Stores, she saw signs of bomb damage everywhere. But already rosebay willow herb and buddleia were sprouting among the rubble; there was deadly nightshade too, and a few imminent brambles as well as, bizarrely, tomato plants and potato haulms. She supposed that somewhere beneath, a greengrocer's shop or barrow, or even the Dig for Victory efforts of a city garden, lay buried, the sprouting shoots now fighting their way towards the light.

There was not much to buy; rationing was still in force and she might have done better in Shrewsbury. There were, though, some rather smarter headscarves than the provinces had to offer, and she treated herself to one of these.

The next bus took her to the women's club, where she had arranged to meet her friend Amaranth for lunch; they had been at college together but unlike Flora, Amaranth had never married. Of course, they were both alone now. Retired from a high position in the civil service, then recalled during the war, she now sat on various committees, did voluntary work for women and children, and looked forward to travelling abroad once more, now that restrictions were being lifted. Paris, perhaps, or Italy... Flora felt vaguely depressed. Her own life, which often seemed crammed with incident and interest (the WI, the flower show, the progress of her pupils) appeared very tame and useless in contrast. The lunch was uninspiring: brown Windsor soup, spam fritters with tinned peas, and stewed prunes with very little custard. Flora was not sorry to announce that she must be on her way; she was going to the theatre. Amaranth looked slightly more impressed on hearing that this was a matinee performance of *Merrie England*, the hit of the season, and that Flora was being escorted by a former pupil from her days in Austria.

Jiri was waiting for her on the steps of the theatre. He held out his arms and embraced her warmly; he was looking quite well, she thought, very smart and trim. Sometimes she wondered what onlookers made of their relationship. She could have been Jiri's mother – many women had children at eighteen – or she might be an aunt, but she suspected that it was all too obvious that she had been his teacher. As they took their seats, he explained that this was his second visit to the show; he knew one of the cast, well, more than one actually, and he was himself working on Sir Walter Raleigh's big number, 'The English Rose', a few bars of which he sang softly. True, his current employment prevented much in the way of singing engagements, but he liked to keep in practice. He had brought chocolates (probably obtained on the black market) and had ordered something for the interval. The overture began as he finished an anecdote, in a whisper that carried throughout the stalls, about the padding in the leading man's tights.

During the interval Flora had tea and he had a pink gin. Perhaps, she thought, it was not his first drink of the day.

--Flora, he said as they left (she was slightly disappointed that he did not suggest going backstage), must you catch the next train? I would like to keep you for a little longer.

She had a timetable; in fact, she knew the trains by heart. Yes, she could stay for a while.

His movements were brisk and agile; only someone who knew him as well as Flora would guess how much he relied on his stick as he led the way to an unobtrusive bar off the Strand, which, once you were inside, was obviously exclusive, expensive and, at this time of day, not crowded. Clearly the doorman, manager, bartender and waiters knew him. The table he chose was tucked into a back room; he ordered another pink gin, sherry for Flora, while a plate of canapes that looked as though rationing was unknown silently appeared. Jiri took one, although Flora knew that he would not eat it.

--This is between ourselves. It goes no further.

He lit a Balkan Sobranie.

--Of course, Jiri. What is it?

--Christa. It seemed to cost him an effort to pronounce the name.

Now that my uncle and Hans, dear Hans, have gone, there is no one else who will care. Flora, she is lost.

--Jiri!

--Yes. In 1943, but I have been able to tell no one. As long as I did not do so, it seemed, perhaps... that it was not true. And even now; we always thought we would know when... and she is somewhere. But she is not here.

Flora covered his hand with hers.

--The *Floritania*. She was on board when the ship was torpedoed. Of course I checked the manifest; she boarded in New York; and I checked the list of survivors. Her name was not there.

--And you have not, you could not...

--No. I almost told David; you know, my friend David Lomax. He was with me when I saw the newspaper report;

in fact, he took me home as I became suddenly unwell. I said nothing, but last year we went to Covent Garden together; it re-opened, you know, with the first performances of Britten's opera *Peter Grimes*. It was… Grime's apprentice, you know, is drowned; so too in the end is the unfortunate Grimes. The music… the sea interludes… And then the moment passed. We went backstage. David was at school with Peter Pears, the tenor who plays Grimes. Peter was three years ahead of David, but with all the music at Lancing College, they knew each other quite well… and there were some other people there that I knew, and Ben, he is so sweet…

Flora had known Jiri for more than forty years, and she realised that this digression could go on for some time.

She sipped her sherry, nibbled a canape (they were delicious) and gently brought Jiri back to the main subject.

--You know, Flora, that after my work in Yorkshire I was posted back to London. Through my work here, it became possible to find… her; of course I did not want to send any message which Bruce Westenberger might intercept, so I sent it to the gallery where she sometimes exhibited her paintings. She wrote back. Flora, she wrote back. Her letters came poste restante, although Magda would probably not have remarked them. At that time, you realise, she was driving an ambulance; the whole crew was Polish, there was great esprit de corps, it was like a family to her; I was working during the day and also as an air raid warden in a rescue squad. We are closer now, but then… Christa was coming to me.

--Jiri! Jiri, what would you have done?

--I don't know. There was a war on, our choices were limited, but we would see each other again, and after that I did not care what became of us and neither did she. At least I know, Flora, that she was on her way to me, that in the end it was me and not Westenberger that she belonged with; but, if I hadn't... called her... she might still be alive today.

Flora, now you know this too. I think I will have another pink gin.

Flora died in February 1952. It was bitterly cold. Paul and Lucilla's baby was expected at any moment and, especially as Magda had not really known Flora well, Jiri said he would attend the funeral alone. The train journey to Shropshire meant an early start, and was long and gruelling; Jiri went to the only hotel in the village, had a cup of tea by the fire, visited the gents' and set out for the church. Latterly, Flora had attended services there and although it was said that she had expressed a preference for cremation, she was to be buried in the churchyard next to her little daughter and close to Mrs Loudon and Beatrice. Jiri valued the opportunity to visit their graves and say a prayer. No one in the congregation, which was mainly composed of local friends with very few relatives (none of the Battrills could come from Canada), had previously met the short, slightly built man in his late fifties, leaning on a stick and warmly dressed in a dark overcoat, hat and scarf, whose voice sounded so beautifully in the hymns. But Flora's solicitor, who was one of her executors, put two and two together. Approaching him in the back room of the pub where tea and sandwiches were being served, he assumed that he was Mr Zellek? Mr Jaroslav von Tarnheim Zellek? Yes, indeed, that is correct.

--Ah. Delighted to meet you. Mrs Loudon named you in her will, Mr Zellek, bequeathing you some few items. I think there is a picture of an Alpine scene with a castle, some books in English and German, and some photographs. If you are travelling by train, they will be too heavy to transport, and I will have them sent to your London address; I believe this is correct? He showed Jiri one of his own cards, which Flora had kept in her address book.

--There are also a few letters and postcards, which I think may have been sent to Mrs Loudon or her late mother-in-law by yourself, and an envelope labelled von Tarnheim, which must have been in her desk for some years, but which I assume to have relevance to your family. I have put these into a separate brown envelope and you might like to take them with you to sort out.

Jiri had a short time before the taxi would arrive to take him back to the station. He asked to use the telephone and called home. Magda answered.

--Jiri! How wonderful! You must have known just when to call! Paul has just rung from St John and St Elizabeth Hospital. They have a beautiful daughter, six pounds, twelve ounces, and Lucilla is doing wonderfully well! She said to give you a message when we could: they are going to call the baby Valerie, as she knows that is a favourite name with you... and of course, darling... her voice faltered... that was what we had chosen if ever we had... and they have always said that this will be my grandchild as much as yours... oh, we must thank God and Our Lady, and tomorrow we can go and see them, so do take care coming home; I will be at the flat when you arrive and you must go straight to bed with a hot water bottle.

In an absolute daze, Jiri sank back in the first class compartment as the train left Shrewsbury (which, apparently, was pronounced Shrowsbry). There must be some sort of pattern, he thought: little Valerie is born on the very day I say goodbye to dear Miss Drake. There really is no such thing as a random occurrence. I must ring the wine merchants; Veuve Clicquot?

He became aware of the brown envelope he was clutching. Removing his gloves, he began to sift through the contents; how sweet that dear Granny Loudon had kept, and passed on, some of those little postcards he had sent her as a boy! He felt his eyes fill with the tears he had been fighting back all day. He stretched his left leg cautiously. It must be the cold making it ache so much; he had really not walked very far, although there had been steps at all the railway stations, and standing about in the churchyard... Now, what was this... something different... a long white envelope, rather discoloured with age, with... could that be Doktor Jonni's handwriting? *von Tarnheim...*

VERNON DAKINS II

In 1962 Vernon Dakins died, aged 75, in Moscow and was given a hero's funeral. His open casket was pictured in grainy press photographs; his features, which had become bloated over the years, were sharpened in death so that Jiri and Magda could readily recognise the dashing Englishman they had known in the Twenties and Thirties. Paul, with typical prudence and circumspection, had obliterated all traces of his godfather from his records and his memories; he had been safely married to Lucy before the news of Dakins's involvement with the absconding diplomats of the early Fifties had broken, and he had somehow escaped media notice.

In due course, a bundle of papers, photographs and memorabilia, carefully worked over by the KGB, appeared at the Russian embassy with directions to Vernon's sister Hilda, who lived in Devon.

Cyril Bowes Barnard and a younger colleague travelled down to deliver it. Over coffee, Cyril explained to Miss Dakins that they would need to examine the contents and if necessary impound anything relevant to national security, although this, he said, was unlikely.

Miss Dakins poured the coffee and proffered a plate of shortbread biscuits. News of Vernon's death, she said, had brought back many memories; but she had never been very close to her elder brother and she had managed to come to terms with his treachery. Much could be explained and forgiven, she hinted, but that was all in the past now; she was having a Mass said for the repose of his soul. Cyril remembered, uncomfortably, that like Jerry Zellek the Dakins were Catholics.

She then left them to it while she walked her three dachshunds; if they required lunch, she added, she could provide something simple.

Their task seemed reasonably straightforward. Newspaper cuttings, photographs of various heavily-clad people walking in Moscow streets, a few letters inviting Vernon to stay at a dacha, come over for dinner; some ornate certificates of honourable membership of Soviet party groups, bills for vodka, little of real interest. Stuck between two demands for payment from a tailor was a flimsy envelope addressed to J.F. v T. Zellek. It had been opened and clumsily resealed. Clearly the contents were known in Moscow.

--Zellek? said the younger man. That rings a bell... who?

--Jerry Zellek. He worked for the Office. Retired in June a couple of years ago, on his sixty-fifth. He was one of Dakins's informants in Germany before the war; Dakins was his son's godfather. Dakins put him in contact with us, but he was never in the Service. I'll take that.

Back in the office, Cyril locked his door, sat at his desk and opened the envelope.

Well, Jiri, you little snake, hearty greetings, as you would say, from beyond the grave, either putative or actual, depending on when you read this. I hope you do read it, because you are more of a traitor than I was, however HM Government may have interpreted it, and you deserve what you are going to get.

Oh yes. I know that the end was sure to come, so that you only did what someone else was bound to do sooner or later. I am pretty sure that it was you who tipped me off, too, and of course you did it all for Magda and Paul, didn't you? But you shopped me, Jiri. I knew you were clever but obviously I underestimated your devious little mind and you latched on to... well, never mind. Among it all I think you began to suspect that our encounter by the holy water stoup wasn't the stuff of romantic fiction, and of course it wasn't. I'd been away from Berlin on a two-year placement in Stockholm and was trying to piece things together. Rosa Seimel had taken refuge with a couple (and I mean a couple) of Austrian musicians. She'd borne a child nine months later, and she had been killed in a riot, her death covered up by the authorities as a tram accident. You weren't difficult to track down, so I went to Mass that morning, and picked you up for the price of a cheap breakfast. And, let's face it, you certainly came cheap in those days. Oh, Jiri, you adorable, sexy, self-absorbed little twat. If I could have fucked you and have done with it, things would have been so much easier. But there was Magda, and the boy, not to mention poor old Heinrich, and the ways you could be useful. Those bridge sessions with the four of us showed me that there aren't too many oddities like you around and both sides like to have them, but I was getting doubtful about recruiting you. Then I saw your poor little body after that beating in Munich, calling out for Christi, not Rosa or Magda. I had to follow that up, and knowing your unreliable streak, there was no way we could have you in the States. I wonder if you ever got there. I did, of course, and when I visited them in Texas, Bruce Westenberger was alive and well. I presume he still is, as I guess you didn't want Paul to have a convicted murderer for a father. Ah, Paul.

But I'm maundering; one needs a lot of vodka to keep warm these days.

So, Jiri darling, and I can see you now, Berlin, Munich then London at the end; we came near, didn't we?

But I've got to give you your comeuppance, tit for tat, as we say in English, and I hope you like the bit of idiom. Of course, as you began to wonder, I did know Rosa before you came on the scene. Do you realise that in English to know a woman has a biblical meaning? Probably not. But you can guess, perhaps? Obviously I didn't enjoy it much, not at all, in fact. Totally in the way of business. She expected it, among comrades, and she was more talkative in bed. You may have noticed.

So. You randy little sod, once she was in your flat, she was available immediately. I've never understood your preference for women, but, let's admit it, there are plenty like you who face both ways. And then there was Paul. How fortunate that Rosa and I were both fair-haired and well-built; apparently your father was

565

the same, and you assumed that Paul took after his mother, plus her father and yours. No problem. Proud father. But just look at him, Jiri. I don't know how old he will be now, but I'll bet he's nothing like you at any stage.

It was an irony that you asked me to be his godfather; maybe I even gave you a few hints, I really don't remember. But it meant that I could keep an eye on him; helping out was just something a godfather does, after all. I moved you to Munich, then to London; the Washington assignment took me out of that, but I was back by Christmas 1937 and maybe I let the guard slip. The rest, as they say, is history.

Let the vodka guide the pen for a bit more. In our business you have to work out what makes people tick. When I followed up the Westenberger story I realised that, though you'd fuck anything in sight, and fall in love three times a month, you never really wanted anyone except Christa. I don't say it was love, that's an overworked four letters. Did you ever read Wuthering Heights? I expect not; Barbara Cartland is more your level. Then, as I say, Paul came along. I wouldn't have thought you had it in you, but you made a better father for him than I could have done. So, darling, I've got you by the balls. I wish.

Goodnight, sweet prince.

V x

Cyril let the page fall. He thought of Jerry Zellek; he had seemed to settle down a bit over the past few years and retirement suited him; lots of music, lots of bridge,

Glyndebourne, Covent Garden, his grandchildren; and recently he'd bought a share in a racehorse. Unlikely on a civil service pension, but then Jerry had always had alternative means of income, some of them probably quite legitimate. The horse was trained by some relative of Jerry's daughter-in-law; it rarely won anything, but allowed access to the owners' enclosure at various racecourses. And Vernon Dakins's whole life had been a series of lies.

Part of Cyril's desk furniture was an ornate table lighter. For a moment he gazed at it. But training was too strong. One never destroyed evidence. The letter would be filed away and that would be it until about 2013, and even then probably no one would look at it. The only problem, really, was whether to file it under Dakins or Zellek.

CODA. NEW YORK 1980

Kennst du den Berg und seinen Wolkensteg?
Das Maultier sucht im Nebel seinen Weg.
In Höhlen wohnt der Drachen alte Brut.
Es stürzt der Fels und über ihn die Flut.
Kennst du ihn wohl?
Dahin, dahin
Geht unser Weg.
O Vater, lass uns ziehn!
(Goethe, Kennst du das Land)

It was most unusual for anyone to visit the showroom without an appointment. Generally clients knew in advance which piece they were interested in; people with items to sell, apart from those eccentric or seedy individuals who sometimes turned up with treasures or fakes, began negotiations well in advance.

Lindi was opening the door; propelled by curiosity, David came out of his office.

A black chauffeur stood in the entrance, ushering in an elderly lady, so elderly that it might not be impolite to call her old.

Bent, with a cane, but of good height at some time; white hair, trendily cut; colourful expensive clothes; varnished nails on arthritic fingers.

--Mr Lomax? American, with a hint of something vaguely familiar.

--Yes.

--Christa Westenberger. The tone implied that he should know who she was.

David searched his brain.

--Ah, yes, the Westenberger Foundation, and Gallery. Please come in; may I offer you something?

--No thank you. Lincoln, come back in thirty minutes.

--Yes, ma'am.

They were seated in David's office.

--Mr Lomax, I think we have met before; or at least, we have been present at the same event.

--Ah. The concert.

--Exactly. I so appreciated the review you had in the *New York Times*.

--Thank you. It was well merited, and I would be happy to think that it contributed to your fundraising success.

--Indeed it did. It led me, Mr Lomax, to find out a little more about such a highly respected music critic, and I discovered that you have another interest.

She waved her hand around the room.

--Zellek. You are Zellek and Lomax. Specialist dealers in *fin de siècle* and *Jugendstil* European glassware. New York showroom.

--Yes, Mrs Westenberger. My business partner is Paul Zellek; he is an accountant based in London, but he is extremely knowledgeable about Central European *Jugendstil*;

indeed, he has one of the most specialised collections anywhere in the world.

His visitor drew a breath.

--I think, Mr Lomax, that Paul Zellek is my second cousin. Or perhaps my first cousin once removed; it depends which system one uses.

Given the age gap between Paul and Mrs Westenberger, David was momentarily sceptical; he then recalled that a second cousin is the son or daughter of one's first cousin.

Jerry? He looked closely at her.

--Then, Mrs Westenberger, you are or were, Christa von Tarnheim?

--Got it in one. Lincoln will be back for me shortly, and I have other people to see. Come and have a drink with me tomorrow, say six?

She handed him a card with her New York address and phone number, got up with the aid of her cane, and moved into the showroom where indeed, Lincoln had materialised.

--Fix yourself a drink. What do I call you?

--David. That's what Jerry did.

--Jerry? That horrible nickname.

She looked very straight at him, and said slowly,

--Jaroslav Felix von Tarnheim Zellek.

Some inspiration led David to raise his martini and say, God rest his soul.

--Thank you. I had thought he would be a little old man by now, if he was still alive.

--He never was. Well, little perhaps! Jerry was sixty-seven when he died.

David realised with a shock that he was now older than that himself; he had never thought of himself as being older than Jerry.

--What happened?

--Road accident. Nineteen sixty-two to three was a terrible winter. Icy crossing, he slipped, then a car hit him; it didn't stop and the police never traced it, but it wouldn't have made any difference if they'd got the driver. They took him to St Marys (that was the nearest hospital) and he could maybe have made it, if he'd been a bit stronger, younger... I don't know.

Christa took a gulp of her bourbon.

--I don't suppose his body could take getting smashed up a second time... I was with him just after the war. I mean, when he'd been in the Ulans.

--Well.

--What else?

--Not much. Magda...

--Oh, yes. Magda.

--She handled it pretty well. He had a priest at the end, of course.

David remembered that Magda had been greatly consoled by the thought that her husband had died trying to recite the Gloria: *Deus Pater omnipotens. Domine Fili unigenite, Iesu Christe; apparently he'd managed the last word, Christe, or that was what it sounded like. David paused and continued,*

--He was buried in the churchyard in the village where they had a weekend cottage. He was happy there, you know.

--David, you loved him. Were you...

--I loved him.

--Yes. Jiri was naughty, always; and he liked to play, gentlemen's mischief, he called it, like the Russians, but really he always preferred women. I suppose that's where Magda came in.

--That woman is a heroine!

--Oh well.

--A couple of years ago she moved in with Paul and Lucy. She's doing well, although not best pleased with the Vatican II reforms. She and Jerry were rather old-style Catholics.

David recalled Jerry's funeral. Magda and Lucy, both staunch Catholics, were sustained in their grief. He and Amanda Sibthorp stood together in shock and despair. Cyril Bowes Barnard had attended; at the wake he had asked David questions about Jerry's last weeks, questions that David had been too exhausted to answer, although he had wondered about them since. Paul, to everyone's surprise, had suffered a devastating nervous breakdown; as part of his recovery he had done a course in European ceramics and glassware, the foundation of his current expertise.

His hostess was still clearly thinking about Magda.

--I guess Magda was like me and Bruce. Second-best isn't so bad. But, David, did she... did Jiri... did she have, it was a plain band with a tiny lapis seal...

--Ah, Jerry's ring! He wore it on his little finger. I think Lucy, that's Paul's wife Lucilla, has it now.

--I'm kind of glad he didn't give it to Magda.

--Magda has some very nice jewellery. Look, if that ring is important to you, I could have a word with Lucy.

--No. It doesn't matter now. And I couldn't get it on these days...

She spread her knotted fingers.

David resumed:

--But, Mrs Westenberger—

--Christa.

--Well, Christa, can I ask you how you lost touch? I don't know much about it but you must have been very close as children.

--Not just as children, David. Perhaps Jiri never told you; we were engaged to be married, then his regiment was mobilised. I went to nurse in north Italy, and next time I saw him he'd been smashed up on the Russian Front. Still, we hoped he was getting better, and when we went to Switzerland, to the Mühlethurnen Institute, it really seemed that he would be pretty much OK.

--Actually he was; you could tell he'd been injured, but it didn't stop him from doing more or less everything he wanted.

--It was in Italy that I met Bruce; the Americans were there too, you know.

She refilled their glasses.

I guess you know how it is in war. Bruce and I, well, I won't say we fell in love, whatever that means.

--Weren't you in love with Jerry?

--In love? It wasn't like that. Oh yes, once or twice, it was romantic, you know, Strauss waltzes, Jiri in his Ulan uniform. He was quite something then, you know. Before he got smashed up, and after he'd been in the Ulans for while, he was all muscle, small, yes, but strong and somehow perfect... apart from his big feet, of course!

David laughed.

--Yes. And they were always freezing cold!

--Well, I guess we did have some romance, apart from that. But mostly... It's hard to describe. We just had each other. Did you ever see that movie, with Merle Oberon? In

Yorkshire? It was terribly corny, but there was just something like us.

Of course, Jerry had, as Paul had said, the literary education of the average woodlouse; Christa obviously shared this family trait.

--I did have an affair with Bruce, though. And of course he was a doctor. And I'd been pregnant, twice in fact, with Jiri, and both times it went of its own accord. According to Bruce, it was because Jiri and I were so closely related; we were first cousins, of course, and my parents were also first cousins, so my mother was a cousin of Jiri's mother as well. I know it sounds complicated, but with families like ours it happened. Of course, Jiri and I never even thought about that. Ignorant, I suppose. Bruce argued that if I married Jiri, we'd never have children, or if we did there would be something terribly wrong with them. He even suggested that it would be morally wrong, whatever that might mean. I was hesitating, and then I heard that Jiri was back at Tarnheim, hardly able to move, deadly ill. I had to go. He needed me so much.

Sorry, Dave, this is coming out scrambled. But Jiri and I ended up in Switzerland, where they could treat his injuries. He was just going to have his second operation when Bruce turned up. Posted back to the States, but said he had to see me again. There was something that went on there in Switzerland. Bruce got quite pally with the institute psychiatrist, and after that he was even more insistent, saying I had to leave with him. My last chance to escape from all of it. And I did. It was a sort of instinct; maybe that's how it was with my mother when she left Tarnheim, and even Aunt Gisela accepting Anton Zellek, although that wasn't quite far enough away. A sort of instinct for flight; perhaps it runs in the family, like so much else. Anyway, I did a terrible thing. I left Jiri. I wrote Miss Drake – you know about her? – and asked her to go to the institute to look after him. And she did, bless her. Bruce and I went to Texas. I was happy, I suppose. Like I said, second best isn't so bad. And I'm sure Jiri was happy, from what I hear. He was always like that: centre of his own little world. Then he somehow tracked me down; that was in the early years of the last war. I think he may have had some means of doing so. I'm not sure exactly what he did, but I think it was connected with the British government in some way.

--He always said he was a civil servant but his language skills were obviously involved, and I do know that in 1938 he somehow managed to get British citizenship for himself, Magda and Paul.

--I'm assuming Paul really is Jiri's son?

--I've no reason to think otherwise.

He refilled their glasses.

--Then, David, in 1943 I decided that I must see him again. I had so many friends whose families were dying in concentration camps, in bombing, and Jiri, my only Jiri, was still alive; so I booked passage on the *Floritania*.

--Which was torpedoed. Jerry thought you'd gone down with her.

--But I wasn't on the ship then, though I did board her in New York. I got off just before she sailed. Bruce and I heard that Carl, our son Charlton, he was a pilot with the US Air Force, had been shot down. It finished Bruce, and it nearly finished me. Carl was our only one, and I blamed Jiri for that: those two miscarriages. And there was Jiri, singing, riding horses, with a son. I couldn't face him then.

David recalled how Jerry had been at that time; not quite as Christa had pictured.

--So. We got through it, or at least I did, and Bruce to an extent. I had my painting, and somehow my work seemed to get, well, different, maybe better. (David heard again something Jerry had said about music: *Perhaps it is the only real thing, after all*). And we set up the foundation, for people like ourselves. It gave us something to hang on to, to make sense of things.

--It has been a wonderful power for good.

--Perhaps. We kept busy, life wasn't so bad, until Bruce got sick. When he was diagnosed we went back to Texas; he wanted to die on the ranch. He told me something. We were going back over our time together, Carl and everything, and how we'd met, and how he came to find me in Switzerland. It was then he said, and at first I didn't believe him, what it really was about me and Jiri. The Swiss shrink was treating Jiri's mother, my aunt Gisela; not dead at all, but hopelessly out of it, and all because, well, according to him, Jiri and I had the same father. Apparently Gisela was pretty crazy anyway, and she and her brother were abnormally close and obsessed with the idea of the exclusive blood of the von Tarnheims; although when they had a child, she flipped, had a guilt trip and tried to... apparently her husband found her about to suffocate Jiri with a pillow. That's when she got hauled off to Switzerland. No, I didn't believe it. I thought it was the drugs Bruce was having. Then things kind of fell into order. We were one and the same, and we came from the same place. Just the two of us, forever. The last of the von Tarnheims.

--Not quite. You forget Paul; and he and Lucy have five children. Lucy was very close to Jerry. The first time she met

Magda and Jerry, I was there with a friend for dinner, and he sang. Lucy's quite musical, unlike Paul, and she fell in love with the voice.

Suddenly David recalled that evening in the Zelleks' London flat, furnished with the furniture they had brought from Munich in 1934, a few pieces of Zellek glassware, the vitrine with the Fabergé animals, the signed photograph of Myra Hess in her fur coat, the portrait of Jerry's mother wearing a blue dress.

--He sang 'Linden Lea'.

--I don't know it.

--No.

He refilled their glasses and they raised them.

--Jaroslav Felix von Tarnheim Zellek.

Christa murmured something that David could not catch, and would not have understood if he had. It meant little bird.

Mon enfant, ma soeur,
Songe à la douceur
D'aller là-bas vivre ensemble!
Aimer à loisir,
Aimer et mourir
Au pays qui te ressemble!
(Charles Baudelaire)

A NOTE ON THE MUSIC

Gareth Bax Williams's composition is of course fictional. Most of the other pieces mentioned can be found on YouTube, usually with recordings from the correct period (1930s/40s). 'Dein ist mein ganzes Herz' (Lehar) and Schubert's 'Ständchen' were both recorded by Josef Schmidt (1904–42), a Romanian/Austrian tenor; Jiri's voice is based on Schmidt's and at one point Jiri says he met him in the twenties when they were both studying under Hermann Weissenborn (1876–1959). Jiri also sings Lehar's 'Girls Were Made to Love and Kiss' in both German and English. This was recorded by Richard Tauber, whose accent in English is similar to Jiri's, although the voice is very different. The version of the duet from *The Pearl Fishers* that inspires Arthur Broadhurst is probably the one by Jussi Björling and Robert Merrill, but the Middle Woodlow Church Hall experience is, anachronistically, more like the 1982 recording by Jerry Hadley and Alan Titus. Hadley, 'the other Jerry', is another source for Jiri's voice. Jiri threatens to sing 'Linden Lea' (Vaughan Williams, words by William Barnes) and does so when his future daughter-in-law comes to dinner;

he would have based his English diction on the tenors John Coates and Heddle Nash. He refers several times to Nash, almost an exact contemporary. Although his social origins and musical training were very different, the English tenor was noted for sauciness and egocentricity like Jiri's and he also underwent trauma in WWI. The 1945 recording of *The Dream of Gerontius* conducted by Malcolm Sergeant with Nash and Gladys Ripley is the guideline for Jerry's performance in Cawley Abbey; Nash also recorded 'When the Bloom Is on the Rye' and is known to have performed 'The Road to the Isles'. Jiri's voice has some of Nash's open, optimistic quality and resonant top notes. 'Drei Lilien', which Jiri sings as a child and which Paul recalls him singing to him in the twenties, is now known as a German marching song of WWII. It is, however, originally a folk song from the 1830s and this is the version referred to. 'Das Lila Lied' is a famous German cabaret song from 1920; it celebrates sexual difference. Other pieces ('Kennst du das Land', 'On Wings of Song', 'Im Frühling', 'Il Mio Tesoro' etc.) are well known and easily found.

SOURCES AND ACKNOWLEDGEMENTS

Two major sources are Jaroslav Hašek's *The Good Soldier Schweik* and Stefan Zweig's *Beware of Pity*. Jiri owes his name to the Czech author, and was originally intended to be a Bohemian Czech, until I realised that this would require a much better knowledge of Czech language, geography, history and culture than mine. So he is something of a melange, coming, as the story indicates, from a small principality in the Austro-Hungarian Empire, with its own language and traditions. Jiri's career in the Uhlans/Ulans owes much to Zweig's Anton Hofmiller, and a few names have been borrowed from *Beware of Pity* (*Ungeduld des Herzens*). His steeplechase experience is less disastrous than Count Vronsky's (*Anna Karenina*). Another important source is *The Diaries of Count Harry Kessler*, especially for cavalry manoeuvres and the Eastern Front in WWI. Sources for Jiri's voice have already been mentioned (see A Note on the Music). See *Singing Against the Tide* (Eleanor Allen) for Heddle Nash, and *Am I Too Loud?* (Gerald Moore) for the mid-century music scene. Vernon Dakins's career owes much to *A Spy Among Friends* (Ben Mcintyre) and *The Untouchable*

(John Banville). *Farewell to Berlin* (Christopher Isherwood) and *A Village in the Third Reich* (Julia Bond) were useful for German life in the 1920s/30s. Some of the Hungarian names are borrowed from novels by Lajos Zilhaly (*Two Prisoners*, *The Dukays*); I discovered his 1928 novel *Something Is Drifting on the Water* well after I'd invented Ferzi Balinkay's novel *Unanchored Vessels* and in fact the two authors have little in common apart from being Hungarian. Jiri's troubled relationship with pistachio ice cream is a homage to *Madame Bovary*. The Zelleks' dentist recalls Laurence Olivier's performance in *Marathon Man*.

The places are a mixture of real and imaginary. Real people including Henry Bainbridge, Felix Yusupov, Josef Schmidt, Kim Philby and others make cameo appearances or are briefly referred to. Fr Armand Sentier has a real-life original; otherwise, characters are entirely fictional.

Inspirational current writers are F R Tallis and Olga Tokarczuk.

Thanks are due to Chris Axford, Michelle Barnett, Eleanor Boulter, Pat Haro, Rena Pope and Emily Stockard, who have read along with Jiri, offering much perceptive comment and kind encouragement. Pat Haro was a wonderfully meticulous first editor. Finally, very many thanks to Beth Archer and the team at Troubador Publishing who have made this book possible.